AN·INLAND·VOYAGE

ARETHVSA   CIGARETTE

AN INLAND VOYAGE

TRAVELS WITH A DONKEY IN
THE CEVENNES

UNDERWOODS
A CHILD'S GARDEN OF VERSES

BY
ROBERT LOUIS STEVENSON

ILLUSTRATED

NEW YORK AND LONDON
THE CO-OPERATIVE PUBLICATION SOCIETY

CONTENTS

AN INLAND VOYAGE

3

TRAVELS WITH A DONKEY IN THE CEVENNES

AN INLAND VOYAGE

PREFACE TO FIRST EDITION

To equip so small a book with a preface is, I am half afraid, to sin against proportion. But a preface is more than an author can resist, for it is the reward of his labors. When the foundation stone is laid, the architect appears with his plans, and struts for an hour before the public eye. So with the writer in his preface: he may have never a word to say, but he must show himself for a moment in the portico, hat in hand, and with an urbane demeanor.

It is best, in such circumstances, to represent a delicate shade of manner between humility and superiority: as if the book had been written by some one else, and you had merely run over it and inserted what was good. But for my part I have not yet learned the trick to that perfection; I am not yet able to dissemble the warmth of my sentiments toward a reader; and if I meet him on the threshold, it is to invite him in with country cordiality.

To say truth, I had no sooner finished reading this little book in proof than I was seized upon by a distressing apprehension. It occurred to me that I might not only be the first to read these pages, but the last as well; that I might have pioneered this very smiling tract

of country all in vain, and find not a soul to follow in
my steps. The more I thought, the more I disliked the
notion; until the distaste grew into a sort of panic terror
and I rushed into this Preface, which is no more than
an advertisement for readers.

What am I to say for my book? Caleb and Joshua
brought back from Palestine a formidable bunch of
grapes; alas! my book produces naught so nourishing;
and for the matter of that, we live in an age when people
prefer a definition to any quantity of fruit.

I wonder, would a negative be found enticing? for,
from the negative point of view, I flatter myself this
volume has a certain stamp. Although it runs to con-
siderably upward of two hundred pages, it contains not
a single reference to the imbecility of God's universe,
nor so much as a single hint that I could have made a
better one myself.—I really do not know where my head
can have been. I seem to have forgotten all that makes
it glorious to be man.—'Tis an omission that renders the
book philosophically unimportant; but I am in hopes the
eccentricity may please in frivolous circles.

To the friend who accompanied me, I owe many
thanks already, indeed I wish I owed him nothing else;
but at this moment I feel toward him an almost exaggerated tenderness. He, at least, will become my reader:
if it were only to follow his own travels alongside of
mine.

R. L. S.

To

SIR WALTER GRINDLAY SIMPSON, Bart.

My dear "Cigarette" — It was enough that you should have shared so liberally in the rains and portages of our voyage; that you should have had so hard a paddle to recover the derelict "Arethusa" on the flooded Oise; and that you should thenceforth have piloted a mere wreck of mankind to Origny Sainte-Benoîte and a supper so eagerly desired. It was perhaps more than enough, as you once somewhat piteously complained, that I should have set down all the strong language to you, and kept the appropriate reflections for myself. I could not in decency expose you to share the disgrace of another and more public shipwreck. But now that this voyage of ours is going into a cheap edition, that peril, we shall hope, is at an end, and I may put your name on the burgee.

But I cannot pause till I have lamented the fate of our two ships. That, sir, was not a fortunate day when we projected the possession of a canal barge; it was not a fortunate day when we shared our day-dream with the most hopeful of day-dreamers. For a while, indeed, the world looked smilingly. The barge was procured and christened, and as the "Eleven Thousand Virgins of Cologne," lay for some months, the admired of all admirers, in a pleasant river and under the walls of an ancient town. M. Mattras, the accomplished carpenter of Moret, had made her a center of emulous labor; and

(9)

you will not have forgotten the amount of sweet champagne consumed in the inn at the bridge end, to give
zeal to the workmen and speed to the work. On the
financial aspect, I would not willingly dwell. The "Eleven
Thousand Virgins of Cologne" rotted in the stream where
she was beautified. She felt not the impulse of the
breeze; she was never harnessed to the patient track-
horse. And when at length she was sold, by the indignant carpenter of Moret, there were sold along with her
the "Arethusa" and the "Cigarette," she of cedar, she,
as we knew so keenly on a portage, of solid-hearted English oak. Now these historic vessels fly the tricolor and
are known by new and alien names.   R. L. S.

AN INLAND VOYAGE

ANTWERP TO BOOM

WE made a great stir in Antwerp Docks. A stevedore and a lot of dock porters took up the two canoes, and ran with them for the slip. A crowd of children followed cheering. The "Cigarette" went off in a splash and a bubble of small breaking water. Next moment the "Arethusa" was after her. A steamer was coming down, men on the paddle-box shouted hoarse warnings, the stevedore and his porters were bawling from the quay. But in a stroke or two the canoes were away out in the middle of the Scheldt, and all steamers, and stevedores, and other 'long-shore vanities were left behind.

The sun shone brightly; the tide was making—four jolly miles an hour; the wind blew steadily, with occasional squalls. For my part, I had never been in a canoe under sail in my life; and my first experiment out in the middle of this big river was not made without some trepidation. What would happen when the wind first caught my little canvas? I suppose it was almost as trying a venture into the regions of the unknown as to publish a first book, or to marry. But my doubts were

not of long duration; and in five minutes you will not
be surprised to learn that I had tied my sheet.

I own I was a little struck by this circumstance
myself; of course, in company with the rest of my fellowmen, I had always tied the sheet in a sailing-boat;
but in so little and cranky a concern as a canoe, and
with these charging squalls, I was not prepared to find
myself follow the same principle; and it inspired me
with some contemptuous views of our regard for life.
It is certainly easier to smoke with the sheet fastened;
but I had never before weighed a comfortable pipe of
tobacco against an obvious risk, and gravely elected for
the comfortable pipe. It is a commonplace, that we cannot answer for ourselves before we have been tried.
But it is not so common a reflection, and surely more
consoling, that we usually find ourselves a great deal
braver and better than we thought. I believe this is
every one's experience: but an apprehension that they
may belie themselves in the future prevents mankind
from trumpeting this cheerful sentiment abroad. I wish
sincerely, for it would have saved me much trouble,
there had been some one to put me in a good heart
about life when I was younger; to tell me how dangers are most portentous on a distant sight; and how
the good in a man's spirit will not suffer itself to be
overlaid, and rarely or never deserts him in the hour of
need. But we are all for tootling on the sentimental
flute in literature; and not a man among us will go
to the head of the march to sound the heady drums.

It was agreeable upon the river. A barge or two
went past laden with hay. Reeds and willows bordered
the stream; and cattle and gray venerable horses came

and hung their mild heads over the embankment. Here and there was a pleasant village among trees, with a noisy shipping yard; here and there a villa in a lawn. The wind served us well up the Scheldt and thereafter up the Rupel; and we were running pretty free when we began to sight the brickyards of Boom, lying for a long way on the right bank of the river. The left bank was still green and pastoral, with alleys of trees along the embankment, and here and there a flight of steps to serve a ferry, where perhaps there sat a woman with her elbows on her knees, or an old gentleman with a staff and silver spectacles. But Boom and its brickyards grew smokier and shabbier with every minute; until a great church with a clock, and a wooden bridge over the river, indicated the central quarters of the town.

Boom is not a nice place, and is only remarkable for one thing: that the majority of the inhabitants have a private opinion that they can speak English, which is not justified by fact. This gave a kind of haziness to our intercourse. As for the Hotel de la Navigation, I think it is the worst feature of the place. It boasts of a sanded parlor, with a bar at one end, looking on the street; and another sanded parlor, darker and colder, with an empty birdcage and a tricolor subscription box by way of sole adornment, where we made shift to dine in the company of three uncommunicative engineer apprentices and a silent bagman. The food, as usual in Belgium, was of a nondescript occasional character; indeed I have never been able to detect anything in the nature of a meal among this pleasing people; they seem to peck and trifle with viands all day long in an amateur spirit: tentatively French, truly German, and somehow falling between the two.

The empty birdcage, swept and garnished, and with no trace of the old piping favorite, save where two wires had been pushed apart to hold its lump of sugar, carried with it a sort of graveyard cheer. The engineer apprentices would have nothing to say to us, nor indeed to the bagman; but talked low and sparingly to one another, or raked us in the gaslight with a gleam of spectacles. For, though handsome lads, they were all (in the Scotch phrase) barnacled.

There was an English maid in the hotel, who had been long enough out of England to pick up all sorts of funny foreign idioms, and all sorts of curious foreign ways, which need not here be specified. She spoke to us very fluently in her jargon, asked us information as to the manners of the present day in England, and obligingly corrected us when we attempted to answer. But as we were dealing with a woman, perhaps our information was not so much thrown away as it appeared. The sex likes to pick up knowledge and yet preserve its superiority. It is good policy, and almost necessary in the circumstances. If a man finds a woman admire him, were it only for his acquaintance with geography, he will begin at once to build upon the admiration. It is only by unintermittent snubbing that the pretty ones can keep us in our place. Men, as Miss Howe or Miss Harlowe would have said, "are such *encroachers.*" For my part, I am body and soul with the women; and after a well-married couple, there is nothing so beautiful in the world as the myth of the divine huntress. It is no use for a man to

take to the woods; we know him; Anthony tried the
same thing long ago, and had a pitiful time of it by
all accounts. But there is this about some women,
which overtops the best gymnosophist among men, that
they suffice to themselves, and can walk in a high and
cold zone without the countenance of any trousered being. I declare, although the reverse of a professed ascetic, I am more obliged to women for this ideal than
I should be to the majority of them, or indeed to any
but one, for a spontaneous kiss. There is nothing so en-
couraging as the spectacle of self-sufficiency. And when
I think of the slim and lovely maidens, running the
woods all night to the note of Diana's horn; moving
among the old oaks, as fancy-free as they; things of the
forest and the starlight not touched by the commotion of
man's hot and turbid life—although there are plenty other
ideals that I should prefer—I find my heart beat at the
thought of this one. 'Tis to fail in life, but to fail
with what a grace! That is not lost which is not regretted. And where—here slips out the male—where
would be much of the glory of inspiring love, if there
were no contempt to overcome?

ON THE WILLEBROEK CANAL

NEXT morning, when we set forth on the Willebroek Canal, the rain began heavy and chill. The water of the canal stood at about the drinking temperature of tea; and under this cold aspersion, the surface was covered with steam. The exhilaration of departure, and the easy motion of the boats under each stroke of the paddles, supported us through this misfortune while it lasted; and when the cloud passed and the sun came out again, our spirits went up above the range of stay-at-home humors. A good breeze rustled and shivered in the rows of trees that bordered the canal. The leaves flickered in and out of the light in tumultuous masses. It seemed sailing weather to eye and ear; but down between the banks, the wind reached us only in faint and desultory puffs. There was hardly enough to steer by. Progress was intermittent and unsatisfactory. A jocular person, of marine antecedents, hailed us from the tow-path with a "C'est vite, mais c'est long."

The canal was busy enough. Every now and then we met or overtook a long string of boats, with great green tillers; high sterns with a window on either side of the rudder, and perhaps a jug or a flower-pot in one of the windows; a dingy following behind; a wo-

:man busied about the day's dinner, and a handful of children. These barges were all tied one behind the other with tow ropes, to the number of twenty-five or thirty; and the line was headed and kept in motion by a steamer of strange construction. It had neither paddle-wheel nor screw; but by some gear not rightly comprehensible to the unmechanical mind, it fetched up over its bow a small bright chain which lay along the bottom of the canal, and paying it out again over the stern, dragged itself forward, link by link, with its whole retinue of loaded skows. Until one had found out the key to the enigma, there was something solemn and uncomfortable in the progress of one of these trains, as it moved gently along the water with nothing to mark its advance but an eddy alongside dying away into the wake.

Of all the creatures of commercial enterprise, a canal barge is by far the most delightful to consider. It may spread its sails, and then you see it sailing high above the tree-tops and the wind-mill, sailing on the aqueduct, sailing through the green corn-lands: the most picturesque of things amphibious. Or the horse plods along at a foot-pace as if there were no such thing as business in the world; and the man dreaming at the tiller sees the same spire on the horizon all day long. It is a mystery how things ever get to their destination at this rate; and to see the barges waiting their turn at a lock, affords a fine lesson of how easily the world may be taken. There should be many contented spirits on board, for such a life is both to travel and to stay at home.

The chimney smokes for dinner as you go along;

the banks of the canal slowly unroll their scenery to contemplative eyes; the barge floats by great forests and through great cities with their public buildings and their lamps at night; and for the bargee, in his floating home, "traveling abed," it is merely as if he were listening to another man's story or turning the leaves of a picture book in which he had no concern. He may take his afternoon walk in some foreign country on the banks of the canal, and then come home to dinner at his own fireside.

There is not enough exercise in such a life for any high measure of health; but a high measure of health is only necessary for unhealthy people. The slug of a fellow, who is never ill nor well, has a quiet time of it in life, and dies all the easier.

I am sure I would rather be a bargee than occupy any position under Heaven that required attendance at an office. There are few callings, I should say, where a man gives up less of his liberty in return for regular meals. The bargee is on shipboard—he is master in his own ship—he can land whenever he will—he can never be kept beating off a lee-shore a whole frosty night when the sheets are as hard as iron; and so far as I can make out, time stands as nearly still with him as is compatible with the return of bed-time or the dinner-hour. It is not easy to see why a bargee should ever die.

Half-way between Willebroek and Villevorde, in a beautiful reach of canal like a squire's avenue, we went ashore to lunch. There were two eggs, a junk of bread, and a bottle of wine on board the "Arethusa"; and two eggs and an Etna cooking apparatus

on board the "Cigarette." The master of the latter
boat smashed one of the eggs in the course of disem-
barkation; but observing pleasantly that it might still be
cooked à la papier, he dropped it into the Etna, in its
covering of Flemish newspaper. We landed in a blink
of fine weather; but we had not been two minutes
ashore, before the wind freshened into half a gale, and
the rain began to patter on our shoulders. We sat as
close about the Etna as we could. The spirits burned
with great ostentation; the grass caught flame every
minute or two, and had to be trodden out; and before
long, there were several burned fingers of the party.
But the solid quantity of cookery accomplished was out
of proportion with so much display; and when we desisted, after two applications of the fire, the sound egg
was little more than loo-warm; and as for à la papier,
it was a cold and sordid fricassee of printer's ink and
broken eggshell. We made shift to roast the other two,
by putting them close to the burning spirits; and that
with better success. And then we uncorked the bottle
of wine, and sat down in a ditch with our canoe aprons
over our knees. It rained smartly. Discomfort, when
it is honestly uncomfortable and makes no nauseous pre-
tensions to the contrary, is a vastly humorous business;
and people well steeped and stupefied in the open air
are in a good vein for laughter. From this point of
view, even egg à la papier, offered by way of food,
may pass muster as a sort of accessory to the fun.
But this manner of jest, although it may be taken in
good part, does not invite repetition; and from that time
forward, the Etna voyaged like a gentleman in the
locker of the "Cigarette."

It is almost unnecessary to mention that when lunch was over and we got aboard again and made sail, the wind promptly died away. The rest of the journey to Villevorde we still spread our canvas to the unfavoring air; and with now and then a puff, and now and then a spell of paddling, drifted along from lock to lock, between the orderly trees.

It was a fine, green, fat landscape; or rather a mere green water-lane, going on from village to village. Things had a settled look, as in places long lived in. Crop-headed children spat upon us from the bridges as we went below, with a true conservative feeling. But even more conservative were the fishermen, intent upon their floats, who let us go by without one glance. They perched upon sterlings and buttresses and along the slope of the embankment, gently occupied. They were indifferent like pieces of dead nature. They did not move any more than if they had been fishing in an old Dutch print. The leaves fluttered, the water lapped, but they continued in one stay like so many churches established by law. You might have trepanned every one of their innocent heads, and found no more than so much coiled fishing line below their skulls. I do not care for your stalwart fellows in india-rubber stockings breasting up mountain torrents with a salmon rod; but I do dearly love the class of man who plies his unfruitful art, forever and a day, by still and depopulated waters.

At the last lock just beyond Villevorde there was a lock mistress who spoke French comprehensibly, and told us we were still a couple of leagues from Brussels. At the same place, the rain began again. It fell in straight, parallel lines; and the surface of the canal was thrown up into an infinity of little crystal fountains. There were no beds to be had in the neighborhood. Nothing for it but to lay the sails aside and address ourselves to steady paddling in the rain.

Beautiful country houses, with clocks and long lines of shuttered windows, and fine old trees standing in groves and avenues, gave a rich and somber aspect in the rain and the deepening dusk to the shores of the canal. I seem to have seen something of the same effect in engravings: opulent landscapes, deserted and overhung with the passage of storm. And throughout we had the escort of a hooded cart, which trotted shabbily along the tow-path, and kept at an almost uniform distance in our wake.

THE ROYAL SPORT NAUTIQUE

THE rain took off near Laeken. But the sun was already down; the air was chill; and we had scarcely a dry stitch between the pair of us. Nay, now we found ourselves near the end of the Allee Verte, and on the very threshold of Brussels, we were confronted by a serious difficulty. The shores were closely lined by canal boats waiting their turn at the lock. Nowhere was there any convenient landing-place; nowhere so much as a stable-yard to leave the canoes in for the night. We scrambled ashore and entered an estaminet where some sorry fellows were drinking with the landlord. The landlord was pretty round with us; he knew of no coach-house or stable-yard, nothing of the sort; and seeing we had come with no mind to drink, he did not conceal his impatience to be rid of us. One of the sorry fellows came to the rescue. Somewhere in the corner of the basin there was a slip, he informed us, and something else besides, not very clearly defined by him, but hopefully construed by his hearers.

Sure enough there was the slip in the corner of the basin; and at the top of it two nice-looking lads in boating clothes. The Arethusa addressed himself to

(22)

these. One of them said there would be no difficulty
about a night's lodging for our boats; and the other,
taking a cigarette from his lips, inquired if they were
made by Searle & Son. The name was quite an in-
troduction. Half-a-dozen other young men came out of
a boat-house bearing the superscription "Royal Sport
Nautique," and joined in the talk. They were all very
polite, voluble and enthusiastic; and their discourse was
interlarded with English boating terms, and the names
of English boat-builders and English clubs. I do not
know, to my shame, any spot in my native land where
I should have been so warmly received by the same
number of people. We were English boating-men, and
the Belgian boating-men fell upon our necks. I wonder
if French Huguenots were as cordially greeted by English Protestants when they came across the Channel
out of great tribulation. But after all, what religion
knits people so closely as a common sport?

The canoes were carried into the boat-house; they
were washed down for us by the Club servants, the
sails were hung out to dry, and everything made as
snug and tidy as a picture. And in the meanwhile we
were led upstairs by our new-found brethren, for so
more than one of them stated the relationship, and
made free of their lavatory. This one lent us soap,
that one a towel, a third and fourth helped us to undo
our bags. And all the time such questions, such assurances of respect and sympathy! I declare I never
knew what glory was before.

"Yes, yes, the Royal Sport Nautique is the oldest
club in Belgium."

"We number two hundred."

"We"—this is not a substantive speech, but an abstract of many speeches, the impression left upon my mind after a great deal of talk; and very youthful, pleasant, natural and patriotic it seems to me to be— "We have gained all races, except those where we were cheated by the French."

"You must leave all your wet things to be dried."

"O! entre frères! In any boat-house in England we should find the same." (I cordially hope they might.)

"En Angleterre, vous employez des sliding-seats, n'est-ce pas?"

"We are all employed in commerce during the day; but in the evening, voyez vous, nous sommes serieux."

These were the words. They were all employed over the frivolous mercantile concerns of Belgium during the day; but in the evening they found some hours for the serious concerns of life. I may have a wrong idea of wisdom, but I think that was a very wise remark. People connected with literature and philosophy are busy all their days in getting rid of second-hand notions and false standards. It is their profession, in the sweat of their brows, by dogged thinking, to recover their old fresh view of life, and distinguish what they really and originally like, from what they have only learned to tolerate perforce. And these Royal Nautical Sportsmen had the distinction still quite legible in their hearts. They had still those clean perceptions of what is nice and nasty, what is interesting and what is dull, which envious old gentlemen refer to as illusions. The nightmare illusion of middle age, the bear's hug of custom gradually squeezing the life out of a man's soul, had not yet begun for these happy-star'd young Belgians.

They still knew that the interest they took in their business was a trifling affair compared to their spontaneous, long-suffering affection for nautical sports. To know what you prefer, instead of humbly saying Amen to what the world tells you you ought to prefer, is to have kept your soul alive. Such a man may be generous; he may be honest in something more than the commercial sense; he may love his friends with an elective, personal sympathy, and not accept them as an adjunct of the station to which he has been called. He may be a man, in short, acting on his own instincts, keeping in his own shape that God made him in; and not a mere crank in the social engine house, welded on principles that he does not understand, and for purposes that he does not care for.

For will any one dare to tell me that business is more entertaining than fooling among boats? He must have never seen a boat, or never seen an office, who says so. And for certain the one is a great deal better for the health. There should be nothing so much a man's business as his amusements. Nothing but money-grubbing can be put forward to the contrary; no one but

> Mammon, the least erected spirit that fell
> From Heaven,

durst risk a word in answer. It is but a lying cant that would represent the merchant and the banker as people disinterestedly toiling for mankind, and then most useful when they are most absorbed in their transactions; for the man is more important than his services. And when my Royal Nautical Sportsman shall have so

far fallen from his hopeful youth that he cannot pluck
up an enthusiasm over anything but his ledger, I venture to doubt whether he will be near so nice a fellow, and whether he would welcome, with so good a
grace, a couple of drenched Englishmen paddling into
Brussels in the dusk.

When we had changed our wet clothes and drunk
a glass of pale ale to the Club's prosperity, one of
their number escorted us to a hotel. He would not
join us at our dinner, but he had no objection to a
glass of wine. Enthusiasm is very wearing; and I begin to understand why prophets were unpopular in Ju-
dea, where they were best known. For three stricken
hours did this excellent young man sit beside us to di-
late on boats and boat-races; and before he left, he
was kind enough to order our bedroom candles.

We endeavored now and again to change the subject; but the diversion did not last a moment: the
Royal Nautical Sportsman bridled, shied, answered the
question, and then breasted once more into the swell-
ing tide of his subject. I call it his subject; but I
think it was he who was subjected. The Arethusa,
who holds all racing as a creature of the devil, found
himself in a pitiful dilemma. He durst not own his
ignorance for the honor of Old England, and spoke
away about English clubs and English oarsmen whose
fame had never before come to his ears. Several times,
and, once above all, on the question of sliding-seats, he
was within an ace of exposure. As for the Cigarette,
who has rowed races in the heat of his blood, but now
disowns these slips of his wanton youth, his case was
still more desperate; for the Royal Nautical proposed

that he should take an oar in one of their eights on
the morrow, to compare the English with the Belgian
stroke. I could see my friend perspiring in his chair
whenever that particular topic came up. And there was
yet another proposal which had the same effect on both
of us. It appeared that the champion canoeist of Europe (as well as most other champions) was a Royal
Nautical Sportsman. And if we would only wait until
the Sunday, this infernal paddler would be so conde-
scending as to accompany us on our next stage. Neither
of us had the least desire to drive the coursers of the
sun against Apollo.

When the young man was gone, we countermanded
our candles, and ordered some brandy and water. The
great billows had gone over our head. The Royal Nautical Sportsmen were as nice young fellows as a man
would wish to see, but they were a trifle too young
and a thought too nautical for us. We began to see
that we were old and cynical; we liked ease and the
agreeable rambling of the human mind about this and
the other subject; we did not want to disgrace our native land by messing an eight, or toiling pitifully in the
wake of the champion canoeist. In short, we had re-
course to flight. It seemed ungrateful, but we tried to
make that good on a card loaded with sincere compliments. And indeed it was no time for scruples; we
seemed to feel the hot breath of the champion on our
necks.

AT MAUBEUGE

PARTLY from the terror we had of our good friends, the Royal Nauticals, partly from the fact that there were no fewer than fifty-five locks between Brussels and Charleroi, we concluded that we should travel by train across the frontier, boats and all. Fifty-five locks in a day's journey was pretty well tantamount to trudging the whole distance on foot, with the canoes upon our shoulders, an object of astonishment to the trees on the canal side, and of honest derision to all right-thinking children.

To pass the frontier, even in a train, is a difficult matter for the Arethusa. He is, somehow or other, a marked man for the official eye. Wherever he journeys, there are the officers gathered together. Treaties are solemnly signed, foreign ministers, embassadors, and consuls sit throned in state from China to Peru, and the Union Jack flutters on all the winds of heaven. Under these safeguards, portly clergymen, schoolmistresses, gentlemen in gray tweed suits, and all the ruck and rabble of British touristry, pour unhindered, "Murray" in hand, over the railways of the continent, and yet the

(28)

slim person of the Arethusa is taken in the meshes, while these great fish go on their way rejoicing. If he travels without a passport, he is cast, without any figure about the matter, into noisome dungeons: if his papers are in order, he is suffered to go his way indeed, but not until he has been humiliated by a general incredulity. He is a born British subject, yet he has never succeeded in persuading a single official of his nationality. He flatters himself he is indifferent honest; yet he is rarely taken for anything better than a spy, and there is no absurd and disreputable means of livelihood but has been attributed to him in some heat of official or popular distrust. . . . .

For the life of me I cannot understand it. I too have been knolled to church, and sat at good men's feasts; but I bear no mark of it. I am as strange as a Jack Indian to their official spectacles. I might come from any part of the globe, it seems, except from where I do. My ancestors have labored in vain, and the glorious Constitution cannot protect me in my walks abroad. It is a great thing, believe me, to present a good normal type of the nation you belong to.

Nobody else was asked for his papers on the way to Maubeuge; but I was; and although I clung to my rights, I had to choose at last between accepting the humiliation and being left behind by the train. I was sorry to give way; but I wanted to get to Maubeuge.

Maubeuge is a fortified town, with a very good inn, the Grand Cerf. It seemed to be inhabited principally by soldiers and bagmen; at least, these were all that we saw, except the hotel servants. We had to stay there some time, for the canoes were in no hurry to follow us, and at last stuck hopelessly in the custom-house until we went back to liberate them. There was nothing to do, nothing to see. We had good meals, which was a great matter; but that was all.

The Cigarette was nearly taken up upon a charge of drawing the fortifications: a feat of which he was hope-lessly incapable. And besides, as I suppose each bel-ligerent nation has a plan of the other's fortified places already, these precautions are of the nature of shutting the stable door after the steed is away. But I have no doubt they help to keep up a good spirit at home. It is a great thing if you can persuade people that they are somehow or other partakers in a mystery. It makes them feel bigger. Even the Freemasons, who have been shown up to satiety, preserve a kind of pride; and not a grocer among them, however honest, harmless and empty-headed he may feel himself to be at bottom, but comes home from one of their cœnacula with a portentous significance for himself.

It is an odd thing, how happily two people, if there are two, can live in a place where they have no ac-quaintance. I think the spectacle of a whole life in which you have no part, paralyzes personal desire. You are content to become a mere spectator. The baker stands in his door; the colonel with his three medals goes by to the cafe at night; the troops drum and trumpet and man the ramparts, as bold as so many lions.

It would task language to say how placidly you be-hold all this. In a place where you have taken some root, you are provoked out of your indifference; you

have a hand in the game; your friends are fighting
with the army. But in a strange town, not small
enough to grow too soon familiar, nor so large as to
have laid itself out for travelers, you stand so far apart
from the business, that you positively forget it would
be possible to go nearer; you have so little human interest around you, that you do not remember yourself
to be a man. Perhaps, in a very short time, you
would be one no longer. Gymnosophists go into a
wood, with all nature seething around them, with romance on every side; it would be much more to the
purpose if they took up their abode in a dull country
town, where they should see just so much of humanity as to keep them from desiring more, and only the
stale externals of man's life. These externals are as
dead to us as so many formalities, and speak a dead
language in our eyes and ears. They have no more
meaning than an oath or a salutation. We are so
much accustomed to see married couples going to
church of a Sunday that we have clean forgotten what
they represent; and novelists are driven to rehabilitate
adultery, no less, when they wish to show us what a
beautiful thing it is for a man and a woman to live
for each other.

One person in Maubeuge, however, showed me something more than his outside. That was the driver of
the hotel omnibus: a mean enough looking little man,
as well as I can remember; but with a spark of something human in his soul. He had heard of our little
journey, and came to me at once in envious sympathy.
How he longed to travel! he told me. How he longed
to be somewhere else, and see the round world before

he went into the grave! "Here I am," said he. "1
drive to the station. Well. And then I drive back
again to the hotel. And so on every day and all the
week round. My God, is that life?" I could not say
I thought it was—for him. He pressed me to tell him
where I had been, and where I hoped to go; and as
he listened, I declare the fellow sighed. Might not this
have been a brave African traveler, or gone to the Indies after Drake? But it is an evil age for the gypsily
inclined among men. He who can sit squarest on a
three-legged stool, he it is who has the wealth and
glory.

I wonder if my friend is still driving the omnibus
for the Grand Cerf? Not very likely, I believe; for I
think he was on the eve of mutiny when we passed
through, and perhaps our passage determined him for
good. Better a thousand times that he should be a
tramp, and mend pots and pans by the wayside, and
sleep under trees, and see the dawn and the sunset
every day above a new horizon. I think I hear you
say that it is a respectable position to drive an omnibus?

Very well. What right has he who likes it not
to keep those who would like it dearly out of this
respectable position? Suppose a dish were not to my
taste, and you told me that it was a favorite among
the rest of the company, what should I conclude from
that? Not to finish the dish against my stomach, I
suppose.

Respectability is a very good thing in its way, but
it does not rise superior to all considerations. I would
not for a moment venture to hint that it was a mat-

ter of taste; but I think I will go as far as this: that
if a position is admittedly unkind, uncomfortable, unnecessary, and superfluously useless, although it were
as respectable as the Church of England, the sooner a
man is out of it, the better for himself and all concerned.

ON THE SAMBRE CANALIZED

TO QUARTES

ABOUT three in the afternoon the whole establishment of the Grand Cerf accompanied us to the water's edge. The man of the omnibus was there with haggard eyes. Poor cagebird! Do I not remember the time when I myself haunted the station, to watch train after train carry its complement of freemen into the night, and read the names of distant places on the time-bills with indescribable longings?

We were not clear of the fortifications before the rain began. The wind was contrary, and blew in furious gusts; nor were the aspects of nature any more clement than the doings of the sky. For we passed through a stretch of blighted country, sparsely covered with brush, but handsomely enough diversified with factory chimneys. We landed in a soiled meadow among some pollards, and there smoked a pipe in a flaw of fair weather. But the wind blew so hard, we could get little else to smoke. There were no natural objects in the neighborhood, but some sordid workshops. A group of children headed by a tall girl stood and watched us from a little distance all the time we stayed. I heartily wonder what they thought of us.

(34)

At Hautmont the lock was almost impassable; the landing-place being steep and high, and the launch at a long distance. Near a dozen grimy workmen lent us a hand. They refused any reward; and, what is much better, refused it handsomely, without conveying any sense of insult. "It is a way we have in our country-side," said they. And a very becoming way it is. In Scotland, where also you will get services for nothing, the good people reject your money as if you had been trying to corrupt a voter. When people take the trouble to do dignified acts, it is worth while to take a little more, and allow the dignity to be common to all concerned. But in our brave Saxon countries, where we plod three score years and ten in the mud, and the wind keeps singing in our ears from birth to burial, we do our good and bad with a high hand and almost offensively; and make even our alms a witness-bearing and an act of war against the wrong.

After Hautmont, the sun came forth again and the wind went down; and a little paddling took us beyond the iron-works and through a delectable land. The river wound among low hills, so that sometimes the sun was at our backs, and sometimes it stood right ahead, and the river before us was one sheet of intolerable glory. On either hand, meadows and orchards bordered, with a margin of sedge and water flowers, upon the river. The hedges were of great height, woven about the trunks of hedgerow elms; and the fields, as they were often very small, looked like a series of bowers along the stream. There was never any prospect; sometimes a hill-top with its trees would look over the nearest hedgerow, just to make a middle distance for the sky;

3—VOL. VII   STEVENSON.

but that was all. The heaven was bare of clouds. The
atmosphere, after the rain, was of enchanting purity.
The river doubled among the hillocks, a shining strip
of mirror glass; and the dip of the paddles set the
flowers shaking along the brink.

In the meadows wandered black and white cattle
fantastically marked. One beast, with a white head
and the rest of the body glossy black, came to the
edge to drink, and stood gravely twitching his ears at
me as I went by, like some sort of preposterous clergyman in a play. A moment after I heard a loud plunge,
and, turning my head, saw the clergyman struggling to
shore. The bank had given way under his feet.

Besides the cattle, we saw no living things except
a few birds and a great many fishermen. These sat
along the edges of the meadows, sometimes with one
rod, sometimes with as many as half a score. They
seemed stupefied with contentment; and when we in-
duced them to exchange a few words with us about
the weather, their voices sounded quiet and far away.
There was a strange diversity of opinion among them
as to the kind of fish for which they set their lures;
although they were all agreed in this, that the river
was abundantly supplied. Where it was plain that no
two of them had ever caught the same kind of fish,
we could not help suspecting that perhaps not any one
of them had ever caught a fish at all. I hope, since
the afternoon was so lovely, that they were one and
all rewarded; and that a silver booty went home in
every basket for the pot. Some of my friends would
cry shame on me for this; but I prefer a man, were
he only an angler, to the bravest pair of gills in all

God's waters. I do not affect fishes unless when cooked in sauce; whereas an angler is an important piece of river scenery, and hence deserves some recognition among canoeists. He can always tell you where you are after a mild fashion; and his quiet presence serves to accentuate the solitude and stillness, and remind you of the glittering citizens below your boat.

The Sambre turned so industriously to and fro among his little hills, that it was past six before we drew near the lock at Quartes. There were some children on the tow-path, with whom the Cigarette fell into a chaffing talk as they ran along beside us. It was in vain that I warned him. In vain I told him, in English, that boys were the most dangerous creatures; and if once you began with them, it was safe to end in a shower of stones. For my own part, whenever anything was addressed to me, I smiled gently and shook my head as though I were an inoffensive person inadequately acquainted with French. For indeed I have had such experience at home, that I would sooner meet many wild animals than a troop of healthy urchins.

But I was doing injustice to these peaceable young Hainaulters. When the Cigarette went off to make inquiries, I got out upon the bank to smoke a pipe and superintend the boats, and became at once the center of much amiable curiosity. The children had been joined by this time by a young woman and a mild lad who had lost an arm; and this gave me more security. When I let slip my first word or so in French, a little girl nodded her head with a comical grown-up air. "Ah, you see," she said, "he understands well enough now; he was just making believe." And the little group laughed together very good-naturedly.

They were much impressed when they heard we came from England; and the little girl proffered the information that England was an island "and a far way from here—bien loin d'ici."

"Ay, you may say that, a far way from here," said the lad with one arm.

I was as nearly home-sick as ever I was in my life; they seemed to make it such an incalculable distance to the place where I first saw the day.

They admired the canoes very much. And I observed one piece of delicacy in these children, which is worthy of record. They had been deafening us for the last hundred yards with petitions for a sail; ay, and they deafended us to the same tune next morning when we came to start; but then, when the canoes were lying empty, there was no word of any such petition. Delicacy? or perhaps a bit of fear for the water in so cranky a vessel? I hate cynicism a great deal worse than I do the devil; unless perhaps the two were the same thing? And yet 'tis a good tonic; the cold tub and bath-towel of the sentiments; and positively necessary to life in cases of advanced sensibility.

From the boats they turned to my costume. They could not make enough of my red sash; and my knife filled them with awe.

"They make them like that in England," said the boy with one arm. I was glad he did not know how badly we make them in England nowadays. "They are for people who go away to sea," he added, "and to defend one's life against great fish."

I felt I was becoming a more and more romantic figure to the little group at every word. And so I suppose I was. Even my pipe, although it was an ordinary French clay, pretty well "trousered," as they call it, would have a rarity in their eyes, as a thing coming from so far away. And if my feathers were not very fine in themselves, they were all from over seas. One thing in my outfit, however, tickled them out of all politeness; and that was the bemired condition of my canvas shoes. I suppose they were sure the mud at any rate was a home product. The little girl (who was the genius of the party) displayed her own sabots in competition; and I wish you could have seen how gracefully and merrily she did it.

The young woman's milk can, a great amphora of hammered brass, stood some way off upon the sward. I was glad of an opportunity to divert public attention from myself, and return some of the compliments I had received. So I admired it cordially both for form and color, telling them, and very truly, that it was as beautiful as gold. They were not surprised. The things were plainly the boast of the country-side. And the children expatiated on the costliness of these *amphoræ*, which sell sometimes as high as thirty francs apiece; told me how they were carried on donkeys, one on either side of the saddle, a brave caparison in themselves; and how they were to be seen all over the district, and at the larger farms in great number and of great size.

PONT-SUR-SAMBRE

WE ARE PEDDLERS

THE Cigarette returned with good news. There were beds to be had some ten minutes' walk from where we were, at a place called Pont. We stowed the canoes in a granary, and asked among the children for a guide. The circle at once widened round us, and our offers of reward were received in dispiriting silence. We were plainly a pair of Bluebeards to the children; they might speak to us in public places, and where they had the advantage of numbers; but it was another thing to venture off alone with two uncouth and legendary characters, who had dropped from the clouds upon their hamlet this quiet afternoon, sashed and beknived, and with a flavor of great voyages. The owner of the granary came to our assistance, singled out one little fellow and threatened him with corporalities; or I suspect we should have had to find the way for ourselves. As it was, he was more frightened at the granary man than the strangers, having perhaps had some experience of the former. But I fancy his little heart must have been going at a fine rate; for he kept trotting at a respectful distance in front, and looking

(40)

back at us with scared eyes. Not otherwise may the children of the young world have guided Jove or one of his Olympian compeers on an adventure.

A miry lane led us up from Quartes with its church and bickering windmill. The hinds were trudging homeward from the fields. A brisk little old woman passed us by. She was seated across a donkey between a pair of glittering milk cans; and, as she went, she kicked jauntily with her heels upon the donkey's side, and scattered shrill remarks among the wayfarers. It was notable that none of the tired men took the trouble to reply.

Our conductor soon led us out of the lane and across country. The sun had gone down, but the west in front of us was one lake of level gold. The path wandered a while in the open, and then passed under a trellis like a bower indefinitely prolonged. On either hand were shadowy orchards; cottages lay low among the leaves and sent their smoke to heaven; every here and there, in an opening, appeared the great gold face of the west.

I never saw the Cigarette in such an idyllic frame of mind. He waxed positively lyrical in praise of country scenes. I was little less exhilarated myself; the mild air of the evening, the shadows, the rich lights and the silence, made a symphonious accompaniment about our walk; and we both determined to avoid towns for the future and sleep in hamlets.

At last the path went between two houses, and turned the party out into a wide muddy high-road, bordered, as far as the eye could reach on either hand, by an unsightly village. The houses stood well back, leaving a ribbon of waste land on either side of the road, where there were stacks of firewood, carts, barrows, rubbish heaps, and a little doubtful grass. Away on the left, a gaunt tower stood in the middle of the street. What it had been in past ages, I know not: probably a hold in time of war; but nowadays it bore an illegible dial-plate in its upper parts, and near the bottom an iron letter-box.

The inn to which we had been recommended at Quartes was full, or else the landlady did not like our looks. I ought to say, that with our long, damp india-rubber bags we presented rather a doubtful type of civilization: like rag and bone men, the Cigarette imagined. "These gentlemen are peddlers?"—Ces messieurs sont des marchands?—asked the landlady. And then, without waiting for an answer, which I suppose she thought superfluous in so plain a case, recommended us to a butcher who lived hard by the tower and took in travelers to lodge.

Thither went we. But the butcher was flitting, and all his beds were taken down. Or else he didn't like our look. As a parting shot, we had "These gentlemen are peddlers?"

It began to grow dark in earnest. We could no longer distinguish the faces of the people who passed us by with an inarticulate good-evening. And the householders of Pont seemed very economical with their oil; for we saw not a single window lighted in all that long village. I believe it is the longest village in the world; but I daresay in our predicament every pace counted three times over. We were much cast down when we came to the last auberge; and looking in at

the dark door, asked timidly if we could sleep there for
the night. A female voice assented in no very friendly
tones. We clapped the bags down and found our way
to chairs.

The place was in total darkness, save a red glow
in the chinks and ventilators of the stove. But now
the landlady lighted a lamp to see her new guests; I
suppose the darkness was what saved us another expul-
sion; for I cannot say she looked gratified at our appearance. We were in a large bare apartment, adorned
with two allegorical prints of Music and Painting, and
a copy of the Law against Public Drunkenness. On
one side, there was a bit of a bar, with some half-a-
dozen bottles. Two laborers sat waiting supper, in attitudes of extreme weariness; a plain-looking lass bustled
about with a sleepy child of two; and the landlady began to derange the pots upon the stove and set some
beafsteak to grill.

"These gentlemen are peddlers?" she asked sharply.
And that was all the conversation forthcoming. We
began to think we might be peddlers after all. I never
knew a population with so narrow a range of conject-
ure as the inn-keepers of Pont-sur-Sambre. But manners and bearing have not a wider currency than bank-
notes. You have only to get far enough out of your
beat, and all your accomplished airs will go for nothing. These Hainaulters could see no difference between
us and the average peddler. Indeed we had some
grounds for reflection while the steak was getting ready,
to see how perfectly they accepted us at their own
valuation, and how our best politeness and best efforts
at entertainment seemed to fit quite suitably with the

character of packmen. At least it seemed a good account of the profession in France, that even before such judges we could not beat them at our own weapons.

At last we were called to table. The two hinds (and one of them looked sadly worn and white in the face, as though sick with overwork and underfeeding) supped off a single plate of some sort of bread-berry, some potatoes in their jackets, a small cup of coffee sweetened with sugar candy, and one tumbler of swipes. The landlady, her son, and the lass aforesaid, took the same.

Our meal was quite a banquet by comparison. We had some beefsteak, not so tender as it might have been, some of the potatoes, some cheese, an extra glass of the swipes, and white sugar in our coffee.

You see what it is to be a gentleman—I beg your pardon, what it is to be a peddler. It had not before occurred to me that a peddler was a great man in a laborer's ale-house; but now that I had to enact the part for an evening, I found that so it was. He has in his hedge quarters somewhat the same pre-eminency as the man who takes a private parlor in a hotel. The more you look into it, the more infinite are the class distinctions among men; and possibly, by a happy dispensation, there is no one at all at the bottom of the scale; no one but can find some superiority over somebody else, to keep up his pride withal.

We were displeased enough with our fare. Particularly the Cigarette; for I tried to make believe that I was amused with the adventure, tough beefsteak and all. According to the Lucretian maxim, our steak should have been flavored by the look of the other people's bread-berry. But we did not find it so in practice. You may have a head knowledge that other people live more poorly than yourself, but it is not agreeable—I was going to say, it is against the etiquette of the universe—to sit at the same table and pick your own superior diet from among their crusts. I had not seen such a thing done since the greedy boy at school with his birthday cake. It was odious enough to witness, I could remember; and I had never thought to play the part myself. But there again you see what it is to be a peddler.

There is no doubt that the poorer classes in our country are much more charitably disposed than their superiors in wealth. And I fancy it must arise a great deal from the comparative indistinction of the easy and the not so easy in these ranks. A workman or a peddler cannot shutter himself off from his less comfortable neighbors. If he treats himself to a luxury, he must do it in the face of a dozen who cannot. And what should more directly lead to charitable thoughts? . . . Thus the poor man, camping out in life, sees it as it is, and knows that every mouthful he puts in his belly has been wrenched out of the fingers of the hungry.

But at a certain stage of prosperity, as in a balloon ascent, the fortunate person passes through a zone of clouds, and sublunary matters are thenceforward hidden from his view. He sees nothing but the heavenly bodies, all in admirable order and positively as good as new. He finds himself surrounded in the most touching manner by the attentions of Providence, and compares himself involuntarily with the lilies and the sky-larks. He does not precisely sing, of course; but then he looks so unassuming in his open Landau! If all the world dined at one table, this philosophy would meet with some rude knocks.

PONT-SUR-SAMBRE

THE TRAVELING MERCHANT

LIKE the lackeys in Molière's farce, when the true nobleman broke in on their high life below stairs, we were destined to be confronted with a real peddler. To make the lesson still more poignant for fallen gentlemen like us, he was a peddler of infinitely more considera- tion than the sort of scurvy fellows we were taken for: like a lion among mice, or a ship of war bearing down upon two cock-boats. Indeed, he did not deserve the name of peddler at all: he was a traveling mer- chant.

I suppose it was about half-past eight when this worthy, Monsieur Hector Gilliard of Maubeuge, turned up at the ale-house door in a tilt cart drawn by a donkey, and cried cheerily on the inhabitants. He was a lean, nervous flibbertigibbet of a man, with some- thing the look of an actor, and something the look of a horse jockey. He had evidently prospered without any of the favors of education; for he adhered with stern simplicity to the masculine gender, and in the course of the evening passed off some fancy futures in a very florid style of architecture. With him came his wife, a comely young woman with her hair tied in a

(47)

yellow kerchief, and their son, a little fellow of four, in a blouse and military *kepi*. It was notable that the child was many degrees better dressed than either of the parents. We were informed he was already at a boarding-school; but the holidays having just commenced, he was off to spend them with his parents on a cruise. An enchanting holiday occupation, was it not? to travel all day with father and mother in the tilt cart full of countless treasures; the green country rattling by on either side, and the children in all the villages contemplating him with envy and wonder? It is better fun, during the holidays, to be the son of a traveling merchant, than son and heir to the greatest cotton spinner in creation. And as for being a reigning prince—indeed I never saw one if it was not Master Gilliard!

While M. Hector and the son of the house were putting up the donkey, and getting all the valuables under lock and key, the landlady warmed up the remains of our beefsteak, and fried the cold potatoes in slices, and Madame Gilliard set herself to waken the boy, who had come far that day, and was peevish and dazzled by the light. He was no sooner awake than he began to prepare himself for supper by eating galette, unripe pears and cold potatoes—with, so far as I could judge, positive benefit to his appetite.

The landlady, fired with motherly emulation, awoke her own little girl; and the two children were confronted. Master Gilliard looked at her for a moment, very much as a dog looks at his own reflection in a mirror before he turns away. He was at that time absorbed in the galette. His mother seemed crestfallen that he should display so little inclination toward the other sex; and expressed her disappointment with some candor and a very proper reference to the influence of years.

Sure enough a time will come when he will pay more attention to the girls, and think a great deal less of his mother: let us hope she will like it as well as she seemed to fancy. But it is odd enough; the very women who profess most contempt for mankind as a sex, seem to find even its ugliest particulars rather lively and high-minded in their own sons.

The little girl looked longer and with more interest, probably because she was in her own house, while he was a traveler and accustomed to strange sights. And besides, there was no galette in the case with her.

All the time of supper, there was nothing spoken of but my young lord. The two parents were both absurdly fond of their child. Monsieur kept insisting on his sagacity: how he knew all the children at school by name; and when this utterly failed on trial, how he was cautious and exact to a strange degree, and if asked anything, he would sit and think—and think, and if he did not know it, "my faith, he wouldn't tell you at all—ma foi, il ne vous le dira pas." Which is certainly a very high degree of caution. At intervals, M. Hector would appeal to his wife, with his mouth full of beefsteak, as to the little fellow's age at such or such a time when he had said or done something memorable; and I noticed that madame usually pooh-poohed these inquiries. She herself was not boastful in her vein; but she never had her fill of caressing the child; and she seemed to take a gentle pleasure in recalling all that was fortunate in his little existence. No schoolboy could have talked more of the holidays which were just beginning and less of the black schooltime which must inevitably follow after. She showed, with a pride perhaps partly mercantile in origin, his pockets preposterously swollen with tops and whistles and string. When she called at a house in the way of business, it appeared he kept her company; and whenever a sale was made, received a sou out of the profit. Indeed they spoiled him vastly, these two good people. But they had an eye to his manners for all that, and reproved him for some little faults in breeding, which occurred from time to time during supper.

On the whole, I was not much hurt at being taken for a peddler. I might think that I ate with greater delicacy, or that my mistakes in French belonged to a different order; but it was plain that these distinctions would be thrown away upon the landlady and the two laborers. In all essential things, we and the Gilliards cut very much the same figure in the ale-house kitchen. M. Hector was more at home, indeed, and took a higher tone with the world; but that was explicable on the ground of his driving a donkey-cart, while we poor bodies tramped afoot. I daresay, the rest of the company thought us dying with envy, though in no ill-sense, to be as far up in the profession as the new arrival.

And of one thing I am sure: that every one thawed and became more humanized and conversible as soon as these innocent people appeared upon the scene. I would not very readily trust the traveling merchant with any extravagant sum of money; but I am sure his heart was in the right place. In this mixed world, if you can find one or two sensible places in a man, above all, if you should find a whole family living together on such pleasant terms you may surely be satisfied, and take the rest for granted; or, what is a great deal better, boldly make up your mind that you can do perfectly well without the rest; and that ten thousand bad traits cannot make a single good one any the less good.

It was getting late. M. Hector lighted a stable lantern and went off to his cart for some arrangements; and my young gentleman proceeded to divest himself of the better part of his raiment, and play gymnastics on his mother's lap, and thence on to the floor, with accompaniment of laughter.

"Are you going to sleep alone?" asked the servant lass.

"There's little fear of that," says Master Gilliard.

"You sleep alone at school," objected his mother. "Come, come, you must be a man."

But he protested that school was a different matter from the holidays; that there were dormitories at school; and silenced the discussion with kisses: his mother smiling, no one better pleased than she.

There certainly was, as he phrased it, very little fear that he should sleep alone; for there was but one bed for the trio. We, on our part, had firmly protested against one man's accommodation for two; and we had a double-bedded pen in the loft of the house, furnished, beside the beds, with exactly three hat pegs and one table. There was not so much as a glass of water. But the window would open, by good fortune.

Some time before I fell asleep the loft was full of the sound of mighty snoring: the Gilliards, and the laborers, and the people of the inn, all at it, I suppose, with one consent. The young moon outside shone very clearly over Pont-sur-Sambre, and down upon the ale-house where all we peddlers were abed.

ON THE SAMBRE CANALIZED

TO LANDRECIES

IN the morning, when we came downstairs, the landlady pointed out to us two pails of water behind the street-door. "Voilà de l'eau pour vous débarbouiller," says she. And so there we made a shift to wash ourselves, while Madame Gilliard brushed the family boots on the outer doorstep, and M. Hector, whistling cheerily, arranged some small goods for the day's campaign in a portable chest of drawers, which formed a part of his baggage. Meanwhile the child was letting off Waterloo crackers all over the floor.

I wonder, by the bye, what they call Waterloo crackers in France; perhaps Austerlitz crackers. There is a great deal in the point of view. Do you remember the Frenchman who, traveling by way of Southampton, was put down in Waterloo Station, and had to drive across Waterloo Bridge? He had a mind to go home again, it seems.

Pont itself is on the river, but whereas it is ten minutes' walk from Quartes by dry land, it is six weary kilometers by water. We left our bags at the inn, and walked to our canoes through the wet orch-

⟨53⟩

ards unencumbered. Some of the children were there to see us off, but we were no longer the mysterious beings of the night before. A departure is much less romantic than an unexplained arrival in the golden evening. Although we might be greatly taken at a ghost's first appearance, we should behold him vanish with comparative equanimity.

The good folk of the inn at Pont, when we called there for the bags, were overcome with marveling. At sight of these two dainty little boats, with a fluttering Union Jack on each, and all the varnish shining from the sponge, they began to perceive that they had entertained angels unawares. The landlady stood upon the bridge, probably lamenting she had charged so little; the son ran to and fro, and called out the neighbors to enjoy the sight; and we paddled away from quite a crowd of wrapt observers. These gentlemen peddlers, indeed! Now you see their quality too late.

The whole day was showery, with occasional drenching plumps. We were soaked to the skin, then partially dried in the sun, then soaked once more. But there were some calm intervals, and one notably, when we were skirting the forest of Mormal, a sinister name to the ear, but a place most gratifying to sight and smell. It looked solemn along the river side, drooping its boughs into the water, and piling them up aloft into a wall of leaves. What is a forest but a city of nature's own, full of hardy and innocuous living things, where there is nothing dead and nothing made with the hands, but the citizens themselves are the houses and public monuments? There is nothing so much alive, and yet so quiet, as a woodland; and a pair of peo-

ple, swinging past in canoes, feel very small and bustling by comparison.

And surely of all smells in the world, the smell of
many trees is the sweetest and most fortifying. The
sea has a rude, pistoling sort of odor, that takes you
in the nostrils like snuff, and carries with it a fine
sentiment of open water and tall ships; but the smell
of a forest, which comes nearest to this in tonic quality, surpasses it by many degrees in the quality of
softness. Again, the smell of the sea has little variety,
but the smell of a forest is infinitely changeful; it varies
with the hour of the day, not in strength merely, but
in character; and the different sorts of trees, as you
go from one zone of the wood to another, seem to live
among different kinds of atmosphere. Usually the resin
of the fir predominates. But some woods are more coquettish in their habits; and the breath of the forest
of Mormal, as it came aboard upon us that showery
afternoon, was perfumed with nothing less delicate than
sweet-briar.

I wish our way had always lain among woods.
Trees are the most civil society. An old oak that has
been growing where he stands since before the Reforma-
tion, taller than many spires, more stately than the
greater part of mountains, and yet a living thing, liable
to sicknesses and death, like you and me: is not that
in itself a speaking lesson in history? But acres on
acres full of such patriarchs contiguously rooted, their
green tops billowing in the wind, their stalwart young-
lings pushing up about their knees: a whole forest,
healthy and beautiful, giving color to the light, giving
perfume to the air: what is this but the most imposing

piece in nature's repertory? Heine wished to lie like Merlin under the oaks of Broceliande. I should not be satisfied with one tree; but if the wood grew together like a banyan grove, I would be buried under the tap-root of the whole; my parts should circulate from oak to oak; and my consciousness should be diffused abroad in all the forest, and give a common heart to that assembly of green spires, so that it also might rejoice in its own loveliness and dignity. I think I feel a thousand squirrels leaping from bough to bough in my vast mausoleum; and the birds and the winds merrily coursing over its uneven, leafy surface.

Alas! the forest of Mormal is only a little bit of a wood, and it was but for a little way that we skirted by its boundaries. And the rest of the time the rain kept coming in squirts and the wind in squalls, until one's heart grew weary of such fitful, scolding weather. It was odd how the showers began when we had to carry the boats over a lock, and must expose our legs. They always did. This is a sort of thing that readily begets a personal feeling against nature. There seems no reason why the shower should not come five minutes before or five minutes after, unless you suppose an intention to affront you. The Cigarette had a mackintosh which put him more or less above these contrarieties. But I had to bear the brunt uncovered. I began to remember that nature was a woman. My companion, in a rosier temper, listened with great satisfaction to my Jeremiads, and ironically concurred. He instanced, as a cognate matter, the action of the tides, "Which," said he, "was altogether designed for the confusion of canoeists, except in so far as it was calculated to minister to a barren vanity on the part of the moon."

At the last lock, some little way out of Landrecies, I refused to go any further; and sat in a drift of rain by the side of the bank, to have a reviving pipe. A vivacious old man, whom I take to have been the devil, drew near and questioned me about our journey. In the fullness of my heart, I laid bare our plans before him. He said it was the silliest enterprise that ever he heard of. Why, did I not know, he asked me, that it was nothing but locks, locks, locks, the whole way? not to mention that, at this season of the year, we should find the Oise quite dry? "Get into a train, my little young man," said he, "and go you away home to your parents." I was so astounded at the man's malice, that I could only stare at him in silence. A tree would never have spoken to me like this. At last, I got out with some words. We had come from Antwerp already, I told him, which was a good long way; and we should do the rest in spite of him. Yes, I said, if there were no other reason, I would do it now, just because he had dared to say we could not. The pleasant old gentleman looked at me sneeringly, made an allusion to my canoe, and marched off, waggling his head.

I was still inwardly fuming, when up came a pair of young fellows, who imagined I was the Cigarette's servant—on a comparison, I suppose, of my bare jersey with the other's mackintosh—and asked me many questions about my place and my master's character. I said he was a good enough fellow, but had this absurd voyage on the head. "Oh, no, no," said one, "you must not say that; it is not absurd; it is very courageous of him." I believe these were a couple of angels sent to give me heart again. It was truly fortifying to re-produce all the old man's insinuations, as if they were original to me in my character of a malcontent foot-man, and have them brushed away like so many flies by these admirable young men.

When I recounted this affair to the Cigarette, "they must have a curious idea of how English servants be-have," says he, dryly, "for you treated me like a brute beast at the lock."

I was a good deal mortified; but my temper had suffered, it is a fact.

AT LANDRECIES

At Landrecies the rain still fell and the wind still blew; but we found a double-bedded room with plenty of furniture, real water-jugs with real water in them, and dinner: a real dinner, not innocent of real wine. After having been a peddler for one night, and a butt for the elements during the whole of the next day, these comfortable circumstances fell on my heart like sunshine. There was an English fruiterer at dinner, traveling with a Belgian fruiterer; in the evening at the cafe, we watched our compatriot drop a good deal of money at corks; and I don't know why, but this pleased us.

It turned out we were to see more of Landrecies than we expected; for the weather next day was simply bedlamite. It is not the place one would have chosen for a day's rest; for it consists almost entirely of fortifications. Within the ramparts, a few blocks of houses, a long row of barracks, and a church, figure, with what countenance they may, as the town. There seems to be no trade; and a shopkeeper from whom I bought a sixpenny flint and steel was so much affected that he filled my pockets with spare flints into the bar-

gain. The only public buildings that had any interest
for us were the hotel and the cafe. But we visited
the church. There lies Marshal Clarke. But as neither
of us had ever heard of that military hero, we bore
the associations of the spot with fortitude.

In all garrison towns, guard-calls, and reveilles, and
such like, make a fine romantic interlude in civic business. Bugles, and drums, and fifes, are of themselves
most excellent things in nature; and when they carry
the mind to marching armies, and the picturesque vi-
cissitudes of war, they stir up something proud in the
heart. But in a shadow of a town like Landrecies, with
little else moving, these points of war made a propor-
tionate commotion. Indeed, they were the only things
to remember. It was just the place to hear the round
going by at night in the darkness, with the solid tramp
of men marching, and the startling reverberations of
the drum. It reminded you, that even this place was
a point in the great warfaring system of Europe, and
might on some future day be ringed about with cannon
smoke and thunder, and make itself a name among
strong towns.

The drum, at any rate, from its martial voice and
notable physiological effect, nay even from its cumbrous
and comical shape, stands alone among the instruments
of noise. And if it be true, as I have heard it said,
that drums are covered with asses' skin, what a picturesque irony is there in that! As if this long-suffering animal's hide had not been sufficiently belabored
during life, now by Lyonnese costermongers, now by
presumptuous Hebrew prophets, it must be stripped from
his poor hinder quarters after death, stretched on a

drum, and beaten night after night round the streets of every garrison town in Europe. And up the heights of Alma and Spicheren, and wherever death has his red flag aflying, and sounds his own potent tuck upon the cannons, there also must the drummer boy, hurrying with white face over fallen comrades, batter and bemaul this slip of skin from the loins of peaceable donkeys.

Generally a man is never more uselessly employed than when he is at this trick of bastinadoing asses' hide. We know what effect it has in life, and how your dull ass will not mend his pace with beating. But in this state of mummy and melancholy survival of itself, when the hollow skin reverberates to the drummer's wrist, and each dub-a-dub goes direct to a man's heart, and puts madness there, and that disposition of the pulses which we, in our big way of talking, nickname Heroism:—is there not something in the nature of a revenge upon the donkey's persecutors? Of old, he might say, you drubbed me up hill and down dale, and I must endure; but now that I am dead, those dull thwacks that were scarcely audible in country lanes have become stirring music in front of the brigade; and for every blow that you lay on my old greatcoat, you will see a comrade stumble and fall.

Not long after the drums had passed the cafe, the Cigarette and the Arethusa began to grow sleepy, and set out for the hotel which was only a door or two away. But although we had been somewhat indifferent to Landrecies, Landrecies had not been indifferent to us. All day, we learned, people had been running out between the squalls to visit our two boats.

Hundreds of persons—so said report, although it fitted ill with our idea of the town—hundreds of persons had inspected them where they lay in a coal-shed. We were becoming lions in Landrecies, who had been only peddlers the night before in Pont.

And now, when we left the cafe, we were pursued and overtaken at the hotel door, by no less a person than the Juge de Paix: a functionary, as far as I can make out, of the character of a Scotch Sheriff Substitute. He gave us his card and invited us to sup with him on the spot, very neatly, very gracefully, as Frenchmen can do these things. It was for the credit of Landrecies, said he; and although we knew very well how little credit we could do the place, we must have been churlish fellows to refuse an invitation so politely introduced.

The house of the Judge was close by; it was a well-appointed bachelor's establishment with a curious collection of old brass warming-pans upon the walls. Some of these were most elaborately carved. It seemed a picturesque idea for a collector. You could not help thinking how many nightcaps had wagged over these warming-pans in past generations; what jests may have been made, and kisses taken, while they were in service; and how often they had been uselessly paraded in the bed of death. If they could only speak, at what absurd, indecorous and tragical scenes had they not been present!

The wine was excellent. When we made the Judge our compliments upon a bottle, "I do not give it you as my worst," said he. I wonder when Englishmen will learn these hospitable graces. They are worth learning; they set off life, and make ordinary moments ornamental.

There were two other Landrecienses present. One was the collector of something or other, I forget what; the other, we were told, was the principal notary of the place. So it happened that we all five more or less followed the law. At this rate, the talk was pretty certain to become technical. The Cigarette expounded the poor laws very magisterially. And a little later I found myself laying down the Scotch Law of Illegitimacy, of which I am glad to say I know nothing. The collector and the notary, who were both married men, accused the Judge, who was a bachelor, of having started the subject. He deprecated the charge, with a conscious, pleased air, just like all the men I have even seen, be they French or English. How strange that we should all, in our unguarded moments, rather like to be thought a bit of a rogue with the women!

As the evening went on, the wine grew more to my taste; the spirits proved better than the wine; the company was genial. This was the highest water mark of popular favor on the whole cruise. After all, being in a Judge's house, was there not something semi-official in the tribute? And so, remembering what a great country France is, we did full justice to our entertainment. Landrecies had been a long while asleep before we returned to the hotel; and the sentries on the ramparts were already looking for daybreak.

SAMBRE AND OISE CANAL

CANAL BOATS

NEXT day we made a late start in the rain. The Judge politely escorted us to the end of the lock under an umbrella. We had now brought ourselves to a pitch of humility in the matter of weather not often attained except in the Scotch Highlands. A rag of blue sky or a glimpse of sunshine set our hearts singing; and when the rain was not heavy, we counted the day almost fair.

Long lines of barges lay one after another along the canal; many of them looking mighty spruce and ship-shape in their jerkin of Archangel tar picked out with white and green. Some carried gay iron railings, and quite a parterre of flower-pots. Children played on the decks, as heedless of the rain as if they had been brought up on Loch Garron side; men fished over the gunwale, some of them under umbrellas; women did their washing; and every barge boasted its mongrel cur by way of watch-dog. Each one barked furiously at the canoes, running alongside until he had got to the end of his own ship, and so passing on the word to the dog aboard the next. We must have seen something like a hundred of these embarkations in the course of that day's paddle, ranged one after another like the houses in a street; and from not one of them were we disappointed of this accompaniment. It was like visiting a menagerie, the Cigarette remarked.

These little cities by the canal side had a very odd effect upon the mind. They seemed, with their flower-pots and smoking chimneys, their washings and dinners, a rooted piece of nature in the scene; and yet, if only the canal below were to open, one junk after another would hoist sail or harness horses and swim away into all parts of France; and the impromptu hamlet would separate, house by house, to the four winds. The chil-dren who played together to-day by the Sambre and Oise Canal, each at his own father's threshold, when and where might they next meet?

For some time past the subject of barges had occu-pied a great deal of our talk, and we had projected an old age on the canals of Europe. It was to be the most leisurely of progresses, now on a swift river at the tail of a steamboat, now waiting horses for days together on some inconsiderable junction. We should be seen pottering on deck in all the dignity of years, our white beards falling into our laps. We were ever to be busied among paintpots; so that there should be no white fresher, and no green more emerald than ours, in all the navy of the canals. There should be books in the cabin, and tobacco jars, and some old Burgundy as red as a November sunset and as odorous as a violet in April. There should be a flageolet whence the Ciga-rette, with cunning touch, should draw melting music under the stars; or perhaps, laying that aside, upraise his voice — somewhat thinner than of yore, and with here and there a quaver, or call it a natural grace note—in rich and solemn psalmody.

All this simmering in my mind, set me wishing to go aboard one of these ideal houses of lounging. I had plenty to choose from, as I coasted one after another, and the dogs bayed at me for a vagrant. At last I saw a nice old man and his wife looking at me with some interest, so I gave them good-day and pulled up alongside. I began with a remark upon their dog, which had somewhat the look of a pointer; thence I slid into a compliment on madame's flowers, and thence into a word in praise of their way of life.

If you ventured on such an experiment in England you would get a slap in the face at once. The life would be shown to be a vile one, not without a side shot at your better fortune. Now, what I like so much in France is the clear unflinching recognition by everybody of his own luck. They all know on which side their bread is buttered, and take a pleasure in showing it to others, which is surely the better part of religion: and they scorn to make a poor mouth over their poverty, which I take to be the better part of manliness. I have heard a woman in quite a better position at home, with a good bit of money in hand, refer to her own child with a horrid whine as "a poor man's child." I would not say such a thing to the Duke of Westminster. And the French are full of this spirit of independence. Perhaps it is the result of republican institutions, as they call them. Much more likely it is because there are so few people really poor, that the whiners are not enough to keep each other in countenance.

The people on the barge were delighted to hear that I admired their state. They understood perfectly well, they told me, how monsieur envied them. Without doubt monsieur was rich; and in that case he might make a canal-boat as pretty as a villa—joli comme un château. And with that they invited me on board their own water villa. They apologized for their cabin; they had not been rich enough to make it as it ought to be.

"The fire should have been here, at this side," explained the husband. "Then one might have a writing-table in the middle—books—and " (comprehensively) "all. It would be quite coquettish—ça serait tout-à-fait coquet." And he looked about him as though the improvements were already made. It was plainly not the first time that he had thus beautified his cabin in imagination; and when next he makes a hit, I should expect to see the writing-table in the middle.

Madame had three birds in a cage. They were no great thing, she explained. Fine birds were so dear. They had sought to get a Hollandais last winter in Rouen (Rouen? thought I; and is this whole mansion, with its dogs and birds and smoking chimneys, so far a traveler as that? and as homely an object among the cliffs and orchards of the Seine as on the green plains of Sambre?)—they had sought to get a Hollandais last winter in Rouen; but these cost fifteen francs apiece—picture it—fifteen francs!

"Pour un tout petit oiseau—For quite a little bird," added the husband.

As I continued to admire, the apologetics died away, and the good people began to brag of their barge, and their happy condition in life, as if they had been Emperor and Empress of the Indies. It was, in the Scotch phrase, a good hearing, and put me in good humor with the world. If people knew what an inspiriting thing it is to hear a man boasting, so long as he boasts of what he really has, I believe they would do it more freely and with a better grace.

They began to ask about our voyage. You should have seen how they sympathized. They seemed half ready to give up their barge and follow us. But these canaletti are only gypsies semi-domesticated. The semi-domestication came out in rather a pretty form. Suddenly madame's brow darkened. "Cependant," she began, and then stopped; and then began again by asking me if I were single?

"Yes," said I.

"And your friend who went by just now?"

He also was unmarried.

Oh, then—all was well. She could not have wives left alone at home; but since there were no wives in the question, we were doing the best we could.

"To see about one in the world," said the husband, "il n'y a que ça—there is nothing else worth while. A man, look you, who sticks in his own village like a bear," he went on, "—very well, he sees nothing. And then death is the end of all. And he has seen nothing."

Madame reminded her husband of an Englishman who had come up this canal in a steamer.

"Perhaps Mr. Moens in the 'Ytene,'" I suggested.

"That's it," assented the husband. "He had his wife and family with him, and servants. He came

ashore at all the locks and asked the name of the villages, whether from boatmen or lock-keepers; and then
he wrote, wrote them down. Oh, he wrote enormously!
I suppose it was a wager.''

A wager was a common enough explanation for our
own exploits, but it seemed an original reason for taking notes.

THE OISE IN FLOOD

BEFORE nine next morning the two canoes were installed on a light country cart at Étreux: and we were soon following them along the side of a pleasant valley full of hop-gardens and poplars. Agreeable villages lay here and there on the slope of the hill; notably, Tupigny, with the hop-poles hanging their garlands in the very street, and the houses clustered with grapes. There was a faint enthusiasm on our passage; weavers put their heads to the windows; children cried out in ecstasy at sight of the two "boaties"—barquettes: and bloused pedestrians, who were acquainted with our charioteer, jested with him on the nature of his freight.

We had a shower or two, but light and flying. The air was clean and sweet among all these green fields and green things growing. There was not a touch of autumn in the weather. And when, at Vadencourt, we launched from a little lawn opposite a mill, the sun broke forth and set all the leaves shining in the valley of the Oise.

The river was swollen with the long rains. From Vadencourt all the way to Origny, it ran with ever quickening speed, taking fresh heart at each mile, and

racing as though it already smelled the sea. The water
was yellow and turbulent, swung with an angry eddy
among half-submerged willows, and made an angry
clatter along stony shores. The course kept turning
and turning in a narrow and well-timbered valley.
Now, the river would approach the side, and run grid-
ing along the chalky base of the hill, and show us a
few open colza fields among the trees. Now, it would
skirt the garden-walls of houses, where we might catch
a glimpse through a doorway, and see a priest pacing
in the checkered sunlight. Again, the foliage closed so
thickly in front that there seemed to be no issue; only
a thicket of willows, overtopped by elms and poplars,
under which the river ran flush and fleet, and where
a kingfisher flew past like a piece of the blue sky. On
these different manifestations, the sun poured its clear
and catholic looks. The shadows lay as solid on the swift
surface of the stream as on the stable meadows. The
light sparkled golden in the dancing poplar leaves, and
brought the hills into communion with our eyes. And
all the while the river never stopped running or took
breath; and the reeds along the whole valley stood
shivering from top to toe.

There should be some myth (but if there is, I know
it not) founded on the shivering of the reeds. There
are not many things in nature more striking to man's
eye. It is such an eloquent pantomime of terror; and
to see such a number of terrified creatures taking
sanctuary in every nook along the shore, is enough to
infect a silly human with alarm. Perhaps they are only
a-cold, and no wonder, standing waist deep in the
stream. Or perhaps they have never got accustomed to

the speed and fury of the river's flux, or the miracle of its continuous body. Pan once played upon their forefathers; and so, by the hands of his river, he still plays upon these later generations down all the valley of the Oise; and plays the same air, both sweet and shrill, to tell us of the beauty and the terror of the world.

The canoe was like a leaf in the current. It took it up and shook it, and carried it masterfully away, like a Centaur carrying off a nymph. To keep some command on our direction required hard and diligent plying of the paddle. The river was in such a hurry for the sea! Every drop of water ran in a panic, like as many people in a frightened crowd. But what crowd was ever so numerous, or so single-minded? All the objects of sight went by at a dance measure; the eyesight raced with the racing river; the exigencies of every moment kept the pegs screwed so tight that our being quivered like a well-tuned instrument; and the blood shook off its lethargy, and trotted through all the highways and byways of the veins and arteries, and in and out of the heart, as if circulation were but a holiday journey, and not the daily moil of three score years and ten. The reeds might nod their heads in warning, and, with tremulous gestures, tell how the river was as cruel as it was strong and cold, and how death lurked in the eddy underneath the willows. But the reeds had to stand where they were; and those who stand still are always timid advisers. As for us, we could have shouted aloud. If this lively and beautiful river were, indeed, a thing of death's contrivance, the old ashen rogue had famously outwitted himself with us. I was living three to the minute. I was scoring points against him every stroke of my paddle, every turn of the stream. I have rarely had better profit of my life.

For I think we may look upon our little private war with death somewhat in this light. If a man knows he will sooner or later be robbed upon a journey, he will have a bottle of the best in every inn, and look upon all his extravagances as so much gained upon the thieves. And above all, where, instead of simply spend-ing, he makes a profitable investment for some of his money, when it will be out of risk of loss. So every bit of brisk living, and above all when it is healthful, is just so much gained upon the wholesale filcher, death. We shall have the less in our pockets, the more in our stomach, when he cries stand and deliver. A swift stream is a favorite artifice of his, and one that brings him in a comfortable thing per annum; but when he and I come to settle our accounts, I shall whistle in his face for these hours upon the upper Oise.

Toward afternoon we got fairly drunken with the sunshine and the exhilaration of the pace. We could no longer contain ourselves and our content. The canoes were too small for us; we must be out and stretch ourselves on shore. And so in a green meadow we bestowed our limbs on the grass, and smoked deifying tobacco and proclaimed the world excellent. It was the last good hour of the day, and I dwell upon it with extreme complacency.

On one side of the valley, high upon the chalky summit of the hill, a plowman with his team appeared and disappeared at regular intervals. At each revela-

tion he stood still for a few seconds against the sky:
for all the world (as the Cigarette declared) like a toy
Burns who had just plowed up the Mountain Daisy.
He was the only living thing within view, unless we
are to count the river.

On the other side of the valley a group of red
roofs and a belfry showed among the foliage. Thence
some inspired bell-ringer made the afternoon musical on
a chime of bells. There was something very sweet and
taking in the air he played; and we thought we had
never heard bells speak so intelligibly, or sing so melodi-
ously, as these. It must have been to some such measure that the spinners and the young maids sang, "Come
away, Death," in the Shakespearian "Illyria." There
is so often a threatening note, something blatant and
metallic, in the voice of bells, that I believe we have
fully more pain than pleasure from hearing them; but
these, as they sounded abroad, now high, now low,
now with a plaintive cadence that caught the ear like
the burthen of a popular song, were always moderate
and tunable, and seemed to fall in with the spirit of
still, rustic places, like the noise of a waterfall or the
babble of a rookery in spring. I could have asked the
bell-ringer for his blessing, good, sedate old man, who
swung the rope so gently to the time of his meditations. I could have blessed the priest or the heritors,
or whoever may be concerned with such affairs in
France, who had left these sweet old bells to gladden
the afternoon, and not held meetings, and made collec-
tions, and had their names repeatedly printed in the
local paper, to rig up a peal of brand-new, brazen,
Birmingham-hearted substitutes, who should bombard

their sides to the provocation of a brand-new bell-
ringer, and fill the echoes of the valley with terror
and riot.

At last the bells ceased, and with their note the
sun withdrew. The piece was at an end; shadow and
silence possessed the valley of the Oise. We took to
the paddle with glad hearts, like people who have sat
out a noble performance, and return to work. The river
was more dangerous here; it ran swifter, the eddies
were more sudden and violent. All the way down we
had had our fill of difficulties. Sometimes it was a
weir which could be shot, sometimes one so shallow and
full of stakes that we must withdraw the boats from
the water and carry them round. But the chief sort of
obstacle was a consequence of the late high winds.
Every two or three hundred yards a tree had fallen
across the river and usually involved more than another
in its fall. Often there was free water at the end, and
we could steer round the leafy promontory and hear
the water sucking and bubbling among the twigs.
Often, again, when the tree reached from bank to
bank, there was room, by lying close, to shoot through
underneath, canoe and all. Sometimes it was necessary
to get out upon the trunk itself and pull the boats
across; and sometimes, where the stream was too impetuous for this, there was nothing for it but to land
and "carry over." This made a fine series of accidents
in the day's career, and kept us aware of ourselves.

Shortly after our re-embarkation, while I was leading by a long way, and still full of a noble, exulting
spirit in honor of the sun, the swift pace, and the
church bells, the river made one of its leonine pounces

round a corner, and I was aware of another fallen tree within a stone-cast. I had my backboard down in a trice, and aimed for a place where the trunk seemed high enough above the water, and the branches not too thick to let me slip below. When a man has just vowed eternal brotherhood with the universe, he is not in a temper to take great determinations coolly, and this, which might have been a very important determination for me, had not been taken under a happy star. The tree caught me about the chest, and while I was yet struggling to make less of myself and get through, the river took the matter out of my hands, and bereaved me of my boat. The "Arethusa" swung round broadside on, leaned over, ejected so much of me as still remained on board, and thus disencumbered, whipped under the tree, righted, and went merrily away down stream.

I do not know how long it was before I scrambled on to the tree to which I was left clinging, but it was longer than I cared about. My thoughts were of a grave and almost somber character, but I still clung to my paddle. The stream ran away with my heels as fast I could pull up my shoulders, and I seemed, by the weight, to have all the water of the Oise in my trouser pockets. You can never know, till you try it; what a dead pull a river makes against a man. Death himself had me by the heels, for this was his last ambuscado, and he must now join personally in the fray. And still I held to my paddle. At last I dragged myself on to my stomach on the trunk, and lay there a breathless sop, with a mingled sense of humor and injustice. A poor figure I must have presented to Burns

upon the hill-top with his team. But there was the
paddle in my hand. On my tomb, if ever I have one,
I mean to get these words inscribed: "He clung to
his paddle."

The Cigarette had gone past a while before; for, as
I might have observed, if I had been a little less
pleased with the universe at the moment, there was a
clear way round the tree-top at the further side. He
had offered his services to haul me out, but as I was
then already on my elbows, I had declined, and sent
him down stream after the truant "Arethusa." The
stream was too rapid for a man to mount with one
canoe, let alone two, upon his hands. So I crawled
along the trunk to shore, and proceeded down the
meadows by the river side. I was so cold that my
heart was sore. I had now an idea of my own, why
the reeds so bitterly shivered. I could have given any
of them a lesson. The Cigarette remarked facetiously,
that he thought I was "taking exercise" as I drew
near, until he made out for certain that I was only
twittering with cold. I had a rub down with a towel,
and donned a dry suit from the india-rubber bag. But
I was not my own man again for the rest of the voyage. I had a queasy sense that I wore my last dry
clothes upon my body. The struggle had tired me;
and perhaps, whether I knew it or not, I was a little
dashed in spirit. The devouring element in the universe had leaped out against me, in this green valley
quickened by a running stream. The bells were all
very pretty in their way, but I had heard some of the
hollow notes of Pan's music. Would the wicked river
drag me down by the heels, indeed? and look so beau-

tiful all the time? Nature's good-humor was only skin-deep after all.

There was still a long way to go by the winding course of the stream, and darkness had fallen, and a late bell was ringing in Origny Sainte-Benoîte, when we arrived.

ORIGNY SAINTE-BENOITE

A BY-DAY

THE next day was Sunday, and the church bells had little rest; indeed I do not think I remember anywhere else so great a choice of services as were here offered to the devout. And while the bells made merry in the sunshine, all the world with his dog was out shooting among the beets and colza.

In the morning a hawker and his wife went down the street at a foot-pace, singing to a very slow, lamentable music "O France, mes amours." It brought everybody to the door; and when our landlady called in the man to buy the words, he had not a copy of them left. She was not the first nor the second who had been taken with the song. There is something very pathetic in the love of the French people, since the war, for dismal patriotic music-making. I have watched a forester from Alsace while some one was singing "Les malheurs de la France," at a baptismal party in the neighborhood of Fontainebleau. He arose from the table and took his son aside, close by where I was standing. "Listen, listen," he said, bearing on the boy's shoulder, "and remember this, my son." A little after

he went out into the garden suddenly, and I could
hear him sobbing in the darkness.

The humiliation of their arms, and the loss of Alsace
and Lorraine, made a sore pull on the endurance of
this sensitive people; and their hearts are still hot, not
so much against Germany as against the Empire. In
what other country will you find a patriotic ditty bring
all the world into the street? But affliction heightens
love; and we shall never know we are Englishmen
until we have lost India. Independent America is still
the cross of my existence; I cannot think of Farmer
George without abhorrence; and I never feel more
warmly to my own land than when I see the stars
and stripes, and remember what our empire might have
been.

The hawker's little book, which I purchased, was a
curious mixture. Side by side with the flippant, rowdy
nonsense of the Paris music-halls, there were many pastoral pieces, not without a touch of poetry, I thought,
and instinct with the brave independence of the poorer
class in France. There you might read how the wood-
cutter gloried in his ax, and the gardener scorned to
be ashamed of his spade. It was not very well written, this poetry of labor, but the pluck of the sentiment redeemed what was weak or wordy in the ex-
pression. The martial and the patriotic pieces, on the
other hand, were tearful, womanish productions one and
all. The poet had passed under the Caudine Forks; he
sang for an army visiting the tomb of its old renown,
with arms reversed; and sang not of victory, but of
death.

There was a number in the hawker's collection

called Conscrits Français, which may rank among the
most dissuasive war-lyrics on record. It would not be
possible to fight at all in such a spirit. The bravest
conscript would turn pale if such a ditty were struck
up beside him on the morning of battle; and whole
regiments would pile their arms to its tune.

If Fletcher of Saltoun is in the right about the influence of national songs, you would say France was come
to a poor pass. But the thing will work its own cure,
and a sound-hearted and courageous people weary at
length of sniveling over their disasters. Already Paul
Deroulède has written some manly military verses.
There is not much of the trumpet note in them, perhaps, to stir a man's heart in his bosom; they lack
the lyrical elation, and move slowly; but they are written in a grave, honorable, stoical spirit, which should
carry soldiers far in a good cause. One feels as if one
would like to trust Deroulède with something. It will
be happy if he can so far inoculate his fellow-country-
men that they may be trusted with their own future.
And in the meantime, here is an antidote to "French
Conscripts" and much other doleful versification.

We had left the boats over-night in the custody of
one whom we shall call Carnival. I did not properly
catch his name, and perhaps that was not unfortunate
for him, as I am not in a position to hand him down
with honor to posterity. To this person's premises we
strolled in the course of the day, and found quite a
little deputation inspecting the canoes. There was a
stout gentleman with a knowledge of the river, which
he seemed eager to impart. There was a very elegant
young gentleman in a black coat, with a smattering of

English, who led the talk at once to the Oxford and
Cambridge Boat Race. And then there were three
handsome girls from fifteen to twenty; and an old
gentleman in a blouse, with no teeth to speak of, and
a strong country accent. Quite the pick of Origny, I
should suppose.

The Cigarette had some mysteries to perform with
his rigging in the coach-house; so I was left to do
the parade single-handed. I found myself very much
of a hero whether I would or not. The girls were full
of little shudderings over the dangers of our journey.
And I thought it would be ungallant not to take my
cue from the ladies. My mishap of yesterday, told in
an off-hand way, produced a deep sensation. It was
Othello over again, with no less than three Desdemonas
and a sprinkling of sympathetic senators in the background. Never were the canoes more flattered, or flattered more adroitly.

"It is like a violin," cried one of the girls in an
ecstasy.

"I thank you for the word, mademoiselle," said I.
"All the more since there are people who call out to
me that it is like a coffin."

"Oh! but it is really like a violin. It is finished like
a violin," she went on.

"And polished like a violin," added a senator.

"One has only to stretch the cords," concluded another, "and then tum-tumty-tum" — he imitated the
result with spirit.

Was not this a graceful little ovation? Where this
people finds the secret of its pretty speeches I cannot
imagine; unless the secret should be no other than a

sincere desire to please? But then **no disgrace is at**-tached in France to saying a thing neatly; whereas in England, to talk like a book is to **give in** one's resignation to society.

The old gentleman in the blouse stole into the coach-house, and somewhat irrelevantly informed the Cigarette that he was the father of the three girls and four more: quite an exploit for a Frenchman.

"You are very fortunate," answered the Cigarette politely.

And the old gentleman, having apparently gained his point, stole away again.

We all got very friendly together. The girls proposed to start with us on the morrow, if you please! And jesting apart, every one was anxious to know the hour of our departure. Now, when you are going to crawl into your canoe from a bad launch, a crowd, however friendly, is undesirable; and so we told them not before twelve, and mentally determined to be off by ten at latest.

Toward evening we went abroad again to post some letters. It was cool and pleasant; the long village was quite empty, except for one or two urchins who followed us as they might have followed a menagerie; the hills and the tree-tops looked in from all sides through the clear air; and the bells were chiming for yet another service.

Suddenly, we sighted the three girls standing, with a fourth sister, in front of a shop on the wide selvage of the roadway. We had been very merry with them a little while ago, to be sure. But what was the etiquette of Origny? Had it been a country road, of

course we should have spoken to them; but here, under the eyes of all the gossips, ought we to do even
as much as bow? I consulted the Cigarette.

"Look," said he.

I looked. There were the four girls on the same
spot; but now four backs were turned to us, very upright and conscious. Corporal Modesty had given the
word of command, and the well-disciplined picket had
gone right-about-face like a single person. They main-
tained this formation all the while we were in sight;
but we heard them tittering among themselves, and
the girl whom we had not met, laughed with open
mouth, and even looked over her shoulder at the
enemy. I wonder was it altogether modesty after all?
or in part a sort of country provocation?

As we were returning to the inn, we beheld something floating in the ample field of golden evening sky,
above the chalk cliffs and the trees that grow along
their summit. It was too high up, too large and too
steady, for a kite; and as it was dark, it could not be
a star. For although a star were as black as ink and
as rugged as a walnut, so amply does the sun bathe
heaven with radiance that it would sparkle like a point
of light for us. The village was dotted with people
with their heads in air; and the children were in a
bustle all along the street and far up the straight road
that climbs the hill, where we could still see them running in loose knots. It was a balloon, we learned, which
had left Saint Quentin at half-past five that evening.
Mighty composedly the majority of the grown people
took it. But we were English, and were soon running
up the hill with the best. Being travelers ourselves in

a small way, we would fain have seen these other travelers alight.

The spectacle was over by the time we gained the top of the hill. All the gold had withered out of the sky, and the balloon had disappeared. Whither? I ask myself; caught up into the seventh heaven? or come safely to land somewhere in that blue uneven distance, into which the roadway dipped and melted before our eyes? Probably the aeronauts were already warming themselves at a farm chimney, for they say it is cold in these unhomely regions of the air. The night fell swiftly. Roadside trees and disappointed sightseers, returning through the meadows, stood out in black against a margin of low red sunset. It was cheerfuler to face the other way, and so down the hill we went, with a full moon, the color of a melon, swinging high above the wooded valley, and the white cliffs behind us faintly reddened by the fire of the chalk kilns.

The lamps were lighted, and the salads were being made in Origny Sainte-Benoîte by the river

ORIGNY SAINTE-BENOÎTE

THE COMPANY AT TABLE

ALTHOUGH we came late for dinner, the company at table treated us to sparkling wine. "That is how we are in France," said one. "Those who sit down with us are our friends." And the rest applauded.

They were three altogether, and an odd trio to pass the Sunday with.

Two of them were guests like ourselves, both men of the north. One ruddy, and of a full habit of body, with copious black hair and beard, the intrepid hunter of France, who thought nothing so small, not even a lark or a minnow, but he might vindicate his prowess by its capture. For such a great, healthy man, his hair flourishing like Samson's, his arteries running buckets of red blood, to boast of these infinitesimal exploits, produced a feeling of disproportion in the world, as when a steam-hammer is set to cracking nuts. The other was a quiet, subdued person, blond and lymphatic and sad, with something the look of a Dane: "Tristes têtes de Danois!" as Gaston Lafenestre used to say.

I must not let that name go by without a word

for the best of all good fellows now gone down into
the dust. We shall never again see Gaston in his forest costume—he was Gaston with all the world, in
affection, not in disrespect—nor hear him wake the
echoes of Fontainebleau with the woodland horn. Never
again shall his kind smile put peace among all races
of artistic men, and make the Englishman at home in
France. Never more shall the sheep, who were not
more innocent at heart than he, sit all unconsciously
for his industrious pencil. He died too early, at the
very moment when he was beginning to put forth
fresh sprouts, and blossom into something worthy of
himself; and yet none who knew him will think he
lived in vain. I never knew a man so little, for whom
yet I had so much affection; and I find it a good test
of others, how much they had learned to understand
and value him. His was indeed a good influence in
life while he was still among us; he had a fresh
laugh, it did you good to see him; and however sad
he may have been at heart, he always bore a bold
and cheerful countenance, and took fortune's worst as
it were the showers of spring. But now his mother
sits alone by the side of Fontainebleau woods, where
he gathered mushrooms in his hardy and penurious
youth.

Many of his pictures found their way across the
channel: besides those which were stolen, when a das-
tardly Yankee left him alone in London with two English pence, and perhaps twice as many words of
English. If any one who reads these lines should have
a scene of sheep, in the manner of Jacques, with this
fine creature's signature, let him tell himself that one

of the kindest and bravest of men has lent a hand to
decorate His lodging. There may be better pictures in
the National Gallery; but not a painter among the
generations had a better heart. Precious in the sight
of the Lord of humanity, the Psalms tell us, is the
death of His saints. It had need to be precious; for it
is very costly, when by the stroke a mother is left
desolate, and the peace-maker, and *peace-looker*, of a
whole society is laid in the ground with Cæsar and the
Twelve Apostles.

There is something lacking among the oaks of Fontainebleau; and when the dessert comes in at Barbizon,
people look to the door for a figure that is gone.

The third of our companions at Origny was no less
a person than the landlady's husband: not properly the
landlord, since he worked himself in a factory during
the day, and came to his own house at evening as a
guest: a man worn to skin and bone by perpetual excitement, with baldish head, sharp features, and swift,
shining eyes. On Saturday, describing some paltry adventure at a duck-hunt, he broke a plate into a score
of fragments. Whenever he made a remark, he would
look all round the table, with his chin raised, and a
spark of green light in either eye, seeking approval.
His wife appeared now and again in the doorway of
the room where she was superintending dinner, with a
"Henri, you forget yourself," or a "Henri, you can
surely talk without making such a noise." Indeed,
that was what the honest fellow could not do. On
the most trifling matter, his eyes kindled, his fist visited
the table, and his voice rolled abroad in changeful
thunder. I never saw such a petard of a man; I

think the devil was in him. He had two favorite expressions: "it is logical," or illogical, as the case might be: and this other, thrown out with a certain bravado, as a man might unfurl a banner, at the beginning of many a long and sonorous story: "I am a proletarian, you see." Indeed, we saw it very well. God forbid that ever I should find him handling a gun in Paris streets. That will not be a good moment for the general public.

I thought his two phrases very much represented the good and evil of his class, and to some extent of his country. It is a strong thing to say what one is, and not be ashamed of it; even although it be in doubtful taste to repeat the statement too often in one evening. I should not admire it in a duke, of course; but as times go, the trait is honorable in a workman. On the other hand, it is not at all a strong thing to put one's reliance upon logic; and our own logic particularly, for it is generally wrong. We never know where we are to end, if once we begin following words or doctors. There is an upright stock in a man's own heart that is trustier than any syllogism; and the eyes, and the sympathies and appetites, know a thing or two that have never yet been stated in controversy. Reasons are as plentiful as blackberries; and, like fisticuffs, they serve impartially with all sides. Doctrines do not stand or fall by their proofs, and are only logical in so far as they are cleverly put. An able controversialist no more than an able general demonstrates the justice of his cause. But France is all gone wandering after one or two big words; it will take some time before they can be satisfied that they are no more than words, however big; and when once that is done, they will perhaps find logic less diverting.

The conversation opened with details of the day's shooting. When all the sportsmen of a village shoot over the village territory pro indiviso, it is plain that many questions of etiquette and priority must arise.

"Here now," cried the landlord, brandishing a plate, "here is a field of beet-root. Well. Here am I then. I advance, do I not? Eh bien! sacristi," and the statement, waxing louder, rolls off into a reverberation of oaths, the speaker glaring about for sympathy, and everybody nodding his head to him in the name of peace.

The ruddy Northman told some tales of his own prowess in keeping order: notably one of a Marquis.

"Marquis," I said, "if you take another step I fire upon you. You have committed a dirtiness, Marquis."

Whereupon, it appeared, the Marquis touched his cap and withdrew.

The landlord applauded noisily. "It was well done," he said. "He did all that he could. He admitted he was wrong." And then oath upon oath. He was no marquis-lover either, but he had a sense of justice in him, this proletarian host of ours.

From the matter of hunting, the talk veered into a general comparison of Paris and the country. The proletarian beat the table like a drum in praise of Paris. "What is Paris? Paris is the cream of France. There are no Parisians: it is you and I and everybody who are Parisians. A man has eighty chances per cent to get on in the world in Paris." And he drew a vivid sketch of the workman in a den no bigger than a dog-hutch, making articles that were to go all over the world. "Eh bien, quoi, c'est magnifique, ça!" cried he.

The sad Northman interfered in praise of a peasant's life; he thought Paris bad for men and women; "centralization," said he—

But the landlord was at his throat in a moment. It was all logical, he showed him; and all magnificent. "What a spectacle! What a glance for an eye!" And the dishes reeled upon the table under a cannonade of blows.

Seeking to make peace, I threw in a word in praise of the liberty of opinion in France. I could hardly have shot more amiss. There was an instant silence, and a great wagging of significant heads. They did not fancy the subject, it was plain; but they gave me to understand that the sad Northman was a martyr on account of his views. "Ask him a bit," said they. "Just ask him."

"Yes, sir," said he in his quiet way, answering me, although I had not spoken, "I am afraid there is less liberty of opinion in France than you may imagine." And with that he dropped his eyes, and seemed to consider the subject at an end.

Our curiosity was mightily excited at this. How, or why, or when, was this lymphatic bagman martyred? We concluded at once it was on some religious question, and brushed up our memories of the Inquisition, which were principally drawn from Poe's horrid story, and the sermon in Tristram Shandy, I believe.

On the morrow we had an opportunity of going further into the question; for when we rose very early to avoid a sympathizing deputation at our departure, we found the hero up before us. He was breaking his fast on white wine and raw onions, in order to keep up the character of martyr, I conclude. We had a long conversation, and made out what we wanted in spite of his reserve. But here was a truly curious circumstance. It seems possible for two Scotchmen and a Frenchman to discuss during a long half hour, and each nationality have a different idea in view throughout. It was not till the very end that we discovered his heresy had been political, or that he suspected our mistake. The terms and spirit in which he spoke of his political beliefs were, in our eyes, suited to religious beliefs. And *vice versa*.

Nothing could be more characteristic of the two countries. Politics are the religion of France; as Nanty Ewart would have said, "A d—d bad religion"; while we, at home, keep most of our bitterness for little differences about a hymn-book, or a Hebrew word which, perhaps, neither of the parties can translate. And perhaps the misconception is typical of many others that may never be cleared up: not only between people of different race, but between those of different sex.

As for our friend's martyrdom, he was a Communist, or perhaps only a Communard, which is a very different thing; and had lost one or more situations in consequence. I think he had also been rejected in marriage; but perhaps he had a sentimental way of considering business which deceived me. He was a mild, gentle creature, anyway; and I hope he has got a better situation, and married a more suitable wife since then.

DOWN THE OISE: TO MOY

CARNIVAL notoriously cheated us at first. Finding us easy in our ways, he regretted having let us off so cheaply; and taking me aside, told me a cock-and-bull story with the moral of another five francs for the narrator. The thing was palpably absurd; but I paid up, and at once dropped all friendliness of manner, and kept him in his place as an inferior with freezing British dignity. He saw in a moment that he had gone too far, and killed a willing horse; his face fell; I am sure he would have refunded if he could only have thought of a decent pretext. He wished me to drink with him, but I would none of his drinks. He grew pathetically tender in his professions; but I walked beside him in silence or answered him in stately courtesies; and when we got to the landing-place, passed the word in English slang to the Cigarette.

In spite of the false scent we had thrown out the day before, there must have been fifty people about the bridge. We were as pleasant as we could be with all but Carnival. We said good-by, shaking hands with the old gentleman who knew the river and the young gentleman who had a smattering of English; but never

a word for Carnival. Poor Carnival, here was a humiliation. He who had been so much identified with
the canoes, who had given orders in our name, who
had shown off the boats and even the boatmen like a
private exhibition of his own, to be now so publicly
shamed by the lions of his caravan! I never saw any-
body look more crestfallen than he. He hung in the
background, coming timidly forward ever and again as
he thought he saw some symptom of a relenting humor,
and falling hurriedly back when he encountered a cold
stare. Let us hope it will be a lesson to him.

I would not have mentioned Carnival's peccadillo had
not the thing been so uncommon in France. This, for
instance, was the only case of dishonesty or even sharp
practice in our whole voyage. We talk very much
about our honesty in England. It is a good rule to
be on your guard wherever you hear great professions
about a very little piece of virtue. If the English could
only hear how they are spoken of abroad, they might
confine themselves for a while to remedying the fact;
and perhaps even when that was done, give us fewer
of their airs.

The young ladies, the graces of Origny, were not
present at our start, but when we got round to the
second bridge, behold it was black with sightseers! We
were loudly cheered, and for a good way below, young
lads and lasses ran along the bank still cheering. What
with current and paddling, we were flashing along like
swallows. It was no joke to keep up with us upon
the woody shore. But the girls picked up their skirts,
as if they were sure they had good ankles, and followed until their breath was out. The last to weary

were the three graces and a couple of companions; and just as they too had had enough, the foremost of the three leaped upon a tree stump and kissed her hand to the canoeists. Not Diana herself, although this was more of a Venus after all, could have done a graceful thing more gracefully. "Come back again!" she cried; and all the others echoed her; and the hills about Origny repeated the words, "Come back." But the river had us round an angle in a twinkling, and we were alone with the green trees and running water.

Come back? There is no coming back, young ladies, on the impetuous stream of life.

The merchant bows unto the seaman's star,
The plowman from the sun his season takes.

And we must all set our pocket watches by the clock of fate. There is a headlong, forth-right tide, that bears away man with his fancies like a straw, and runs fast in time and space. It is full of curves like this, your winding river of the Oise; and lingers and returns in pleasant pastorals; and yet, rightly thought upon, never returns at all. For though it should revisit the same acre of meadow in the same hour, it will have made an ample sweep between whiles; many little streams will have fallen in; many exhalations risen toward the sun; and even although it were the same acre, it will no more be the same river of Oise. And thus, O graces of Origny, although the wandering fortune of my life should carry me back again to where you await death's whistle by the river, that will not be the old I who walks the street; and those wives and mothers, say, will those be you?

There was never any mistake about the Oise, as a matter of fact. In these upper reaches, it was still in a prodigious hurry for the sea. It ran so fast and merrily, through all the windings of its channel, that I strained my thumb, fighting with the rapids, and had to paddle all the rest of the way with one hand turned up. Sometimes, it had to serve mills; and being still a little river, ran very dry and shallow in the meanwhile. We had to put our legs out of the boat, and shove ourselves off the sand of the bottom with our feet. And still it went on its way singing among the poplars and making a green valley in the world. After a good woman, and a good book, and tobacco, there is nothing so agreeable on earth as a river. I forgave it its attempt on my life; which was after all one part owing to the unruly winds of heaven that had blown down the tree, one part to my own mismanagement, and only a third part to the river itself, and that not out of malice, but from its great pre-occupation over its business of getting to the sea. A difficult business, too; for the detours it had to make are not to be counted. The geographers seem to have given up the attempt; for I found no map represent the infinite contortion of its course. A fact will say more than any of them. After we had been some hours, three if I mistake not, flitting by the trees at this smooth, break-neck gallop, when we came upon a hamlet and asked where we were, we had got no further than four kilo-meters (say two miles and a half) from Origny. If it were not for the honor of the thing (in the Scotch saying), we might almost as well have been standing still.

We lunched on a meadow inside a parallelogram of poplars. The leaves danced and prattled in the wind all round about us. The river hurried on meanwhile, and seemed to chide at our delay. Little we cared. The river knew where it was going; not so we: the less our hurry, where we found good quarters and a pleasant theater for a pipe. At that hour, stockbrokers were shouting in Paris Bourse for two or three per cent; but we minded them as little as the sliding stream, and sacrificed a hecatomb of minutes to the gods of tobacco and digestion. Hurry is the resource of the faithless. Where a man can trust his own heart, and those of his friends, to-morrow is as good as to-day. And if he die in the meanwhile, why then, there he dies, and the question is solved.

We had to take to the canal in the course of the afternoon; because, where it crossed the river, there was, not a bridge, but a siphon. If it had not been for an excited fellow on the bank we should have paddled right into the siphon, and thenceforward not paddled any more. We met a man, a gentleman, on the tow-path, who was much interested in our cruise. And I was witness to a strange seizure of lying suffered by the Cigarette; who, because his knife came from Norway, narrated all sorts of adventures in that country, where he has never been. He was quite feverish at the end, and pleaded demoniacal possession.

Moy (pronounce Moÿ) was a pleasant little village, gathered round a château in a moat. The air was perfumed with hemp from neighboring fields. At the Golden Sheep we found excellent entertainment. German shells from the siege of La Fère, Nürnberg fig-

ures, gold fish in a bowl, and all manner of knick-
knacks, embellished the public room. The landlady was
a stout, plain, short-sighted, motherly body, with something not far short of a genius for cookery. She had
a guess of her excellence herself. After every dish was
sent in she would come and look on at the dinner for
a while, with puckered, blinking eyes. "C'est bon,
n'est-ce pas?" she would say; and when she had received a proper answer, she disappeared into the kitchen.
That common French dish, partridge and cabbages, became a new thing in my eyes at the Golden Sheep;
and many subsequent dinners have bitterly disappointed
me in consequence. Sweet was our rest in the Golden
Sheep at Moy.

LA FERE OF CURSED MEMORY

WE lingered in Moy a good part of the day, for we were fond of being philosophical, and scorned long journeys and early starts on principle. The place, moreover, invited to repose. People in elaborate shooting costumes sallied from the chateau with guns and gamebags; and this was a pleasure in itself, to remain behind while these elegant pleasure-seekers took the first of the morning. In this way, all the world may be an aristocrat, and play the duke among marquises, and the reigning monarch among dukes, if he will only outvie them in tranquillity. An imperturbable demeanor comes from perfect patience. Quiet minds cannot be perplexed or frightened, but go on in fortune or misfortune at their own private pace, like a clock during a thunderstorm.

We made a very short day of it to La Fère; but the dusk was falling, and a small rain had begun before we stowed the boats. La Fère is a fortified town in a plain, and has two belts of rampart. Between the first and the second extends a region of waste land and cultivated patches. Here and there along the wayside were posters forbidding trespass in the name of

military engineering. At last, a second gateway admitted us to the town itself. Lighted windows looked
gladsome, whiffs of comfortable cookery came abroad
upon the air. The town was full of the military reserve, out for the French Autumn maneuvers, and the
reservists walked speedily and wore their formidable
greatcoats. It was a fine night to be within doors
over dinner, and hear the rain upon the windows.

The Cigarette and I could not sufficiently congratu-
late each other on the prospect, for we had been told
there was a capital inn at La Fère. Such a dinner as
we were going to eat! such beds as we were to sleep
in!—and all the while the rain raining on houseless folk
over all the poplared country-side! It made our mouths
water. The inn bore the name of some woodland animal, stag, or hart, or hind, I forget which. But I
shall never forget how spacious and how eminently
habitable it looked as we drew near. The carriage entry was lighted up, not by intention, but from the
mere superfluity of fire and candle in the house. A
rattle of many dishes came to our ears; we sighted
a great field of tablecloth; the kitchen glowed like a
forge and smelled like a garden of things to eat.

Into this, the inmost shrine, and physiological heart,
of a hostlery, with all its furnaces in action, and all
its dressers charged with viands, you are now to suppose us making our triumphal entry, a pair of damp
rag-and-bone men, each with a limp india-rubber bag
upon his arm. I do not believe I have a sound view
of that kitchen; I saw it through a sort of glory: but
it seemed to me crowded with the snowy caps of cook-
men, who all turned round from their saucepans and

looked at us with surprise. There was no doubt about the landlady, however: there she was, heading her army, a flushed, angry woman, full of affairs. Her I asked politely—too politely, thinks the Cigarette—if we could have beds: she surveying us coldly from head to foot.

"You will find beds in the suburb," she remarked. "We are too busy for the like of you."

If we could make an entrance, change our clothes, and order a bottle of wine, I felt sure we could put things right; so said I: "If we cannot sleep, we may at least dine"—and was for depositing my bag.

What a terrible convulsion of nature was that which followed in the landlady's face! She made a run at us, and stamped her foot.

"Out with you—out of the door!" she screeched. "Sortez! sortez! sortez par la porte!"

I do not know how it happened, but next moment we were out in the rain and darkness, and I was cursing before the carriage entry like a disappointed mendicant. Where were the boating men of Belgium? where the Judge and his good wines? and where the graces of Origny? Black, black was the night after the firelit kitchen; but what was that to the blackness in our heart? This was not the first time that I have been refused a lodging. Often and often have I planned what I should do if such a misadventure happened to me again. And nothing is easier to plan. But to put in execution, with the heart boiling at the indignity? Try it; try it only once; and tell me what you did.

It is all very fine to talk about tramps and morality. Six hours of police surveillance (such as I have had), or one brutal rejection from an inn door, change your views upon the subject like a course of lectures. As long as you keep in the upper regions, with all the world bowing to you as you go, social arrangements have a very handsome air; but once get under the wheels, and you wish society were at the devil. I will give most respectable men a fortnight of such a life, and then I will offer them twopence for what remains of their morality.

For my part, when I was turned out of the Stag, or the Hind, or whatever it was, I would have set the temple of Diana on fire, if it had been handy. There was no crime complete enough to express my disapproval of human institutions. As for the Cigarette, I never knew a man so altered. "We have been taken for peddlers again," said he. "Good God, what it must be to be a peddler in reality!" He particularized a complaint for every joint in the landlady's body. Timon was a philanthropist alongside of him. And then, when he was at the top of his maledictory bent, he would suddenly break away and begin whimperingly to commiserate the poor. "I hope to God," he said—and I trust the prayer was answered—"that I shall never be uncivil to a peddler." Was this the imperturbable Cigarette? This, this was he. Oh, change beyond report, thought, or belief!

Meantime the heaven wept upon our heads; and the windows grew brighter as the night increased in darkness. We trudged in and out of La Fère streets; we saw shops, and private houses where people were copiously dining; we saw stables where carters' nags had plenty of fodder and clean straw; we saw no end of

reservists, who were very sorry for themselves this wet
night, I doubt not, and yearned for their country
homes; but had they not each man his place in La
Fère barracks? And we, what had we?

There seemed to be no other inn in the whole town.
People gave us directions, which we followed as best
we could, generally with the effect of bringing us out
again upon the scene of our disgrace. We were very
sad people indeed by the time we had gone all over
La Fère; and the Cigarette had already made up his
mind to lie under a poplar and sup off a loaf of bread.
But right at the other end, the house next the town-
gate was full of light and bustle. "Bazin, aubergiste,
loge à pied," was the sign. "À la Croix de Malte."
There were we received.

The room was full of noisy reservists drinking and
smoking; and we were very glad indeed when the
drums and bugles began to go about the streets, and
one and all had to snatch shakoes and be off for the
barracks.

Bazin was a tall man, running to fat: soft-spoken,
with a delicate, gentle face. We asked him to share
our wine; but he excused himself, having pledged reservists all day long. This was a very different type
of the workman-innkeeper from the bawling disputatious
fellow at Origny. He also loved Paris, where he had
worked as a decorative painter in his youth. There
were such opportunities for self-instruction there, he
said. And if any one has read Zola's description of
the workman's marriage party visiting the Louvre, they
would do well to have heard Bazin by way of antidote. He had delighted in the museums in his youth.

"One sees there little miracles of work," he said; "that is what makes a good workman; it kindles a spark." We asked him how he managed in La Fère. "I am married," he said, "and I have my pretty children. But frankly, it is no life at all. From morning to night, I pledge a pack of good enough fellows who know nothing."

It faired as the night went on, and the moon came out of the clouds. We sat in front of the door, talking softly with Bazin. At the guard-house opposite, the guard was being forever turned out, as trains of field artillery kept clanking in out of the night, or patrols of horsemen trotted by in their cloaks. Madame Bazin came out after a while; she was tired with her day's work, I suppose; and she nestled up to her husband and laid her head upon his breast. He had his arm about her and kept gently patting her on the shoulder. I think Bazin was right, and he was really married. Of how few people can the same be said!

Little did the Bazins know how much they served us. We were charged for candles, for food and drink, and for the beds we slept in. But there was nothing in the bill for the husband's pleasant talk; nor for the pretty spectacle of their married life. And there was yet another item uncharged. For these people's politeness really set us up again in our own esteem. We had a thirst for consideration; the sense of insult was still hot in our spirits; and civil usage seemed to restore us to our position in the world.

How little we pay our way in life! Although we have our purses continually in our hand, the better part of service goes still unrewarded. But I like to fancy that a grateful spirit gives as good as it gets. Perhaps the Bazins knew how much I liked them? perhaps they also were healed of some slights by the thanks that I gave them in my manner?

DOWN THE OISE

THROUGH THE GOLDEN VALLEY

BELOW La Fère the river runs through a piece of open pastoral country; green, opulent, loved by breeders; called the Golden Valley. In wide sweeps, and with a swift and equable gallop, the ceaseless stream of water visits and makes green the fields. Kine, and horses, and little humorous donkeys, browse together in the meadows, and come down in troops to the riverside to drink. They make a strange feature in the landscape; above all when startled, and you see them galloping to and fro, with their incongruous forms and faces. It gives a feeling as of great, unfenced pampas, and the herds of wandering nations. There were hills in the distance upon either hand; and on one side, the river sometimes bordered on the wooded spurs of Coucy and St. Gobain.

The artillery were practicing at La Fère; and soon the cannon of heaven joined in that loud play. Two continents of cloud met and exchanged salvos overhead; while all round the horizon we could see sunshine and clear air upon the hills. What with the guns and the thunder, the herds were all frighted in the Golden Valley. We could see them tossing their heads, and running to and fro in timorous indecision; and when they had made up their minds, and the donkey followed the horse, and the cow was after the donkey, we could hear their hoofs thundering abroad over the meadows. It had a martial sound, like cavalry charges. And altogether, as far as the ears are concerned, we had a very rousing battle piece, performed for our amusement.

At last the guns and the thunder dropped of; the sun shone on the wet meadows; the air was scented with the breath of rejoicing trees and grass; and the river kept unweariedly carrying us on at its best pace. There was a manufacturing district about Chauny; and after that the banks grew so high that they hid the adjacent country, and we could see nothing but clay sides, and one willow after another. Only, here and there, we passed by a village or a ferry, and some wondering child upon the bank would stare after us until we turned the corner. I daresay we continued to paddle in that child's dreams for many a night after.

Sun and shower alternated like day and night, making the hours longer by their variety. When the showers were heavy I could feel each drop striking through my jersey to my warm skin; and the accumulation of small shocks put me nearly beside myself. I decided I should buy a mackintosh at Noyon. It is nothing to get wet; but the misery of these individual pricks of cold all over my body at the same instant of time made me flail the water with my paddle like a madman. The Cigarette was greatly amused by these ebullitions. It gave him something else to look at, besides clay banks and willows.

All the time, the river stole away like a thief in

straight places, or swung round corners with an eddy; the willows nodded and were undermined all day long; the clay banks tumbled in; the Oise, which had been so many centuries making the Golden Valley, seemed to have changed its fancy, and be bent upon undoing its performance. What a number of things a river does, by simply following Gravity in the innocence of its heart!

NOYON CATHEDRAL

NOYON stands about a mile from the river, in a little plain surrounded by wooded hills, and entirely covers an eminence with its tile roofs, surmounted by a long, straight-backed cathedral with two stiff towers. As we got into the town, the tile roofs seemed to tumble uphill one upon another, in the oddest disorder; but for all their scrambling, they did not attain above the knees of the cathedral, which stood, upright and solemn, over all. As the streets drew near to this presiding genius, through the market-place under the Hôtel de Ville, they grew emptier and more composed. Blank walls and shuttered windows were turned to the great edifice, and grass grew on the white causeway. "Put off thy shoes from off thy feet, for the place whereon thou standest is holy ground." The Hôtel du Nord, nevertheless, lights its secular tapers within a stone cast of the church; and we had the superb east-end before our eyes all morning from the window of our bedroom. I have seldom looked on the east-end of a church with more complete sympathy. As it flanges out in three wide terraces, and settles down broadly on the earth, it looks like the poop of some great old battle ship.

Hollow-backed buttresses carry vases, which figure for the stern-lanterns. There is a roll in the ground, and the towers just appear above the pitch of the roof, as though the good ship were bowing lazily over an Atlantic swell. At any moment it might be a hundred feet away from you, climbing the next billow. At any moment a window might open, and some old admiral thrust forth a cocked hat, and proceed to take an observation. The old admirals sail the sea no longer; the old ships of battle are all broken up, and live only in pictures; but this, that was a church before ever they were thought upon, is still a church, and makes as brave an appearance by the Oise. The cathedral and the river are probably the two oldest things for miles around; and certainly they have both a grand old age.

The Sacristan took us to the top of one of the towers, and showed us the five bells hanging in their loft. From above, the town was a tesselated pavement of roofs and gardens; the old line of rampart was plainly traceable; and the Sacristan pointed out to us, far across the plain, in a bit of gleaming sky between two clouds, the towers of Château Coucy.

I find I never weary of great churches. It is my favorite kind of mountain scenery. Mankind was never so happily inspired as when it made a cathedral: a thing as single and specious as a statue to the first glance, and yet, on examination, as lively and interesting as a forest in detail. The height of spires cannot be taken by trigonometry; they measure absurdly short, but how tall they are to the admiring eye! And where we have so many elegant proportions, growing one out of the other, and all together into one, it seems as if proportion transcended itself and became something different and more imposing. I could never fathom how a man dares to lift up his voice to preach in a cathedral. What is he to say that will not be an anti-climax? For though I have heard a considerable variety of sermons, I never yet heard one that was so expressive as a cathedral. 'Tis the best preacher itself, and preaches day and night; not only telling you of man's art and aspirations in the past, but convicting your own soul of ardent sympathies; or rather, like all good preachers, it sets you preaching to yourself;—and every man is his own doctor of divinity in the last resort.

As I sat outside of the hotel in the course of the afternoon, the sweet groaning thunder of the organ floated out of the church like a summons. I was not averse, liking the theater so well, to sit out an act or two of the play, but I could never rightly make out the nature of the service I beheld. Four or five priests and as many choristers were singing Miserere before the high altar when I went in. There was no congregation but a few old women on chairs and old men kneeling on the pavement. After a while a long train of young girls, walking two and two, each with a lighted taper in her hand, and all dressed in black with a white veil, came from behind the altar and began to descend the nave; the four first carrying a Virgin and Child upon a table. The priests and choristers arose from their knees and followed after, singing "Ave Mary" as they went. In this order, they made the circuit of the cathedral, passing twice before me where I leaned against a pillar. The priest who seemed of most consequence was a strange, down-looking old man. He kept mum-

bling prayers with his lips; but as he looked upon me
darkling, it did not seem as if prayer were uppermost
in his heart. Two others, who bore the burden of the
chant, were stout, brutal, military-looking men of forty,
with bold, over-fed eyes; they sang with some lusti-
ness, and trolled forth "Ave Mary" like a garrison
catch. The little girls were timid and grave. As they
footed slowly up the aisle, each one took a moment's
glance at the Englishman; and the big nun who played
marshal fairly stared him out of countenance. As for
the choristers, from first to last they misbehaved as
only boys can misbehave; and cruelly marred the performance with their antics.

I understood a great deal of the spirit of what went
on. Indeed it would be difficult not to understand the
Miserere, which I take to be the composition of an
atheist. If it ever be a good thing to take such despondency to heart, the Miserere is the right music and
a cathedral a fit scene. So far I am at one with the
Catholics:—an odd name for them, after all? But why,
in God's name, these holiday choristers? why these
priests who steal wandering looks about the congregation while they feign to be at prayer? why this fat
nun, who rudely arranges her procession and shakes
delinquent virgins by the elbow? why this spitting, and
snuffing, and forgetting of keys, and the thousand and
one little misadventures that disturb a frame of mind,
laboriously edified with chants and organings? In any
play-house reverend fathers may see what can be done
with a little art, and how, to move high sentiments,
it is necessary to drill the supernumeraries and have
every stool in its proper place.

One other circumstance distressed me. I could bear a Miserere myself, having had a good deal of open air exercise of late; but I wished the old people somewhere else. It was neither the right sort of music nor the right sort of divinity, for men and women who have come through most accidents by this time, and probably have an opinion of their own upon the tragic element in life. A person up in years can generally do his own Miserere for himself; although I notice that such a one often prefers Jubilate Deo for his ordinary singing. On the whole, the most religious exercise for the aged is probably to recall their own experience; so many friends dead, so many hopes disappointed, so many slips and stumbles, and withal so many bright days and smiling providences; there is surely the matter of a very eloquent sermon in all this.

On the whole, I was greatly solemnized. In the little pictorial map of our whole Inland Voyage which my fancy still preserves, and sometimes unrolls for the amusement of odd moments, Noyon cathedral figures on a most preposterous scale, and must be nearly as large as a department. I can still see the faces of the priests as if they were at my elbow, and hear "Ave Maria, ora pro nobis" sounding through the church. All Noyon is blotted out for me by these superior memories; and I do not care to say more about the place. It was but a stack of brown roofs at the best, where I believe people live very reputably in a quiet way; but the shadow of the church falls upon it when the sun is low, and the five bells are heard in all quarters, telling that the organ has begun. If ever I join the Church of Rome, I shall stipulate to be Bishop of Noyon on the Oise.

DOWN THE OISE: TO COMPIEGNE

THE most patient people grow weary at last with being continually wetted with rain; except of course in the Scotch Highlands, where there are not enough fine intervals to point the difference. That was like to be our case, the day we left Noyon. I remember nothing of the voyage; it was nothing but clay banks and willows, and rain; incessant, pitiless, beating rain: until we stopped to lunch at a little inn at Pimprez, where the canal ran very near the river. We were so sadly drenched that the landlady lighted a few sticks in the chimney for our comfort; there we sat in a steam of vapor, lamenting our concerns. The husband donned a game bag and strode out to shoot; the wife sat in a far corner watching us. I think we were worth looking at. We grumbled over the misfortune of La Fère; we forecast other La Fères in the future—although things went better with the Cigarette for spokesman; he had more aplomb altogether than I; and a dull, positive way of approaching a landlady that carried off the india-rubber bags. Talking of La Fère put us talking of the reservists.

"Reservery," said he, "seems a pretty mean way to spend one's autumn holiday."

"About as mean," returned I dejectedly, "as canoe-ing."

"These gentlemen travel for their pleasure?" asked the landlady, with unconscious irony.

It was too much. The scales fell from our eyes. Another wet day, it was determined, and we put the boats into the train.

The weather took the hint. That was our last wet-ting. The afternoon faired up: grand clouds still voy-aged in the sky, but now singly, and with a depth of blue around their path; and a sunset, in the daintiest rose and gold, inaugurated a thick night of stars and a month of unbroken weather. At the same time, the river began to give us a better outlook into the coun-try. The banks were not so high, the willows disap-peared from along the margin, and pleasant hills stood all along its course and marked their profile on the sky.

In a little while, the canal, coming to its last lock, began to discharge its water-houses on the Oise; so that we had no lack of company to fear. Here were all our old friends; the "Deo Gratias" of Conde and the "Four Sons of Aymon" journeyed cheerily down stream along with us; we exchanged waterside pleasantries with the steersman perched among the lumber, or the driver hoarse with bawling to his horses; and the children came and looked over the side as we paddled by. We had never known all this while how much we missed them; but it gave us a fillip to see the smoke from their chimneys.

A little below this junction, we made another meet-ing of yet more account. For there we were joined by the Aisne, already a far-traveled river and fresh out of

Champagne. Here ended the adolescence of the Oise;
this was his marriage day; thenceforward he had a
stately, brimming march, conscious of his own dignity
and sundry dams. He became a tranquil feature in the
scene. The trees and towns saw themselves in him, as
in a mirror. He carried the canoes lightly on his broad
breast; there was no need to work hard against an
eddy: but idleness became the order of the day, and
mere straightforward dipping of the paddle, now on this
side, now on that, without intelligence or effort. Truly
we were coming into halcyon weather upon all accounts,
and were floated toward the sea like gentlemen.

We made Compiègne, as the sun was going down:
a fine profile of a town above the river. Over the
bridge, a regiment was parading to the drum. People
loitered on the quay, some fishing, some looking idly
at the stream. And as the two boats shot in along
the water, we could see them pointing them out and
speaking one to another. We landed at a floating lavatory, where the washerwomen were still beating the
clothes.

AT COMPIEGNE

WE put up at a big, bustling hotel in Compiègne, where nobody observed our presence.

Reservery and general militarismus (as the Germans call it) was rampant. A camp of conical white tents without the town looked like a leaf out of a picture Bible; sword-belts decorated the walls of the cafes; and the streets kept sounding all day long with military music. It was not possible to be an Englishman and avoid a feeling of elation; for the men who followed the drums were small, and walked shabbily. Each man inclined at his own angle, and jolted to his own convenience, as he went. There was nothing of the superb gait with which a regiment of tall Highlanders moves behind its music, solemn and inevitable, like a natural phenomenon. Who, that has seen it, can forget the drum-major pacing in front, the drummers' tiger-skins, the pipers' swinging plaids, the strange elastic rhythm of the whole regiment footing it in time—and the bang of the drum, when the brasses cease, and the shrill pipes take up the martial story in their place?

A girl, at school in France, began to describe one of our regiments on parade, to her French schoolmates; and as she went on, she told me, the recollection grew so vivid, she became so proud to be the countrywoman of such soldiers, and so sorry to be in another country, that her voice failed her and she burst into tears. I have never forgotten that girl; and I think she very nearly deserves a statue. To call her a young lady, with all its niminy associations, would be to offer her an insult. She may rest assured of one thing; although she never should marry a heroic general, never see any great or immediate result of her life, she will not have lived in vain for her native land.

But though French soldiers show to ill-advantage on parade, on the march they are gay, alert, and willing like a troop of fox-hunters. I remember once seeing a company pass through the forest of Fontainebleau, on the Chailly road, between the Bas Breau and the Reine Blanche. One fellow walked a little before the rest, and sang a loud, audacious marching song. The rest bestirred their feet, and even swung their muskets in time. A young officer on horseback had hard ado to keep his countenance at the words. You never saw anything so cheerful and spontaneous as their gait; schoolboys do not look more eagerly at hare and hounds; and you would have thought it impossible to tire such willing marchers.

My great delight in Compiègne was the town-hall. I doted upon the town-hall. It is a monument of Gothic insecurity, all turreted, and gargoyled, and slashed, and bedizened with half a score of architectural fancies. Some of the niches are gilt and painted; and in a great square panel in the center, in black relief on a gilt ground, Louis XII. rides upon a pacing horse, with hand on hip, and head thrown back.

There is royal arrogance in every line of him; the
stirruped foot projects insolently from the frame; the
eye is hard and proud; the very horse seems to be
treading with gratification over prostrate serfs, and to
have the breath of the trumpet in his nostrils. So rides
forever, on the front of the town-hall, the good king
Louis XII., the father of his people.

Over the king's head, in the tall center turret, appears the dial of a clock; and high above that, three
little mechanical figures, each one with a hammer in
his hand, whose business it is to chime out the hours
and halves and quarters for the burgesses of Compiègne.
The center figure has a gilt breast-plate; the two others
wear gilt trunk-hose; and they all three have elegant,
flapping hats like cavaliers. As the quarter approaches,
they turn their heads and look knowingly one to the
other; and then, kling go the three hammers on three
little bells below. The hour follows, deep and sonorous,
from the interior of the tower; and the gilded gentlemen rest from their labors with contentment.

I had a great deal of healthy pleasure from their
maneuvers, and took good care to miss as few per-
formances as possible; and I found that even the Cigarette, while he pretended to despise my enthusiasm, was
more or less a devotee himself. There is something
highly absurd in the exposition of such toys to the
outrages of winter on a housetop. They would be more
in keeping in a glass case before a Nürnberg clock.
Above all, at night, when the children are abed, and
even grown people are snoring under quilts, does it
not seem impertinent to leave these ginger-bread figures
winking and tinkling to the stars and the rolling moon?

The gargoyles may fitly enough twist their ape-like heads; fitly enough may the potentate bestride his charger, like a centurion in an old German print of the Via Dolorosa; but the toys should be put away in a box among some cotton, until the sun rises and the children are abroad again to be amused.

In Compiègne post-office, a great packet of letters awaited us; and the authorities were, for this occasion only, so polite as to hand them over upon application.

In some ways, our journey may be said to end with this letter-bag at Compiègne. The spell was broken. We had partly come home from that moment.

No one should have any correspondence on a journey; it is bad enough to have to write; but the receipt of letters is the death of all holiday feeling.

"Out of my country and myself I go." I wish to take a dive among new conditions for a while, as into another element. I have nothing to do with my friends or my affections for the time; when I came away, I left my heart at home in a desk, or sent it forward with my portmanteau to await me at my destination. After my journey is over, I shall not fail to read your admirable letters with the attention they deserve. But I have paid all this money, look you, and paddled all these strokes, for no other purpose than to be abroad; and yet you keep me at home with your perpetual communications. You tug the string, and I feel that I am a tethered bird. You pursue me all over Europe with the little vexations that I came away to avoid. There is no discharge in the war of life, I am well aware; but shall there not be so much as a week's furlough?

We were up by six, the day we were to leave. They had taken so little note of us that I hardly thought they would have condescended on a bill. But they did, with some smart particulars too; and we paid in a civilized manner to an uninterested clerk, and went out of that hotel, with the india-rubber bags, unremarked. No one cared to know about us. It is not possible to rise before a village; but Compiègne was so grown a town that it took its ease in the morning; and we were up and away while it was still in dressing-gown and slippers. The streets were left to people washing doorsteps; nobody was in full dress but the cavaliers upon the town-hall; they were all washed with dew, spruce in their gilding, and full of intelligence and a sense of professional responsibility. Kling, went they on the bells for the half-past six, as we went by. I took it kind of them to make me this parting compliment; they never were in better form, not even at noon upon a Sunday.

There was no one to see us off but the early washerwomen — early and late — who were already beating the linen in their floating lavatory on the river. They were very merry and matutinal in their ways; plunged their arms boldly in, and seemed not to feel the shock. It would be dispiriting to me, this early beginning and first cold dabble, of a most dispiriting day's work. But I believe they would have been as unwilling to change days with us, as we could be to change with them. They crowded to the door to watch us paddle away into the thin sunny mists upon the river; and shouted heartily after us till we were through the bridge.

CHANGED TIMES

THERE is a sense in which those mists never rose from off our journey; and from that time forth they lie very densely in my note-book. As long as the Oise was a small rural river, it took us near by people's doors, and we could hold a conversation with natives in the riparian fields. But now that it had grown so wide, the life along shore passed us by at a distance. It was the same difference as between a great public highway and a country bypath that wanders in and out of cottage gardens. We now lay in towns, where nobody troubled us with questions; we had floated into civilized life, where people pass without salutation. In sparsely inhabited places, we make all we can of each encounter; but when it comes to a city, we keep to ourselves, and never speak unless we have trodden on a man's toes. In these waters, we were no longer strange birds, and nobody supposed we had traveled further than from the last town. I remember, when we came into L'Isle Adam, for instance, how we met dozens of pleasure-boats outing it for the afternoon, and there was nothing to distinguish the true voyager from the amateur, except, perhaps, the filthy condition of my sail. The company in one boat actually thought they recognized me for a neighbor. Was there ever anything more wounding? All the romance had come down to that. Now, on the upper Oise, where nothing sailed as a general thing but fish, a pair of canoeists could not be thus vulgarly explained away; we were strange and picturesque intruders; and out of people's wonder sprang a sort of light and passing intimacy all along our route. There is nothing but tit for tat in this world, though sometimes it be a little difficult to trace: for the scores are older than we ourselves, and there has never yet been a settling-day since things were. You get entertainment pretty much in proportion as you give. As long as we were a sort of odd wanderers, to be stared at and followed like a quack doctor or a caravan, we had no want of amusement in return; but as soon as we sank into commonplace ourselves, all whom we met were similarly disenchanted. And here is one reason of a dozen, why the world is dull to dull persons.

In our earlier adventures there was generally something to do, and that quickened us. Even the showers of rain had a revivifying effect, and shook up the brain from torpor. But now, when the river no longer ran in a proper sense, only glided seaward with an even, outright, but imperceptible speed, and when the sky smiled upon us day after day without variety, we began to slip into that golden doze of the mind which follows upon much exercise in the open air. I have stupefied myself in this way more than once; indeed, I dearly love the feeling; but I never had it to the same degree as when paddling down the Oise. It was the apotheosis of stupidity.

We ceased reading entirely. Sometimes, when I found a new paper, I took a particular pleasure in reading a single number of the current novel; but I never could bear more than three instalments; and even the second was a disappointment. As soon as the tale became in any way perspicuous, it lost all merit in my eyes; only a single scene, or, as is the way with these feuilletons, half a scene, without antecedent or consequence, like a piece of a dream, had the knack of fixing my interest. The less I saw of the novel, the better I liked it: a pregnant reflection. But for the most part, as I said, we neither of us read anything in the world, and employed the very little while we were awake between bed and dinner in poring upon maps. I have always been fond of maps, and can voyage in an atlas with the greatest enjoyment. The names of places are singularly inviting; the contour of coasts and rivers is enthralling to the eye; and to hit, in a map, upon some place you have heard of before, makes history a new possession. But we thumbed our charts, on these evenings, with the blankest unconcern. We cared not a fraction for this place or that. We stared at the sheet as children listen to their rattle; and read the names of towns or villages to forget them again at once. We had no romance in the matter; there was nobody so fancy-free. If you had taken the maps away while we were studying them most intently, it is a fair bet whether we might not have continued to study the table with the same delight.

About one thing we were mightily taken up, and that was eating. I think I made a god of my belly. I remember dwelling in imagination upon this or that

dish till my mouth watered; and long before we got
in for the night my appetite was a clamant, instant
annoyance. Sometimes we paddled alongside for a
while and whetted each other with gastronomical fancies
as we went. Cake and sherry, a homely refection, but
not within reach upon the Oise, trotted through my
head for many a mile; and once, as we were approaching Verberie, the Cigarette brought my heart into my
mouth by the suggestion of oyster patties and Sauterne.

I suppose none of us recognize the great part that
is played in life by eating and drinking. The appetite
is so imperious that we can stomach the least interesting viands, and pass off a dinner hour thankfully
enough on bread and water; just as there are men
who must read something, if it were only Bradshaw's
Guide. But there is a romance about the matter after
all. Probably the table has more devotees than love;
and I am sure that food is much more generally entertaining than scenery. Do you give in, as Walt Whit-
man would say, that you are any the less immortal for
that? The true materialism is to be ashamed of what
we are. To detect the flavor of an olive is no less a
piece of human perfection, than to find beauty in the
colors of the sunset.

Canoeing was easy work. To dip the paddle at the
proper inclination, now right, now left; to keep the
head down stream; to empty the little pool that gathered in the lap of the apron; to screw up the eyes
against the glittering sparkles of sun upon the water;
or now and again to pass below the whistling tow-rope
of the "Deo Gratias" of Conde, or the "Four Sons of
Aymon"—there was not much art in that; certain silly

muscles managed it between sleep and waking; and meanwhile the brain had a whole holiday, and went to sleep. We took in, at a glance, the larger features of the scene; and beheld, with half an eye, bloused fishes and dabbling washerwomen on the bank. Now and again we might be half wakened by some church spire, by a leaping fish, or by a trail of river grass that clung about the paddle and had to be plucked off and thrown away. But these luminous intervals were only partially luminous. A little more of us was called into action, but never the whole. The central bureau of nerves, what in some moods we call Ourselves, enjoyed its holiday without disturbance, like a Government Office. The great wheels of intelligence turned idly in the head, like fly-wheels, grinding no grist. I have gone on for half an hour at a time, counting my strokes and forgetting the hundreds. I flatter myself the beasts that perish could not underbid that, as a low form of consciousness. And what a pleasure it was! What a hearty, tolerant temper did it bring about! There is nothing captious about a man who has attained to this, the one possible apotheosis in life, the Apotheosis of Stupidity; and he begins to feel dignified and long-œvous like a tree.

There was one odd piece of practical metaphysics which accompanied what I may call the depth, if I must not call it the intensity, of my abstraction. What philosophers call *me* and *not me*, *ego* and *non ego*, preoccupied me whether I would or no. There was less *me* and more *not me* than I was accustomed to expect. I looked on upon somebody else, who managed the paddling; I was aware of somebody else's feet against

the stretcher; my own body seemed to have no more
intimate relation to me than the canoe, or the river,
or the river banks. Nor this alone: something inside
my mind, a part of my brain, a province of my proper
being, had thrown off allegiance and set up for itself,
or perhaps for the somebody else who did the paddling.
I had dwindled into quite a little thing in a corner of
myself. I was isolated in my own skull. Thoughts
presented themselves unbidden; they were not my
thoughts, they were plainly some one else's; and I
considered them like a part of the landscape. I take
it, in short, that I was about as near Nirvana as
would be convenient in practical life; and if this be
so, I make the Buddhists my sincere compliments; 'tis
an agreeable state, not very consistent with mental
brilliancy, not exactly profitable in a money point of
view, but very calm, golden and incurious, and one
that sets a man superior to alarms. It may be best
figured by supposing yourself to get dead drunk, and
yet keep sober to enjoy it. I have a notion that open
air laborers must spend a large portion of their days
in this ecstatic stupor, which explains their high composure and endurance. A pity to go to the expense of
laudanum, when here is a better paradise for nothing!

This frame of mind was the great exploit of our
voyage, take it all in all. It was the furthest piece
of travel accomplished. Indeed, it lies so far from
beaten paths of language, that I despair of getting the
reader into sympathy with the smiling, complacent idiocy
of my condition; when ideas came and went like motes
in a sunbeam; when trees and church spires along the
bank surged up, from time to time, into my notice,

like solid objects through a rolling cloudland; when the rhythmical swish of boat and paddle in the water became a cradle-song to lull my thoughts asleep; when a piece of mud on the deck was sometimes an intolerable eyesore, and sometimes quite a companion for me, and the object of pleased consideration;—and all the time, with the river running and the shores changing upon either hand, I kept counting my strokes and forgetting the hundreds, the happiest animal in France.

DOWN THE OISE

CHURCH INTERIORS

WE made our first stage below Compiègne to Pont Sainte Maxence. I was abroad a little after six the next morning. The air was biting and smelled of frost. In an open place, a score of women wrangled together over the day's market; and the noise of their negotiation sounded thin and querulous like that of sparrows on a winter's morning. The rare passengers blew into their hands, and shuffled in their wooden shoes to set the blood agog. The streets were full of icy shadow, although the chimneys were smoking overhead in golden sunshine. If you wake early enough at this season of the year, you may get up in December to break your fast in June.

I found my way to the church; for there is always something to see about a church, whether living worshipers or dead men's tombs; you find there the deadliest earnest, and the hollowest deceit; and even where it is not a piece of history, it will be certain to leak out some contemporary gossip. It was scarcely so cold in the church as it was without, but it looked colder. The white nave was positively arctic to the eye; and the tawdriness of a continental altar looked more for-

lorn than usual in the solitude and the bleak air. Two
priests sat in the chancel, reading and waiting peni-
tents; and out in the nave, one very old woman was
engaged in her devotions. It was a wonder how she
was able to pass her beads when healthy young people
were breathing in their palms and slapping their chest;
but though this concerned me, I was yet more dis-
pirited by the nature of her exercises. She went from
chair to chair, from altar to altar, circumnavigating the
church. To each shrine she dedicated an equal number of beads and an equal length of time. Like a
prudent capitalist with a somewhat cynical view of the
commercial prospect, she desired to place her supplica-
tions in a great variety of heavenly securities. She
would risk nothing on the credit of any single inter-
cessor. Out of the whole company of saints and angels,
not one but was to suppose himself her champion elect
against the Great Assizes! I could only think of it as
a dull, transparent jugglery, based upon unconscious
unbelief.

She was as dead an old woman as ever I saw; no
more than bone and parchment, curiously put together.
Her eyes, with which she interrogated mine, were vacant of sense. It depends on what you call seeing,
whether you might not call her blind. Perhaps she had
known love: perhaps borne children, suckled them and
given them pet names. But now that was all gone
by, and had left her neither happier nor wiser; and
the best she could do with her mornings was to come
up here into the cold church and juggle for a slice of
heaven. It was not without a gulp that I escaped into
the streets and the keen morning air. Morning? why,

how tired of it she would be before night! and if she
did not sleep, how then? It is fortunate that not many
of us are brought up publicly to justify our lives at
the bar of three score years and ten; fortunate that
such a number are knocked opportunely on the head in
what they call the flower of their years, and go away
to suffer for their follies in private somewhere else.
Otherwise, between sick children and discontented old
folk, we might be put out of all conceit of life.

I had need of all my cerebral hygiene during that
day's paddle: the old devotee stuck in my throat sorely.
But I was soon in the seventh heaven of stupidity;
and knew nothing but that somebody was paddling a
canoe, while I was counting his strokes and forgetting
the hundreds. I used sometimes to be afraid I should
remember the hundreds; which would have made a
toil of a pleasure; but the terror was chimerical, they
went out of my mind by enchantment, and I knew no
more than the man in the moon about my only occupation.

At Creil, where we stopped to lunch, we left the
canoes in another floating lavatory, which, as it was
high noon, was packed with washerwomen, red-handed
and loud-voiced; and they and their broad jokes are
about all I remember of the place. I could look up
my history books, if you were very anxious, and tell
you a date or two; for it figured rather largely in the
English wars. But I prefer to mention a girls' boarding-school, which had an interest for us because it was
a girls' boarding-school, and because we imagined we
had rather an interest for it. At least—there were the
girls about the garden; and here were we on the river;

and there was more than one handkerchief waved as
we went by. It caused quite a stir in my heart; and
yet how we should have wearied and despised each
other, these girls and I, if we had been introduced at
a croquet party! But this is a fashion I love: to kiss
the hand or wave a handkerchief to people I shall
never see again, to play with possibility, and knock in
a peg for fancy to hang upon. It gives the traveler
a jog, reminds him that he is not a traveler everywhere, and that his journey is no more than a siesta
by the way on the real march of life.

The church at Creil was a nondescript place in the
inside, splashed with gaudy lights from the windows,
and picked out with medallions of the Dolorous Way.
But there was one oddity, in the way of an *ex voto*,
which pleased me hugely: a faithful model of a canal
boat, swung from the vault, with a written aspiration
that God should conduct the "Saint Nicolas" of Creil
to a good haven. The thing was neatly executed, and
would have made the delight of a party of boys on
the waterside. But what tickled me was the gravity
of the peril to be conjured. You might hang up the
model of a sea-going ship, and welcome: one that is
to plow a furrow round the world, and visit the tropic
or the frosty poles, runs dangers that are well worth
a candle and a mass. But the "Saint Nicolas" of Creil,
which was to be tugged for some ten years by patient
draught horses, in a weedy canal, with the poplars
chattering overhead, and the skipper whistling at the
tiller; which was to do all its errands in green, inland
places, and never got out of sight of a village belfry
in all its cruising. why, you would have thought, it

anything could be done without the intervention of Providence, it would be that! But perhaps the skipper was a humorist: or perhaps a prophet, reminding people of the seriousness of life by this preposterous token.

At Creil, as at Noyon, Saint Joseph seemed a favorite saint on the score of punctuality. Day and hour can be specified; and grateful people do not fail to specify them on a votive tablet, when prayers have been punctually and neatly answered. Whenever time is a consideration, Saint Joseph is the proper intermediary. I took a sort of pleasure in observing the vogue he had in France, for the good man plays a very small part in my religion at home. Yet I could not help fearing that, where the Saint is so much commended for exactitude, he will be expected to be very grateful for his tablet.

This is foolishness to us Protestants; and not of great importance anyway. Whether people's gratitude for the good gifts that come to them be wisely conceived or dutifully expressed, is a secondary matter, after all, so long as they feel gratitude. The true ignorance is when a man does not know that he has received a good gift, or begins to imagine that he has got it for himself. The self-made man is the funniest windbag after all! There is a marked difference between decreeing light in chaos, and lighting the gas in a metropolitan back-parlor with a box of patent matches; and do what we will, there is always something made to our hand, if it were only our fingers.

But there was something worse than foolishness placarded in Creil Church. "The Association of the Living Rosary" (of which I had never previously heard) is responsible for that. This association was founded, according to the printed advertisement, by a brief of Pope Gregory Sixteenth, on the 17th of January, 1832: according to a colored bas-relief, it seems to have been founded, some time or other, by the Virgin giving one rosary to Saint Dominic, and the Infant Saviour giving another to Saint Catherine of Sienna. Pope Gregory is not so imposing, but he is nearer hand. I could not distinctly make out whether the association was entirely devotional, or had an eye to good works; at least it is highly organized: the names of fourteen matrons and misses were filled in for each week of the month as associates, with one other, generally a married woman, at the top for Zelatrice: the choragus of the band. Indulgences, plenary and partial, follow on the performance of the duties of the association. "The partial indulgences are attached to the recitation of the rosary." On "the recitation of the required dizaine," a partial indulgence promptly follows. When people serve the kingdom of Heaven with a pass-book in their hands, I should always be afraid lest they should carry the same commercial spirit into their dealings with their fellow-men, which would make a sad and sordid business of this life.

There is one more article, however, of happier import. "All these indulgences," it appeared, "are applicable to souls in purgatory." For God's sake, ye ladies of Creil, apply them all to the souls in purgatory without delay! Burns would take no hire for his last songs, preferring to serve his country out of unmixed love. Suppose you were to imitate the exciseman, mesdames, and even if the souls in purgatory were not greatly bettered, some souls in Creil upon the Oise would find themselves none the worse either here or hereafter.

I cannot help wondering, as I transcribe these notes, whether a Protestant born and bred is in a fit state to understand these signs, and do them what justice they deserve; and I cannot help answering that he is not. They cannot look so merely ugly and mean to the faithful as they do to me. I see that as clearly as a proposition in Euclid. For these believers are neither weak nor wicked. They can put up their tablet commending Saint Joseph for his dispatch, as if he were still a village carpenter; they can "recite the required dizaine," and metaphorically pocket the indulgence, as if they had done a job for heaven; and then they can go out and look down unabashed upon this wonderful river flowing by, and up without confusion at the pin-point stars, which are themselves great worlds full of flowing rivers greater than the Oise. I see it as plainly, I say, as a proposition in Euclid, that my Protestant mind has missed the point, and that there goes with these deformities some higher and more religious spirit than I dream.

I wonder if other people would make the same allowances for me? Like the ladies of Creil, having recited my rosary of toleration, I look for my indulgence on the spot.

PRÉCY AND THE MARIONETTES

WE made Precy about sundown. The plain is rich
with tufts of poplar. In a wide, luminous curve, the
Oise lay under the hillside. A faint mist began to
rise and confound the different distances together. There
was not a sound audible but that of the sheep-bells in
some meadows by the river, and the creaking of a cart
down the long road that descends the hill. The villas
in their gardens, the shops along the street, all seemed
to have been deserted the day before; and I felt inclined
to walk discreetly as one feels in a silent forest. All
of a sudden, we came round a corner, and there, in a
little green round the church, was a bevy of girls in
Parisian costumes playing croquet. Their laughter and
the hollow sound of ball and mallet, made a cheery
stir in the neighborhood; and the look of these slim
figures, all corseted and ribboned, produced an answer-
able disturbance in our hearts. We were within sniff
of Paris, it seemed. And here were females of our
own species playing croquet, just as if Precy had been
a place in real life, instead of a stage in the fairy land
of travel. For, to be frank, the peasant woman is
scarcely to be counted as a woman at all, and after

having passed by such a succession of people in petticoats digging and hoeing and making dinner, this company of coquettes under arms made quite a surprising
feature in the landscape, and convinced us at once of
being fallible males.

The inn at Precy is the worst inn in France. Not
even in Scotland have I found worse fare. It was kept
by a brother and sister, neither of whom was out of
their teens. The sister, so to speak, prepared a meal
for us; and the brother, who had been tippling, came
in and brought with him a tipsy butcher, to entertain
us as we ate. We found pieces of loo-warm pork among
the salad, and pieces of unknown yielding substance in
the ragoût. The butcher entertained us with pictures
of Parisian life, with which he professed himself well
acquainted; the brother sitting the while on the edge
of the billiard table, toppling precariously, and sucking
the stump of a cigar. In the midst of these diversions,
bang went a drum past the house, and a hoarse voice
began issuing a proclamation. It was a man with
marionettes announcing a performance for that evening.

He had set up his caravan and lighted his candles
on another part of the girl's croquet green, under one
of those open sheds which are so common in France
to shelter markets; and he and his wife, by the time
we strolled up there, were trying to keep order with
the audience.

It was the most absurd contention. The show-people
had set out a certain number of benches; and all who
sat upon them were to pay a couple of sous for the
accommodation. They were always quite full—a bumper
house—as long as nothing was going forward; but let

the show-woman appear with an eye to a collection,
and at the first rattle of her tambourine, the audience
slipped off the seats, and stood round on the outside
with their hands in their pockets. It certainly would
have tried an angel's temper. The showman roared
from the proscenium; he had been all over France,
and nowhere, nowhere, "not even on the borders of
Germany," had he met with such misconduct. Such
thieves and rogues and rascals, as he called them! And
every now and again, the wife issued on another round,
and added her shrill quota to the tirade. I remarked
here, as elsewhere, how far more copious is the female
mind in the material of insult. The audience laughed
in high good humor over the man's declamations; but
they bridled and cried aloud under the woman's pungent
sallies. She picked out the sore points. She had the
honor of the village at her mercy. Voices answered
her angrily out of the crowd, and received a smarting
retort for their trouble. A couple of old ladies beside
me, who had duly paid for their seats, waxed very
red and indignant, and discoursed to each other audi-
bly about the impudence of these mountebanks; but as
soon as the show-woman caught a whisper of this, she
was down upon them with a swoop: if mesdames could
persuade their neighbors to act with common honesty,
the mountebanks, she assured them, would be polite
enough: mesdames had probably had their bowl of
soup, and perhaps a glass of wine that evening; the
mountebanks also had a taste for soup, and did not
choose to have their little earnings stolen from them
before their eyes. Once, things came as far as a brief
personal encounter between the showman and some lads,

in which the former went down as readily as one of
his own marionettes to a peal of jeering laughter.

I was a good deal astonished at this scene, because
I am pretty well acquainted with the ways of French
strollers, more or less artistic; and have always found
them singularly pleasing. Any stroller must be dear to
the right-thinking heart; if it were only as a living
protest against offices and the mercantile spirit, and as
something to remind us that life is not by necessity
the kind of thing we generally make it. Even a German band, if you see it leaving town in the early
morning for a campaign in country places, among trees
and meadows, has a romantic flavor for the imagination. There is nobody, under thirty, so dead but his
heart will stir a little at sight of a gypsies' camp.
"We are not cotton-spinners all;" or, at least, not all
through. There is some life in humanity yet: and
youth will now and again find a brave word to say
in dispraise of riches, and throw up a situation to go
strolling with a knapsack.

An Englishman has always special facilities for intercourse with French gymnasts; for England is the
natural home of gymnasts. This or that fellow, in his
tights and spangles, is sure to know a word or two
of English, to have drunk English aff-'n-aff, and perhaps performed in an English music-hall. He is a countryman of mine by profession. He leaps, like the Belgian boating men, to the notion that I must be an
athlete myself.

But the gymnast is not my favorite; he has little
or no tincture of the artist in his composition; his soul
is small and pedestrian, for the most part, since his

profession makes no call upon it, and does not accustom him to high ideas. But if a man is only so much of an actor that he can stumble through a farce, he is made free of a new order of thoughts. He has something else to think about beside the money-box. He has a pride of his own, and, what is of far more importance, he has an aim before him that he can never quite attain. He has gone upon a pilgrimage that will last him his life-long, because there is no end to it short of perfection. He will better upon himself a little day by day; or even if he has given up the attempt, he will always remember that once upon a time he had conceived this high ideal, that once upon a time he had fallen in love with a star. " 'Tis better to have loved and lost." Although the moon should have nothing to say to Endymion, although he should settle down with Audrey and feed pigs, do you not think he would move with a better grace, and cherish higher thoughts to the end? The louts he meets at church never had a fancy above Audrey's snood; but there is a reminiscence in Endymion's heart that, like a spice, keeps it fresh and haughty.

To be even one of the outskirters of art, leaves a fine stamp on a man's countenance. I remember once dining with a party in the inn at Chateau Landon. Most of them were unmistakable bagmen; others well-to-do peasantry; but there was one young fellow in a blouse, whose face stood out from among the rest surprisingly. It looked more finished; more of the spirit looked out through it; it had a living, expressive air, and you could see that his eyes took things in. My companion and I wondered greatly who and what he could be. It was fair time in Chateau Landon, and when we went along to the booths, we had our question answered; for there was our friend busily fiddling for the peasants to caper to. He was a wandering violinist.

A troop of strollers once came to the inn where I was staying, in the department of Seine et Marne. There was a father and mother; two daughters, brazen, blowsy huzzies, who sang and acted, without an idea of how to set about either; and a dark young man, like a tutor, a recalcitrant house-painter, who sang and acted not amiss. The mother was the genius of the party, so far as genius can be spoken of with regard to such a pack of incompetent humbugs; and her husband could not find words to express his admiration for her comic countryman. "You should see my old woman," said he, and nodded his beery countenance. One night, they performed in the stable-yard, with flaring lamps: a wretched exhibition, coldly looked upon by a village audience. Next night, as soon as the lamps were lighted, there came a plump of rain, and they had to sweep away their baggage as fast as possible, and make off to the barn where they harbored, cold, wet, and supperless. In the morning, a dear friend of mine, who has as warm a heart for strollers as I have myself, made a little collection, and sent it by my hands to comfort them for their disappointment. I gave it to the father; he thanked me cordially, and we drank a cup together in the kitchen, talking of roads, and audiences, and hard times.

When I was going, up got my old stroller, and off with his hat. "I am afraid," said he, "that monsieur will think me altogether a beggar; but I have another demand to make upon him." I began to hate him on the spot. "We play again to-night," he went on. "Of course, I shall refuse to accept any more money from monsieur and his friends, who have been already so liberal. But our programme of to-night is something truly creditable; and I cling to the idea that monsieur will honor us with his presence." And then, with a shrug and a smile: "Monsieur understands—the vanity of an artist!" Save the mark! The vanity of an artist! That is the kind of thing that reconciles me to life: a ragged, tippling, incompetent old rogue, with the manners of a gentleman, and the vanity of an artist, to keep up his self-respect!

But the man after my own heart is M. de Vauversin. It is nearly two years since I saw him first, and indeed I hope I may see him often again. Here is his first programme, as I found it on the breakfast table, and have kept it ever since as a relic of bright days:

"MESDAMES ET MESSIEURS—Mademoiselle Ferrario et M. de Vauversin auront l'honneur de chanter ce soir les morceaux suivants.

"Mademoiselle Ferrario chantera — Mignon'— Oiseaux Legers—France—Des Français dorment là—Le château bleu—Où voulez-vous aller?

"M. de Vauversin—Madame Fontaine et M. Robinet —Les plongeurs à cheval—Le Mari mecontent—Tais-toi, gamin—Mon voisin l'original—Heureux comme ça—Comme on est trompe."

They made a stage at one end of the salle-à-manger. And what a sight it was to see M. de Vauversin, with

a cigarette in his mouth, twanging a guitar, and following Mademoiselle Ferrario's eyes with the obedient,
kindly look of a dog! The entertainment wound up
with a tombola, or auction of lottery tickets: an admirable amusement, with all the excitement of gam-
bling, and no hope of gain to make you ashamed of
your eagerness; for there, all is loss; you make haste
to be out of pocket; it is a competition who shall lose
most money for the benefit of M. de Vauversin and
Mdlle. Ferrario.

M. de Vauversin is a small man, with a great head
of black hair, a vivacious and engaging air, and a
smile that would be delightful if he had better teeth.
He was once an actor in the Châtelet; but he con-
tracted a nervous affection from the heat and glare of
the footlights, which unfitted him for the stage. At
this crisis Mademoiselle Ferrario, otherwise Mademoiselle
Rita of the Alcazar, agreed to share his wandering fortunes. "I could never forget the generosity of that
lady," said he. He wears trousers so tight that it
has long been a problem to all who know him how he
manages to get in and out of them. He sketches a
little in water-colors; he writes verses; he is the most
patient of fishermen, and spent long days at the bottom of the inn garden fruitlessly dabbling a line in the
clear river.

You should hear him recounting his experiences over
a bottle of wine; such a pleasant vein of talk as he
has, with a ready smile at his own mishaps, and every
now and then a sudden gravity, like a man who should
hear the surf roar while he was telling the perils of
the deep. For it was no longer ago than last night,

perhaps, that the receipts only amounted to a franc and a half, to cover three francs of railway fare and two of board and lodging. The Maire, a man worth a million of money, sat in the front seat, repeatedly applauding Mdlle. Ferrario, and yet gave no more than three sous the whole evening. Local authorities look with such an evil eye upon the strolling artist. Alas! I know it well, who have been myself taken for one, and pitilessly incarcerated on the strength of the misapprehension. Once, M. de Vauversin visited a commissary of police for permission to sing. The commissary, who was smoking at his ease, politely doffed his hat upon the singer's entrance. "Mr. Commissary," he began, "I am an artist." And on went the commissary's hat again. No courtesy for the companions of Apollo! "They are as degraded as that," said M. de Vauversin, with a sweep of his cigarette.

But what pleased me most was one outbreak of his, when we had been talking all the evening of the rubs, indignities, and pinchings of his wandering life. Some one said, it would be better to have a million of money down, and Mdlle. Ferrario admitted that she would prefer that mightily. "Eh bien, moi non;—not I," cried De Vauversin, striking the table with his hand. "If any one is a failure in the world, is it not I? I had an art, in which I have done things well—as well as some—better perhaps than others; and now it is closed against me. I must go about the country gathering coppers and singing nonsense. Do you think I regret my life? Do you think I would rather be a fat burgess, like a calf? Not I! I have had moments when I have been applauded on the boards: I think nothing of that; but I have known in my own mind some-times, when I had not a clap from the whole house, that I had found a true intonation, or an exact and speaking gesture; and then, messieurs, I have known what pleasure was, what it was to do a thing well, what it was to be an artist. And to know what art is, is to have an interest forever, such as no burgess can find in his petty concerns. Tenez, messieurs, je vais vous le dire—it is like a religion.''

Such, making some allowance for the tricks of mem-ory and the inaccuracies of translation, was the profes-sion of faith of M. de Vauversin. I have given him his own name, lest any other wanderer should come across him, with his guitar and cigarette, and Mdlle. Ferrario; for should not all the world delight to honor this unfortunate and loyal follower of the Muses? May Apollo send him rimes hitherto undreamed of; may the river be no longer scanty of her silver fishes to his lure; may the cold not pinch him on long winter rides, nor the village jack-in-office affront him with unseemly manners; and may he never miss Mdlle. Ferrario from his side, to follow with his dutiful eyes and accompany on the guitar!

The marionettes made a very dismal entertainment. They performed a piece, called "Pyramus and Thisbe," in five mortal acts, and all written in Alexandrines fully as long as the performers. One marionette was the king; another the wicked counselor; a third, credited with exceptional beauty, represented Thisbe; and then there were guards, and obdurate fathers, and walking gentlemen. Nothing particular took place during the two or three acts that I sat out; but you will be pleased

to learn that the unities were properly respected, and
the whole piece, with one exception, moved in harmony
with classical rules. That exception was the comic countryman, a lean marionette in wooden shoes, who spoke
in prose and in a broad patois much appreciated by
the audience. He took unconstitutional liberties with
the person of his sovereign; kicked his fellow marionettes in the mouth with his wooden shoes, and whenever none of the versifying suitors were about, made
love to Thisbe on his own account in comic prose.

This fellow's evolutions, and the little prologue, in
which the showman made a humorous eulogium of his
troop, praising their indifference to applause and hisses,
and their single devotion to their art, were the only
circumstances in the whole affair that you could fancy
would so much as raise a smile. But the villagers of
Precy seemed delighted. Indeed, so long as a thing is
an exhibition, and you pay to see it, it is nearly certain to amuse. If we were charged so much a head
for sunsets, or if God sent round a drum before the
hawthorns came in flower, what a work should we not
make about their beauty! But these things, like good
companions, stupid people early cease to observe: and
the Abstract Bagman tittups past in his spring gig,
and is positively not aware of the flowers along the
lane, or the scenery of the weather overhead.

BACK TO THE WORLD

Of the next two days' sail little remains in my mind, and nothing whatever in my note-book. The river streamed on steadily through pleasant riverside landscapes. Washerwomen in blue dresses, fishers in blue blouses, diversified the green banks; and the relation of the two colors was like that of the flower and the leaf in the *forget-me-not*. A symphony in *forget-me-not;* I think Theophile Gautier might thus have characterized that two days' panorama. The sky was blue and cloudless; and the sliding surface of the river held up, in smooth places, a mirror to the heaven and the shores. The washerwomen hailed us laughingly; and the noise of trees and water made an accompaniment to our dozing thoughts, as we fleeted down the stream.

The great volume, the indefatigable purpose of the river, held the mind in chain. It seemed now so sure of its end, so strong and easy in its gait, like a grown man full of determination. The surf was roaring for it on the sands of Havre.

For my own part, slipping along this moving thoroughfare in my fiddle-case of a canoe, I also was beginning to grow aweary for my ocean. To the civilized man, there must come, sooner or later, a desire for civilization. I was weary of dipping the paddle; I was weary of living on the skirts of life; I wished to be in the thick of it once more; I wished to get to work; I wished to meet people who understood my own speech, and could meet with me on equal terms, as a man, and no longer as a curiosity.

And so a letter at Pontoise decided us, and we drew up our keels for the last time out of that river of Oise that had faithfully piloted them, through rain and sunshine, for so long. For so many miles had this fleet and footless beast of burden charioted our fortunes, that we turned our back upon it with a sense of separation. We had made a long detour out of the world, but now we were back in the familiar places, where life itself makes all the running, and we are carried to meet adventure without a stroke of the paddle. Now we were to return, like the voyager in the play, and see what rearrangements fortune had perfected the while in our surroundings; what surprsies stood ready made for us at home; and whither and how far the world had voyaged in our absence. You may paddle all day long; but it is when you come back at nightfall, and look in at the familiar room, that you find Love or Death awaiting you beside the stove; and the most beautiful adventures are not those we go to seek.

END OF "AN INLAND VOYAGE"

TRAVELS WITH A DONKEY
IN THE CEVENNES

MY DEAR SIDNEY COLVIN,

THE journey which this little book is to describe was very agreeable and fortunate for me. After an uncouth beginning, I had the best of luck to the end. But we are all travelers in what John Bunyan calls the wilderness of this world—all, too, travelers with a donkey; and the best that we find in our travels is an honest friend. He is a fortunate voyager who finds many. We travel, indeed, to find them. They are the end and the reward of life. They keep us worthy of ourselves; and when we are alone, we are only nearer to the absent.

Every book is, in an intimate sense, a circular letter to the friends of him who writes it. They alone take his meaning; they find private messages, assurances of love, and expressions of gratitude, dropped for them in every corner. The public is but a generous patron who defrays the postage. Yet though the letter is directed to all, we have an old and kindly custom of addressing it on the outside to one. Of what shall a man be proud, if he is not proud of his friends? And so, my dear Sidney Colvin, it is with pride that I sign myself affectionately yours,   R. L. S.

VELAY

"Many are the mighty things, and naught is more mighty than man. . . . He masters by his devices the tenant of the fields."—SOPHOCLES

"Who hath loosed the bands of the wild ass?"—JOB

THE DONKEY, THE PACK, AND THE PACK-SADDLE

IN a little place called Le Monastier, in a pleasant highland valley fifteen miles from Le Puy, I spent about a month of fine days. Monastier is notable for the making of lace, for drunkenness, for freedom of language, and for unparalleled political dissension. There are adherents of each of the four French parties—Legitimists, Orleanists, Imperialists, and Republicans—in this little mountain town; and they all hate, loathe, decry, and calumniate each other. Except for business purposes, or to give each other the lie in a tavern brawl, they have laid aside even the civility of speech. 'Tis a mere mountain Poland. In the midst of this Babylon I found myself a rallying-point; every one was anxious to be kind and helpful to the stranger. This was not merely from the natural hospitality of mountain people, nor even from the surprise with which I was regarded as a man living of his own free will in Le Monastier, when he might just as well have lived

(153)

anywhere else in this big world; it arose a good deal
from my projected excursion southward through the Cevennes. A traveler of my sort was a thing hitherto
unheard of in that district. I was looked upon with
contempt, like a man who should project a journey to
the moon, but yet with a respectful interest, like one
setting forth for the inclement Pole. All were ready
to help in my preparations; a crowd of sympathizers
supported me at the critical moment of a bargain; not
a step was taken but was heralded by glasses round
and celebrated by a dinner or a breakfast.

It was already hard upon October before I was
ready to set forth, and at the high altitudes over
which my road lay there was no Indian summer to be
looked for. I was determined, if not to camp out, at
least to have the means of camping out in my possession; for there is nothing more harassing to an easy
mind than the necessity of reaching shelter by dusk,
and the hospitality of a village inn is not always to
be reckoned sure by those who trudge on foot. A tent,
above all for a solitary traveler, is troublesome to pitch,
and troublesome to strike again; and even on the march
it forms a conspicuous feature in your baggage. A
sleeping-sack, on tne other hand, is always ready—you
have only to get into it; it serves a double purpose—
a bed by night, a portmanteau by day; and it does
not advertise your intention of camping out to every
curious passer-by. This is a huge point. If the camp
is not secret, it is but a troubled resting-place; you
become a public character; the convivial rustic visits
your bedside after an early supper; and you must sleep
with one eye open, and be up before the day. I de-

cided on a sleeping-sack; and after repeated visits to
Le Puy, and a deal of high living for myself and my
advisers, a sleeping-sack was designed, constructed, and
triumphally brought home.

This child of my invention was nearly six feet
square, exclusive of two trianglar flaps to serve as a
pillow by night and as the top and bottom of the sack
by day. I call it "the sack," but it was never a
sack by more than courtesy: only a sort of long roll
or sausage, green water-proof cart-cloth without and
blue sheep's fur within. It was commodious as a va-
lise, warm and dry for a bed. There was luxurious
turning room for one; and at a pinch the thing might
serve for two. I could bury myself in it up to the
neck; for my head I trusted to a fur cap, with a hood
to fold down over my ears, and a band to pass under
my nose like a respirator; and in case of heavy rain
I proposed to make myself a little tent, or tentlet, with
my water-proof coat, three stones, and a bent branch.

It will readily be conceived that I could not carry
this huge package on my own, merely human, shoulders. It remained to choose a beast of burden. Now,
a horse is a fine lady among animals, flighty, timid,
delicate in eating, of tender health; he is too valuable
and too restive to be left alone, so that you are chained
to your brute as to a fellow galley-slave; a dangerous
road puts him out of his wits; in short, he's an uncertain and exacting ally, and adds thirty-fold to the
troubles of the voyager. What I required was something cheap and small and hardy, and of a stolid and
peaceful temper; and all these requisites pointed to a
donkey.

There dwelt an old man in Monastier, of rather un-
sound intellect according to some, much followed by
street-boys, and known to fame as Father Adam. Father
Adam had a cart, and to draw the cart a diminutive
she-ass, not much bigger than a dog, the color of a
mouse, with a kindly eye and a determined under-jaw.
There was something neat and high-bred, a quakerish
elegance, about the rogue that hit my fancy on the
spot. Our first interview was in Monastier market-place.
To prove her good temper, one child after another was
set upon her back to ride, and one after another went
head over heels into the air; until a want of confidence began to reign in youthful bosoms, and the experiment was discontinued from a dearth of subjects. I
was already backed by a deputation of my friends; but
as if this were not enough, all the buyers and sellers
came round and helped me in the bargain; and the
ass and I and Father Adam were the center of a hub-
bub for near half an hour. At length she passed into
my service for the consideration of sixty-five francs and
a glass of brandy. The sack had already cost eighty
francs and two glasses of beer; so that Modestine, as
I instantly baptized her, was upon all accounts the
cheaper article. Indeed, that was as it should be; for
she was only an appurtenance of my mattress, or self-
acting bedstead on four castors.

I had a last interview with Father Adam in a bil-
liard-room at the witching hour of dawn, when I administered the brandy. He professed himself greatly
touched by the separation, and declared he had often
bought white bread for the donkey when he had been
content with black bread for himself; but this, accord-

ing to the best authorities, must have been a flight of
fancy. He had a name in the village for brutally mis-
using the ass; yet it is certain that he shed a tear,
and the tear made a clean mark down one cheek.

By the advice of a fallacious local saddler, a leather
pad was made for me with rings to fasten on my bundle; and I thoughtfully completed my kit and arranged
my toilet. By way of armory and utensils, I took a
revolver, a little spirit-lamp and pan, a lantern and
some halfpenny candles, a jack-knife and a large leather
flask. The main cargo consisted of two entire changes
of warm clothing—besides my traveling wear of country velveteen, pilot-coat, and knitted spencer — some
books, and my railway-rug, which, being also in the
form of a bag, made me a double castle for cold
nights. The permanent larder was represented by cakes
of chocolate and tins of Bologna sausage. All this, except what I carried about my person, was easily stowed
into the sheepskin bag; and by good fortune I threw
in my empty knapsack, rather for convenience of carriage than from any thought that I should want it
on my journey. For more immediate needs, I took a
leg of cold mutton, a bottle of Beaujolais, an empty
bottle to carry milk, an egg-beater, and a considerable
quantity of black bread and white, like Father Adam,
for myself and donkey, only in my scheme of things
the destinations were reversed.

Monastrians, of all shades of thought in politics,
had agreed in threatening me with many ludicrous misadventures, and with sudden death in many surprising
forms. Cold, wolves, robbers, above all the nocturnal
practical joker, were daily and eloquently forced on my

attention. Yet in these vaticinations, the true, patent danger was left out. Like Christian, it was from my pack I suffered by the way. Before telling my own mishaps, let me, in two words, relate the lesson of my experience. If the pack is well strapped at the ends, and hung at full length—not doubled, for your life— across the pack-saddle, the traveler is safe. The saddle will certainly not fit, such is the imperfection of our transitory life; it will assuredly topple and tend to overset; but there are stones on every roadside, and a man soon learns the art of correcting any tendency to overbalance with a well-adjusted stone.

On the day of my departure I was up a little after five; by six, we began to load the donkey; and ten minutes after, my hopes were in the dust. The pad would not stay on Modestine's back for half a moment. I returned it to its maker, with whom I had so contumelious a passage that the street outside was crowded from wall to wall with gossips looking on and listening. The pad changed hands with much vivacity; perhaps it would be more descriptive to say that we threw it at each other's heads; and, at any rate, we were very warm and unfriendly, and spoke with a deal of freedom.

I had a common donkey pack-saddle—a barde, as they call it — fitted upon Modestine; and once more loaded her with my effects. The doubled sack, my pilot-coat (for it was warm, and I was to walk in my waistcoat), a great bar of black bread, and an open basket containing the white bread, the mutton, and the bottles were all corded together in a very elaborate system of knots, and I looked on the result with fatu-

ous content. In such a monstrous deck-cargo, all poised
above the donkey's shoulders, with nothing below to
balance, on a brand-new pack-saddle that had not yet
been worn to fit the animal, and fastened with brand-
new girths that might be expected to stretch and slacken
by the way, even a very careless traveler should have
seen disaster brewing. That elaborate system of knots,
again, was the work of too many sympathizers to be
very artfully designed. It is true they tightened the
cords with a will; as many as three at a time would
have a foot against Modestine's quarters, and be hauling with clinched teeth; but I learned afterward that
one thoughtful person, without any exercise of force,
can make a more solid job than half a dozen heated
and enthusiastic grooms. I was then but a novice;
even after the misadventure of the pad nothing could
disturb my security, and I went forth from the stable-
door as an ox goeth to the slaughter.

THE GREEN DONKEY-DRIVER

THE bell of Monastier was just striking nine as I got quit of these preliminary troubles and descended the hill through the common. As long as I was within sight of the windows, a secret shame and the fear of some laughable defeat withheld me from tampering with Modestine. She tripped along upon her four small hoofs with a sober daintiness of gait; from time to time she shook her ears or her tail; and she looked so small under the bundle that my mind misgave me. We got across the ford without difficulty—there was no doubt about the matter, she was docility itself—and once on the other bank, where the road begins to mount through pine-woods, I took in my right hand the unhallowed staff, and with a quaking spirit applied it to the donkey. Modestine brisked up her pace for perhaps three steps, and then relapsed into her former minuet. Another application had the same effect, and so with the third. I am worthy the name of an Englishman, and it goes against my conscience to lay my hand rudely on a female. I desisted, and looked her all over from head to foot; the poor brute's knees were trem-

bling and her breathing was distressed; it was plain
that she could go no faster on a hill. God forbid,
thought I, that I should brutalize this innocent creature; let her go at her own pace, and let me patiently
follow.

What that pace was, there is no word mean enough
to describe; it was something as much slower than a
walk as a walk is slower than a run; it kept me hanging on each foot for an incredibble length of time; in
five minutes it exhausted the spirit and set up a fever
in all the muscles of the leg. And yet I had to keep
close at hand and measure my advance exactly upon
hers; for if I dropped a few yards into the rear, or
went on a few yards ahead, Modestine came instantly
to a halt and began to browse. The thought that this
was to last from here to Alais nearly broke my heart.
Of all conceivable journeys, this promised to be the
most tedious. I tried to tell myself it was a lovely
day; I tried to charm my foreboding spirit with tobacco; but I had a vision ever present to me of the
long, long roads, up hill and down dale, and a pair of
figures ever infinitesimally moving, foot by foot, a yard
to the minute, and, like things enchanted in a nightmare, approaching no nearer to the goal.

In the meantime there came up behind us a tall
peasant, perhaps forty years of age, of an ironical
snuffy countenance, and arrayed in the green tail-coat
of the country. He overtook us hand over hand, and
stopped to consider our pitiful advance.

"Your donkey," says he, "is very old?"

I told him, I believed not.

Then, he supposed, we had come far.

I told him, we had but newly left Monastier.

"Et vous marchez comme ça!" cried he; and, throwing back his head, he laughed long and heartily. I watched him, half prepared to feel offended, until he had satisfied his mirth; and then, "You must have no pity on these animals," said he; and, plucking a switch out of a thicket, he began to lace Modestine about the stern-works, uttering a cry. The rogue pricked up her ears and broke into a good round pace, which she kept up without flagging, and without exhibiting the least symptom of distress, as long as the peasant kept beside us. Her former panting and shaking had been, I regret to say, a piece of comedy.

My deus ex machinâ, before he left me, supplied some excellent, if inhumane, advice; presented me with the switch, which he declared she would feel more tenderly than my cane; and finally taught me the true cry or masonic word of donkey-drivers, "Proot!" All the time, he regarded me with a comical incredulous air, which was embarrassing to confront; and smiled over my donkey-driving, as I might have smiled over his orthography, or his green tail-coat. But it was not my turn for the moment.

I was proud of my new lore, and thought I had learned the art to perfection. And certainly Modestine did wonders for the rest of the forenoon, and I had a breathing space to look about me. It was Sabbath; the mountain-fields were all vacant in the sunshine; and as we came down through St. Martin de Frugères, the church was crowded to the door, there were people kneeling without upon the steps, and the sound of the priest's chanting came forth out of the dim interior. It

gave me a home feeling on the spot; for I am a countryman of the Sabbath, so to speak, and all Sabbath
observances, like a Scotch accent, strike in me mixed
feelings, grateful and the reverse. It is only a traveler,
hurrying by like a person from another planet, who
can rightly enjoy the peace and beauty of the great
ascetic feast. The sight of the resting country does his
spirit good. There is something better than music in
the wide unusual silence; and it disposes him to amiable thoughts, like the sound of a little river or the
warmth of sunlight.

In this pleasant humor I came down the hill to
where Goudet stands in a green end of a valley, with
Chateau Beaufort opposite upon a rocky steep, and the
stream, as clear as crystal, lying in a deep pool between them. Above and below, you may hear it wim-
pling over the stones, an amiable stripling of a river,
which it seems absurd to call the Loire. On all sides,
Goudet is shut in by mountains; rocky footpaths, prac-
ticable at best for donkeys, join it to the outer world
of France; and the men and women drink and swear,
in their green corner, or look up at the snow-clad
peaks in winter from the threshold of their homes, in
an isolation, you would think, like that of Homer's
Cyclops.

But it is not so; the postman reaches Goudet
with the letter-bag; the aspiring youth of Goudet are
within a day's walk of the railway at Le Puy; and
here in the inn you may find an engraved portrait of
the host's nephew, Regis Senac, "Professor of Fencing
and Champion of the two Americas," a distinction
gained by him, along with the sum of five hundred

dollars, at Tammany Hall, New York, on the 10th April, 1876.

I hurried over my midday meal, and was early forth again. But, alas, as we climbed the interminable hill upon the other side, "Proot!" seemed to have lost its virtue. I prooted like a lion, I prooted mellifluously like a sucking-dove; but Modestine would be neither softened nor intimidated. She held doggedly to her pace; nothing but a blow would move her, and that only for a second. I must follow at her heels, incessantly belaboring. A moment's pause in this ignoble toil, and she relapsed into her own private gait. I think I never heard of any one in as mean a situation. I must reach the lake of Bouchet, where I meant to camp, before sundown, and, to have even a hope of this, I must instantly maltreat this uncomplaining animal. The sound of my own blows sickened me. Once, when I looked at her, she had a faint resemblance to a lady of my acquaintance who formerly loaded me with kindness; and this increased my horror of my cruelty.

To make matters worse, we encountered another donkey, ranging at will upon the roadside; and this other donkey chanced to be a gentleman. He and Modestine met nickering for joy, and I had to separate the pair and beat down their young romance with a renewed and feverish bastinado. If the other donkey had had the heart of a male under his hide, he would have fallen upon me tooth and hoof; and this was a kind of consolation—he was plainly unworthy of Modestine's affection. But the incident saddened me, as did everything that spoke of my donkey's sex.

It was blazing hot up the valley, windless, with vehement sun upon my shoulders; and I had to labor so consistently with my stick that the sweat ran into my eyes. Every five minutes, too, the pack, the basket, and the pilot-coat would take an ugly slew to one side or the other; and I had to stop Modestine, just when I had got her to a tolerable pace of about two miles an hour, to tug, push, shoulder, and readjust the load. And at last, in the village of Ussel, saddle and all, the whole hypothec turned round and groveled in the dust below the donkey's belly. She, none better pleased, incontinently drew up and seemed to smile; and a party of one man, two women, and two children came up, and, standing round me in a half-circle, encouraged her by their example.

I had the devil's own trouble to get the thing righted; and the instant I had done so, without hesitation, it toppled and fell down upon the other side. Judge if I was hot! And yet not a hand was offered to assist me. The man, indeed, told me I ought to have a package of a different shape. I suggested, if he knew nothing better to the point in my predicament, he might hold his tongue. And the good-natured dog agreed with me smilingly. It was the most despicable fix. I must plainly content myself with the pack for Modestine, and take the following items for my own share of the portage: a cane, a quart flask, a pilot-jacket heavily weighted in the pockets, two pounds of black bread, and an open basket full of meats and bottles. I believe I may say I am not devoid of greatness of soul; for I did not recoil from this infamous burden. I disposed it, Heaven knows how, so as to be mildly portable, and then proceeded to steer Modestine through the village. She tried, as was indeed her invariable habit, to enter every house and every courtyard in the whole length; and, encumbered as I was, without a hand to help myself, no words can render an idea of my difficulties. A priest, with six or seven others, was examining a church in process of repair, and he and his acolytes laughed loudly as they saw my plight. I remembered having laughed myself when I had seen good men struggling with adversity in the person of a jackass, and the recollection filled me with penitence. That was in my old light days, before this trouble came upon me. God knows at least that I shall never laugh again, thought I. But, oh, what a cruel thing is a farce to those engaged in it!

A little out of the village, Modestine, filled with the demon, set her heart upon a byroad, and positively refused to leave it. I dropped all my bundles, and, I am ashamed to say, struck the poor sinner twice across the face. It was pitiful to see her lift up her head with shut eyes, as if waiting for another blow. I came very near crying; but I did a wiser thing than that, and sat squarely down by the roadside to consider my situation under the cheerful influence of tobacco and a nip of brandy. Modestine, in the meanwhile, munched some black bread with a contrite hypocritical air. It was plain that I must make a sacrifice to the gods of shipwreck. I threw away the empty bottle destined to carry milk; I threw away my own white bread, and, disdaining to act by general average, kept the black bread for Modestine; lastly, I threw away the cold leg of mutton and the egg-whisk, although this last was

dear to my heart. Thus I found room for everything
in the basket, and even stowed the boating-coat on the
top. By means of an end of cord I slung it under
one arm; and although the cord cut my shoulder, and
the jacket hung almost to the ground, it was with a
heart greatly lightened that I set forth again.

I had now an arm free to thrash Modestine, and
cruelly I chastised her. If I were to reach the lake-
side before dark, she must bestir her little shanks to
some tune. Already the sun had gone down into a
windy-looking mist; and although there were still a few
streaks of gold far off to the east on the hills and the
black fir-woods, all was cold and gray about our onward path. An infinity of little country byroads led
hither and thither among the fields. It was the most
pointless labyrinth. I could see my destination overhead, or rather the peak that dominates it; but choose
as I pleased, the roads always ended by turning away
from it, and sneaking back toward the valley, or north-
ward along the margin of the hills. The failing light,
the waning color, the naked, unhomely, stony country
through which I was traveling, threw me into some
despondency. I promise you, the stick was not idle; I
think every decent step that Modestine took must have
cost me at least two emphatic blows. There was not
another sound in the neighborhood but that of my
unwearying bastinado.

Suddenly, in the midst of my toils, the load once
more bit the dust, and, as by enchantment, all the
cords were simultaneously loosened, and the road scattered with my dear possessions. The packing was to
begin again from the beginning; and as I had to in-

vent a new and better system, I do not doubt but I
lost half an hour. It began to be dusk in earnest as
I reached a wilderness of turf and stones. It had the
air of being a road which should lead everywhere at
the same time; and I was falling into something not
unlike despair when I saw two figures stalking toward
me over the stones. They walked one behind the other
like tramps, but their pace was remarkable. The son
led the way, a tall, ill-made, somber, Scotch-looking
man; the mother followed, all in her Sunday's best,
with an elegantly-embroidered ribbon to her cap, and a
new felt hat atop, and proffering, as she strode along
with kilted petticoats, a string of obscene and blas-
phemous oaths.

I hailed the son and asked him my direction. He
pointed loosely west and northwest, muttered an inaudible comment, and, without slacking his pace for an
instant, stalked on, as he was going, right athwart my
path. The mother followed without so much as raising
her head. I shouted and shouted after them, but they
continued to scale the hillside, and turned a deaf ear
to my outcries. At last, leaving Modestine by herself,
I was constrained to run after them, hailing the while.
They stopped as I drew near, the mother still cursing;
and I could see she was a handsome, motherly, respect-
able-looking woman. The son once more answered me
roughly and inaudibly, and was for setting out again.
But this time I simply collared the mother, who was
nearest me, and, apologizing for my violence, declared
that I could not let them go until they had put me
on my road. They were neither of them offended—
rather mollified than otherwise; told me I had only to

follow them; and then the mother asked me what I
wanted by the lake at such an hour. I replied, in the
Scotch manner, by inquiring if she had far to go herself. She told me, with another oath, that she had an
hour and a half's road before her. And then, without
salutation, the pair strode forward again up the hillside
in the gathering dusk.

I returned for Modestine, pushed her briskly forward,
and, after a sharp ascent of twenty minutes, reached
the edge of a plateau. The view, looking back on
my day's journey, was both wild and sad. Mount
Mezenc and the peaks beyond St. Julien stood out in
trenchant gloom against a cold glitter in the east; and
the intervening field of hills had fallen together into
one broad wash of shadow, except here and there the
outline of a wooded sugar-loaf in black, here and there
a white irregular patch to represent a cultivated farm,
and here and there a blot where the Loire, the Ga-
zeille, or the Laussonne wandered in a gorge.

Soon we were on a high-road, and surprise seized
on my mind as I beheld a village of some magnitude
close at hand; for I had been told that the neighborhood of the lake was uninhabited except by trout. The
road smoked in the twilight with children driving home
cattle from the fields; and a pair of mounted stride-
legged women, hat and cap and all, dashed past me
at a hammering trot from the canton where they had
been to church and market. I asked one of the children where I was. At Bouchet St. Nicolas, he told
me.

Thither, about a mile south of my destination,
and on the other side of a respectable summit, had

these confused roads and treacherous peasantry conducted me. My shoulder was cut, so that it hurt
sharply; my arm ached like toothache from perpetual
beating; I gave up the lake and my design to camp,
and asked for the auberge.

I HAVE A GOAD

THE auberge of Bouchet St. Nicolas was among the least pretentious I have ever visited; but I saw many more of the like upon my journey. Indeed, it was typical of these French highlands. Imagine a cottage of two stories, with a bench before the door; the stable and kitchen in a suite, so that Modestine and I could hear each other dining; furniture of the plainest, earthern floors, a single bedchamber for travelers, and that without any convenience but beds. In the kitchen cooking and eating go forward side by side, and the family sleep at night. Any one who has a fancy to wash must do so in public at the common table. The food is sometimes spare; hard fish and omelette have been my portion more than once; the wine is of the smallest, the brandy abominable to man; and the visit of a fat sow, grouting under the table and rubbing against your legs, is no impossible accompaniment to dinner.

But the people of the inn, in nine cases out of ten, show themselves friendly and considerate. As soon as you cross the doors you cease to be a stranger; and although these peasantry are rude and forbidding on the highway, they show a tincture of kind breeding when you share their hearth. At Bouchet, for instance, I uncorked my bottle of Beaujolais, and asked the host to join me. He would take but little.

"I am an amateur of such wine, do you see?" he said, "and I am capable of leaving you not enough."

In these hedge-inns the traveler is expected to eat with his own knife; unless he ask, no other will be supplied: with a glass, a whang of bread, and an iron fork, the table is completely laid. My knife was cordially admired by the landlord of Bouchet, and the spring filled him with wonder.

"I should never have guessed that," he said. "I would bet," he added, weighing it in his hand, "that this cost you not less than five francs."

When I told him it had cost me twenty, his jaw dropped.

He was a mild, handsome, sensible, friendly old man, astonishingly ignorant. His wife, who was not so pleasant in her manners, knew how to read, although I do not suppose she ever did so. She had a share of brains and spoke with a cutting emphasis, like one who ruled the roast.

"My man knows nothing," she said, with an angry nod; "he is like the beasts."

And the old gentleman signified acquiescence with his head. There was no contempt on her part, and no shame on his; the facts were accepted loyally, and no more about the matter.

I was tightly cross-examined about my journey; and the lady understood in a moment, and sketched out what I should put into my book when I got home.

"Whether people harvest or not in such or such a place; if there were forests; studies of manners; what, for example, I and the master of the house say to you; the beauties of Nature, and all that." And she interrogated me with a look.

"It is just that," said I.

"You see," she added to her husband, "I understood that."

They were both much interested by the story of my misadventures.

"In the morning," said the husband, "I will make you something better than your cane. Such a beast as that feels nothing; it is in the proverb—dur comme un âne; you might beat her insensible with a cudgel, and yet you would arrive nowhere."

Something better! I little knew what he was offering.

The sleeping-room was furnished with two beds. I had one; and I will own I was a little abashed to find a young man and his wife and child in the act of mounting into the other. This was my first experience of the sort; and if I am always to feel equally silly and extraneous, I pray God it be my last as well. I kept my eyes to myself, and know nothing of the woman except that she had beautiful arms, and seemed no whit embarrassed by my appearance. As a matter of fact, the situation was more trying to me than to the pair. A pair keep each other in countenance; it is the single gentleman who has to blush. But I could not help attributing my sentiments to the husband, and sought to conciliate his tolerance with a cup of brandy from my flask. He told me that he was a cooper of Alais traveling to St. Etienne in search of work, and that in his spare moments he followed the fatal calling of a maker of matches. Me he readily enough divined to be a brandy merchant.

I was up first in the morning (Monday, September 23), and hastened my toilet guiltily, so as to leave a clear field for madam, the cooper's wife. I drank a bowl of milk, and set off to explore the neighborhood of Bouchet. It was perishing cold, a gray, windy, wintry morning; misty clouds flew fast and low; the wind piped over the naked platform; and the only speck of color was away behind Mount Mezenc and the eastern hills, where the sky still wore the orange of the dawn.

It was five in the morning, and four thousand feet above the sea; and I had to bury my hands in my pockets and trot. People were trooping out to the labors of the field by twos and threes, and all turned round to stare upon the stranger. I had seen them coming back last night, I saw them going afield again; and there was the life of Bouchet in a nutshell.

When I came back to the inn for a bit of breakfast, the landlady was in the kitchen combing out her daughter's hair; and I made her my compliments upon its beauty.

"Oh, no," said the mother; "it is not so beautiful as it ought to be. Look, it is too fine."

Thus does a wise peasantry console itself under adverse physical circumstances, and, by a startling democratic process, the defects of the majority decide the type of beauty.

"And where," said I, "is monsieur?"

"The master of the house is upstairs," she answered, "making you a goad."

Blessed be the man who invented goads! Blessed the innkeeper of Bouchet St. Nicolas, who introduced me to their use! This plain wand, with an eighth of an inch of pin, was indeed a scepter when he put it in my hands. Thenceforward Modestine was my slave. A prick, and she passed the most inviting stable-door. A prick, and she broke forth into a gallant little trot-let that devoured the miles. It was not a remarkable speed, when all was said; and we took four hours to cover ten miles at the best of it. But what a heavenly change since yesterday! No more wielding of the ugly cudgel; no more flailing with an aching arm; no more broadsword exercise, but a discreet and gentlemanly fence. And what although now and then a drop of blood should appear on Modestine's mouse-colored wedge-like rump? I should have preferred it otherwise, in-deed; but yesterday's exploits had purged my heart of all humanity. The perverse little devil, since she would not be taken with kindness, must even go with pricking.

It was bleak and bitter cold, and, except a caval-cade of stride-legged ladies and a pair of post-runners, the road was dead solitary all the way to Pradelles. I scarce remember an incident but one. A handsome foal with a bell about his neck came charging up to us upon a stretch of common, sniffed the air martially as one about to do great deeds, and, suddenly thinking otherwise in his green young heart, put about and gal-loped off as he had come, the bell tinkling in the wind. For a long while afterward I saw his noble attitude as he drew up, and heard the note of his

bell; and when I struck the high-road, the song of
the telegraph-wires seemed to continue the same music.

Pradelles stands on a hillside, high above the Allier,
surrounded by rich meadows. They were cutting after-
math on all sides, which gave the neighborhood, this
gusty autumn morning, an untimely smell of hay. On
the opposite bank of the Allier the land kept mounting
for miles to the horizon: a tanned and sallow autumn
landscape, with black blots of fir-wood and white roads
wandering through the hills. Over all this the clouds
shed a uniform and purplish shadow, sad and somewhat menacing, exaggerating height and distance, and
throwing into still higher relief the twisted ribbons of
the highway. It was a cheerless prospect, but one
stimulating to a traveler. For I was now upon the
limit of Velay, and all that I beheld lay in another
county—wild Gevaudan, mountainous, uncultivated, and
but recently disforested from terror of the wolves.

Wolves, alas, like bandits, seem to flee the traveler's
advance; and you may trudge through all our comfortable Europe, and not meet with an adventure worth
the name. But here, if anywhere, a man was on the
frontiers of hope. For this was the land of the ever-
memorable BEAST, the Napoleon Bonaparte of wolves.
What a career was his! He lived ten months at free
quarters in Gevaudan and Vivarais; he ate women
and children and "shepherdesses celebrated for their
beauty"; he pursued armed horsemen; he has been
seen at broad noonday chasing a postchaise and out-
rider along the king's high-road, and chaise and out-
rider fleeing before him at the gallop. He was placarded like a political offender, and ten thousand francs

were offered for his head. And yet, when he was shot and sent to Versailles, behold! a common wolf, and even small for that. "Though I could reach from pole to pole," sang Alexander Pope; the Little Corporal shook Europe; and if all wolves had been as this wolf, they would have changed the history of man. M. Elie Berthet has made him the hero of a novel, which I have read, and do not wish to read again.

I hurried over my lunch, and was proof against the landlady's desire that I should visit our Lady of Pradelles, "who performed many miracles, although she was of wood"; and before three-quarters of an hour I was goading Modestine down the steep descent that leads to Langogne on the Allier. On both sides of the road, in big dusty fields, farmers were preparing for next spring. Every fifty yards a yoke of great-necked stolid oxen were patiently haling at the plow. I saw one of these mild formidable servants of the glebe, who took a sudden interest in Modestine and me. The furrow down which he was journeying lay at an angle to the road, and his head was solidly fixed to the yoke like those of caryatides below a ponderous cornice; but he screwed round his big honest eyes and followed us with a ruminating look, until his master bade him turn the plow and proceed to reascend the field. From all these furrowing plowshares, from the feet of oxen, from a laborer here and there who was breaking the dry clods with a hoe, the wind carried away a thin dust like so much smoke. It was a fine, busy, breathing, rustic landscape; and as I continued to descend, the highlands of Gevaudan kept mounting in front of me against the sky.

I had crossed the Loire the day before; now I was to cross the Allier; so near are these two confluents in their youth. Just at the bridge of Langogne, as the long-promised rain was beginning to fall, a lassie of some seven or eight addressed me in the sacramental phrase, "D'où 'st que vous venez?" She did it with so high an air that she set me laughing; and this cut her to the quick. She was evidently one who reckoned on respect, and stood looking after me in silent dudgeon, as I crossed the bridge and entered the county of Gevaudan.

UPPER GÉVAUDAN

*"The way also here was very wearisome through dirt
and slabbiness; nor was there on all this ground so much
as one inn or victualing-house wherein to refresh the feebler
sort."*—PILGRIM'S PROGRESS

A CAMP IN THE DARK

THE next day (Tuesday, September 24), it was two
o'clock in the afternoon before I got my journal written up and my knapsack repaired, for I was determined
to carry my knapsack in the future and have no more
ado with baskets; and half an hour afterward I set out
for Le Cheylard l'Eveque, a place on the borders of
the forest of Mercoire. A man, I was told, should
walk there in an hour and a half; and I thought it
scarce too ambitious to suppose that a man encumbered
with a donkey might cover the same distance in four
hours.

All the way up the long hill from Langogne it rained
and hailed alternately; the wind kept freshening steadily,
although slowly; plentiful hurrying clouds—some drag-
ging veils of straight rain-shower, others massed and
luminous as though promising snow—careered out of the
north and followed me along my way. I was soon out
of the cultivated basin of the Allier, and away from
the plowing oxen, and suchlike sights of the country.

Moor, heathery marsh, tracts of rock and pines, woods of birch all jeweled with the autumn yellow, here and there a few naked cottages and bleak fields—these were the characters of the country. Hill and valley followed valley and hill; the little green and stony cattle-tracks wandered in and out of one another, split into three or four, died away in marshy hollows, and began again sporadically on hillsides or at the borders of a wood.

There was no direct road to Cheylard, and it was no easy affair to make a passage in this uneven country and through this intermittent labyrinth of tracks. It must have been about four o'clock when I struck Sagnerousse, and went on my way rejoicing in a sure point of departure. Two hours afterward, the dusk rapidly falling, in a lull of the wind, I issued from a fir-wood where I had long been wandering, and found, not the looked-for village, but another marish bottom among rough-and-tumble hills. For some time past I had heard the ringing of cattle-bells ahead; and now, as I came out of the skirts of the wood, I saw near upon a dozen cows and perhaps as many more black figures, which I conjectured to be children, although the mist had almost unrecognizably exaggerated their forms. These were all silently following each other round and round in a circle, now taking hands, now breaking up with chains and reverences. A dance of children appeals to very innocent and lively thoughts; but, at nightfall on the marshes, the thing was eerie and fantastic to behold. Even I, who am well enough read in Herbert Spencer, felt a sort of silence fall for an instant on my mind. The next, I was pricking Modestine forward, and guiding her like an unruly ship through the open. In a path, she went doggedly ahead of her own accord, as before a fair wind; but once on the turf or among heather, and the brute became demented. The tendency of lost travelers to go round in a circle was developed in her to the degree of passion, and it took all the steering I had in me to keep even a decently straight course through a single field.

While I was thus desperately tacking through the bog, children and cattle began to disperse, until only a pair of girls remained behind. From these I sought direction on my path. The peasantry in general were but little disposed to counsel a wayfarer. One old devil simply retired into his house, and barricaded the door on my approach; and I might beat and shout myself hoarse, he turned a deaf ear. Another, having given me a direction which, as I found afterward, I had misunderstood, complacently watched me going wrong without adding a sign. He did not care a stalk of parsley if I wandered all night upon the hills! As for these two girls, they were a pair of impudent sly sluts, with not a thought but mischief. One put out her tongue at me, the other bade me follow the cows; and they both giggled and jogged each other's elbows. The Beast of Gevaudan ate about a hundred children of this district; I began to think of him with sympathy.

Leaving the girls, I pushed on through the bog, and got into another wood and upon a well-marked road. It grew darker and darker. Modestine, suddenly beginning to smell mischief, bettered the pace of her own accord, and from that time forward gave me no trouble. It was the first sign of intelligence I had occasion to remark in her. At the same time, the wind freshened into half a gale, and another heavy discharge of rain came flying up out of the north. At the other side of the wood I sighted some red windows in the dusk. This was the hamlet of Fouzilhic; three houses on a hillside, near a wood of birches. Here I found a delightful old man, who came a little way with me in the rain to put me safely on the road for Cheylard. He would hear of no reward; but shook his hands above his head almost as if in menace, and refused volubly and shrilly, in unmitigated patois.

All seemed right at last. My thoughts began to turn upon dinner and a fireside, and my heart was agreeably softened in my bosom. Alas, and I was on the brink of new and greater miseries! Suddenly, at a single swoop, the night fell. I have been abroad in many a black night, but never in a blacker. A glimmer of rocks, a glimmer of the track where it was well beaten, a certain fleecy density, or night within night, for a tree—this was all that I could discriminate. The sky was simply darkness overhead; even the flying clouds pursued their way invisibly to human eyesight. I could not distinguish my hand at arms-length from the track, nor my goad, at the same distance, from the meadows or the sky.

Soon the road that I was following split, after the fashion of the country, into three or four in a piece of rocky meadow. Since Modestine had shown such a fancy for beaten roads, I tried her instinct in this predicament. But the instinct of an ass is what might be expected from the name; in half a minute she was clambering round and round among some bowlders, as lost a donkey as you would wish to see. I should have camped long before had I been properly provided; but as this was to be so short a stage, I had brought no wine, no bread for myself, and little over a pound for my lady-friend. Add to this, that I and Modestine were both handsomely wetted by the showers. But now, if I could have found some water, I should have camped at once in spite of all. Water, however, being entirely absent, except in the form of rain, I determined to return to Fouzilhic, and ask a guide a little further on my way—"a little further lend thy guiding hand."

The thing was easy to decide, hard to accomplish. In this sensible roaring blackness I was sure of nothing but the direction of the wind. To this I set my face; the road had disappeared, and I went across country, now in marshy opens, now baffled by walls unscalable to Modestine, until I came once more in sight of some red windows. This time they were differently disposed. It was not Fouzilhic, but Fouzilhac, a hamlet little distant from the other in space, but worlds away in the spirit of its inhabitants. I tied Modestine to a gate, and groped forward, stumbling among rocks, plunging midleg in bog, until I gained the entrance of the village. In the first lighted house there was a woman who would not open to me. She could do nothing, she cried to me through the door, being alone and lame; but if I would apply at the next house, there was a man who could help me if he had a mind.

They came to the next door in force, a man, two women, and a girl, and brought a pair of lanterns to examine the wayfarer. The man was not ill-looking, but had a shifty smile. He leaned against the door-post, and heard me state my case. All I asked was a guide as far as Cheylard.

"C'est que, voyez-vous, il fait noir," said he.

I told him that was just my reason for requiring help.

"I understand that," said he, looking uncomfortable; "mais—c'est—de la peine."

I was willing to pay, I said. He shook his head. I rose as high as ten francs; but he continued to shake his head.

"Name your own price, then," said I.

"Ce n'est pas ca," he said at length, and with evident difficulty; "but I am not going to cross the door —mais je ne sortirai pas de la porte."

I grew a little warm, and asked him what he proposed that I should do.

"Where are you going beyond Cheylard?" he asked by way of answer.

"That is no affair of yours," I returned, for I was not going to indulge his bestial curiosity; "it changes nothing in my present predicament."

"C'est vrai, ca," he acknowledged, with a laugh; "oui, c'est vrai. Et d'où venez vous?"

A better man than I might have felt nettled.

"Oh," said I, "I am not going to answer any of your questions, so you may spare yourself the trouble of putting them. I am late enough already; I want help. If you will not guide me yourself, at least help me to find some one else who will."

"Hold on," he cried suddenly. "Was it not you who passed in the meadow while it was still day?"

"Yes, yes," said the girl, whom I had not hitherto

recognized; "it was monsieur; I told him to follow the cow."

"As for you, mademoiselle," said I, "you are a *farceuse.*"

"And," added the man, "what the devil have you done to be still here?"

What the devil, indeed! But there I was. "The great thing," said I, "is to make an end of it;" and once more proposed that he should help me to find a guide.

"C'est que," he said again, "c'est que—il fait noir."

"Very well," said I; "take one of your lanterns."

"No," he cried, drawing a thought backward, and again intrenching himself behind one of his former phrases; "I will not cross the door."

I looked at him. I saw unaffected terror struggling on his face with unaffected shame; he was smiling piti-fully and wetting his lip with his tongue, like a de-tected schoolboy. I drew a brief picture of my state, and asked him what I was to do.

"I don't know," he said; "I will not cross the door."

Here was the Beast of Gevaudan, and no mistake.

"Sir," said I, with my most commanding manners, "you are a coward."

And with that I turned my back upon the family party, who hastened to retire within their fortifications; and the famous door was closed again, but not till I had overheard the sound of laughter. Filia barbara pater barbarior. Let me say it in the plural: the Beasts of Gevaudan.

The lanterns had somewhat dazzled me, and I plowed

distressfully among stones and rubbish-heaps. All the other houses in the village were both dark and silent; and though I knocked at here and there a door, my knocking was unanswered. It was a bad business; I gave up Fouzilhac with my curses. The rain had stopped, and the wind, which still kept rising, began to dry my coat and trousers. "Very well," thought I, "water or no water, I must camp." But the first thing was to return to Modestine. I am pretty sure I was twenty minutes groping for my lady in the dark; and if it had not been for the unkindly services of the bog, into which I once more stumbled, I might have still been groping for her at the dawn. My next business was to gain the shelter of a wood, for the wind was cold as well as boisterous. How, in this well-wooded district, I should have been so long in finding one, is another of the insoluble mysteries of this day's adventures; but I will take my oath that I put near an hour to the discovery.

At last black trees began to show upon my left, and, suddenly crossing the road, made a cave of unmitigated blackness right in front. I call it a cave without exaggeration; to pass below that arch of leaves was like entering a dungeon. I felt about until my hand encountered a stout branch, and to this I tied Modestine, a haggard, drenched, desponding donkey. Then I lowered my pack, laid it along the wall on the margin of the road, and unbuckled the straps. I knew well enough where the lantern was; but where were the candles? I groped and groped among the tumbled articles, and, while I was thus groping, suddenly I touched the spirit-lamp. Salvation! This would serve

my turn as well. The wind roared unwearyingly among
the trees; I could hear the boughs tossing and the
leaves churning through half a mile of forest; yet the
scene of my encampment was not only as black as the
pit, but admirably sheltered. At the second match
the wick caught flame. The light was both livid and
shifting; but it cut me off from the universe, and
doubled the darkness of the surrounding night.

I tied Modestine more conveniently for herself, and
broke up half the black bread for her supper, reserving
the other half against the morning. Then I gathered
what I should want within reach, took off my wet boots
and gaiters, which I wrapped in my waterproof, arranged
my knapsack for a pillow under the flap of my sleeping-bag, insinuated my limbs into the interior, and
buckled myself in like a bambino. I opened a tin of
Bologna sausage and broke a cake of chocolate, and
that was all I had to eat. It may sound offensive, but
I ate them together, bite by bite, by way of bread
and meat. All I had to wash down this revolting
mixture was neat brandy: a revolting beverage in itself. But I was rare and hungry; ate well, and smoked
one of the best cigarettes in my experience. Then I
put a stone in my straw hat, pulled the flap of my
fur cap over my neck and eyes, put my revolver ready
to my hand, and snuggled well down among the sheep-
skins.

I questioned at first if I were sleepy, for I felt my
heart beating faster than usual, as if with an agreeable
excitement to which my mind remained a stranger. But
as soon as my eyelids touched, that subtle glue leaped
between them, and they would no more come separate.

The wind among the trees was my lullaby. Sometimes it sounded for minutes together with a steady even rush, not rising nor abating; and again it would swell and burst like a great crashing breaker, and the trees would patter me all over with big drops from the rain of the afternoon. Night after night, in my own bedroom in the country, I have given ear to this perturbing concert of the wind among the woods; but whether it was a difference in the trees, or the lie of the ground, or because I was myself outside and in the midst of it, the fact remains that the wind sang to a different tune among these woods of Gevaudan. I hearkened and hearkened; and meanwhile sleep took gradual possession of my body and subdued my thoughts and senses; but still my last waking effort was to listen and distinguish, and my last conscious state was one of wonder at the foreign clamor in my ears.

Twice in the course of the dark hours—once when a stone galled me underneath the sack, and again when the poor patient Modestine, growing angry, pawed and stamped upon the road—I was recalled for a brief while to consciousness, and saw a star or two overhead, and the lace-like edge of the foliage against the sky. When I awoke for the third time (Wednesday, September 25), the world was flooded with a blue light, the mother of the dawn. I saw the leaves laboring in the wind and the ribbon of the road; and, on turning my head, there was Modestine tied to a beech, and standing half across the path in an attitude of inimitable patience. I closed my eyes again, and set to thinking over the experience of the night. I was surprised to find how easy and pleasant it had been, even in this tempestuous weather.

The stone which annoyed me would not have been there, had I not been forced to camp blindfold in the opaque night; and I had felt no other inconvenience, except when my feet encountered the lantern or the second volume of "Peyrat's Pastors of the Desert" among the mixed contents of my sleeping-bag; nay more, I had felt not a touch of cold, and awakened with unusually lightsome and clear sensations.

With that, I shook myself, got once more into my boots, and gaiters, and, breaking up the rest of the bread for Modestine, strolled about to see in what part of the world I had awakened. Ulysses, left on Ithaca, and with a mind unsettled by the goddess, was not more pleasantly astray. I have been after an adventure all my life, a pure dispassionate adventure, such as befell early and heroic voyagers; and thus to be found by morning in a random woodside nook in Gevaudan—not knowing north from south, as strange to my surroundings as the first man upon the earth, an inland castaway—was to find a fraction of my day-dreams realized. I was on the skirts of a little wood of birch, sprinkled with a few beeches; behind, it adjoined another wood of fir; and in front, it broke up and went down in open order into a shallow and meadowy dale. All around there were bare hill-tops, some near, some far away, as the perspective closed or opened, but none apparently much higher than the rest. The wind huddled the trees. The golden specks of autumn in the birches tossed shiveringly. Overhead the sky was full of strings and shreds of vapor, flying, vanishing, reappearing, and turning about an axis like tumblers, as the wind hounded them through heaven. It was wild

weather and famishing cold. I ate some chocolate, swal-
lowed a mouthful of brandy, and smoked a cigarette
before the cold should have time to disable my fingers.
And by the time I had got all this done, and had
made my pack and bound it on the pack-saddle, the
day was tiptoe on the threshold of the east. We had
not gone many steps along the lane before the sun,
still invisible to me, sent a glow of gold over some
cloud mountains that lay ranged along the eastern sky.

The wind had us on the stern, and hurried us bit-
ingly forward. I buttoned myself into my coat, and
walked on in a pleasant frame of mind with all men,
when suddenly, at a corner, there was Fouzilhic once
more in front of me. Nor only that, but there was
the old gentleman who had escorted me so far the
night before, running out of his house at sight of me,
with hands upraised in horror.

"My poor boy!" he cried, "what does this mean?"

I told him what had happened. He beat his old
hands like clappers in a mill, to think how lightly he
had let me go; but when he heard of the man of
Fouzilhac, anger and depression seized upon his mind.

"This time, at least," said he, "there shall be no
mistake."

And he limped along, for he was very rheumatic,
for about half a mile, and until I was almost within
sight of Cheylard, the destination I had hunted for so
long.

CHEYLARD AND LUC

CANDIDLY, it seemed little worthy of all this search-
ing. A few broken ends of village, with no particular
street, but a succession of open places heaped with logs
and fagots; a couple of tilted crosses, a shrine to our
Lady of all Graces on the summit of a little hill; and
all this, upon a rattling highland river, in the corner
of a naked valley. What went ye out for to see?
thought I to myself. But the place had a life of its
own. I found a board commemorating the liberalities
of Cheylard for the past year, hung up, like a banner,
in the diminutive and tottering church. In 1877, it appeared, the inhabitants subscribed forty-eight francs ten
centimes for the "Work of the Propagation of the
Faith." Some of this, I could not help hoping, would
be applied to my native land. Cheylard scrapes together
halfpence for the darkened souls in Edinburgh; while
Balquidder and Dunrossness bemoan the ignorance of
Rome. Thus, to the high entertainment of the angels,
do we pelt each other with evangelists, like schoolboys
bickering in the snow.

The inn was again singularly unpretentious. The
whole furniture of a not ill-to-do family was in the
kitchen: the beds, the cradle, the clothes, the plate-

rack, the meal-chest, and the photograph of the parish priest. There were five children, one of whom was set to its morning prayers at the stair-foot soon after my arrival, and a sixth would ere long be forthcoming. I was kindly received by these good folk. They were much interested in my misadventure. The wood in which I had slept belonged to them; the man of Fou-zilhac they thought a monster of iniquity, and counseled me warmly to summon him at law—"because I might have died." The good wife was horror-stricken to see me drink over a pint of uncreamed milk.

"You will do yourself an evil," she said. "Permit me to boil it for you."

After I had begun the morning on this delightful liquor, she having an infinity of things to arrange, I was permitted, nay requested, to make a bowl of chocolate for myself. My boots and gaiters were hung up to dry, and, seeing me trying to write my journal on my knee, the eldest daughter let down a hinged table in the chimney-corner for my convenience. Here I wrote, drank my chocolate, and finally ate an omelette before I left. The table was thick with dust; for, as they explained, it was not used except in winter weather. I had a clear look up the vent, through brown agglom-erations of soot and blue vapor, to the sky; and when-ever a handful of twigs was thrown on to the fire my legs were scorched by the blaze.

The husband had begun life as a muleteer, and when I came to charge Modestine showed himself full of the prudence of his art. "You will have to change this package," said he; "it ought to be in two parts, and then you might have double the weight."

I explained that I wanted no more weight; and for no donkey hitherto created would I cut my sleeping-bag in two.

"It fatigues her, however," said the innkeeper; "it fatigues her greatly on the march. Look."

Alas, there were her two forelegs no better than raw beef on the inside, and blood was running from under her tail. They told me when I left, and I was ready to believe it, that before a few days I should come to love Modestine like a dog. Three days had passed, we had shared some misadventures, and my heart was still as cold as a potato toward my beast of burden. She was pretty enough to look at; but then she had given proof of dead stupidity, redeemed indeed by patience, but aggravated by flashes of sorry and ill-judged light-heartedness. And I own this new discovery seemed another point against her. What the devil was the good of a she-ass if she could not carry a sleeping-bag and a few necessaries? I saw the end of the fable rapidly approaching, when I should have to carry Modestine. Æsop was the man to know the world! I assure you I set out with heavy thoughts upon my short day's march.

It was not only heavy thoughts about Modestine that weighted me upon the way; it was a leaden business altogether. For first, the wind blew so rudely that I had to hold on the pack with one hand from Cheylard to Luc; and second, my road lay through one of the most beggarly countries in the world. It was like the worst of the Scotch Highlands, only worse; cold, naked, and ignoble, scant of wood, scant of eather, scant of life. A road and some fences broke the unvarying waste, and the line of the road was marked by upright pillars, to serve in time of snow.

Why any one should desire to visit either Luc or Cheylard is more than my much-inventing spirit can suppose. For my part, I travel not to go anywhere, but to go. I travel for travel's sake. The great affair is to move; to feel the needs and hitches of our life more nearly; to come down off this feather-bed of civilization, and find the globe granite underfoot and strewn with cutting flints. Alas, as we get up in life, and are more preoccupied with our affairs, even a holiday is a thing that must be worked for. To hold a pack upon a pack-saddle against a gale out of the freezing north is no high industry, but it is one that serves to occupy and compose the mind. And when the present is so exacting, who can annoy himself about the future?

I came out at length above the Allier. A more unsightly prospect at this season of the year it would be hard to fancy. Shelving hills rose round it on all sides, here dabbled with wood and fields, there rising to peaks alternately naked and hairy with pines. The color throughout was black or ashen, and came to a point in the ruins of the castle of Luc, which pricked up impudently from below my feet, carrying on a pinnacle a tall white statue of Our Lady, which, I heard with interest, weighed fifty quintals, and was to be dedicated on the sixth of October. Through this sorry landscape trickled the Allier and a tributary of nearly equal size, which came down to join it through a broad nude valley in Vivarais. The weather had somewhat lightened, and the clouds massed in squadron; but the fierce wind still hunted them through heaven, and cast great ungainly splashes of shadow and sunlight over the scene.

Luc itself was a straggling double file of houses wedged between hill and river. It had no beauty, nor was there any notable feature, save the old castle overhead with its fifty quintals of brand-new Madonna. But the inn was clean and large. The kitchen, with its two box-beds hung with clean check curtains, with its wide stone chimney, its chimney-shelf four yards long and garnished with lanterns and religious statuettes, its array of chests and pair of ticking clocks, was the very model of what a kitchen ought to be; a melodrama kitchen, suitable for bandits or noblemen in disguise. Nor was the scene disgraced by the landlady, a handsome, silent, dark old woman, clothed and hooded in black like a nun. Even the public bedroom had a character of its own, with the long deal tables and benches, where fifty might have dined, set out as for a harvest-home, and the three box-beds along the wall. In one of these, lying on straw and covered with a pair of table-napkins, did I do penance all night long in goose-flesh and chattering teeth, and sigh from time to time as I awakened for my sheepskin sack and the lee of some great wood.

OUR LADY OF THE SNOWS

"I behold
The House, the Brotherhood austere—
And what am I, that I am here?"
—MATTHEW ARNOLD

FATHER APOLLINARIS

NEXT morning (Thursday, September 20) I took the road in a new order. The sack was no longer doubled, but hung at full length across the saddle, a green sausage six feet long with a tuft of blue wool hanging out of either end. It was more picturesque, it spared the donkey, and, as I began to see, it would insure stability, blow high, blow low. But it was not without a pang that I had so decided. For although I had purchased a new cord, and made all as fast as I was able, I was yet jealously uneasy lest the flaps should tumble out and scatter my effects along the line of march.

My way lay up the bald valley of the river, along the march of Vivarais and Gevaudan. The hills of Gevaudan on the right were a little more naked, if anything, than those of Vivarais upon the left, and the former had a monopoly of a low dotty underwood that grew thickly in the gorges and died out in soli-

(196)

tary burrs upon the shoulders and the summits. Black bricks of fir-wood were plastered here and there upon both sides, and here and there were cultivated fields. A railway ran beside the river; the only bit of railway in Gevaudan, although there are many proposals afoot and surveys being made, and even, as they tell me, a station standing ready built in Mende. A year or two hence and this may be another world. The desert is beleaguered. Now may some Languedocian Wordsworth turn the sonnet into patois: "Mountains and vales and floods, heard YE that whistle?"

At a place called La Bastide I was directed to leave the river, and follow a road that mounted on the left among the hills of Vivarais, the modern Ardèche; for I was now come within a little way of my strange destination, the Trappist monastery of our Lady of the Snows. The sun came out as I left the shelter of a pine-wood, and I beheld suddenly a fine wild landscape to the south. High rocky hills, as blue as sapphire, closed the view, and between these lay ridge upon ridge, heathery, craggy, the sun glittering on veins of rock, the underwood clambering in the hollows, as rude as God made them at the first. There was not a sign of man's hand in all the prospect; and indeed not a trace of his passage, save where generation after generation had walked in twisted footpaths, in and out among the beeches, and up and down upon the channeled slopes. The mists, which had hitherto beset me, were now broken into clouds, and fled swiftly and shone brightly in the sun. I drew a long breath. It was grateful to come, after so long, upon a scene of some attraction for the human heart. I own I like

definite form in what my eyes are to rest upon; and
if landscapes were sold, like the sheets of characters of
my boyhood, one penny plain and twopence colored, I
should go the length of twopence every day of my life.

But if things had grown better to the south, it was
still desolate and inclement near at hand. A spidery
cross on every hill-top marked the neighborhood of a
religious house; and a quarter of a mile beyond, the
outlook southward opening out and growing bolder with
every step, a white statue of the Virgin at the corner
of a young plantation directed the traveler to our Lady
of the Snows. Here, then, I struck leftward, and pursued my way, driving my secular donkey before me,
and creaking in my secular boots and gaiters, toward
the asylum of silence.

I had not gone very far ere the wind brought to
me the clanging of a bell, and somehow, I can scarce
tell why, my heart sank within me at the sound. I
have rarely approached anything with more unaffected
terror than the monastery of our Lady of the Snows.
This it is to have had a Protestant education. And
suddenly, on turning a corner, fear took hold on me
from head to foot—slavish superstitious fear; and though
I did not stop in my advance, yet I went on slowly,
like a man who should have passed a bourne unno-
ticed, and strayed into the country of the dead. For
there upon the narrow new-made road, between the
stripling pines, was a mediæval friar, fighting with a
barrowful of turfs. Every Sunday of my childhood I
used to study the "Hermits" of Marco Sadeler—enchanting prints, full of wood and field and mediæval landscapes, as large as a county, for the imagination to

go a traveling in; and here, sure enough, was one of
Marco Sadeler's heroes. He was robed in white like
any specter, and the hood falling back, in the instancy
of his contention with the barrow, disclosed a pate as
bald and yellow as a skull. He might have been
buried any time these thousand years, and all the lively
parts of him resolved into earth and broken up with
the farmer's harrow.

I was troubled besides in my mind as to etiquette.
Durst I address a person who was under a vow of silence? Clearly not. But drawing near, I doffed my cap
to him with a far-away superstitious reverence. He
nodded back, and cheerfully addressed me. Was I going to the monastery? Who was I? An Englishman?
Ah, an Irishman, then?

"No," I said, "a Scotsman."

A Scotsman? Ah, he had never seen a Scotsman
before. And he looked me all over, his good, honest,
brawny countenance shining with interest, as a boy
might look upon a lion or an alligator. From him I
learned with disgust that I could not be received at
our Lady of the Snows; I might get a meal, perhaps,
but that was all. And then, as our talk ran on, and
it turned out that I was not a peddler, but a literary
m'n, who drew landscapes and was going to write a
book, he changed his manner of thinking as to my
reception (for I fear they respect persons even in a
Trappist monastery), and told me I must be sure to
ask for the Father Prior, and state my case to him in
full. On second thoughts he determined to go down
with me himself: he thought he could manage for me
better. Might he say that I was a geographer?

No; I thought, in the interests of truth, he positively might not.

"Very well, then" (with disappointment), "an author."

It appeared he had been in a seminary with six young Irishmen, all priests long since, who had received newspapers and kept him informed of the state of ecclesiastical affairs in England. And he asked me eagerly after Dr. Pusey, for whose conversion the good man had continued ever since to pray night and morning.

"I thought he was very near the truth," he said; "and he will reach it yet; there is so much virtue in prayer."

He must be a stiff ungodly Protestant who can take anything but pleasure in this kind and hopeful story. While he was thus near the subject, the good father asked me if I were a Christian; and when he found I was not, or not after his way, he glossed it over with great good-will.

The road which we were following, and which this stalwart father had made with his own two hands within the space of a year, came to a corner, and showed us some white buildings a little further on beyond the wood. At the same time, the bell once more sounded abroad. We were hard upon the monastery. Father Apollinaris (for that was my companion's name) stopped me.

"I must not speak to you down there," he said. "Ask for the Brother Porter, and all will be well. But try to see me as you go out again through the wood, where I may speak to you. I am charmed to have made your acquaintance."

And then suddenly raising his arms, flapping his fingers, and crying out twice, "I must not speak, I must not speak!" he ran away in front of me, and disappeared into the monastery door.

I own this somewhat ghastly eccentricity went a good way to revive my terrors. But where one was so good and simple, why should not all be alike? I took heart of grace, and went forward to the gate as fast as Modestine, who seemed to have a disaffection for monasteries, would permit. It was the first door, in my acquaintance of her, which she had not shown an indecent haste to enter. I summoned the place in form, though with a quaking heart. Father Michael, the Father Hospitaler, and a pair of brown-robed brothers came to the gate and spoke with me a while. I think my sack was the great attraction; it had already beguiled the heart of poor Apollinaris, who had charged me on my life to show it to the Father Prior. But whether it was my address, or the sack, or the idea speedily published among that part of the brotherhood who attend on strangers that I was not a peddler after all, I found no difficulty as to my reception. Modestine was led away by a layman to the stables, and I and my pack were received into our Lady of the Snows.

THE MONKS

FATHER MICHAEL, a pleasant, fresh-faced, smiling man, perhaps of thirty-five, took me to the pantry, and gave me a glass of liqueur to stay me until dinner. We had some talk, or rather I should say he listened to my prattle indulgently enough, but with an abstracted air, like a spirit with a thing of clay. And truly when I remember that I descanted principally on my appetite, and that it must have been by that time more than eighteen hours since Father Michael had so much as broken bread, I can well understand that he would find an earthly savor in my conversation. But his manner, though superior, was exquisitely gracious; and I find I have a lurking curiosity as to Father Michael's past.

The whet administered, I was left alone for a little in the monastery garden. This is no more than the main court, laid out in sandy paths and beds of parti-colored dahlias, and with a fountain and a black statue of the Virgin in the center. The buildings stand around it four-square, bleak, as yet unseasoned by the years and weather, and with no other features than a belfry and a pair of slated gables. Brothers in white,

brothers in brown, passed silently along the sanded
alleys; and when I first came out, three hooded monks
were kneeling on the terrace at their prayers. A naked
hill commands the monastery upon one side, and the
wood commands it on the other. It lies exposed to
wind; the snow falls off and on from October to May,
and sometimes lies six weeks on end; but if they stood
in Eden, with a climate like heaven's, the buildings
themselves would offer the same wintry and cheerless
aspect; and for my part, on this wild September day,
before I was called to dinner, I felt chilly in and out.

When I had eaten well and heartily, Brother Ambrose, a hearty conversible Frenchman (for all those who
wait on strangers have the liberty to speak), led me
to a little room in that part of the building which is
set apart for MM. les retraitants. It was clean and
whitewashed, and furnished with strict necessaries, a
crucifix, a bust of the late Pope, the "Imitation" in
French, a book of religious meditations, and the life
of Elizabeth Seton, evangelist, it would appear, of North
America and of New England in particular. As far as
my experience goes, there is a fair field for some more
evangelization in these quarters; but think of Cotton
Mather! I should like to give him a reading of this
little work in heaven, where I hope he dwells; but
perhaps he knows all that already, and much more;
and perhaps he and Mrs. Seton are the dearest friends,
and gladly unite their voices in the everlasting psalm.
Over the table, to conclude the inventory of the room,
hung a set of regulations for MM. les retraitants: what
services they should attend, when they were to tell
their beads or meditate, and when they were to rise

and go to rest. At the foot was a notable N.B.: "Le temps libre est employe à l'examen de conscience, à la confession, à faire de bonnes resolutions," etc. To make good resolutions, indeed! You might talk as fruitfully of making the hair grow on your head.

I had scarce explored my niche when Brother Ambrose returned. An English boarder, it appeared, would like to speak with me. I professed my willingness, and the friar ushered in a fresh, young, little Irishman of fifty, a deacon of the Church, arrayed in strict canonicals, and wearing on his head what, in default of knowledge, I can only call the ecclesiastical shako. He had lived seven years in retreat at a convent of nuns in Belgium, and now five at our Lady of the Snows; he never saw an English newspaper; he spoke French imperfectly, and had he spoken it like a native, there was not much chance of conversation where he dwelt. With this, he was a man eminently sociable, greedy of news, and simple-minded like a child. If I was pleased to have a guide about the monastery, he was no less delighted to see an English face and hear an English tongue.

He showed me his own room, where he passed his time among breviaries, Hebrew Bibles, and the Waverley novels. Thence he led me to the cloisters, into the chapter-house, through the vestry, where the brothers' gowns and broad straw hats were hanging up, each with his religious name upon a board—names full of legendary suavity and interest, such as Basil, Hilarion, Raphael, or Pacifique; into the library, where were all the works of Veuillot and Chateaubriand, and the "Odes et Ballades," if you please, and even Moliere, to say nothing of innumerable Fathers and a great variety of local and general historians. Thence my good Irishman took me round the workshops, where brothers bake bread, and make cartwheels, and take photographs; where one superintends a collection of curiosities, and another a gallery of rabbits. For in a Trappist monastery each monk has an occupation of his own choice, apart from his religious duties and the general labors of the house. Each must sing in the choir, if he has a voice and ear, and join in the haymaking if he has a hand to stir; but in his private hours, although he must be occupied, he may be occupied on what he likes. Thus I was told that one brother was engaged with literature; while Father Apollinaris busies himself in making roads, and the Abbot employs himself in binding books. It is not so long since this Abbot was consecrated, by the way; and on that occasion, by a special grace, his mother was permitted to enter the chapel and witness the ceremony of consecration. A proud day for her to have a son a mitered abbot; it makes you glad to think they let her in.

In all these journeyings to and fro, many silent fathers and brethren fell in our way. Usually they paid no more regard to our passage than if we had been a cloud; but sometimes the good deacon had a permission to ask of them, and it was granted by a peculiar movement of the hands, almost like that of a dog's paws in swimming, or refused by the usual negative signs, and in either case with lowered eyelids and a certain air of contrition, as of a man who was steering very close to evil.

The monks, by special grace of their Abbot, were

still taking two meals a day; but it was already time
for their grand fast, which begins somewhere in September and lasts till Easter, and during which they
eat but once in the twenty-four hours, and that at two
in the afternoon, twelve hours after they have begun
the toil and vigil of the day. Their meals are scanty,
but even of these they eat sparingly; and though each
is allowed a small carafe of wine, many refrain from
this indulgence. Without doubt, the most of mankind
grossly overeat themselves; our meals serve not only
for support, but as a hearty and natural diversion from
the labor of life. Yet, though excess may be hurtful,
I should have thought this Trappist regimen defective.
And I am astonished, as I look back, at the freshness of face and cheerfulness of manner of all whom
I beheld. A happier nor a healthier company I should
scarce suppose that I have ever seen. As a matter of
fact, on this bleak upland, and with the incessant occupation of the monks, life is of an uncertain tenure,
and death no infrequent visitor, at our Lady of the
Snows. This, at least, was what was told me. But if
they die easily, they must live healthily in the meantime, for they seemed all firm of flesh and high in
color; and the only morbid sign that I could observe,
an unusual brilliancy of eye, was one that served rather
to increase the general impression of vivacity and
strength.

Those with whom I spoke were singularly sweet
tempered, with what I can only call a holy cheerfulness in air and conversation. There is a note, in the
direction to visitors, telling them not to be offended at
the curt speech of those who wait upon them, since it

is proper to monks to speak little. The note might have been spared; to a man the hospitalers were all brimming with innocent talk, and, in my experience of the monastery, it was easier to begin than to break off a conversation. With the exception of Father Michael, who was a man of the world, they showed themselves full of kind and healthy interest in all sorts of subjects —in politics, in voyages, in my sleeping-sack—and not without a certain pleasure in the sound of their own voices.

As for those who are restricted to silence, I can only wonder how they bear their solemn and cheerless isolation. And yet, apart from any view of mortification, I can see a certain policy, not only in the exclusion of women, but in this vow of silence. I have had some experience of lay phalansteries, of an artistic, not to say a bacchanalian, character; and seen more than one association easily formed and yet more easily dispersed. With a Cistercian rule, perhaps they might have lasted longer. In the neighborhood of women it is but a touch-and-go association that can be formed among defenseless men; the stronger electricity is sure to triumph; the dreams of boyhood, the schemes of youth, are abandoned after an interview of ten minutes, and the arts and sciences, and professional male jollity, deserted at once for two sweet eyes and a caressing accent. And next after this, the tongue is the great divider.

I am almost ashamed to pursue this worldly criticism of a religious rule; but there is yet another point in which the Trappist order appeals to me as a model of wisdom. By two in the morning the clapper goes upon

the bell, and so on, hour by hour, and sometimes quarter by quarter, till eight, the hour of rest; so infinitesimally is the day divided among different occupa-
tions. The man who keeps rabbits, for example, hurries
from his hutches to the chapel, the chapter-room, or
the refectory, all day long: every hour he has an
office to sing, a duty to perform; from two, when he
rises in the dark, till eight, when he returns to receive
the comfortable gift of sleep, he is upon his feet and
occupied with manifold and changing business. I know
many persons, worth several thousands in the year, who
are not so fortunate in the disposal of their lives. Into
how many houses would not the note of the monastery-
bell, dividing the day into manageable portions, bring
peace of mind and healthful activity of body! We speak
of hardships, but the true hardship is to be a dull fool,
and permitted to mismanage life in our own dull and
foolish manner.

From this point of view, we may perhaps better
understand the monk's existence. A long novitiate and
every proof of constancy of mind and strength of body
is required before admission to the order; but I could
not find that many were discouraged. In the photog-
rapher's studio, which figures so strangely among the
outbuildings, my eye was attracted by the portrait of
a young fellow in the uniform of a private of foot.
This was one of the novices, who came of the age for
service, and marched and drilled and mounted guard
for the proper time among the garrison of Algiers.
Here was a man who had surely seen both sides of
life before deciding; yet as soon as he was set free
from service he returned to finish his novitiate.

This austere rule entitles a man to heaven as by right. When the Trappist sickens, he quits not his habit; he lies in the bed of death as he has prayed and labored in his frugal and silent existence; and when the Liberator comes, at the very moment, even before they have carried him in his robe to lie his little last in the chapel among continual chantings, joy-bells break forth, as if for a marriage, from the slated belfry, and proclaim throughout the neighborhood that another soul has gone to God.

At night, under the conduct of my kind Irishman, I took my place in the gallery to hear compline and Salve Regina, with which the Cistercians bring every day to a conclusion. There were none of those circumstances which strike the Protestant as childish or as tawdry in the public offices of Rome. A stern simplicity, heightened by the romance of the surroundings, spoke directly to the heart. I recall the whitewashed chapel, the hooded figures in the choir, the lights alternately occluded and revealed, the strong manly singing, the silence that ensued, the sight of cowled heads bowed in prayer, and then the clear trenchant beating of the bell, breaking in to show that the last office was over and the hour of sleep had come; and when I remember, I am not surprised that I made my escape into the court with somewhat whirling fancies, and stood like a man bewildered in the windy starry night.

But I was weary; and when I had quieted my spirits with Elizabeth Seton's memoirs—a dull work—the cold and the raving of the wind among the pines —for my room was on that side of the monastery which adjoins the woods—disposed me readily to slumber. I was wakened at black midnight, as it seemed, though it was really two in the morning, by the first stroke upon the bell. All the brothers were then hurrying to the chapel; the dead in life, at this untimely hour, were already beginning the uncomforted labors of their day. The dead in life—there was a chill reflection. And the words of a French song came back into my memory, telling of the best of our mixed existence:

> " Que t'as de belles filles,
>   Giroflé !
>   Girofla !
>   Que t'as de belles filles,
>   *L'Amour les comptera !*"

And I blessed God that I was free to wander, free to nope, and free to love.

THE BOARDERS

BUT there was another side to my residence at our Lady of the Snows. At this late season there were not many boarders; and yet I was not alone in the public part of the monastery. This itself is hard by the gate, with a small dining-room on the ground-floor, and a whole corridor of cells similar to mine upstairs. I have stupidly forgotten the board for a regular retraitant; but it was somewhere between three and five francs a day, and I think most probably the first. Chance visitors like myself might give what they chose as a free-will offering, but nothing was demanded. I may mention that when I was going away, Father Michael refused twenty francs as excessive. I explained the reasoning which led me to offer him so much; but even then, from a curious point of honor, he would not accept it with his own hand. "I have no right to refuse for the monastery," he explained, "but I should prefer if you would give it to one of the brothers."

I had dined alone, because I arrived late; but at supper I found two other guests. One was a country parish priest, who had walked over that morning from the seat of his cure near Mende to enjoy four days of solitude and prayer. He was a grenadier in person, with the hale color and circular wrinkles of a peasant; and as he complained much of how he had been impeded by his skirts upon the march, I have a vivid fancy portrait of him, striding along, upright, big-boned, with kilted cassock, through the bleak hills of Gevaudan. The other was a short, grizzling, thick-set man, from forty-five to fifty, dressed in tweed with a knitted spencer, and the red ribbon of a decoration in his buttonhole. This last was a hard person to classify. He was an old soldier, who had seen service and risen to the rank of commandant; and he retained some of the brisk decisive manners of the camp. On the other hand, as soon as his resignation was accepted, he had come to our Lady of the Snows as a boarder, and, after a brief experience of its ways, had decided to remain as a novice. Already the new life was beginning to modify his appearance; already he had acquired somewhat of the quiet and smiling air of the brethren; and he was as yet neither an officer nor a Trappist, but partook of the character of each. And certainly here was a man in an interesting nick of life. Out of the noise of cannon and trumpets, he was in the act of passing into this still country bordering on the grave, where men sleep nightly in their grave-clothes, and, like phantoms, communicate by signs.

At supper we talked politics. I make it my business, when I am in France, to preach political goodwill and moderation, and to dwell on the example of Poland, much as some alarmists in England dwell on the example of Carthage. The priest and the commandant assured me of their sympathy with all I said, and made a heavy sighing over the bitterness of contemporary feeling.

"Why, you cannot say anything to a man with which he does not absolutely agree," said I, "but he flies up at you in a temper."

They both declared that such a state of things was antichristian.

While we were thus agreeing what should my tongue stumble upon but a word in praise of Gambetta's moderation. The old soldier's countenance was instantly suffused with blood; with the palms of his hands he beat the table like a naughty child.

"Comment, monsieur?" he shouted. "Comment? Gambetta moderate? Will you dare to justify these words?"

But the priest had not forgotten the tenor of our talk. And suddenly in the height of his fury the old soldier found a warning look directed on his face; the absurdity of his behavior was brought home to him in a flash; and the storm came to an abrupt end, without another word.

It was only in the morning, over our coffee (Friday, September 27), that this couple found out I was a heretic. I suppose I had misled them by some admiring expressions as to the monastic life around us; and it was only by a pointblank question that the truth came out. I had been tolerantly used both by simple Father Apollinaris and astute Father Michael; and the good Irish deacon, when he heard of my religious weakness, had only patted me upon the shoulder and said, "You must be a Catholic and come to heaven." But I was now among a different sect of orthodox.

These two men were bitter and upright and narrow, like the worst of Scotsmen, and indeed, upon my heart, I fancy they were worse. The priest snorted aloud like a battle-horse.

"Et vous pretendez mourir dans cette espèce de croyance?" he demanded; and there is no type used by mortal printers large enough to qualify his accent.

I humbly indicated that I had no design of changing.

But he could not away with such a monstrous attitude. "No, no," he cried; "you must change. You have come here, God has led you here, and you must embrace the opportunity."

I made a slip in policy; I appealed to the family affections, though I was speaking to a priest and a soldier, two classes of men circumstantially divorced from the kind and homely ties of life.

"Your father and mother?" cried the priest. "Very well; you will convert them in their turn when you go home."

I think I see my father's face! I would rather tackle the Gætulian lion in his den than embark on such an enterprise against the family theologian.

But now the hunt was up; priest and soldier were in full cry for my conversion; and the Work of the Propagation of the Faith, for which the people of Cheylard subscribed forty-eight francs ten centimes during 1877, was being gallantly pursued against myself. It was an odd but most effective proselytizing. They never sought to convince me in argument, where I might have attempted some defense; but took it for granted that I was both ashamed and terrified at my position, and urged me solely on the point of time. Now, they said, when God had led me to our Lady of the Snows, now was the appointed hour.

"Do not be withheld by false shame," observed the priest, for my encouragement.

For one who feels very similarly to all sects of religion, and who has never been able, even for a moment, to weigh seriously the merit of this or that creed on the eternal side of things, however much he may see to praise or blame upon the secular and temporal side, the situation thus created was both unfair and painful. I committed my second fault in tact, and tried to plead that it was all the same thing in the end, and we were all drawing near by different sides to the same kind and undiscriminating Friend and Father. That, as it seems to lay-spirits, would be the only gospel worthy of the name. But different men think differently; and this revolutionary aspiration brought down the priest with all the terrors of the law. He launched into harrowing details of hell. The damned, he said—on the authority of a little book which he had read not a week before, and which, to add conviction to conviction, he had fully intended to bring along with him in his pocket—were to occupy the same attitude through all eternity in the midst of dismal tortures. And as he thus expatiated, he grew in nobility of aspect with his enthusiasm.

As a result the pair concluded that I should seek out the Prior, since the Abbot was from home, and lay my case immediately before him.

"C'est mon conseil comme ancien militaire," observed the commandant; "et celui de monsieur comme prêtre."

"Oui," added the cure, sententiously nodding; "comme ancien militaire—et comme prêtre."

At this moment, while I was somewhat embarrassed how to answer, in came one of the monks, a little brown fellow, as lively as a grig, and with an Italian accent, who threw himself at once into the contention, but in a milder and more persuasive vein, as befitted one of these pleasant brethren. Look at *him*, he said. The rule was very hard; he would have dearly liked to stay in his own country, Italy—it was well known how beautiful it was, the beautiful Italy; but then there were no Trappists in Italy; and he had a soul to save; and here he was.

I am afraid I must be, at bottom, what a cheerful Indian critic has dubbed me, "a faddling hedonist"; for this description of the brother's motives gave me somewhat of a shock. I should have preferred to think he had chosen the life for its own sake, and not for ulterior purposes; and this shows how profoundly I was out of sympathy with these good Trappists, even when I was doing my best to sympathize. But to the cure the argument seemed decisive.

"Hear that!" he cried. "And I have seen a marquis here, a marquis, a marquis"—he repeated the holy word three times over—"and other persons high in society; and generals. And here, at your side, is this gentleman, who has been so many years in armies—decorated, an old warrior. And here he is, ready to dedicate himself to God."

I was by this time so thoroughly embarrassed that I pled cold feet, and made my escape from the apartment. It was a furious windy morning, with a sky

much cleared, and long and potent intervals of sunshine; and I wandered until dinner in the wild country toward the east, sorely staggered and beaten upon
by the gale, but rewarded with some striking views.

At dinner the Work of the Propagation of the
Faith was recommenced, and on this occasion still more
distastefully to me. The priest asked me many questions as to the contemptible faith of my fathers, and
received my replies with a kind of ecclesiastical titter.

"Your sect," he said once; "for I think you will
admit it would be doing it too much honor to call it
a religion."

"As you please, monsieur," said I. "La parole est
à vous."

At length I grew annoyed beyond endurance; and
although he was on his own ground, and, what is
more to the purpose, an old man, and so holding a
claim upon my toleration, I could not avoid a protest
against this uncivil usage. He was sadly discounte-
nanced.

"I assure you," he said, "I have no inclination to
laugh in my heart. I have no other feeling but interest in your soul."

And there ended my conversion. Honest man! he
was no dangerous deceiver; but a country parson, full
of zeal and faith. Long may he tread Gevaudan with
his kilted skirts—a man strong to walk and strong to
comfort his parishioners in death! I daresay he would
beat bravely through a snowstorm where his duty called
him; and it is not always the most faithful believer
who makes the cunningest apostle.

UPPER GÉVAUDAN

(CONTINUED)

> *" The bed was made, the room was fit,*
> *By punctual eve the stars were lit;*
> *The air was still, the water ran;*
> *No need there was for maid or man,*
> *When we put up, my ass and I,*
> *At God's green caravanserai."*
>
> —OLD PLAY

ACROSS THE GOULET

THE wind fell during dinner, and the sky remained clear; so it was under better auspices that I loaded Modestine before the monastery gate. My Irish friend accompanied me so far on the way. As we came through the wood, there was Père Apollinaire hauling his barrow; and he too quitted his labors to go with me for perhaps a hundred yards, holding my hand between both of his in front of him. I parted first from one and then from the other with unfeigned regret, but yet with the glee of the traveler who shakes off the dust of one stage before hurrying forth upon another. Then Modestine and I mounted the course of the Allier, which here led us back into Gevaudan toward its sources in the forest of Mercoire. It was but an inconsiderable burn before we left its guidance.

(218)

Thence, over a hill, our way lay through a naked plateau, until we reached Chasseradès at sundown.

The company in the inn-kitchen that night were all men employed in survey for one of the projected railways. They were intelligent and conversible, and we decided the future of France over hot wine, until the state of the clock frightened us to rest. There were four beds in the little upstairs room; and we slept six. But I had a bed to myself, and persuaded them to leave the window open.

"He, bourgeois; il est cinq heures!" was the cry that wakened me in the morning (Saturday, September 28). The room was full of a transparent darkness, which dimly showed me the other three beds and the five different nightcaps on the pillows. But out of the window the dawn was growing ruddy in a long belt over the hill-tops, and day was about to flood the plateau. The hour was inspiriting; and there seemed a promise of calm weather, which was perfectly fulfilled. I was soon under way with Modestine. The road lay for a while over the plateau, and then descended through a precipitous village into the valley of the Chassezac. This stream ran among green meadows, well hidden from the world by its steep banks; the broom was in flower, and here and there was a hamlet sending up its smoke.

At last the path crossed the Chassezac upon a bridge, and, forsaking this deep hollow, set itself to cross the mountain of La Goulet. It wound up through Lestampes by upland fields and woods of beech and birch, and with every corner brought me into an acquaintance with some new interest. Even in the gully of the Chassezac my ear had been struck by a noise like that of a great bass bell ringing at the distance of many miles; but this, as I continued to mount and draw nearer to it, seemed to change in character, and I found at length that it came from some one leading flocks afield to the note of a rural horn. The narrow street of Lestampes stood full of sheep, from wall to wall—black sheep and white, bleating with one accord like the birds in spring, and each one accompanying himself upon the sheep-bell round his neck. It made a pathetic concert, all in treble. A little higher, and I passed a pair of men in a tree with pruning-hooks, and one of them was singing the music of a bourrée. Still further, and when I was already threading the birches, the crowing of cocks came cheerfully up to my ears, and along with that the voice of a flute discoursing a deliberate and plaintive air from one of the upland villages. I pictured to myself some grizzled, apple-cheeked, country schoolmaster fluting in his bit of a garden in the clear autumn sunshine. All these beautiful and interesting sounds filled my heart with an unwonted expectation; and it appeared to me that, once past this range which I was mounting, I should descend into the garden of the world. Nor was I deceived, for I was now done with rains and winds and a bleak country. The first part of my journey ended here; and this was like an induction of sweet sounds into the other and more beautiful.

There are other degrees of *feyness*, as of punishment, besides the capital; and I was now led by my good spirits into an adventure which I relate in the interest of future donkey-drivers. The road zigzagged

so widely on the hillside that I chose a short cut by
map and compass, and struck through the dwarf woods
to catch the road again upon a higher level. It was
my one serious conflict with Modestine. She would
none of my short cut; she turned in my face, she
backed, she reared; she, whom I had hitherto imagined to be dumb, actually brayed with a loud hoarse
flourish, like a cock crowing for the dawn. I plied the
goad with one hand; with the other, so steep was the
ascent, I had to hold on the pack-saddle. Half a dozen
times she was nearly over backward on the top of me;
half a dozen times, from sheer weariness of spirit, I
was nearly giving it up, and leading her down again
to follow the road. But I took the thing as a wager,
and fought it through. I was surprised, as I went on
my way again, by what appeared to be chill rain-drops
falling on my hand, and more than once looked up in
wonder at the cloudless sky. But it was only sweat
which came dropping from my brow.

Over the summit of the Goulet there was no marked
road—only upright stones posted from space to space to
guide the drovers. The turf underfoot was springy and
well scented. I had no company but a lark or two,
and met but one bullock-cart between Lestampes and
Bleymard. In front of me I saw a shallow valley, and
beyond that the range of the Lozère, sparsely wooded
and well enough modeled in the flanks, but straight
and dull in outline. There was scarce a sign of cul-
ture; only about Bleymard, the white high-road from
Villefort to Mende traversed a range of meadows, set
with spiry poplars, and sounding from side to side with
the bells of flocks and herds.

A NIGHT AMONG THE PINES

FROM Bleymard after dinner, although it was already late, I set out to scale a portion of the Lozere. An ill-marked stony drove road guided me forward; and I met nearly half a dozen bullock-carts descending from the woods, each laden with a whole pine-tree for the winter's firing. At the top of the woods, which do not climb very high upon this cold ridge, I struck leftward by a path among the pines, until I hit on a dell of green turf, where a streamlet made a little spout over some stones to serve me for a water-tap. "In a more sacred or sequestered bower . . . nor nymph, nor faunus, haunted." The trees were not old, but they grew thickly round the glade: there was no outlook, except northeastward upon distant hill-tops, or straight upward to the sky; and the encampment felt secure and private like a room. By the time I had made my arrangements and fed Modestine, the day was already beginning to decline. I buckled myself to the knees into my sack and made a hearty meal; and as soon as the sun went down I pulled my cap over my eyes and fell asleep.

Night is a dead monotonous period under a roof;

but in the open world it passes lightly, with its stars and dews and perfumes, and the hours are marked by changes in the face of Nature. What seems a kind of temporal death to people choked between walls and curtains, is only a light and living slumber to the man who sleeps afield. All night long he can hear Nature breathing deeply and freely; even as she takes her rest, she turns and smiles; and there is one stirring hour unknown to those who dwell in houses, when a wakeful influence goes abroad over the sleeping hemisphere, and all the outdoor world are on their feet. It is then that the cock first crows, not this time to announce the dawn, but like a cheerful watchman speeding the course of night. Cattle awake on the meadows; sheep break their fast on dewy hillsides, and change to a new lair among the ferns; and houseless men, who have lain down with the fowls, open their dim eyes and behold the beauty of the night.

At what inaudible summons, at what gentle touch of Nature, are all these sleepers thus recalled in the same hour to life? Do the stars rain down an influence, or do we share some thrill of mother earth below our resting bodies? Even shepherds and old countryfolk, who are the deepest read in these arcana, have not a guess as to the means or purpose of this nightly resurrection. Toward two in the morning they declare the thing takes place; and neither know nor inquire further. And at least it is a pleasant incident. We are disturbed in our slumber only, like the luxurious Montaigne, "that we may the better and more sensibly relish it." We have a moment to look upon the stars. And there is a special pleasure for some minds in the reflection that we share the impulse with all outdoor creatures in our neighborhood, that we have escaped out of the Bastille of civilization, and are become, for the time being, a mere kindly animal and a sheep of Nature's flock.

When that hour came to me among the pines, I wakened thirsty. My tin was standing by me half full of water. I emptied it at a draught; and feeling broad awake after this internal cold aspersion, sat upright to make a cigarette. The stars were clear, colored, and jewel-like, but not frosty. A faint silvery vapor stood for the Milky Way. All around me the black fir-points stood upright and stock-still. By the whiteness of the pack-saddle, I could see Modestine walking round and round at the length of her tether; I could hear her steadily munching at the sward; but there was not another sound, save the indescribable quiet talk of the runnel over the stones. I lay lazily smoking and studying the color of the sky, as we call the void of space, from where it showed a reddish gray behind the pines to where it showed a glossy blue-black between the stars. As if to be more like a peddler, I wear a silver ring. This I could see faintly shining as I raised or lowered the cigarette; and at each whiff the inside of my hand was illuminated, and became for a second the highest light in the landscape.

A faint wind, more like a moving coolness than a stream of air, passed down the glade from time to time; so that even in my great chamber the air was being renewed all night long. I thought with horror of the inn at Chasserades and the congregated night-caps; with horror of the nocturnal prowesses of clerks

and students, of hot theaters and pass-keys and close
rooms. I have not often enjoyed a more serene possession of myself, nor felt more independent of material
aids. The outer world, from which we cower into our
houses, seemed after all a gentle habitable place; and
night after night a man's bed, it seemed, was laid and
waiting for him in the fields, where God keeps an open
house. I thought I had rediscovered one of those truths
which are revealed to savages and hid from political
economists: at the least, I had discovered a new pleasure for myself. And yet even while I was exulting in
my solitude I became aware of a strange lack. I wished
a companion to lie near me in the starlight, silent and
not moving, but ever within touch. For there is a fel-
lowship more quiet even than solitude, and which,
rightly understood, is solitude made perfect. And to
live out of doors with the woman a man loves is of
all lives the most complete and free.

As I thus lay, between content and longing, a faint
noise stole toward me through the pines. I thought, at
first, it was the crowing of cocks or the barking of
dogs at some very distant farm; but steadily and gradually it took articulate shape in my ears, until I became aware that a passenger was going by upon the
high-road in the valley, and singing loudly as he went.
There was more of good-will than grace in his performance; but he trolled with ample lungs; and the
sound of his voice took hold upon the hillside and set
the air shaking in the leafy glens. I have heard people passing by night in sleeping cities; some of them
sang; one, I remember, played loudly on the bagpipes.
I have heard the rattle of a cart or carriage spring up

suddenly after hours of stillness, and pass, for some minutes, within the range of my hearing as I lay abed. There is a romance about all who are abroad in the black hours, and with something of a thrill we try to guess their business. But here the romance was double: first, this glad passenger, lighted internally with wine, who sent up his voice in music through the night; and then I, on the other hand, buckled into my sack, and smoking alone in the pine woods between four and five thousand feet toward the stars.

When I awoke again (Sunday, September 29) many of the stars had disappeared; only the stronger companions of the night still burned visibly overhead; and away toward the east I saw a faint haze of light upon the horizon, such as had been the Milky Way when I was last awake. Day was at hand. I lighted my lantern, and by its glowworm light put on my boots and gaiters; then I broke up some bread for Modestine, filled my can at the water tap, and lighted my spirit-lamp to boil myself some chocolate. The blue darkness lay long in the glade where I had so sweetly slumbered; but soon there was a broad streak of orange melting into gold along the mountain-tops of Vivarais. A solemn glee possessed my mind at this gradual and lovely coming in of day. I heard the runnel with delight; I looked round me for something beautiful and unexpected; but the still black pine-trees, the hollow glade, the munching ass, remained unchanged in figure. Nothing had altered but the light, and that, indeed, shed over all a spirit of life and of breathing peace, and moved me to a strange exhilaration.

I drank my water chocolate, which was hot if it

was not rich, and strolled here and there, and up and down about the glade. While I was thus delaying, a gush of steady wind, as long as a heavy sigh, poured direct out of the quarter of the morning. It was cold, and set me sneezing. The trees near at hand tossed their black plumes in its passage; and I could see the thin distant spires of pine along the edge of the hill rock slightly to and fro against the golden east. Ten minutes after, the sunlight spread at a gallop along the hillside, scattering shadows and sparkles, and the day had come completely.

I hastened to prepare my pack, and tackle the steep ascent that lay before me; but I had something on my mind. It was only a fancy; yet a fancy will sometimes be importunate. I had been most hospitably received and punctually served in my green caravanserai. The room was airy, the water excellent, and the dawn had called me to a moment. I say nothing of the tapestries or the inimitable ceiling, nor yet of the view which I commanded from the windows; but I felt I was in some one's debt for all this liberal entertainment. And so it pleased me, in a half-laughing way, to leave pieces of money on the turf as I went along, until I had left enough for my night's lodging. I trust they did not fall to some rich and churlish drover.

THE COUNTRY OF THE CAMISARDS

"We traveled in the print of olden wars;
Yet all the land was green;
And love we found, and peace,
Where fire and war had been.
They pass and smile, the children of the
sword—
No more the sword they wield;
And oh, how deep the corn
Along the battlefield!"

—W. P. BANNATYNE

ACROSS THE LOZÈRE

THE track that I had followed in the evening soon
died out, and I continued to follow over a bald turf
ascent a row of stone pillars, such as had conducted
me across the Goulet. It was already warm. I tied
my jacket on the pack, and walked in my knitted
waistcoat. Modestine herself was in high spirits, and
broke of her own accord, for the first time in my experience, into a jolting trot that set the oats swashing
in the pocket of my coat. The view, back upon the
northern Gevaudan, extended with every step; scarce a
tree, scarce a house, appeared upon the fields of wild
hill that ran north, east, and west, all blue and gold
in the haze and sunlight of the morning. A multitude
(228)

of little birds kept sweeping and twittering about my
path; they perched on the stone pillars, they pecked and
strutted on the turf, and I saw them circle in volleys
in the blue air, and show, from time to time, trans-
lucent flickering wings between the sun and me.

Almost from the first moment of my march, a faint
large noise, like a distant surf, had filled my ears.
Sometimes I was tempted to think it the voice of a
neighboring waterfall, and sometimes a subjective result
of the utter stillness of the hill. But as I continued
to advance, the noise increased and became like the
hissing of an enormous tea-urn, and at the same time
breaths of cool air began to reach me from the direction of the summit. At length I understood. It was
blowing stiffly from the south upon the other slope of
the Lozere, and every step that I took I was drawing
nearer to the wind.

Although it had been long desired, it was quite un-
expectedly at last that my eyes rose above the summit.
A step that seemed no way more decisive than many
other steps that had preceded it—and, "like stout Cortez
when, with eagle eyes, he stared on the Pacific," I
took possession, in my own name, of a new quarter of
the world. For behold, instead of the gross turf rampart I had been mounting for so long, a view into the
hazy air of heaven, and a land of intricate blue hills
below my feet.

The Lozere lies nearly east and west, cutting Gevaudan into two unequal parts; its highest point, this
Pic de Finiels, on which I was then standing, rises
upward of five thousand six hundred feet above the
sea, and in clear weather commands a view over all

lower Languedoc to the Mediterranean Sea. I have
spoken with people who either pretended or believed
that they had seen, from the Pic de Finiels, white
ships sailing by Montpellier and Cette. Behind was the
upland northern country through which my way had
lain, peopled by a dull race, without wood, without
much grandeur of hill-form, and famous in the past
for little beside wolves. But in front of me, half veiled
in sunny haze, lay a new Gevaudan, rich, picturesque,
illustrious for stirring events. Speaking largely, I was
in the Cevennes at Monastier, and during all my journey; but there is a strict and local sense in which
only this confused and shaggy country at my feet has
any title to the name, and in this sense the peasantry
employ the word. These are the Cevennes with an
emphasis: the Cevennes of the Cevennes. In that un-
decipherable labyrinth of hills, a war of bandits, a war
of wild beasts, raged for two years between the Grand
Monarch with all his troops and marshals on the one
hand, and a few thousand Protestant mountaineers upon
the other. A hundred and eighty years ago, the Camisards held a station even on the Lozere, where I
stood; they had an organization, arsenals, a military
and religious hierarchy; their affairs were "the discourse
of every coffee-house" in London; England sent fleets
in their support; their leaders prophesied and murdered;
with colors and drums, and the singing of old French
psalms, their bands sometimes affronted daylight, marched
before walled cities, and dispersed the generals of the
king; and sometimes at night, or in masquerade, possessed themselves of strong castles, and avenged treach-
ery upon their allies and cruelty upon their foes. There,

a hundred and eighty years ago, was the chivalrous Roland, "Count and Lord Roland, generalissimo of the Protestants in France," grave, silent, imperious, pock-marked ex-dragoon, whom a lady followed in his wanderings out of love. There was Cavalier, a baker's apprentice with a genius for war, elected brigadier of Camisards at seventeen, to die at fifty-five the English governor of Jersey. There again was Castanet, a partisan leader in a voluminous peruke and with a taste for controversial divinity. Strange generals, who moved apart to take counsel with the God of Hosts, and fled or offered battle, set sentinels or slept in an unguarded camp, as the Spirit whispered to their hearts! And there, to follow these and other leaders, was the rank and file of prophets and disciples, bold, patient, indefatigable, hardy to run upon the mountains, cheering their rough life with psalms, eager to fight, eager to pray, listening devoutly to the oracles of brainsick children, and mystically putting a grain of wheat among the pewter balls with which they charged their muskets.

I had traveled hitherto through a dull district, and in the track of nothing more notable than the child-eating Beast of Gevaudan, the Napoleon Bonaparte of wolves. But now I was to go down into the scene of a romantic chapter—or, better, a romantic footnote—in the history of the world. What was left of all this bygone dust and heroism? I was told that Protestantism still survived in this head seat of Protestant resistance; so much the priest himself had told me in the monastery parlor. But I had yet to learn if it were a bare survival, or a lively and generous tradition. Again, if in the northern Cevennes the people are narrow in religious judgments, and more filled with zeal than charity, what was I to look for in this land of persecution and reprisal—in a land where the tyranny of the Church produced the Camisard rebellion, and the terror of the Camisards threw the Catholic peasantry into legalized revolt upon the other side, so that Camisard and Florentin skulked for each other's lives among the mountains?

Just on the brow of the hill, where I paused to look before me, the series of stone pillars came abruptly to an end; and only a little below, a sort of track appeared and began to go down a breakneck slope, turning like a corkscrew as it went. It led into a valley between falling hills, stubbly with rocks like a reaped field of corn, and floored further down with green meadows. I followed the track with precipitation; the steepness of the slope, the continual agile turning of the line of the descent, and the old unwearied hope of finding something new in a new country, all conspired to lend me wings. Yet a little lower and a stream began, collecting itself together out of many fountains, and soon making a glad noise among the hills. Sometimes it would cross the track in a bit of waterfall, with a pool, in which Modestine refreshed her feet.

The whole descent is like a dream to me, so rapidly was it accomplished. I had scarcely left the summit ere the valley had closed round my path, and the sun beat upon me, walking in a stagnant lowland atmosphere. The track became a road, and went up and down in easy undulations. I passed cabin after cabin, but all seemed deserted; and I saw not a human creature, nor heard any sound except that of the stream. I was, however, in a different country from the day before. The stony skeleton of the world was here vigorously displayed to sun and air. The slopes were steep and changeful. Oak-trees clung along the hills, well grown, wealthy in leaf, and touched by the autumn with strong and luminous colors. Here and there another stream would fall in from the right or the left, down a gorge of snow-white and tumultuary bowlders. The river in the bottom (for it was rapidly growing a river, collecting on all hands as it trotted on its way) here foamed a while in desperate rapids, and there lay in pools of the most enchanting sea-green shot with watery browns. As far as I have gone, I have never seen a river of so changeful and delicate a hue; crystal was not more clear, the meadows were not by half so green; and at every pool I saw I felt a thrill of longing to be out of these hot, dusty, and material garments, and bathe my naked body in the mountain air and water. All the time as I went on I never forgot it was the Sabbath; the stillness was a perpetual reminder; and I heard in spirit the church-bells clamoring all over Europe, and the psalms of a thousand churches.

At length a human sound struck upon my ear—a cry strangely modulated between pathos and derision; and looking across the valley, I saw a little urchin sitting in a meadow, with his hands about his knees, and dwarfed to almost comical smallness by the distance. But the rogue had picked me out as I went down the road, from oak-wood on to oak-wood, driving Modestine; and he made me the compliments of the new country in this tremulous high-pitched salutation. And as all noises are lovely and natural at a sufficient distance, this also, coming through so much clean hill air and crossing all the green valley, sounded pleasant to my ear, and seemed a thing rustic, like the oaks or the river.

A little after, the stream that I was following fell into the Tarn at Pont de Montvert of bloody memory.

PONT DE MONTVERT

ONE of the first things I encountered in Pont de Montvert was, if I remember rightly, the Protestant temple; but this was but the type of other novelties. A subtle atmosphere distinguishes a town in England from a town in France, or even in Scotland. At Carlisle you can see you are in one country; at Dumfries, thirty miles away, you are as sure that you are in the other. I should find it difficult to tell in what particulars Pont de Montvert differed from Monastier or Langogne, or even Bleymard; but the difference existed, and spoke eloquently to the eyes. The place, with its houses, its lanes, its glaring river-bed, wore an indescribable air of the South.

All was Sunday bustle in the streets and in the public-house, as all had been Sabbath peace among the mountains. There must have been near a score of us at dinner by eleven before noon; and after I had eaten and drunken, and sat writing up my journal, I suppose as many more came dropping in one after another, or by twos and threes. In crossing the Lozere I had not only come among new natural features, but moved into the territory of a different race. These people, as they hurriedly dispatched their viands in an intricate sword-play of knives, questioned and answered me with a degree of intelligence which excelled all that I had met, except among the railway folk at Chasserades. They had open telling faces, and were lively both in speech and manner. They not only entered thoroughly into the spirit of my little trip, but more than one declared, if he were rich enough, he would like to set forth on such another.

Even physically there was a pleasant change. I had not seen a pretty woman since I left Monastier, and there but one. Now of the three who sat down with me to dinner, one was certainly not beautiful—a poor timid thing of forty, quite troubled at this roaring table d'hôte, whom I squired and helped to wine, and pledged and tried generally to encourage, with quite a contrary effect; but the other two, both married, were both more handsome than the average of women. And Clarisse? What shall I say of Clarisse? She waited the table with a heavy placable nonchalance, like a performing cow; her great gray eyes were steeped in amorous languor; her features, although fleshy, were of an original and accurate design; her mouth had a curl; her nostril spoke of dainty pride; her cheek fell into strange and interesting lines. It was a face capable of strong emotion, and, with training, it offered the promise of delicate sentiment. It seemed pitiful to see so good a model left to country admirers and a country way of thought. Beauty should at least have touched society; then, in a moment, it throws off a weight that lay upon it, it becomes conscious of itself, it puts on an elegance, learns a gait and a carriage of

the head, and, in a moment, patet dea. Before I left
I assured Clarisse of my hearty admiration. She took
it like milk, without embarrassment or wonder, merely
looking at me steadily with her great eyes; and I own
the result upon myself was some confusion. If Clarisse
could read English, I should not dare to add that her
figure was unworthy of her face. Hers was a case for
stays; but that may perhaps grow better as she gets up
in years.

Pont de Montvert, or Greenhill Bridge, as we might
say at home, is a place memorable in the story of the
Camisards. It was here that the war broke out; here
that those southern Covenanters slew their Archbishop
Sharpe. The persecution on the one hand, the febrile
enthusiasm on the other, are almost equally difficult to
understand in these quiet modern days, and with our
easy modern beliefs and disbeliefs. The Protestants were
one and all beside their right minds with zeal and sorrow. They were all prophets and prophetesses. Children
at the breast would exhort their parents to good works.
"A child of fifteen months at Quissac spoke from its
mother's arms, agitated and sobbing, distinctly and with
a loud voice." Marshal Villars has seen a town where
all the women "seemed possessed by the devil," and
had trembling fits, and uttered prophecies publicly upon
the streets. A prophetess of Vivarais was hanged at
Montpellier because blood flowed from her eyes and
nose, and she declared that she was weeping tears of
blood for the misfortunes of the Protestants. And it
was not only women and children. Stalwart dangerous
fellows, used to swing the sickle or to wield the forest
ax, were likewise shaken with strange paroxysms, and

spoke oracles with sobs and streaming tears. A persecution unsurpassed in violence had lasted near a score of years, and this was the result upon the persecuted; hanging, burning, breaking on the wheel, had been in vain; the dragoons had left their hoof-marks over all the country-side; there were men rowing in the galleys, and women pining in the prisons of the Church; and not a thought was changed in the heart of any upright Protestant.

Now the head and forefront of the persecution—after Lamoignon de Bâvile—François de Langlade du Chayla (pronounce Chéïla), Archpriest of the Cevennes and Inspector of Missions in the same country, had a house in which he sometimes dwelt in the town of Pont de Montvert. He was a conscientious person, who seems to have been intended by nature for a pirate, and now fifty-five, an age by which a man has learned all the moderation of which he is capable. A missionary in his youth in China, he there suffered martyrdom, was left for dead, and only succored and brought back to life by the charity of a pariah. We must suppose the pariah devoid of second sight, and not purposely malicious in this act. Such an experience, it might be thought, would have cured a man of the desire to persecute; but the human spirit is a thing strangely put together; and, having been a Christian martyr, Du Chayla became a Christian persecutor. The Work of the Propagation of the Faith went roundly forward in his hands. His house in Pont de Montvert served him as a prison. There he plucked out the hairs of the beard, and closed the hands of his prisoners upon live coal, to convince them that they were deceived in their opinions. And yet had not he himself tried and proved the inefficacy of these carnal arguments among the Buddhists in China?

Not only was life made intolerable in Languedoc, but flight was rigidly forbidden. One Massip, a muleteer, and well acquainted with the mountain-paths, had already guided several troops of fugitives in safety to Geneva; and on him, with another convoy, consisting mostly of women dressed as men, Du Chayla, in an evil hour for himself, laid his hands. The Sunday following, there was a conventicle of Protestants in the woods of Altefage upon Mount Bouges; where there stood up one Seguier—Spirit Seguier, as his companions called him—a woolcarder, tall, black-faced, and toothless, but a man full of prophecy. He declared, in the name of God, that the time for submission had gone by, and they must betake themselves to arms for the deliverance of their brethren and the destruction of the priests.

The next night, July 24, 1702, a sound disturbed the Inspector of Missions as he sat in his prison-house at Pont de Montvert; the voices of many men upraised in psalmody drew nearer and nearer through the town. It was ten at night; he had his court about him, priests, soldiers, and servants, to the number of twelve or fifteen; and now, dreading the insolence of a conventicle below his very windows, he ordered forth his soldiers to report. But the psalm-singers were already at his door, fifty strong, led by the inspired Seguier, and breathing death. To their summons, the archpriest made answer like a stout old persecutor, and bade his garrison fire upon the mob. One Camisard (for, accord-

ing to some, it was in this night's work that they
came by the name) fell at this discharge; his comrades
burst in the door with hatchets and a beam of wood,
overran the lower story of the house, set free the
prisoners, and finding one of them in the vine, a sort
of Scavenger's Daughter of the place and period, re-
doubled in fury against Du Chayla, and sought by
repeated assaults to carry the upper floors. But he, on
his side, had given absolution to his men, and they
bravely held the staircase.

"Children of God," cried the prophet, "hold your
hands. Let us burn the house, with the priest and the
satellites of Baal."

The fire caught readily. Out of an upper window
Du Chayla and his men lowered themselves into the
garden by means of knotted sheets; some escaped across
the river under the bullets of the insurgents; but the
archpriest himself fell, broke his thigh, and could only
crawl into the hedge. What were his reflections as
this second martyrdom drew near? A poor, brave, be-
sotted, hateful man, who had done his duty resolutely
according to his light both in the Cevennes and China.
He found at least one telling word to say in his defense; for when the roof fell in and the upbursting
flames discovered his retreat, and they came and dragged
him to the public place of the town, raging and calling him damned—"if I be damned," said he, "why
should you also damn yourselves?"

Here was a good reason for the last; but in the
course of his inspectorship he had given many stronger
which all told in a contrary direction; and these he
was now to hear. One by one, Seguier first, the

Camisards drew near and stabbed him. "This," they said, "is for my father broken on the wheel. This for my brother in the galleys. That for my mother or my sister imprisoned in your cursed convents." Each gave his blow and his reason; and then all kneeled and sang psalms around the body till the dawn. With the dawn, still singing, they defiled away toward Frugeres, further up the Tarn, to pursue the work of vengeance, leaving Du Chayla's prison-house in ruins, and his body pierced with two-and-fifty wounds upon the public place.

'Tis a wild night's work, with its accompaniment of psalms; and it seems as if a psalm must always have a sound of threatening in that town upon the Tarn. But the story does not end, even so far as concerns Pont de Montvert, with the departure of the Camisards. The career of Seguier was brief and bloody. Two more priests and a whole family at Ladeveze, from the father to the servants, fell by his hand or by his orders; and yet he was but a day or two at large, and restrained all the time by the presence of the soldiery. Taken at length by a famous soldier of fortune, Captain Poul, he appeared unmoved before his judges.

"Your name?" they asked.

"Pierre Seguier."

"Why are you called Spirit?"

"Because the Spirit of the Lord is with me."

"Your domicile?"

"Lately in the desert, and soon in heaven."

"Have you no remorse for your crimes?"

"I have committed none. *My soul is like a garden full of shelter and of fountains.*"

At Pont de Montvert, on the twelfth of August, he

had his right hand stricken from his body, and was burned alive. And his soul was like a garden? So perhaps was the soul of Du Chayla, the Christian martyr. And perhaps if you could read in my soul, or I could read in yours, our own composure might seem little less surprising.

Du Chayla's house still stands, with a new roof, beside one of the bridges of the town; and if you are curious you may see the terrace-garden into which he dropped.

IN THE VALLEY OF THE TARN

A NEW road leads from Pont de Montvert to Florac by the valley of the Tarn; a smooth sandy ledge, it runs about half-way between the summit of the cliffs and the river in the bottom of the valley; and I went in and out, as I followed it, from bays of shadow into promontories of afternoon sun. This was a pass like that of Killiecrankie; a deep turning gully in the hills, with the Tarn making a wonderful hoarse uproar far below, and craggy summits standing in the sunshine high above. A thin fringe of ash-trees ran about the hill-tops, like ivy on a ruin; but on the lower slopes, and far up every glen, the Spanish chestnut-trees stood each four-square to heaven under its tented foliage. Some were planted, each on its own terrace no larger than a bed; some, trusting in their roots, found strength to grow and prosper and be straight and large upon the rapid slopes of the valley; others, where there was a margin to the river, stood marshaled in a line and mighty like cedars of Lebanon. Yet even where they grew most thickly they were not to be thought of as a wood, but as a herd of stalwart individuals; and the dome of each tree stood forth sepa-

rate and large, and as it were a little hill, from among
the domes of its companions. They gave forth a faint
sweet perfume which pervaded the air of the afternoon;
autumn had put tints of gold and tarnish in the green;
and the sun so shone through and kindled the broad
foliage, that each chestnut was relieved against another,
not in shadow, but in light. A humble sketcher here
laid down his pencil in despair.

I wish I could convey a notion of the growth of
these noble trees; of how they strike out boughs like
the oak, and trail sprays of drooping foliage like the
willow; of how they stand on upright fluted columns
like the pillars of a church; or, like the olive, from
the most shattered bole can put out smooth and youthful shoots, and begin a new life upon the ruins of the
old. Thus they partake of the nature of many different trees; and even their prickly top-knots, seen near
at hand against the sky, have a certain palm-like air
that impresses the imagination. But their individuality,
although compounded of so many elements, is but the
richer and the more original. And to look down upon
a level filled with these knolls of foliage, or to see a
clan of old unconquerable chestnuts cluster "like herded
elephants" upon the spur of a mountain, is to rise to
higher thoughts of the powers that are in Nature.

Between Modestine's laggard humor and the beauty
of the scene, we made little progress all that afternoon;
and at last, finding the sun, although still far from
setting, was already beginning to desert the narrow valley of the Tarn, I began to cast about for a place to
camp in. This was not easy to find; the terraces were
too narrow, and the ground, where it was unterraced,

was usually too steep for a man to lie upon. I should have slipped all night, and awakened toward morning with my feet or my head in the river.

After perhaps a mile, I saw, some sixty feet above the road, a little plateau large enough to hold my sack, and securely parapeted by the trunk of an aged and enormous chestnut. Thither, with infinite trouble, I goaded and kicked the reluctant Modestine, and there I hastened to unload her. There was only room for myself upon the plateau, and I had to go nearly as high again before I found so much as standing room for the ass. It was on a heap of rolling stones, on an artificial terrace, certainly not five feet square in all. Here I tied her to a chestnut, and having given her corn and bread and made a pile of chestnut-leaves, of which I found her greedy, I descended once more to my own encampment.

The position was unpleasantly exposed. One or two carts went by upon the road; and as long as daylight lasted I concealed myself, for all the world like a hunted Camisard, behind my fortification of vast chestnut trunk; for I was passionately afraid of discovery and the visit of jocular persons in the night. Moreover, I saw that I must be early awake; for these chestnut gardens had been the scene of industry no further gone than on the day before. The slope was strewn with lopped branches, and here and there a great package of leaves was propped against a trunk; for even the leaves are serviceable, and the peasants use them in winter by way of fodder for their animals. I picked a meal in fear and trembling, half lying down to hide myself from the road; and I daresay

I was as much concerned as if I had been a scout from Joani's band above upon the Lozere, or from Salomon's across the Tarn, in the old times of psalm-singing and blood. Or, indeed, perhaps more; for the Camisards had a remarkable confidence in God; and a tale comes back into my memory of how the Count of Gevaudan, riding with a party of dragoons and a notary at his saddlebow to enforce the oath of fidelity in all the country hamlets, entered a valley in the woods, and found Cavalier and his men at dinner, gayly seated on the grass, and their hats crowned with box-tree garlands, while fifteen women washed their linen in the stream. Such was a field festival in 1703; at that date Antony Watteau would be painting similar subjects.

This was a very different camp from that of the night before in the cool and silent pine-woods. It was warm and even stifling in the valley. The shrill song of frogs, like the tremolo note of a whistle with a pea in it, rang up from the riverside before the sun was down. In the growing dusk, faint rustlings began to run to and fro among the fallen leaves; from time to time a faint chirping or cheaping noise would fall upon my ear; and from time to time I thought I could see the movement of something swift and indistinct between the chestnuts. A profusion of large ants swarmed upon the ground; bats whisked by, and mosquitoes droned overhead. The long boughs with their bunches of leaves hung against the sky like garlands; and those imme-diately above and around me had somewhat the air of a trellis which should have been wrecked and half overthrown in a gale of wind.

Sleep for a long time fled my eyelids; and just as I was beginning to feel quiet stealing over my limbs, and settling densely on my mind, a noise at my head startled me broad awake again, and, I will frankly confess it, brought my heart into my mouth. It was such a noise as a person would make scratching loudly with a finger-nail, it came from under the knapsack which served me for a pillow, and it was thrice re-peated before I had time to sit up and turn about. Nothing was to be seen, nothing more was to be heard, but a few of these mysterious rustlings far and near, and the ceaseless accompaniment of the river and the frogs. I learned next day that the chestnut gardens are infested by rats; rustling, chirping, and scraping were probably all due to these; but the puzzle, for the moment, was insoluble, and I had to compose myself for sleep, as best I could, in wondering uncertainty about my neighbors.

I was wakened in the gray of the morning (Mon-day, September 30) by the sound of footsteps not far off upon the stones, and opening my eyes, I beheld a peasant going by among the chestnuts by a footpath that I had not hitherto observed. He turned his head neither to the right nor to the left, and disappeared in a few strides among the foliage. Here was an escape! But it was plainly more than time to be moving. The peasantry were abroad; scarce less terrible to me in my nondescript position than the soldiers of Captain Poul to an undaunted Camisard. I fed Modestine with what haste I could; but as I was returning to my sack, I saw a man and a boy come down the hillside in a direction crossing mine. They unintelligibly hailed me, and I replied with inarticulate but cheerful sounds and hurried forward to get into my gaiters.

The pair, who seemed to be father and son, came slowly up to the plateau, and stood close beside me for some time in silence. The bed was open, and I saw with regret my revolver lying patently disclosed on the blue wool. At last, after they had looked me all over, and the silence had grown laughably embarrassing, the man demanded, in what seemed unfriendly tones:

"You have slept here?"

"Yes," said I. "As you see."

"Why?" he asked.

"My faith," I answered lightly, "I was tired."

He next inquired where I was going and what I had had for dinner; and then, without the least transition, "C'est bien," he added, "come along." And he and his son, without another word, turned off to the next chestnut-tree but one, which they set to pruning. The thing had passed off more simply than I hoped. He was a grave respectable man; and his unfriendly voice did not imply that he thought he was speaking to a criminal, but merely to an inferior.

I was soon on the road, nibbling a cake of chocolate and seriously occupied with a case of conscience. Was I to pay for my night's lodging? I had slept ill, the bed was full of fleas in the shape of ants, there was no water in the room, the very dawn had neglected to call me in the morning. I might have missed a train, had there been any in the neighborhood to catch. Clearly, I was dissatisfied with my entertainment; and I decided I should not pay unless I met a beggar.

The valley looked even lovelier by morning; and

soon the road descended to the level of the river. Here, in a place where many straight and prosperous chest- nuts stood together, making an aisle upon a swarded terrace, I made my morning toilet in the water of the Tarn. It was marvelously clear, thrillingly cool; the soap-suds disappeared as if by magic in the swift cur- rent, and the white bowlders gave one a model for cleanliness. To wash in one of God's rivers in the open air seems to me a sort of cheerful solemnity or semi-pagan act of worship. To dabble among dishes in a bedroom may perhaps make clean the body; but the imagination takes no share in such a cleansing. I went on with a light and peaceful heart, and sang psalms to the spiritual ear as I advanced.

Suddenly up came an old woman, who pointblank demanded alms.

"Good," thought I; "here comes the waiter with the bill."

And I paid for my night's lodging on the spot. Take it how you please, but this was the first and the last beggar that I met with during all my tour.

A step or two further I was overtaken by an old man in a brown nightcap, clear-eyed, weather-beaten, with a faint excited smile. A little girl followed him, driving two sheep and a goat; but she kept in our wake, while the old man walked beside me and talked about the morning and the valley. It was not much past six; and for healthy people who have slept enough that is an hour of expansion and of open and trustful talk.

"Connaissez-vous le Seigneur?" he said at length.

I asked him what Seigneur he meant; but he only

repeated the question with more emphasis and a look in his eyes denoting hope and interest.

"Ah," said I, pointing upward, "I understand you now. Yes, I know Him; He is the best of acquaintances."

The old man said he was delighted. "Hold," he added, striking his bosom; "it makes me happy here." There were a few who knew the Lord in these valleys, he went on to tell me; not many, but a few. "Many are called," he quoted, "and few chosen."

"My father," said I, "it is not easy to say who know the Lord; and it is none of our business. Protestants and Catholics, and even those who worship stones, may know Him and be known by Him; for He has made all."

I did not know I was so good a preacher.

The old man assured me he thought as I did, and repeated his expressions of pleasure at meeting me. "We are so few," he said. "They call us Moravians here; but down in the department of Gard, where there are also a good number, they are called Derbists, after an English pastor."

I began to understand that I was figuring, in questionable taste, as a member of some sect to me unknown; but I was more pleased with the pleasure of my companion than embarrassed by my own equivocal position. Indeed, I can see no dishonesty in not avowing a difference; and especially in these high matters, where we have all a sufficient assurance that, whoever may be in the wrong, we ourselves are not completely in the right. The truth is much talked about; but this old man in a brown nightcap showed himself so simple, sweet, and friendly that I am not unwilling to profess myself his convert. He was, as a matter of fact, a Plymouth Brother. Of what that involves in the way of doctrine I have no idea nor the time to inform myself; but I know right well that we are all embarked upon a troublesome world, the children of one Father, striving in many essential points to do and to become the same. And although it was somewhat in a mistake that he shook hands with me so often and showed himself so ready to receive my words, that was a mistake of the truth-finding sort. For charity begins blindfold; and only through a series of similar misapprehensions rises at length into a settled principle of love and patience, and a firm belief in all our fellowmen. If I deceived this good old man, in the like manner I would willingly go on to deceive others. And if ever at length, out of our separate and sad ways, we should all come together into one common house, I have a hope, to which I cling dearly, that my mountain Plymouth Brother will hasten to shake hands with me again.

Thus, talking like Christian and Faithful by the way, he and I came down upon a hamlet by the Tarn. It was but a humble place, called La Vernede, with less than a dozen houses, and a Protestant chapel on a knoll. Here he dwelt; and here, at the inn, I ordered my breakfast. The inn was kept by an agreeable young man, a stone-breaker on the road, and his sister, a pretty and engaging girl. The village schoolmaster dropped in to speak with the stranger. And these were all Protestants—a fact which pleased me more than I should have expected; and, what pleased

me still more, they seemed all upright and simple people. The Plymouth Brother hung round me with a
sort of yearning interest, and returned at least thrice
to make sure I was enjoying my meal.   His behavior touched me deeply at the time, and even now
moves me in recollection. He feared to intrude, but he
would not willingly forego one moment of my society; and he seemed never weary of shaking me by
the hand.

When all the rest had drifted off to their day's
work, I sat for near half an hour with the young mistress of the house, who talked pleasantly over her seam
of the chestnut harvest, and the beauties of the Tarn,
and old family affections, broken up when young folk
go from home, yet still subsisting. Hers, I am sure,
was a sweet nature, with a country plainness and much
delicacy underneath; and he who takes her to his heart
will doubtless be a fortunate young man.

The valley below La Vernede pleased me more and
more as I went forward. Now the hills approached
from either hand, naked and crumbling, and walled in
the river between cliffs; and now the valley widened
and became green. The road led me past the old castle
of Miral on a steep; past a battlemented monastery,
long since broken up and turned into a church and
parsonage; and past a cluster of black roofs, the village of Cocures, sitting among vineyards and meadows
and orchards thick with red apples, and where, along
the highway, they were knocking down walnuts from
the roadside trees, and gathering them in sacks and
baskets. The hills, however much the vale might open,
were still tall and bare, with cliffy battlements and

here and there a pointed summit; and the Tarn still rattled through the stones with a mountain noise. I had been led, by bagmen of a picturesque turn of mind, to expect a horrific country after the heart of Byron; but to my Scotch eyes it seemed smiling and plentiful, as the weather still gave an impression of high summer to my Scotch body; although the chestnuts were already picked out by the autumn, and the poplars, that here began to mingle with them, had turned into pale gold against the approach of winter.

There was something in this landscape, smiling although wild, that explained to me the spirit of the Southern Covenanters. Those who took to the hills for conscience' sake in Scotland had all gloomy and bedeviled thoughts; for once that they received God's comfort they would be twice engaged with Satan; but the Camisards had only bright and supporting visions. They dealt much more in blood, both given and taken; yet I find no obsession of the Evil One in their records. With a light conscience, they pursued their life in these rough times and circumstances. The soul of Seguier, let us not forget, was like a garden. They knew they were on God's side, with a knowledge that has no parallel among the Scots; for the Scots, although they might be certain of the cause, could never rest confident of the person.

"We flew," says one old Camisard, "when we heard the sound of psalm-singing, we flew as if with wings. We felt within us an animating ardor, a transporting desire. The feeling cannot be expressed in words. It is a thing that must have been experienced to be understood. However weary we might be, we thought no more of our weariness and grew light, so soon as the psalms fell upon our ears."

The valley of the Tarn and the people whom I met at La Vernede not only explain to me this passage, but the twenty years of suffering which those, who were so stiff and so bloody when once they betook themselves to war, endured with the meekness of children and the constancy of saints and peasants.

FLORAC

ON a branch of the Tarn stands Florac, the seat of
a subprefecture, with an old castle, an alley of planes,
many quaint street-corners, and a live fountain welling
from the hill. It is notable, besides, for handsome
women, and as one of the two capitals, Alais being
the other, of the country of the Camisards.

The landlord of the inn took me, after I had eaten,
to an adjoining cafe, where I, or rather my journey,
became the topic of the afternoon. Every one had some
suggestion for my guidance; and the subprefectorial map
was fetched from the subprefecture itself, and much
thumbed among coffee-cups and glasses of liqueur. Most
of these kind advisers were Protestant, though I observed
that Protestant and Catholic intermingled in a very easy
manner; and it surprised me to see what a lively memory
still subsisted of the religious war. Among the hills of
the southwest, by Mauchline, Cumnock, or Carsphairn, in
isolated farms or in the manse, serious Presbyterian people
still recall the days of the great persecution, and the
graves of local martyrs are still piously regarded. But in
towns and among the so-called better classes, I fear that
these old doings have become an idle tale. If you met

a mixed company in the King's Arms at Wigton, it is not likely that the talk would run on Covenanters. Nay, at Muirkirk of Glenluce, I found the beadle's wife had not so much as heard of Prophet Peden. But these Cevenols were proud of their ancestors in quite another sense; the war was their chosen topic; its exploits were their own patent of nobility; and where a man or a race has had but one adventure, and that heroic, we must expect and pardon some prolixity of reference. They told me the country was still full of legends hitherto uncollected; I heard from them about Cavalier's descendants—not direct descendants, be it understood, but only cousins or nephews—who were still prosperous people in the scene of the boy-general's exploits; and one farmer had seen the bones of old combatants dug up into the air of an afternoon in the nineteenth century, in a field where the ancestors had fought, and the great-grandchildren were peaceably ditching.

Later in the day one of the Protestant pastors was so good as to visit me: a young man, intelligent and polite, with whom I passed an hour or two in talk. Florac, he told me, is part Protestant, part Catholic; and the difference in religion is usually doubled by a difference in politics. You may judge of my surprise, coming as I did from such a babbling purgatorial Poland of a place as Monastier, when I learned that the population lived together on very quiet terms; and there was even an exchange of hospitalities between households thus doubly separated. Black Camisard and White Camisard, militiaman and Miquelet and dragoon, Protestant prophet and Catholic cadet of the White Cross, they had all been sabering and shooting, burning, pillaging, and murdering, their hearts hot with indignant passion; and here, after a hundred and seventy years, Protestant is still Protestant, Catholic still Catholic, in mutual toleration and mild amity of life. But the race of man, like that indomitable nature whence it sprang, has medicating virtues of its own; the years and seasons bring various harvests; the sun returns after the rain; and mankind outlives sæcular animosities, as a single man awakens from the passions of a day. We judge our ancestors from a more divine position; and the dust being a little laid with several centuries, we can see both sides adorned with human virtues and fighting with a show of right.

I have never thought it easy to be just, and find it daily even harder than I thought. I own I met these Protestants with delight and a sense of coming home. I was accustomed to speak their language, in another and deeper sense of the word than that which distinguishes between French and English; for the true babel is a divergence upon morals. And hence I could hold more free communication with the Protestants, and judge them more justly, than the Catholics. Father Apollinaris may pair off with my mountain Plymouth Brother as two guileless and devout old men; yet I ask myself if I had as ready a feeling for the virtues of the Trappist; or had I been a Catholic, if I should have felt so warmly to the dissenter of La Vernede. With the first I was on terms of mere forbearance; but with the other, although only on a misunderstanding and by keeping on selected points, it was still possible to hold converse and exchange some honest thoughts. In this world of imperfection we gladly wel-

come even partial intimacies. And if we find but one
to whom we can speak out of our heart freely, with
whom we can walk in love and simplicity without dis-
simulation, we have no ground of quarrel with the
world or God.

IN THE VALLEY OF THE MIMENTE

On Tuesday, October 1, we left Florac late in the afternoon, a tired donkey and tired donkey-driver. A little way up the Tarnon, a covered bridge of wood introduced us into the valley of the Mimente. Steep rocky red mountains overhung the stream; great oaks and chestnuts grew upon the slopes or in stony terraces; here and there was a red field of millet or a few apple-trees studded with red apples; and the road passed hard by two black hamlets, one with an old castle atop to please the heart of the tourist.

It was difficult here again to find a spot fit for my encampment. Even under the oaks and chestnuts the ground had not only a very rapid slope, but was heaped with loose stones; and where there was no timber the hills descended to the stream in a red precipice tufted with heather. The sun had left the highest peak in front of me, and the valley was full of the lowing sound of herdsmen's horns as they recalled the flocks into the stable, when I spied a bight of meadow some way below the roadway in an angle of the river. Thither I descended, and, tying Modestine provisionally to a tree, proceeded to investigate the neighborhood. A

gray pearly evening shadow filled the glen; objects at
a little distance grew indistinct and melted bafflingly
into each other; and the darkness was rising steadily
like an exhalation. I approached a great oak which
grew in the meadow, hard by the river's brink; when
to my disgust the voices of children fell upon my ear,
and I beheld a house round the angle on the other
bank. I had half a mind to pack and begone again,
but the growing darkness moved me to remain. I had
only to make no noise until the night was fairly come,
and trust to the dawn to call me early in the morning. But it was hard to be annoyed by neighbors in
such a great hotel.

A hollow underneath the oak was my bed. Before
I had fed Modestine and arranged my sack, three stars
were already brightly shining, and the others were beginning dimly to appear. I slipped down to the river,
which looked very black among its rocks, to fill my
can; and dined with a good appetite in the dark, for I
scrupled to light a lantern while so near a house. The
moon, which I had seen, a pallid crescent, all afternoon, faintly illuminated the summit of the hills, but
not a ray fell into the bottom of the glen where I was
lying. The oak rose before me like a pillar of darkness; and overhead the heartsome stars were set in the
face of the night. No one knows the stars who has
not slept, as the French happily put it, à la belle
etoile. He may know all their names and distances
and magnitudes, and yet be ignorant of what alone
concerns mankind, their serene and gladsome influence
on the mind. The greater part of poetry is about the
stars; and very justly, for they are themselves the

most classical of poets. These same far-away worlds, sprinkled like tapers or shaken together like a diamond dust upon the sky, had looked not otherwise to Roland or Cavalier, when, in the words of the latter, they had "no other tent but the sky, and no other bed than my mother earth."

All night a strong wind blew up the valley, and the acorns fell pattering over me from the oak. Yet, on this first night of October, the air was as mild as May, and I slept with the fur thrown back.

I was much disturbed by the barking of a dog, an animal that I fear more than any wolf. A dog is vastly braver, and is besides supported by the sense of duty. If you kill a wolf, you meet with encouragement and praise; but if you kill a dog, the sacred rights of property and the domestic affections come clamoring round you for redress. At the end of a fagging day, the sharp cruel note of a dog's bark is in itself a keen annoyance; and to a tramp like myself, he represents the sedentary and respectable world in its most hostile form. There is something of the clergyman or the lawyer about this engaging animal; and if he were not amenable to stones, the boldest man would shrink from traveling afoot. I respect dogs much in the domestic circle; but on the highway or sleeping afield, I both detest and fear them.

I was wakened next morning (Wednesday, October 2) by the same dog—for I knew his bark—making a charge down the bank, and then, seeing me sit up, retreating again with great alacrity. The stars were not yet quite extinguished. The heaven was of that enchanting mild gray-blue of the early morn. A still

clear light began to fall, and the trees on the hillside
were outlined sharply against the sky. The wind had
veered more to the north, and no longer reached me
in the glen; but as I was going on with my preparations, it drove a white cloud very swiftly over the hill-
top; and looking up, I was surprised to see the cloud
dyed with gold. In these high regions of the air, the
sun was already shining as at noon. If only the clouds
traveled high enough, we should see the same thing all
night long. For it is always daylight in the fields of
space.

As I began to go up the valley, a draught of wind
came down it out of the seat of the sunrise, although
the clouds continued to run overhead in an almost contrary direction. A few steps further, and I saw a
whole hillside gilded with the sun; and still a little
beyond, between two peaks, a center of dazzling brilliancy appeared floating in the sky, and I was once
more face to face with the big bonfire that occupies
the kernel of our system.

I met but one human being that forenoon, a dark
military-looking wayfarer, who carried a gamebag on a
baldric; but he made a remark that seems worthy of
record. For when I asked him if he were Protestant
or Catholic—

"Oh," said he, "I make no shame of my religion.
I am a Catholic."

He made no shame of it! The phrase is a piece of
natural statistics; for it is the language of one in a
minority. I thought with a smile of Bavile and his
dragoons, and how you may ride rough-shod over a
religion for a century, and leave it only the more lively

for the friction. Ireland is still Catholic; the Cevennes still Protestant. It is not a basketful of law-papers, nor the hoofs and pistol-butts of a regiment of horse, that can change one tittle of a plowman's thoughts. Outdoor rustic people have not many ideas, but such as they have are hardy plants and thrive flourishingly in persecution. One who has grown a long while in the sweat of laborious noons, and under the stars at night, a frequenter of hills and forests, an old honest countryman, has, in the end, a sense of communion with the powers of the universe, and amicable relations toward his God. Like my mountain Plymouth Brother, he knows the Lord. His religion does not repose upon a choice of logic; it is the poetry of the man's experience, the philosophy of the history of his life. God, like a great power, like a great shining sun, has appeared to this simple fellow in the course of years, and become the ground and essence of his least reflections; and you may change creeds and dogmas by authority, or proclaim a new religion with the sound of trumpets, if you will; but here is a man who has his own thoughts, and will stubbornly adhere to them in good and evil. He is a Catholic, a Protestant, or a Plymouth Brother, in the same indefeasible sense that a man is not a woman, or a woman not a man. For he could not vary from his faith, unless he could eradicate all memory of the past, and, in a strict and not a conventional meaning, change his mind.

THE HEART OF THE COUNTRY

I WAS now drawing near to Cassagnas, a cluster of black roofs upon the hillside, in this wild valley, among chestnut gardens, and looked upon in the clear air by many rocky peaks. The road along the Mimente is yet new, nor have the mountaineers recovered their surprise when the first cart arrived at Cassagnas. But although it lay thus apart from the current of men's business, this hamlet had already made a figure in the history of France. Hard by, in caverns of the mountain, was one of the five arsenals of the Camisards; where they laid up clothes and corn and arms against necessity, forged bayonets and sabers, and made themselves gunpowder with willow charcoal and saltpeter boiled in kettles. To the same caves, amid this multifarious industry, the sick and wounded were brought up to heal; and there they were visited by the two surgeons, Chabrier and Tavan, and secretly nursed by women of the neighborhood.

Of the five legions into which the Camisards were divided, it was the oldest and the most obscure that had its magazines by Cassagnas. This was the band of Spirit Seguier; men who had joined their voices

with his in the 68th Psalm as they marched down by
night on the archpriest of the Cevennes. Seguier, pro-
moted to heaven, was succeeded by Salomon Couderc,
whom Cavalier treats in his memoirs as chaplain-gen-
eral to the whole army of the Camisards. He was a
prophet; a great reader of the heart, who admitted
people to the sacrament or refused them by "intentively
viewing every man" between the eyes; and had the
most of the Scriptures off by rote. And this was surely
happy; since in a surprise in August 1703, he lost his
mule, his portfolios, and his Bible. It is only strange
that they were not surprised more often and more
effectually; for this legion of Cassagnas was truly
patriarchal in its theory of war, and camped without
sentries, leaving that duty to the angels of the God
for whom they fought. This is a token, not only of
their faith, but of the trackless country where they
harbored. M. de Caladon, taking a stroll one fine day,
walked without warning into their midst, as he might
have walked into "a flock of sheep in a plain," and
found some asleep and some awake and psalm-singing.
A traitor had need of no recommendation to insinuate
himself among their ranks, beyond "his faculty of singing psalms"; and even the prophet Salomon "took him
into a particular friendship." Thus, among their intricate hills, the rustic troop subsisted; and history can
attribute few exploits to them but sacraments and
ecstasies.

People of this tough and simple stock will not, as
I have just been saying, prove variable in religion; nor
will they get nearer to apostasy than a mere external
conformity like that of Naaman in the house of Rim-

mon. When Louis XVI., in the words of the edict, "convinced by the uselessness of a century of persecutions, and rather from necessity than sympathy," granted at last a royal grace of toleration, Cassagnas was still Protestant; and to a man, it is so to this day. There is, indeed, one family that is not Protestant, but neither is it Catholic. It is that of a Catholic cure in revolt, who has taken to his bosom a schoolmistress. And his conduct, it's worth noting, is disapproved by the Protestant villagers.

"It is a bad idea for a man," said one, "to go back from his engagements."

The villagers whom I saw seemed intelligent after a countrified fashion, and were all plain and dignified in manner. As a Protestant myself, I was well looked upon, and my acquaintance with history gained me further respect. For we had something not unlike a religious controversy at table, a gendarme and a merchant with whom I dined being both strangers to the place and Catholics. The young men of the house stood round and supported me; and the whole discussion was tolerantly conducted, and surprised a man brought up among the infinitesimal and contentious differences of Scotland. The merchant, indeed, grew a little warm, and was far less pleased than some others with my historical acquirements. But the gendarme was mighty easy over it all.

"It's a bad idea for a man to change," said he; and the remark was generally applauded.

That was not the opinion of the priest and soldier at our Lady of the Snows. But this is a different race; and perhaps the same great-heartedness that up-

held them to resist, now enables them to differ in a
kind spirit. For courage respects courage; but where
a faith has been trodden out, we may look for a mean
and narrow population. The true work of Bruce and
Wallace was the union of the nations; not that they
should stand apart a while longer, skirmishing upon
their borders; but that, when the time came, they
might unite with self-respect.

The merchant was much interested in my journey,
and thought it dangerous to sleep afield.

"There are the wolves," said he; "and then it is
known you are an Englishman. The English have always long purses, and it might very well enter into
some one's head to deal you an ill blow some night."

I told him I was not much afraid of such accidents; and at any rate judged it unwise to dwell upon
alarms or consider small perils in the arrangement of
life. Life itself, I submitted, was a far too risky business as a whole to make each additional particular of
danger worth regard. "Something," said I, "might
burst in your inside any day of the week, and there
would be an end of you, if you were locked into your
room with three turns of the key."

"Cependant," said he, "coucher dehors!"

"God," said I, "is everywhere."

"Cependant, coucher dehors!" he repeated, and his
voice was eloquent of terror.

He was the only person, in all my voyage, who saw
anything hardy in so simple a proceeding; although
many considered it superfluous. Only one, on the other
hand, professed much delight in the idea; and that was
my Plymouth Brother, who cried out, when I told him

I sometimes preferred sleeping under the stars to a close
and noisy alehouse, "Now I see that you know the
Lord!"

The merchant asked me for one of my cards as I
was leaving, for he said I should be something to talk
of in the future, and desired me to make a note of
his request and reason; a desire with which I have thus
complied.

A little after two I struck across the Mimente, and
took a rugged path southward up a hillside covered
with loose stones and tufts of heather. At the top, as
is the habit of the country, the path disappeared; and
I left my she-ass munching heather, and went forward
alone to seek a road.

I was now on the separation of two vast water-
sheds; behind me all the streams were bound for the
Garonne and the Western Ocean; before me was the
basin of the Rhone. Hence, as from the Lozere, you
can see in clear weather the shining of the Gulf of
Lyons; and perhaps from here the soldiers of Salomon
may have watched for the topsails of Sir Cloudesley
Shovel, and the long-promised aid from England. You
may take this ridge as lying in the heart of the country of the Camisards; four of the five legions camped
all round it and almost within view—Salomon and Joani
to the north, Castanet and Roland to the south; and
when Julien had finished his famous work, the devastation of the High Cevennes, which lasted all through
October and November 1703, and during which four
hundred and sixty villages and hamlets were, with fire
and pickax, utterly subverted, a man standing on this
eminence would have looked forth upon a silent, smoke-

less, and dispeopled land. Time and man's activity have now repaired these ruins; Cassagnas is once more roofed and sending up domestic smoke; and in the chestnut gardens, in low and leafy corners, many a prosperous farmer returns, when the day's work is done, to his children and bright hearth. And still it was perhaps the wildest view of all my journey. Peak upon peak, chain upon chain of hills ran surging southward, channeled and sculptured by the winter streams, feathered from head to foot with chestnuts, and here and there breaking out into a coronal of cliffs. The sun, which was still far from setting, sent a drift of misty gold across the hill-tops, but the valleys were already plunged in a profound and quiet shadow. ·

A very old shepherd, hobbling on a pair of sticks, and wearing a black cap of liberty, as if in honor of his nearness to the grave, directed me to the road for St. Germain de Calberte. There was something solemn in the isolation of this infirm and ancient creature. Where he dwelt, how he got upon this high ridge, or how he proposed to get down again, were more than I could fancy. Not far off upon my right was the famous Plan de Font Morte, where Poul with his Armenian saber slashed down the Camisards of Seguier. This, methought, might be some Rip van Winkle of the war, who had lost his comrades, fleeing before Poul, and wandered ever since upon the mountains. It might be news to him that Cavalier had surrendered, or Roland had fallen fighting with his back against an olive. And while I was thus working on my fancy, I heard him hailing in broken tones, and saw him waving me to come back with one of his two sticks. I

had already got some way past him; but, leaving
Modestine once more, retraced my steps.

Alas, it was a very commonplace affair. The old
gentleman had forgot to ask the peddler what he sold,
and wished to remedy this neglect.

I told him sternly, "Nothing."

"Nothing?" cried he.

I repeated "Nothing," and made off.

It's odd to think of, but perhaps I thus became as
inexplicable to the old man as he had been to me.

The road lay under chestnuts, and though I saw a
hamlet or two below me in the vale, and many lone
houses of the chestnut farmers, it was a very solitary
march all afternoon; and the evening began early underneath the trees. But I heard the voice of a woman
singing some sad, old, endless ballad not far off. It
seemed to be about love and a bel amoureux, her
handsome sweetheart; and I wished I could have taken
up the strain and answered her, as I went on upon
my invisible woodland way, weaving, like Pippa in the
poem, my own thoughts with hers. What could I have
told her? Little enough; and yet all the heart requires.
How the world gives and takes away, and brings
sweethearts near, only to separate them again into distant and strange lands; but to love is the great amu-
let which makes the world a garden; and "hope, which
comes to all," outwears the accidents of life, and reaches
with tremulous hand beyond the grave and death. Easy
to say: yea, but also, by God's mercy, both easy and
grateful to believe!

We struck at last into a wide white high-road carpeted with noiseless dust. The night had come; the

moon had been shining for a long while upon the opposite mountain; when on turning a corner my donkey and I issued ourselves into her light. I had emptied out my brandy at Florac, for I could bear the stuff no longer, and replaced it with some generous and scented Volnay; and now I drank to the moon's sacred majesty upon the road. It was but a couple of mouthfuls; yet I became thenceforth unconscious of my limbs, and my blood flowed with luxury. Even Modestine was inspired by this purified nocturnal sunshine, and bestirred her little hoofs as to a livelier measure. The road wound and descended swiftly among masses of chestnuts. Hot dust rose from our feet and flowed away. Our two shadows—mine deformed with the knapsack, hers comically bestridden by the pack—now lay before us clearly outlined on the road, and now, as we turned a corner, went off into the ghostly distance, and sailed along the mountain like clouds. From time to time a warm wind rustled down the valley, and set all the chestnuts dangling their bunches of foliage and fruit; the ear was filled with whispering music, and the shadows danced in tune. And next moment the breeze had gone by, and in all the valley nothing moved except our traveling feet. On the opposite slope, the monstrous ribs and gullies of the mountain were faintly designed in the moonshine; and high overhead, in some lone house, there burned one lighted window, one square spark of red in the huge field of sad nocturnal coloring.

At a certain point, as I went downward, turning many acute angles, the moon disappeared behind the hill; and I pursued my way in great darkness, until another turning shot me without preparation into St.

Germain de Calberte. The place was asleep and silent, and buried in opaque night. Only from a single open door some lamplight escaped upon the road to show me that I was come among men's habitations. The two last gossips of the evening, still talking by a garden wall, directed me to the inn. The landlady was getting her chicks to bed; the fire was already out, and had, not without grumbling, to be rekindled; half an hour later, and I must have gone supperless to roost.

THE LAST DAY

WHEN I awoke (Thursday, October 3), and, hearing a great flourishing of cocks and chuckling of contented hens, betook me to the window of the clean and comfortable room where I had slept the night, I looked forth on a sunshiny morning in a deep vale of chestnut gardens. It was still early, and the cockcrows, and the slanting lights, and the long shadows encouraged me to be out and look round me.

St. Germain de Calberte is a great parish nine leagues round about. At the period of the wars, and immediately before the devastation, it was inhabited by two hundred and seventy-five families, of which only nine were Catholic; and it took the cure seventeen September days to go from house to house on horseback for a census. But the place itself, although capital of a canton, is scarce larger than a hamlet. It lies terraced across a steep slope in the midst of mighty chestnuts. The Protestant chapel stands below upon a shoulder; in the midst of the town is the quaint old Catholic church.

It was here that poor Du Chayla, the Christian

martyr, kept his library and held a court of mission-
aries; here he had built his tomb, thinking to lie
among a grateful population whom he had redeemed
from error; and hither on the morrow of his death
they brought the body, pierced with two-and-fifty
wounds, to be interred. Clad in his priestly robes, he
was laid out in state in the church. The cure, taking
his text from Second Samuel, twentieth chapter and
twelfth verse, "And Amasa wallowed in his blood in
the highway," preached a rousing sermon, and exhorted
his brethren to die each at his post, like their unhappy
and illustrious superior. In the midst of this eloquence
there came a breeze that Spirit Seguier was near at
hand; and behold! all the assembly took to their horses'
heels, some east, some west, and the cure himself as
far as Alais.

Strange was the position of this little Catholic me-
tropolis, a thimbleful of Rome, in such a wild and
contrary neighborhood. On the one hand, the legion of
Salomon overlooked it from Cassagnas; on the other, it
was cut off from assistance by the legion of Roland at
Mialet. The cure, Louvrelenil, although he took a panic
at the archpriest's funeral, and so hurriedly decamped
to Alais, stood well by his isolated pulpit, and thence
uttered fulminations against the crimes of the Protestants. Salomon besieged the village for an hour and a
half, but was beat back. The militiamen, on guard
before the cure's door, could be heard, in the black
hours, singing Protestant psalms and holding friendly
talk with the insurgents. And in the morning, although
not a shot had been fired, there would not be a round
of powder in their flasks. Where was it gone? All

handed over to the Camisards for a consideration. Untrusty guardians for an isolated priest!

That these continual stirs were once busy in St. Germain de Calberte, the imagination with difficulty receives; all is now so quiet, the pulse of human life now beats so low and still in this hamlet of the mountains. Boys followed me a great way off, like a timid sort of lion-hunters; and people turned round to have a second look, or came out of their houses, as I went by. My passage was the first event, you would have fancied, since the Camisards. There was nothing rude or forward in this observation; it was but a pleased and wondering scrutiny, like that of oxen or the human infant; yet it wearied my spirits, and soon drove me from the street.

I took refuge on the terraces, which are here greenly carpeted with sward, and tried to imitate with a pencil the inimitable attitudes of the chestnuts as they bear up their canopy of leaves. Ever and again a little wind went by, and the nuts dropped all around me, with a light and dull sound, upon the sward. The noise was as of a thin fall of great hailstones; but there went with it a cheerful human sentiment of an approaching harvest and farmers rejoicing in their gains. Looking up, I could see the brown nut peering through the husk, which was already gaping; and between the stems the eye embraced an amphitheater of hill, sunlit and green with leaves.

I have not often enjoyed a place more deeply. I moved in an atmosphere of pleasure, and felt light and quiet and content. But perhaps it was not the place alone that so disposed my spirit. Perhaps some one

was thinking of me in another country; or perhaps
some thought of my own had come and gone unno-
ticed, and yet done me good. For some thoughts, which
sure would be the most beautiful, vanish before we can
rightly scan their features; as though a god, traveling
by our green highways, should but ope the door, give
one smiling look into the house, and go again forever.
Was it Apollo, or Mercury, or Love with folded wings?
Who shall say? But we go the lighter about our business, and feel peace and pleasure in our hearts.

I dined with a pair of Catholics. They agreed in
the condemnation of a young man, a Catholic, who had
married a Protestant girl and gone over to the religion
of his wife. A Protestant born they could understand
and respect; indeed, they seemed to be of the mind of
an old Catholic woman, who told me that same day
there was no difference between the two sects, save
that "wrong was more wrong for the Catholic," who
had more light and guidance; but this of a man's
desertion filled them with contempt.

"It is a bad idea for a man to change," said one.

It may have been accidental, but you see how this
phrase pursued me; and for myself, I believe it is the
current philosophy in these parts. I have some difficulty
in imagining a better. It's not only a great flight of
confidence for a man to change his creed and go out
of his family for heaven's sake; but the odds are—nay,
and the hope is—that, with all this great transition in
the eyes of man, he has not changed himself a hairs-
breadth to the eyes of God. Honor to those who do
so, for the wrench is sore. But it argues something
narrow, whether of strength or weakness, whether of

the prophet or the fool, in those who can take a sufficient interest in such infinitesimal and human operations, or who can quit a friendship for a doubtful process of the mind. And I think I should not leave my old creed for another, changing only words for other words; but by some brave reading, embrace it in spirit and truth, and find wrong as wrong for me as for the best of other communions.

The phylloxera was in the neighborhood; and instead of wine we drank at dinner a more economical juice of the grape—La Parisienne, they call it. It is made by putting the fruit whole into a cask with water; one by one the berries ferment and burst; what is drunk during the day is supplied at night in water; so, with ever another pitcher from the well, and ever another grape exploding and giving out its strength, one cask of Parisienne may last a family till spring. It is, as the reader will anticipate, a feeble beverage, but very pleasant to the taste.

What with dinner and coffee, it was long past three before I left St. Germain de Calberte. I went down beside the Gardon of Mialet, a great glaring watercourse devoid of water, and through St. Etienne de Vallée Française, or Val Francesque, as they used to call it; and toward evening began to ascend the hill of St. Pierre. It was a long and steep ascent. Behind me an empty carriage returning to St. Jean du Gard kept hard upon my tracks, and near the summit overtook me. The driver, like the rest of the world, was sure I was a peddler; but, unlike others, he was sure of what I had to sell. He had noticed the blue wool which hung out of my pack at either end; and from

this he had decided, beyond my power to alter his de-
cision, that I dealt in blue-wool collars, such as decorate the neck of the French draught-horse.

I had hurried to the topmost powers of Modestine,
for I dearly desired to see the view upon the other
side before the day had faded. But it was night when
I reached the summit; the moon was riding high and
clear; and only a few gray streaks of twilight lingered
in the west. A yawning valley, gulfed in blackness,
lay like a hole in created nature at my feet; but the
outline of the hills was sharp against the sky. There
was Mount Aigoal, the stronghold of Castanet. And
Castanet, not only as an active undertaking leader, deserves some mention among Camisards; for there is a
spray of rose among his laurel; and he showed how,
even in a public tragedy, love will have its way. In
the high tide of war he married, in his mountain
citadel, a young and pretty lass called Mariette. There
were great rejoicings; and the bridegroom released five-
and-twenty prisoners in honor of the glad event. Seven
months afterward Mariette, the Princess of the Cevennes, as they called her in derision, fell into the
hands of the authorities, where it was like to have
gone hard with her. But Castanet was a man of execution, and loved his wife. He fell on Valleraugue,
and got a lady there for a hostage; and for the first
and last time in that war there was an exchange of
prisoners. Their daughter, pledge of some starry night
upon Mount Aigoal, has left descendants to this day.

Modestine and I—it was our last meal together—had
a snack upon the top of St. Pierre, I on a heap of
stones, she standing by me in the moonlight and de-

corously eating bread out of my hand. The poor brute would eat more heartily in this manner; for she had a sort of affection for me, which I was soon to betray.

It was a long descent upon St. Jean du Gard, and we met no one but a carter, visible afar off by the glint of the moon on his extinguished lantern.

Before ten o'clock we had got in and were at supper; fifteen miles and a stiff hill in little beyond six hours!

FAREWELL, MODESTINE

ON examination, on the morning of October fourth, Modestine was pronounced unfit for travel. She would need at least two days' repose according to the hostler; but I was now eager to reach Alais for my letters; and, being in a civilized country of stage-coaches, I determined to sell my lady-friend and be off by the diligence that afternoon. Our yesterday's march, with the testimony of the driver who had pursued us up the long hill of St. Pierre, spread a favorable notion of my donkey's capabilities. Intending purchasers were aware of an unrivaled opportunity. Before ten I had an offer of twenty-five francs; and before noon, after a desperate engagement, I sold her, saddle and all, for five-and-thirty. The pecuniary gain is not obvious, but I had bought freedom into the bargain.

St. Jean du Gard is a large place and largely Protestant. The maire, a Protestant, asked me to help him in a small matter which is itself characteristic of the country. The young women of the Cevennes profit by the common religion and the difference of the language to go largely as governesses into England; and here was one, a native of Mialet, struggling with English circulars from two different agencies in London. I gave what help I could; and volunteered some advice, which struck me as being excellent.

One thing more I note. The phylloxera has ravaged the vineyards in this neighborhood; and in the early morning, under some chestnuts by the river, I found a party of men working with a cider-press. I could not at first make out what they were after, and asked one fellow to explain.

"Making cider," he said. "Oui, c'est comme ça. Comme dans le nord!"

There was a ring of sarcasm in his voice: the country was going to the devil.

It was not until I was fairly seated by the driver, and rattling through a rocky valley with dwarf olives, that I became aware of my bereavement. I had lost Modestine. Up to that moment I had thought I hated her; but now she was gone,

> "And, O,
> The difference to me!"

For twelve days we had been fast companions; we had traveled upward of a hundred and twenty miles, crossed several respectable ridges, and jogged along with our six legs by many a rocky and many a boggy byroad. After the first day, although sometimes I was hurt and distant in manner, I still kept my patience; and as for her, poor soul! she had come to regard me as a god. She loved to eat out of my hand. She was patient, elegant in form, the color of an ideal mouse, and inimitably small. Her faults were those of her race

and sex; her virtues were her own. Farewell, and if
forever—

Father Adam wept when he sold her to me; after
I had sold her in my turn, I was tempted to follow
his example; and being alone with a stage-driver and
four or five agreeable young men, I did not hesitate
to yield to my emotion.

CONTENTS

UNDERWOODS

BOOK I.—IN ENGLISH

BOOK II.—IN SCOTS

A CHILD'S GARDEN OF VERSES

THE CHILD ALONE

GARDEN DAYS

ENVOYS

UNDERWOODS

DEDICATION

THERE are men and classes of men that stand
above the common herd: the soldier, the sailor,
and the shepherd not infrequently; the artist
rarely; rarelier still, the clergyman; the physician
almost as a rule. He is the flower (such as it
is) of our civilization; and when that stage of
man is done with, and only remembered to be
marveled at in history, he will be thought to
have shared as little as any in the defects of the
period, and most notably exhibited the virtues of
the race. Generosity he has, such as is possible
to those who practice an art, never to those
who drive a trade; discretion, tested by a
hundred secrets; tact, tried in a thousand em-
barrassments; and what are more important,
Heraclean cheerfulness and courage. So it is
that he brings air and cheer into the sickroom,
and often enough, though not so often as he
wishes, brings healing.

Gratitude is but a lame sentiment; thanks,

when they are expressed, are often more embarrassing than welcome; and yet I must set forth
mine to a few out of many doctors who have
brought me comfort and help: to Dr. Willey of
San Francisco, whose kindness to a stranger it
must be as grateful to him, as it is touching to
me, to remember; to Dr. Karl Ruedi of Davos, the
good genius of the English in his frosty mountains; to Dr. Herbert of Paris, whom I knew
only for a week, and to Dr. Caissot of Montpellier, whom I knew only for ten days, and who
have yet written their names deeply in my
memory; to Dr. Brandt of Royat; to Dr. Wake-
field of Nice; to Dr. Chepmell, whose visits
make it a pleasure to be ill; to Dr. Horace
Dobell, so wise in counsel; to Sir Andrew Clark,
so unwearied in kindness; and to that wise
youth, my uncle, Dr. Balfour.

I forget as many as I remember; and I ask
both to pardon me, these for silence, those for
inadequate speech. But one name I have kept
on purpose to the last, because it is a household
word with me, and because if I had not received
favors from so many hands and in so many
quarters of the world, it should have stood upon
this page alone: that of my friend Thomas Bod-
ley Scott of Bournemouth. Will he accept this,
although shared among so many, for a dedication

to himself? and when next my ill-fortune (which has thus its pleasant side) brings him hurrying to me when he would fain sit down to meat or lie down to rest, will he care to remember that he takes this trouble for one who is not fool enough to be ungrateful?

R. L. S.

Skerryvore,
Bournemouth.

NOTE

THE human conscience has fled of late the troublesome domain of conduct for what I should have supposed to be the less congenial field of art: there she may now be said to rage, and with special severity in all that touches dialect; so that in every novel the letters of the alphabet are tortured, and the reader wearied, to commemorate shades of mispronunciation. Now, spelling is an art of great difficulty in my eyes, and I am inclined to lean upon the printer, even in common practice, rather than to venture abroad upon new quests. And the Scots tongue has an orthography of its own, lacking neither "authority nor author." Yet the temptation is great to lend a little guidance to the bewildered Englishman. Some simple phonetic artifice might defend your verses from barbarous mishandling, and yet not injure any vested interest. So it seems at first; but there are rocks ahead. Thus, if I wish the diphthong *ou* to have its proper value, I may write *oor* instead of *our;* many have done so and lived, and the pillars of the universe remained unshaken. But if I did so, and came presently to *doun*, which is the classical Scots spelling of the English *down*, I should begin to feel uneasy; and if I went on a little further, and came to a classical Scots word, like *stour* or *dour* or *clour*, I should know precisely where I was—that is to say, that I was out of sight of land on those high seas of spelling reform in which so many strong swimmers have toiled vainly. To some the situation is exhilarating; as for me, I give one bubbling cry and sink. The compromise at which I have arrived is inde-fensible, and I have no thought of trying to defend it. As I have stuck for the most part to the proper spelling, I append a table of some common vowel sounds which no one need con-sult; and just to prove that I belong to my age and have in me the stuff of a reformer, I have used modification marks throughout. Thus I can tell myself, not without pride, that I have added a fresh stumbling-block for English readers, and to a page of print in my native tongue have lent a new uncouthness. *Sed non nobis.*

I note again, that among our new dialecticians, the local habitat of every dialect is given to the square mile. I could not emulate this nicety if I desired; for I simply wrote my Scots as well as I was able, not caring if it hailed from Lauderdale or Angus, from the Mearns or Galloway; if I had ever heard a good word, I used it without shame; and when Scots was lacking, or the rhyme jibbed, I was glad (like my betters) to fall back on English. For all that, I own to a friendly feeling for the tongue of Fergusson and of Sir Walter, both Edinburgh men; and I confess that Burns has always sounded in my ear like something partly foreign. And indeed I am from the Lothians myself; it is there I heard the language spoken about my childhood; and it is in the drawling Lothian voice that I repeat it to myself. Let the precisians call my speech that of the Lothians. And if it be not pure, alas! what matters it? The day draws near when this illustrious and malleable tongue shall be quite forgotten; and Burns's Ayrshire, and Dr. Macdonald's Aberdeen-awa', and Scott's brave, metropolitan utterance will be all equally the ghosts of speech. Till then I would love to have my hour as a native Maker, and be read by my own countryfolk in our own dying language: an ambition surely rather of the heart than of the head, so restricted as it is in prospect of endurance, so parochial in bounds of space.

BOOK I — IN ENGLISH

I

ENVOY

Go, little book, and wish to all
Flowers in the garden, meat in the hall,
A bin of wine, a spice of wit,
A house with lawns inclosing it,
A living river by the door,
A nightingale in the sycamore!

II

A SONG OF THE ROAD

THE gauger walked with willing foot,
And aye the gauger played the flute;
And what should Master Gauger play
But *Over the hills and far away?*

Whene'er I buckle on my pack
And foot it gayly in the track,
O pleasant gauger, long since dead,
I hear you fluting on ahead.

You go with me the self-same way—
The self-same air for me you play;
For I do think and so do you
It is the tune to travel to.

For who would gravely set his face
To go to this or t'other place?
There's nothing under heav'n so blue
That's fairly worth the traveling to.

On every hand the roads begin,
And people walk with zeal therein;
But wheresoe'er the highways tend,
Be sure there's nothing at the end.

Then follow you, wherever hie
The traveling mountains of the sky.
Or let the streams in civil mode
Direct your choice upon a road;

For one and all, or high or low,
Will lead you where you wish to go;
And one and all go night and day
Over the hills and far away!

Forest of Montargis, 1878.

III

THE CANOE SPEAKS

On the great streams the ships may go
About men's business to and fro.
But I, the egg-shell pinnace, sleep
On crystal waters ankle-deep:
I, whose diminutive design,
Of sweeter cedar, pithier pine,
Is fashioned on so frail a mold,
A hand may launch, a hand withhold:
I, rather, with the leaping trout
Wind, among lilies, in and out;
I, the unnamed, inviolate,
Green, rustic rivers navigate;
My dipping paddle scarcely shakes
The berry in the bramble-brakes;
Still forth on my green way I wend
Beside the cottage garden-end;
And by the nested angler fare,
And take the lovers unaware.
By willow wood and water-wheel
Speedily fleets my touching keel;
By all retired and shady spots
Where prosper dim forget-me-nots;
By meadows where at afternoon
The growing maidens troop in June

To loose their girdles on the grass.
Ah! speedier than before the glass
The backward toilet goes; and swift
As swallows quiver, robe and shift
And the rough country stockings lie
Around each young divinity.
When, following the recondite brook,
Sudden upon this scene I look,
And light with unfamiliar face
On chaste Diana's bathing-place,
Loud ring the hills about and all
The shallows are abandoned. . . .

IV

IT is the season now to go
About the country high and low,
Among the lilacs hand in hand,
And two by two in fairy land.

The brooding boy, the sighing maid,
Wholly fain and half afraid,
Now meet along the hazel'd brook
To pass and linger, pause and look.

A year ago, and blithely paired,
Their rough-and-tumble play they shared;

They kissed and quarreled, laughed and
    cried,
A year ago at Eastertide.

With bursting heart, with fiery face,
She strove against him in the race;
He, unabashed, her garter saw,
That now would touch her skirts with
    awe.

Now by the stile ablaze she stops,
And his demurer eyes he drops;
Now they exchange averted sighs
Or stand and marry silent eyes.

And he to her a hero is,
And sweeter she than primroses;
Their common silence dearer far
Than nightingale and mavis are.

Now when they sever wedded hands,
Joy trembles in their bosom-strands,
And lovely laughter leaps and falls
Upon their lips in madrigals.

V

THE HOUSE BEAUTIFUL

A naked house, a naked moor,
A shivering pool before the door,
A garden bare of flowers and fruit,
And poplars at the garden foot:
Such is the place that I live in,
Bleak without and bare within.

Yet shall your ragged moor receive
The incomparable pomp of eve,
And the cold glories of the dawn
Behind your shivering trees be drawn;
And when the wind from place to place
Doth the unmoored cloud-galleons chase,
Your garden gloom and gleam again,
With leaping sun, with glancing rain.
Here shall the wizard moon ascend
The heavens, in the crimson end
Of day's declining splendor; here
The army of the stars appear.
The neighbor hollows dry or wet,
Spring shall with tender flowers beset;
And oft the morning muser see
Larks rising from the broomy lea,
And every fairy wheel and thread
Of cobweb dew-bediamonded.

When daisies go, shall winter time
Silver the simple grass with rime;
Autumnal frosts enchant the pool
And make the cart-ruts beautiful;
And when snow-bright the moor expands
How shall your children clap their hands!
To make this earth our hermitage,
A cheerful and a changeful page,
God's bright and intricate device
Of days and seasons doth suffice.

VI

A VISIT FROM THE SEA

FAR from the loud sea beaches
    Where he goes fishing and crying,
Here in the inland garden
    Why is the sea-gull flying?

Here are no fish to dive for;
    Here is the corn and lea;
Here are the green trees rustling.
    Hie away home to sea!

Fresh is the river water
    And quiet among the rushes;

This is no home for the sea-gull
  But for the rooks and thrushes.

Pity the bird that has wandered!
  Pity the sailor ashore!
Hurry him home to the ocean,
  Let him come here no more.

High on the sea-cliff ledges
  The white gulls are trooping and
      crying,
Here among rooks and roses,
  Why is the sea-gull flying?

———

VII

TO A GARDENER

FRIEND, in my mountain-side demesne,
My plain-beholding, rosy, green
And linnet-haunted garden-ground,
Let still the esculents abound.
Let first the onion flourish there,
Rose among roots, the maiden-fair,
Wine-scented and poetic soul
Of the capacious salad bowl.

Let thyme the mountaineer (to dress
The tinier birds) and wading cress,
The lover of the shallow brook,
From all my plots and borders look.
Nor crisp and ruddy radish, nor
Pease-cods for the child's pinafore
Be lacking; nor of salad clan
The last and least that ever ran
About great nature's garden-beds.
Nor thence be missed the speary heads
Of artichoke; nor thence the bean
That gathered innocent and green
Outsavors the belauded pea.

These tend, I prithee; and for me,
Thy most long-suffering master, bring
In April, when the linnets sing
And the days lengthen more and more
At sundown to the garden door.
And I, being provided thus,
Shall, with superb asparagus,
A book, a taper, and a cup
Of country wine, divinely sup.

La Solitude, Hyères.

VIII

TO MINNIE

(With a Hand-Glass)

A PICTURE-FRAME for you to fill,
    A paltry setting for your face,
A thing that has no worth until
    You lend it something of your grace,

I send (unhappy I that sing
    Laid by a while upon the shelf)
Because I would not send a thing
    Less charming than you are yourself.

And happier than I, alas!
    (Dumb thing, I envy its delight),
'Twill wish you well, the looking-glass,
    And look you in the face to-night.

1869.

IX

TO K. de M.

A LOVER of the moorland bare
And honest country winds, you were;
The silver-skimming rain you took;
And loved the floodings of the brook,

Dew, frost and mountains, fire and seas,
Tumultuary silences,
Winds that in darkness fifed a tune,
And the high-riding, virgin moon.

And as the berry, pale and sharp,
Springs on some ditch's counterscarp
In our ungenial, native north—
You put your frosted wildings forth,
And on the heath, afar from man,
A strong and bitter virgin ran.

The berry ripened keeps the rude
And racy flavor of the wood;
And you that loved the empty plain
All redolent of wind and rain,
Around you still the curlew sings—
The freshness of the weather clings—
The maiden jewels of the rain
Sit in your dabbled locks again.

X

TO N. V. de G. S.

THE unfathomable sea, and time, and tears,
The deeds of heroes and the crimes of kings
Dispart us; and the river of events
Has, for an age of years, to east and west

More widely borne our cradles. Thou to me
Art foreign, as when seamen at the dawn
Descry a land far off and know not which.
So I approach uncertain; so I cruise
Round thy mysterious islet, and behold
Surf and great mountains and loud river-bars,
And from the shore hear inland voices call.
Strange is the seaman's heart; he hopes, he
      fears;
Draws closer and sweeps wider from that
      coast;
Last, his rent sail refits, and to the deep
His shattered prow uncomforted puts back.
Yet as he goes he ponders at the helm
Of that bright island; where he feared to
      touch,
His spirit re-adventures; and for years,
Where by his wife he slumbers safe at home,
Thoughts of that land revisit him; he sees
The eternal mountains beckon, and awakes
Yearning for that far home that might have
      been.

XI

TO WILL. H. LOW

YOUTH now flees on feathered foot
Faint and fainter sounds the flute,
Rarer songs of gods; and still
Somewhere on the sunny hill,
Or along the winding stream,
Through the willows, flits a dream;
Flits, but shows a smiling face,
Flees, but with so quaint a grace,
None can choose to stay at home,
All must follow, all must roam.
This is unborn beauty: she
Now in air floats high and free,
Takes the sun and breaks the blue;—
Late with stooping pinion flew
Raking hedgerow trees, and wet
Her wing in silver streams, and set
Shining foot on temple roof:
Now again she flies aloof,
Coasting mountain clouds and kiss't
By the evening's amethyst.

In wet wood and miry lane,
Still we pant and pound in vain;
Still with leaden foot we chase
Waning pinion, fainting face;

Still with gray hair we stumble on,
Till, behold, the vision gone!
Where hath fleeting beauty led?
To the doorway of the dead.
Life is over, life was gay:
We have come the primrose way.

XII

TO MRS. WILL. H. LOW

Even in the bluest noonday of July,
There could not run the smallest breath of wind
But all the quarter sounded like a wood;
And in the checkered silence and above
The hum of city cabs that sought the Bois,
Suburban ashes shivered into song.
A patter and a chatter and a chirp
And a long-dying hiss—it was as though
Starched old brocaded dames through all the
        house
Had trailed a strident skirt, or the whole sky
Even in a wink had over-brimmed in rain.
Hark, in these shady parlors, how it talks
Of the near autumn, how the smitten ash
Trembles and augurs floods! O not too long

In these inconstant latitudes delay,
O not too late from the unbeloved north
Trim your escape! For soon shall this low roof
Resound indeed with rain, soon shall your eyes
Search the foul garden, search the darkened
    rooms,
Nor find one jewel but the blazing log.

18 Rue Vernier, Paris.

XIII

TO H. F. BROWN

(Written During a Dangerous Sickness)

I SIT and wait a pair of oars
On cis-Elysian river-shores.
Where the immortal dead have sate,
'Tis mine to sit and meditate;
To re-ascend life's rivulet,
Without remorse, without regret;
And sing my *Alma Genetrix*
Among the willows of the Styx.

And lo, as my serener soul
Did these unhappy shores patrol,
And wait with an attentive ear
The coming of the gondolier,

Your fire-surviving roll I took,
Your spirited and happy book;*
Whereon, despite my frowning fate,
It did my soul so recreate
That all my fancies fled away
On a Venetian holiday.

Now, thanks to your triumphant
    care,
Your pages clear as April air,
The sails, the bells, the birds, I
    know,
And the far-off Friulan snow;
The land and sea, the sun and
    shade,
And the blue even lamp-inlaid,
For this, for these, for all, O friend,
For your whole book from end to
    end—
For Paron Piero's muttonham—
I your defaulting debtor am.

Perchance, reviving, yet may I
To your sea-paven city hie,
And in a *felze*, some day yet
Light at your pipe my cigarette.

---

* "Life on the Lagoons," by H. F. Brown, originally burned in the fire at Messrs. Kegan Paul, Trench & Co.'s.

XIV

TO ANDREW LANG

Dear Andrew, with the brindled hair,
Who glory to have thrown in air,
High over arm, the trembling reed,
By Ale and Kail, by Till and Tweed;
An equal craft of hand you show
The pen to guide, the fly to throw:
I count you happy starred; for God,
When He with inkpot and with rod
Endowed you, bade your fortune lead
Forever by the crooks of Tweed,
Forever by the woods of song
And lands that to the Muse belong;
Or if in peopled streets, or in
The abhorred pedantic sanhedrim,
It should be yours to wander, still
Airs of the morn, airs of the hill,
The plovery Forest and the seas
That break about the Hebrides,
Should follow over field and plain
And find you at the window-pane;
And you again see hill and peel,
And the bright springs gush at your
        heel.

So went the fiat forth, and so
Garrulous like a brook you go,
With sound of happy mirth and sheen
Of daylight—whether by the green
You fare that moment, or the gray;
Whether you dwell in March or May
Or whether treat of reels and rods
Or of the old unhappy gods:
Still like a brook your page has shone
And your ink sings of Helicon.

XV

ET TU IN ARCADIA VIXISTI

(TO R. A. M. S.)

In ancient tales, O friend, thy spirit dwelt;
There, from of old, thy childhood passed; and
there
High expectation, high delights and deeds,
Thy fluttering heart with hope and terror moved.
And thou hast heard of yore the Blatant Beast,
And Roland's horn, and that war-scattering shout
Of all-unarmed Achilles, ægis-crowned.
And perilous lands thou sawest, sounding shores
And seas and forests drear, island and dale

And mountain dark. For thou with Tristram
    rod'st
Or Bedevere, in farthest Lyonesse
Thou hadst a booth in Samarcand, whereat
Side-looking Magians trafficked; thence, by night,
An Afreet snatched thee, and with wings upbore
Beyond the Aral mount; or hoping gain,
Thou, with a jar of money didst embark
For Balsorah, by sea. But chiefly thou
In that clear air took'st life; in Arcady
The haunted, land of song; and by the wells
Where most the gods frequent. There Chiron
    old,
In the Pelethronian antre, taught thee lore:
The plants, he taught, and by the shining stars
In forests dim to steer. There hast thou seen
Immortal Pan dance secret in a glade,
And, dancing, roll his eyes; these where they
    fell,
Shed glee, and through the congregated oaks
A flying horror winged; while all the earth
To the god's pregnant footing thrilled within.
Or whiles, beside the sobbing stream, he breathed,
In his clutched pipe unformed and wizard
    strains
Divine yet brutal; which the forest heard,
And thou, with awe; and far upon the plain
The unthinking plowman started and gave ear.

Now things there are that, upon him who sees,
A strong vocation lay; and strains there are
That whoso hears shall hear for evermore.
For evermore thou hear'st a mortal Pan
And those melodious godheads, ever young
And ever quiring on the mountains old.

What was this earth, child of the gods, to thee?
Forth from thy dreamland thou, a dreamer cam'st
And in thine ears the olden music rang,
And in thy mind the doings of the dead,
And those heroic ages long forgot.
To a so fallen earth, alas! too late,
Alas! in evil days, thy steps return,
To list at noon for nightingales, to grow
A dweller on the beach till Argo come
That came long since, a lingerer by the pool
Where that desired angel bathes no more.

As when the Indian to Dakota comes
Or farthest Idaho, and where he dwelt,
He with his clan, a humming city finds;
Thereon a while, amazed, he stares, and then
To right and leftward, like a questing dog,
Seeks first the ancestral altars, then the hearth
Long cold with rains, and where old terror lodged
And where the dead. So thee undying Hope,
With all her pack, hunts screaming through the
        years:

Here, there, thou fleest; but nor here nor there
The pleasant gods abide, the glory dwells.

That, that was not Apollo, not the god.
This was not Venus, though she Venus seemed
A moment.   And though fair yon river move,
She, all the way from disenchanted fount
To seas unhallowed runs; the gods forsook
Long since her trembling rushes; from her plains
Disconsolate, long since adventure fled;
And now although the inviting river flows
And every poplared cape and every bend
Or willowy islet, win upon thy soul
And to thy hopeful shallop whisper speed;
Yet hope not thou at all; hope is no more;
And O, long since the golden groves are dead
The faery cities vanished from the land!

XVI

TO W. E. HENLEY

THE year runs through her phases; rain and sun,
Springtime and summer pass; winter succeeds;
But one pale season rules the house of death.
Cold falls the imprisoned daylight; fell disease
By each lean pallet squats, and pain and sleep
Toss gaping on the pillows.

But O thou!
Uprise and take thy pipe. Bid music flow,
Strains by good thoughts attended, like the
     spring
The swallows follow over land and sea.
Pain sleeps at once; at once, with open eyes,
Dozing despair awakes. The shepherd sees
His flock come bleating home; the seaman hears
Once more the cordage rattle. Airs of home!
Youth, love and roses blossom; the gaunt ward
Dislimns and disappears, and, opening out,
Shows brooks and forests, and the blue beyond
Of mountains.

Small the pipe; but oh! do thou,
Peak-faced and suffering piper, blow therein
The dirge of heroes dead; and to these sick,
These dying, sound the triumph over death.
Behold! each greatly breathes; each tastes a joy
Unknown before, in dying; for each knows
A hero dies with him—though unfulfilled,
Yet conquering truly—and not dies in vain

So is pain cheered, death comforted; the house
Of sorrow smiles to listen. Once again—
O thou, Orpheus and Heracles, the bard
And the deliverer, touch the stops again!

XVII

HENRY JAMES

WHO comes to-night? We ope the doors in vain.
Who comes? My bursting walls, can you contain
The presences that now together throng
Your narrow entry, as with flowers and song,
As with the air of life, the breath of talk?
Lo, how these fair immaculate women walk
Behind their jocund maker; and we see
Slighted *De Mauves*, and that far different she,
Gressie, the trivial sphynx; and to our feast
Daisy and *Barb* and *Chancellor* (she not least!)
With all their silken, all their airy kin,
Do like unbidden angels enter in.
But he, attended by these shining names,
Comes (best of all) himself—our welcome James.

XVIII

THE MIRROR SPEAKS

WHERE the bells peal far at sea
Cunning fingers fashioned me.
There on palace walls I hung
While that Consuelo sung;

But I heard, though I listened well,
Never a note, never a trill,
Never a beat of the chiming bell.
There I hung and looked, and there
In my gray face, faces fair
Shone from under shining hair.
Well I saw the poising head,
But the lips moved and nothing said;
And when lights were in the hall,
Silent moved the dancers all.

So a while I glowed, and then
Fell on dusty days and men;
Long I slumbered packed in straw,
Long I none but dealers saw;
Till before my silent eye
One that sees came passing by.

Now with an outlandish grace,
To the sparkling fire I face
In the blue room at Skerryvore;
Where I wait until the door
Open, and the Prince of Men,
Henry James, shall come again.

XIX

KATHARINE

WE see you as we see a face
That trembles in a forest place
Upon the mirror of a pool
Forever quiet, clear and cool;
And in the wayward glass appears
To hover between smiles and tears
Elfin and human, airy and true,
And backed by the reflected blue.

———

XX

TO F. J. S.

I READ, dear friend, in your dear face
Your life's tale told with perfect grace;
The river of your life I trace
Up the sun-checkered, devious bed
To the far-distant fountain-head.

Not one quick beat of your warm heart,
Nor thought that came to you apart,
Pleasure nor pity, love nor pain
Nor sorrow, has gone by in vain;

But as some lone, wood-wandering child
Brings home with him at evening mild
The thorns and flowers of all the wild,
From your whole life, O fair and true
Your flowers and thorns you bring with you

XXI

REQUIEM

UNDER the wide and starry sky,
Dig the grave and let me lie.
Glad did I live and gladly die,
   And I laid me down with a will.

This be the verse you grave for me:
Here he lies where he longed to be;
Home is the sailor, home from sea,
   And the hunter home from the hill.

XXII

THE CELESTIAL SURGEON

IF I have faltered more or less
In my great task of happiness;
If I have moved among my race
And shown no glorious morning face;

If beams from happy human eyes
Have moved me not; if morning skies,
Books, and my food, and summer rain
Knocked on my sullen heart in vain:—
Lord, thy most pointed pleasure take
And stab my spirit broad awake;
Or, Lord, if too obdurate I,
Choose thou, before that spirit die,
A piercing pain, a killing sin,
And to my dead heart run them in!

XXIII

OUR LADY OF THE SNOWS

OUT of the sun, out of the blast,
Out of the world, alone I passed
Across the moor and through the wood
To where the monastery stood.
There neither lute nor breathing fife,
Nor rumor of the world of life,
Nor confidences low and dear,
Shall strike the meditative ear.
Aloof, unhelpful, and unkind,
The prisoners of the iron mind,
Where nothing speaks except the bell
The unfraternal brothers dwell.

Poor, passionate men, still clothed afresh
With agonizing folds of flesh;
Whom the clear eyes solicit still
To some bold output of the will,
While fairy Fancy far before
And musing Memory-Hold-the-door
Now to heroic death invite
And now uncurtain fresh delight:
O, little boots it thus to dwell
On the remote unneighbored hill!

O, to be up and doing, O
Unfearing and unshamed to go
In all the uproar and the press
About my human business!
My undissuaded heart I hear
Whisper courage in my ear.
With voiceless calls, the ancient earth
Summons me to a daily birth.
Thou, O my love, ye, O my friends—
The gist of life, the end of ends—
To laugh, to love, to live, to die,
Ye call me by the ear and eye!

Forth from the casemate, on the plain
Where honor has the world to gain,
Pour forth and bravely do your part,
O knights of the unshielded heart!

Forth and forever forward!—out
From prudent turret and redoubt,
And in the mellay charge amain,
To fall, but yet to rise again!
Captive? ah, still, to honor bright,
A captive soldier of the right!
Or free and fighting, good with ill?
Unconquering but unconquered still!

And ye, O brethren, what if God,
When from heav'n's top he spies
          abroad,
And sees on this tormented stage
The noble war of mankind rage:
What if his vivifying eye,
O monks, should pass your corner by?
For still the Lord is Lord of might;
In deeds, in deeds, he takes delight;
The plow, the spear, the laden barks,
The field, the founded city, marks;
He marks the smiler of the streets,
The singer upon garden seats;
He sees the climber in the rocks:
To him the shepherd folds his flocks.
For those he loves that underprop
With daily virtues heaven's top,
And bear the falling sky with ease,
Unfrowning carvatides.

Those he approves that ply the trade,
That rock the child, that wed the maid,
That with weak virtues, weaker hands,
Sow gladness on the peopled lands,
And still with laughter, song and shout,
Spin the great wheel of earth about.

But ye? O ye who linger still,
Here in your fortress on the hill,
With placid face, with tranquil breath,
The unsought volunteers of death,
Our cheerful General on high
With careless looks may pass you by.

————

XXIV

Not yet, my soul, these friendly fields desert,
Where thou with grass, and rivers, and the breeze,
And the bright face of day, thy dalliance hadst;
Where to thine ear first sang the enraptured
        birds;
Where love and thou that lasting bargain made.
The ship rides trimmed, and from the eternal
        shore
Thou hearest airy voices; but not yet
Depart, my soul, not yet a while depart.

Freedom is far, rest far. Thou art with life
Too closely woven, nerve with nerve entwined;
Service still craving service, love for love,
Love for dear love, still suppliant with tears.
Alas, not yet thy human task is done!
A bond at birth is forged; a debt doth lie
Immortal on mortality. It grows—
By vast rebound it grows, unceasing growth;
Gift upon gift, alms upon alms, upreared,
From man, from God, from nature, till the soul
At that so huge indulgence stands amazed.

Leave not, my soul, the unfoughten field, nor
    leave
Thy debts dishonored, nor thy place desert
Without due service rendered. For thy life,
Up, spirit, and defend that fort of clay,
Thy body, now beleaguered; whether soon
Or late she fall; whether to-day thy friends
Bewail thee dead, or, after years, a man
Grown old in honor and the friend of peace.
Contend, my soul, for moments and for hours;
Each is with service pregnant; each reclaimed
Is as a kingdom conquered, where to reign.
As when a captain rallies to the fight
His scattered legions, and beats ruin back,
He, on the field, encamps, well pleased in mind.
Yet surely him shall fortune overtake,

Him smite in turn, headlong his ensigns drive;
And that dear land, now safe, to-morrow fall.
But he, unthinking, in the present good
Solely delights, and all the camps rejoice.

———

XXV

It is not yours, O mother, to complain,
Not, mother, yours to weep,
Though nevermore your son again
Shall to your bosom creep,
Though nevermore again you watch your
        baby sleep.

Though in the greener paths of earth,
Mother and child no more
We wander; and no more the birth
Of me whom once you bore
Seems still the brave reward that once it
        seemed of yore;

Though as all passes, day and night,
The seasons and the years,
From you, O mother, this delight,
This also disappears—
Some profit yet survives of all your pangs
        and tears.

The child, the seed, the grain of corn,
The acorn on the hill,
Each for some separate end is born
In season fit, and still
Each must in strength arise to work the
almighty will.

So from the hearth the children flee,
By that almighty hand
Austerely led; so one by sea
Goes forth, and one by land;
Nor aught of all man's sons escape from
that command.

So from the sally each obeys
The unseen almighty nod;
So till the ending all their ways
Blindfolded loth have trod:
Nor knew their task at all, but were the
tools of God.

And as the fervent smith of yore
Beat out the glowing blade,
Nor wielded in the front of war
The weapons that he made,
But in the tower at home still plied his
ringing trade;

So like a sword the son shall roam
On nobler missions sent;

And as the smith remained at home
In peaceful turret pent,
So sits the while at home the mother
　　well content.

XXVI

THE SICK CHILD

Child

O MOTHER, lay your hand on my brow!
O mother, mother, where am I now?
Why is the room so gaunt and great?
Why am I lying awake so late?

Mother

Fear not at all: the night is still;
Nothing is here that means you ill—
Nothing but lamps the whole town through,
And never a child awake but you.

Child

Mother, mother, speak low in my ear,
Some of the things are so great and near,
Some are so small and far away,
I have a fear that I cannot say.
What have I done, and what do I fear,
And why are you crying, mother dear?

Mother

Out in the city, sounds begin
Thank the kind God, the carts come in!
An hour or two more, and God is so kind,
The day shall be blue in the window-blind,
Then shall my child go sweetly asleep,
And dream of the birds and the hills of
  sheep.

XXVII

IN MEMORIAM F. A. S.

YET, O stricken heart, remember, O remember
  How of human days he lived the better part.
April came to bloom and never dim December
  Breathed its killing chills upon the head or
    heart.

Doomed to know not Winter, only Spring, a
    being
  Trod the flowery April blithely for a while,
Took his fill of music, joy of thought and
    seeing,
  Came and stayed and went, nor ever ceased
    to smile.

Came and stayed and went, and now when all
   is finished,
You alone have crossed the melancholy stream,
Yours the pang, but his, O his, the undiminished
   Undecaying gladness, undeparted dream.

All that life contains of torture, toil, and treason,
   Shame, dishonor, death, to him were but a
   name.
Here, a boy, he dwelt through all the singing
   season
   And ere the day of sorrow departed as he
   came.

Davos, 1881.

XXVIII

TO MY FATHER

Peace and her huge invasion to these shores
Puts daily home; innumerable sails
Dawn on the far horizon and draw near;
Innumerable loves, uncounted hopes
To our wild coasts, not darkling now, approach:
Not now obscure, since thou and thine are there,
And bright on the lone isle, the foundered reef,
The long, resounding foreland, Pharos stands.

These are thy works, O father, these thy crown;
Whether on high the air be pu..., they shine
Along the yellowing sunset, and all night
Among the unnumbered stars of God they shine;
Or whether fogs arise and far and wide
The low sea-level drown—each finds a tongue
And all night long the tolling bell resounds:
So shine, so toll, till night be overpast,
Till the stars vanish, till the sun return,
And in the haven rides the fleet secure.

In the first hour, the seaman in his skiff
Moves through the unmoving bay, to where the
      town
Its earliest smoke into the air upbreathes
And the rough hazels climb along the beach.
To the tugg'd oar the distant echo speaks.
The ship lies resting, where by reef and roost
Thou and thy lights have led her like a child.

This hast thou done, and I—can I be base?
I must arise, O father, and to port
Some lost, complaining seaman pilot home.

XXIX

IN THE STATES

WITH half a heart I wander here
  As from an age gone by
A brother—yet though young in years,
  An elder brother, I.

You speak another tongue than mine,
  Though both were English born.
I toward the night of time decline,
  You mount into the morn.

Youth shall grow great and strong and
    free,
  But age must still decay:
To-morrow for the States—for me,
  England and Yesterday.

San Francisco.

———

XXX

A PORTRAIT

I AM a kind of farthing dip,
  Unfriendly to the nose and eyes;
A blue-behinded ape, I skip
  Upon the trees of Paradise.

At mankind's feast, I take my place
In solemn, sanctimonious state,
And have the air of saying grace
While I defile the dinner-plate.

I am "the smiler with the knife,"
The battener upon garbage, I—
Dear Heaven, with such a rancid life,
Were it not better far to die?

Yet still, about the human pale,
I love to scamper, love to race,
To swing by my irreverent tail
All over the most holy place;

And when at length, some golden day,
The unfailing sportsman, aiming at,
Shall bag, me—all the world shall say,
Thank God, and there's an end of that!

XXXI

Sing clearlier, Muse, or evermore be still,
Sing truer or no longer sing!
No more the voice of melancholy Jacques
To wake a weeping echo in the hill;
But as the boy, the pirate of the spring,
From the green elm a living linnet takes,
One natural verse recapture—then be still.

XXXII

*A CAMP**

THE bed was made, the room was fit
By punctual eve the stars were lit;
The air was still, the water ran,
No need was there for maid or man,
When we put up, my ass and I,
At God's green caravanserai.

———

XXXIII

THE COUNTRY OF THE CAMISARDS†

WE traveled in the print of olden wars,
    Yet all the land was green
    And love we found, and peace,
    Where fire and war had been.

They pass and smile, the children of the sword—
    No more the sword they wield;
    And O, how deep the corn
    Along the battlefield!

---

*From "Travels with a Donkey."   † Ibid.

XXXIV

SKERRYVORE

For love of lovely words and for the sake
Of those, my kinsmen and my countrymen,
Who early and late in the windy ocean toiled
To plant a star for seamen, where was then
The surfy haunt of seals and cormorants:
I, on the lintel of this cot, inscribe
The name of a strong tower.

XXXV

SKERRYVORE: The Parallel

Here all is sunny, and when the truant gull
Skims the green level of the lawn, his wing
Dispetals roses; here the house is framed
Of kneaded brick and the plumed mountain pine,
Such clay as artists fashion and such wood
As the tree-climbing urchin breaks. But there
Eternal granite hewn from the living isle
And dowelled with brute iron, rears a tower
That from its wet foundation to its crown
Of glittering glass, stands, in the sweep of
        winds,
Immovable, immortal, eminent.

XXXVI

My house, I say. But hark to the sunny doves
That make my roof the arena of their loves,
That gyre about the gable all day long
And fill the chimneys with their murmurous
      song:
Our house, they say; and *mine*, the cat declares
And spreads his golden fleece upon the chairs;
And *mine*, the dog, and rises stiff with wrath
If any alien foot profane the path.
So too the buck that trimmed my terraces,
Our whilome gardener, called the garden his;
Who now, deposed, surveys my plain abode
And his late kingdom, only from the road.

———

XXXVII

My body which my dungeon is,
And yet my parks and palaces:—
   Which is so great that there I go
All the day long to and fro,
And when the night begins to fall
Throw down my bed and sleep, while all
The building hums with wakefulness—
Even as a child of savages

When evening takes her on her way,
(She having roamed a summer's day
Along the mountain-sides and scalp)
Sleeps in an antre of that alp:—
 Which is so broad and high that there,
As in the topless fields of air,
My fancy soars like to a kite
And faints in the blue infinite:—
 Which is so strong, my strongest throes
And the rough world's besieging blows
Not break it, and so weak withal,
Death ebbs and flows in its loose wall
As the green sea in fishers' nets,
And tops its topmost parapets:—
 Which is so wholly mine that I
Can wield its whole artillery, ·
And mine so little, that my soul
Dwells in perpetual control,
And I but think and speak and do
As my dead fathers move me to:—
 If this born body of my bones
The beggared soul so barely owns,
What money passed from hand to hand,
What creeping custom of the land,
What deed of author or assign,
Can make a house a thing of mine?

XXXVIII

Say not of me that weakly I declined
The labors of my sires, and fled the sea,
The towers we founded and the lamps we lit,
To play at home with paper like a child.
But rather say: *In the afternoon of time*
A strenuous family dusted from its hands
The sand of granite, and beholding far
Along the sounding coast its pyramids
And tall memorials catch the dying sun,
Smiled well content, and to this childish task
Around the fire addressed its evening hours.

BOOK II — IN SCOTS

TABLE OF COMMON SCOTTISH VOWEL SOUNDS

ae
ai, } — open A as in rare.

a'
au } — AW as in law.
aw

ea — open E as in mere, but this with exceptions, as heather —
heather, wean — wain, lear — lair.

ee
ei } — open E as in mere.
ie

oa — open O as in more.

ou — doubled O as in poor.

ow — OW as in Bower.

u — doubled O as in poor.

ui or û before R — (say roughly) open A as in rare.

ui or û before any other consonant — (say roughly) close I as in grin.

y — open I as in kite.

i — pretty nearly what you please, much as in English. Heaven guide
the reader through that labyrinth! But in Scots it dodges usually
from the short I, as in grin, to the open E, as in mere. Find and
blind, I may remark, are pronounced to rhyme with the preterite
of grin.

I

THE MAKER TO POSTERITY

Far 'yont amang the years to be
When a' we think, an' a' we see,
An' a' we luve, 's been dung ajee
    By time's rouch shouther,
An' what was richt and wrang for me
    Lies mangled throu'ther,

It's possible—it's hardly mair—
That some ane, ripin' after lear—
Some auld professor or young heir,
    If still there's either—
May find an' read me, an' be sair
    Perplexed, puir brither!

"What tongue does your auld bookie speak?"
He'll spier; an' I, his mou to steik:
"No bein' fit to write in Greek,
    I wrote in Lallan,
Dear to my heart as the peat reek,
    Auld as Tantallon.

"*Few spak it than, an' noo there's nane.*
My puir auld sangs lie a' their lane,
Their sense, that aince was braw an' plain,
        Tint a'thegether,
Like runes upon a standin' stane
        Amang the heather.

"*But think not you the brae to speel;*
You, tae, maun chow the bitter peel;
For a' your lear, for a' your skeel,
        Ye're nane sae lucky;
An' things are mebbe waur than weel
        For you, my buckie.

"'*The hale concern (baith hens an' eggs,*
Baith books an' writers, stars an' clegs)
Noo stachers upon lowsent legs
        An' wears awa';
The tack o' mankind, near the dregs,
        Rins unco law.

"*Your book, that in some braw new tongue,*
Ye wrote or prentit, preached or sung,
Will still be just a bairn, an' young
        In fame an' years,
Whan the hale planet's guts are dung
        About your ears;

"*An' you, sair gruppin' to a spar*
Or whammled wi' some bleezin' star,

Cryin' to ken whaur deil ye are,
  Hame, France, or Flanders—
Whang sindry like a railway car
  An' flie in danders."

II

ILLE TERRARUM

FRAE nirly, nippin', Eas'lan' breeze,
Frae Norlan' snaw, an' haar o' seas,
Weel happit in your gairden trees,
    A bonny bit,
Atween the muckle Pentland's knees,
    Secure ye sit.

Beeches an' aiks entwine their theek,
An' firs, a stench, auld-farrant clique.
A' simmer day, your chimleys reek,
    Couthy and bien;
An' here an' there your windies keek
    Amang the green.

A pickle plats an' paths an' posies,
A wheen auld gillyflowers an' roses:
A ring o' wa's the hale incloses
    Frae sheep or men;
An' there the auld housie beeks an' dozes
    A' by her lane.

The gairdner crooks his weary back
A' day in the pitaty-track,
Or mebbe stops a while to crack
    Wi' Jane the cook,
Or at some buss, worm-eaten-black,
    To gie a look.

Frae the high hills the curlew ca's;
The sheep gang baaing by the wa's;
Or whiles a clan o' roosty craws
    Cangle together;
The wild bees seek the gairden raws.
    Weariet wi' heather.

Or in the gloamin' douce an' gray
The sweet-throat mavis tunes her lay;
The herd comes linkin' doun the brae;
    An' by degrees
The muckle siller müne maks way
    Amang the trees.

Here aft hae I, wi' sober heart,
For meditation sat apairt,
When orra loves or kittle art
    Perplexed my mind;
Here socht a balm for ilka smart
    O' humankind.

Here aft, weel neukit by my lane,
Wi' Horace, or perhaps Montaigne,

The mornin' hours hae come an' gane
    Abüne my heid—
I wadnae gi'en a chucky-stane
    For a' I'd read.

But noo the auld city, street by street,
An' winter fu' o' snaw an' sleet,
A while shut in my gangrel feet
    An' goavin' mettle;
Noo is the soopit ingle sweet,
    An' liltin' kettle.

An' noo the winter winds complain;
Cauld lies the glaur in ilka lane;
On draigled hizzie, tautit wean
    An' drucken lads,
In the mirk nicht, the winter rain
    Dribbles an' blads.

Whan bugles frae the Castle rock,
An' beaten drums wi' dowie shock,
Wauken, at cauld-rife sax o'clock,
    My chitterin' frame,
I mind me on the kintry cock,
    The kintry hame.

I mind me on yon bonny bield;
An' Fancy traivels far afield

To gaither a' that gairdens yield
    O' sun an' Simmer:
To hearten up a dowie chield,
    Fancy's the limmer!

———

III

WHEN aince Aprile has fairly come,
An' birds may bigg in winter's lum,
An' pleisure's spreid for a' and some
    O' whatna state,
Love, wi' her auld recruitin' drum,
    Than taks the gate.

The heart plays dunt wi' main an'
    micht;
The lasses' een are a' sae bricht,
Their dresses are sae braw an' ticht,
    The bonny birdies!—
Puir winter virtue at the sicht
    Gangs heels ower hurdies.

An' aye as love frae land to land
Tirls the drum wi' eident hand,
A' men collect at her command,
    Toun-bred or land'art,
An' follow in a denty band
    Her gaucy standart.

An' I, wha sang o' rain an' snaw,
An' weary winter weel awa',
Noo busk me in a jacket braw,
    An' tak my place
I' the ram-stam, harum-scarum raw,
    Wi' smilin' face.

IV

A MILE AN' A BITTOCK

A MILE an' a bittock, a mile or twa,
Abüne the burn, ayont the law,
Davie an' Donal' an' Cherlie an' a',
    An' the müne was shinin' clearly!

Ane went hame wi' the ither, an' then
The ither went hame wi' the ither twa men,
An' baith wad return him the service again,
    An' the müne was shinin' clearly!

The clocks were chappin' in house an' ha',
Eleeven, twal an' ane an' twa;
An' the guidman's face was turnt to the wa',
    An' the müne was shinin' clearly!

A wind got up frae affa the sea,
It blew the stars as clear's could be,
It blew in the een of a' o' the three,
    An' the müne was shinin' clearly!

Noo, Davie was first to get sleep in his head,
" The best o' frien's maun twine," he said;
" I'm weariet, an' here I'm awa' to my bed."
An' the müne was shinin' clearly!

Twa o' them walkin' an' crackin' their lane,
The mornin' licht cam gray an' plain,
An' the birds they yammert on stick an'
        stane,
    An' the müne was shinin' clearly!

O years ayont, O years awa',
My lads, ye'll mind whate'er befa'—
My lads, ye'll mind on the bield o' the law,
    When the müne was shinin' clearly.

———

V

A LOWDEN SABBATH MORN

THE clinkum-clank o' Sabbath bells
Noo to the hoastin' rookery swells,
Noo faintin' laigh in shady dells,
        Sounds far an' near,
An' through the simmer kintry tells
        Its tale o' cheer.

An' noo, to that melodious play,
A' deidly awn the quiet sway—
A' ken their solemn holiday,
    Bestial an' human,
The singin' lintie on the brae,
    The restin' plou'man.

He, mair than a' the lave o' men,
His week completit joys to ken;
Half-dressed, he daunders out an' in,
    Perplext wi' leisure;
An' his raxt limbs he'll rax again
    Wi' painfü' pleesure.

The steerin' mither strang afit
Noo shoos the bairnies but a bit;
Noo cries them ben, their Sinday shüit
    To scart upon them,
Or sweeties in their pouch to pit,
    Wi' blessin's on them.

The lasses, clean frae tap to taes,
Are busked in crunklin' underclaes;
The gartened hose, the weel-filled stays,
    The nakit shift,
A' bleached on bonny greens for days,
    An' white's the drift.

An' noo to face the kirkward mile:
The guidman's hat o' dacent style,

The blackit shoon, we noo maun fyle
    As white's the miller:
A waefü' peety tae, to spile
    The warth o' siller.

Our Marg'et, aye sae keen to crack,
Douce-stappin' in the stoury track,
Her emeralt goun a' kiltit back
    Frae snawy coats,
White-ankled, leads the kirkward pack
    Wi' Dauvit Groats.

A thocht ahint, in runkled breeks
A' spiled wi' lyin' by for weeks,
The guidman follows closs, an' cleiks
    The sonsie missis;
His sarious face at aince bespeaks
    The day that this is.

And aye an' while we nearer draw
To whaur the kirton lies alaw,
Mair neebors, comin' saft an' slaw
    Frae here an' there,
The thicker thrang the gate an' caw
    The stour in air.

But hark! the bells frae nearer clang;
To rowst the slaw, their sides they
    bang;

An' see! black coats a'ready thrang
    The green kirkyaird,
And at the yett, the chestnuts spang
    That brocht the laird.

The solemn elders at the plate
Stand drinkin' deep the pride o' state.
That practiced hands as gash an' great
    As Lords o' Session;
The later named, a wee thing blate
    In their expression.

The prentit stanes that mark the deid,
Wi' lengthened lip, the sarious read;
Syne wag a moraleesin' heid,
    An' then an' there
Their hirplin' practice an' their creed
    Try hard to square.

It's here our Merren lang has lain.
A wee bewast the table-stane;
An' yon's the grave o' Sandy Blane;
    An' further ower,
The mither's brithers, dacent men!
    Lie a' the fower.

Here the guidman sall bide awee
To dwall amang the deid; to see

Auld faces clear in fancy's e'e;
 Belike to hear
Auld voices fa'in' saft an' slee
 On fancy's ear.

Thus, on the day o' solemn things,
The bell that in the steeple swings
To fauld a scaittered faim'ly rings
 Its walcome screed;
An' just a wee thing nearer brings
 The quick an' deid.

But noo the bell is ringin' in;
To tak their places, folk begin;
The minister himsel' will shune
 Be up the gate,
Filled fu' wi' clavers about sin
 An' man's estate.

The tünes are up—*French.* to be shüre.
The faithfü' *French*, an' twa-three ma
The auld prezentor, hoastin' sair,
 Wales out the portions,
An' yirks the tüne into the air
 Wi' queer contortions.

Follows the prayer, the readin' next,
An' than the fisslin' for the text—

The twa-three last to find it, vext
   But kind o' proud;
An' than the peppermints are raxed,
   An' southernwood.

For noo's the time whan pows are
   seen
Nid-noddin' like a mandareen;
When tenty mithers stap a preen
   In sleepin' weans;
An' nearly half the parochine
   Forget their pains.

There's just a waukrif' twa or three:
Thrawn commentautors sweer to 'gree.
Weans glowrin' at the bumblin' bee
   On windie-glasses,
Or lads that tak a keek a-glee
   At sonsie lasses.

Himsel', meanwhile, frae whaur he cocks
An' bobs belaw the soundin'-box,
The treesures of his words unlocks
   Wi' prodigality,
An' deals some unco dingin' knocks
   To infidality.

Wi' sappy unction, hoo he burkes
The hopes o' men that trust in works,

Expounds the fau'ts o' ither kirks,
  An' shaws the best o' them
No muckle better than mere Turks,
  When a's confessed o' them.

Bethankit! what a bonny creed!
What mair would ony Christian need?—
The braw words rumm'le ower his heid,
  Nor steer the sleeper;
An' in their restin' graves, the deid
  Sleep aye the deeper.

NOTE.—It may be guessed by some that I had a certain parish in my eye, and this makes it proper I should add a word of disclamation. In my time there have been two ministers in that parish. Of the first I have a special reason to speak well, even had there been any to think ill. The second I have often met in private and long (in the due phrase) "sat under" in his church, and neither here nor there have I heard an unkind or ugly word upon his lips. The preacher of the text had thus no original in that particular parish; but when I was a boy, he might have been observed in many others; he was then (like the schoolmaster) abroad; and by recent advices, it would seem he has not yet entirely disappeared.

VI

THE SPAEWIFE

O, I wad like to ken—to the beggar-wife says I—
Why chops are guid to brander and nane sae
    guid to fry.
An' siller, that's sae braw to keep, is brawer still
    to gi'e.
—*It's gey an' easy spierin'*, says the beggar-wife
    to me.

O, I wad like to ken—to the beggar-wife says I—
Hoo a' things come to be whaur we find them
    when we try,
The lasses in their claes an' the fishes in the sea.
—*It's gey an' easy spierin'*, says the beggar-wife
    'to me.

O, I wad like to ken—to the beggar-wife says I—
Why lads are a' to sell an' lasses a' to buy;
An' naebody for dacency but barely twa or three
—*It's gey an' easy spierin'*, says the beggar-wife
    to me.

O, I wad like to ken—to the beggar-wife says I—
Gin death's as shüre to men as killin' is to kye,
Why God has filled the yearth sae fu' o' tasty
    things to pree.
—*It's gey an' easy spierin'*, says the beggar-wife
    to me.

O, I wad like to ken—to the beggar-wife says I—
The reason o' the cause an' the wherefore o' the
    why,
Wi' mony anither riddle brings the tear into
    my e'e.
—*It's gey an' easy speirin'*, says the beggar-wife
    to me.

VII

THE BLAST—1875

IT's rainin'. Weet's the gairden sod
Weet the lang roads whaur gangrels plod—
A maist unceevil thing o' God
      In mid July—
If ye'll just curse the sneckdraw, dod!
      An' sae wull I!

He's a braw place in heev'n, ye ken,
An' lea's us puir, forjaskit men
Clamjamfried in the but and ben
      He ca's the earth—
A wee bit inconvenient den
      No muckle worth;

An' whiles, at orra times, keeks out,
Sees what puir mankind are about;

An' if He can, I've little doubt,
    Upsets their plans;
He hates a' mankind, brainch and root,
    An' a' that's man's.

An' whiles, whan they tak heart again,
An' life i' the sun looks braw an' plain,
Doun comes a jaw o' droukin' rain
    Upon their honors—
God sends a spate outower the plain,
    Or mebbe thun'ers.

Lord safe us, life's an unco thing!
Simmer an' Winter, Yule an' Spring,
The damned, dour-heartit seasons bring
    A feck o' trouble.
I wadna try't to be a king—
    No, nor for double.

But since we're in it, willy-nilly,
We maun be watchfü', wise an' skilly
An' no mind ony ither billy,
    Lassie nor God.
But drink—that's my best counsel till 'e
    Sae tak the nod.

VIII

THE COUNTERBLAST—1886

My bonny man, the warld, it's true,
Was made for neither me nor you;
It's just a place to warstle through,
          As Job confessed o't;
And aye the best that we'll can do
          Is mak the best o't.

There's rowth o' wrang, I'm free to say:
The simmer brunt, the winter blae,
The face of earth a' fyled wi' clay
          An' dour wi' chuckies,
An' life a rough an' land'art play
          For country buckies.

An' food's anither name for clart;
An' beasts an' brambles bite an' scart;
An' what would WE be like, my heart!
          If bared o' claethin'?
—Aweel, I cannae mend your cart:
          It's that or naethin'.

A feck o' folk frae first to last
Have through this queer experience passed;
Twa-three, I ken, just damn an' blast
          The hale transaction;
But twa-three ithers, east an' wast,
          Fand satisfaction.

Whaur braid the briery muirs expand,
A waefü' an' a weary land,
The bumblebees, a gowden band,
　　　　Are blithely hingin';
An' there the canty wanderer fand
　　　　The laverock singin'.

Trout in the burn grow great as herr'n',
The simple sheep can find their fair'n';
The wind blaws clean about the cairn
　　　　Wi' caller air;
The muircock an' the barefit bairn
　　　　Are happy there.

Sic-like the howes o' life to some:
Green loans whaur they ne'er fash their
　　　　thumb,
But mark the muckle winds that come.
　　　　Soopin' an' cool,
Or hear the powrin' burnie drum
　　　　In the shilfa's pool.

The evil wi' the guid they tak;
They ca' a gray thing gray, no black;
To a steigh brae, a stubborn back
　　　　Addressin' daily;
An' up the rude, unbieldy track
　　　　O' life, gang gayly.

What you would like's a palace ha',
Or Sinday parlor dink an' braw
Wi' a' things ordered in a raw
          By denty leddies.
Weel, than, ye cannae hae't: that's a'
          That to be said is.

An' since at life ye've taen the grue,
An' winnae blithely hirsle through,
Ye've fund the very thing to do—
          That's to drink speerit;
An' shüne we'll hear the last o' you—
          An' blithe to hear it!

The shoon ye coft, the life ye lead,
Ithers will heir when aince ye're deid;
They'll heir your tasteless bite o' breid,
          An' find it sappy;
They'll to your dulefü' house succeed,
          An' there be happy.

As whan a glum an' fractious wean
Has sat an' sullened by his lane
Till, wi' a rowstin' skelp, he's taen
          An' shoo'd to bed—
The ither bairns a' fa' to play'n',
          As gleg's a gled.

IX

THE COUNTERBLAST IRONICAL

It's strange that God should fash to frame
    The yearth and lift sae hie,
An' clean forget to explain the same
    To a gentleman like me.

They gutsy, donnered ither folk,
    Their weird they weel may dree;
But why present a pig in a poke
    To a gentleman like me?

They ither folk their parritch eat
    An' sup their sugared tea;
But the mind is no to be wyled wi' meat
    Wi' a gentleman like me.

They ither folk, they court their joes
    At gloamin' on the lea;
But they're made of a commoner clay, I suppose.
    Than a gentleman like me.

They ither folk, for richt or wrang,
    They suffer, bleed, or dee;
But a' thir things are an emp'y sang
    Tu a gentleman like me.

It's a different thing that I demand,
    Tho' humble as can be—
A statement fair in my Maker's hand
    To a gentleman like me:

A clear account writ fair an' broad,
    An' a plain apologie;
Or the deevil a ceevil word to God
    From a gentleman like me.

X

THEIR LAUREATE TO AN ACADEMY CLASS DINNER CLUB

DEAR Thamson class, whaure'er I gang
It aye comes ower me wi' a spang:
"Lordsake! they Thamson lads—(deil hang
        Or else Lord mend them!)—
An' that wanchancy annual sang
        I ne'er can send them!"

Straucht, at the name a trusty tyke,
My conscience girrs ahint the dyke;
Straucht on my hinderlands I fyke
        To find a rhyme t' ye;
Pleased—although mebbe no pleased-like—
        To gie my time t' ye.

"Weel," an' says you, wi' heavin' breist,
"Sae far, sae guid, but what's the neist?
Yearly we gaither to the feast,
  A' hopefu' men—
Yearly we skelloch 'Hang the beast—
  Nae sang again!'"

My lads, an' what am I to say?
Ye shürely ken the Muse's way:
Yestreen, as gleg's a tyke—the day,
  Thrawn like a cuddy:
Her conduc', that to her's a play,
  Deith to a body.

Aft whan I sat an' made my mane,
Aft whan I labored burd-alane
Fishin' for rhymes an' findin' nane,
  Or nane were fit for ye—
Ye judged me cauld's a chucky stane—
  No car'n' a bit for ye!

But saw ye ne'er some pingein' bairn
As weak as a pitaty-par'n'—
Less üsed wi' guidin' horse-shoe airn
  Than steerin' crowdie—
Packed aff his lane, by moss an' cairn,
  To ca' the howdie.

Wae's me, for the puir callant than!
He wambles like a poke o' bran,

An' the lowse rein, as hard's he can,
    Pu's, trem'lin' handit;
Till, blaff! upon his hinderlan'
    Behauld him landit.

Sic-like—I awn the weary fac'—
Whan on my muse the gate I tak,
An' see her gleed e'e raxin' back
    To keek ahint her;—
To me the brig of heev'n gangs black
    As blackest winter.

"Lordsake! we're aff," thinks I, *"but whaur?*
On what abhorred and whinny scaur,
Or whammled in what sea o' glaur,
    Will she desert me?
An' will she just disgrace? or waur—
    Will she no hurt me?"

Kittle the quaere! But at least
The day I've backed the fashious beast,
While she, wi' mony a spang an' reist,
    Flang heels ower bonnet;
An' a' triumphant—for your feast,
    Hae! there's your sonnet!

XI

EMBRO HIE KIRK

THE Lord Himsel' in former days
Waled out the proper tünes for praise
An' named the proper kind o' claes
    For folk to preach in:
Preceese and in the chief o' ways
    Important teachin'.

He ordered a' things, late and air';
He ordered folk to stand at prayer
(Although I cannae just mind where
    He gave the warnin'),
An' pit pomatum on their hair
    On Sabbath mornin'.

The hale o' life by His commands
Was ordered to a body's hands;
But see! this *corpus juris* stands
    By a' forgotten;
An' God's religion in a' lands
    Is deid an' rotten.

While thus the lave o' mankind's lost,
O' Scotland still God maks his boast—

Puir Scotland, on whase barren coast
　　A score or twa
Auld wives wi' mutches an' a hoast
　　Still keep His law.

In Scotland, a wheen canty, plain,
Douce kintry-leevin' folk retain
The Truth—or did so aince—alane
　　Of a' men leevin';
An' noo just twa o' them remain—
　　Just Begg an' Niven.

For noo, unfaithfü' to the Lord
Auld Scotland joins the rebel horde;
Her human hymn-books on the board
　　She noo displays:
An' Embro Hie Kirk's been restored
　　In popish ways.

O *punctum temporis* for action
To a' o' the reformin' faction,
If yet, by ony act or paction,
　　Thocht, word, or sermon,
This dark an' damnable transaction
　　Micht yet determine!

For see—as Doctor Begg explains—
Hoo easy 't's düne! a pickle weans,

Wha in the Hie Street gaither stanes
    By his instruction,
The uncovenantit, pentit panes
    Ding to destruction.

Up, Niven, or ower late—an' dash
Laigh in the glaur that carnal hash;
Let spires and pews wi' gran' stramash
    Thegether fa';
The rumlin' kist o' whustles smash
    In pieces sma'.

Noo choose ye out a walie hammer;
About the knottit buttress clam'er;
Alang the steep roof stoyt an' stammer,
    A gate mis-chancy;
On the aul' spire, the bells' hie cha'mer,
    Dance your bit dancie.

Ding, devel, dunt, destroy, an' ruin,
Wi' carnal stanes the square bestrewin',
Till your loud chaps frae Kyle to Fruin,
    Frae hell to heeven,
Tell the guid wark that baith are doin'—
    Baith Begg an' Niven.

XII

THE SCOTSMAN'S RETURN FROM ABROAD

(In a letter from Mr. Thomson to Mr. Johnstone)

In mony a foreign pairt I've been,
An' mony an unco ferlie seen,
Since, Mr. Johnstone, you and I
Last walkit upon Cocklerye.
Wi' gleg, observant een, I pass't
By sea an' land, through East an' Wast,
And still in ilka age an' station
Saw naething but abomination.
In thir uncovenantit lands
The gangrel Scot uplifts his hands
At lack of a' sectarian füsh'n,
An' cauld religious destitütion.
He rins, puir man, frae place to place,
Tries a' their graceless means o' grace,
Preacher on preacher, kirk on kirk—
This yin a stot an' thon a stirk—
A bletherin' clan, no warth a preen,
As bad as Smith of Aiberdeen!

At last, across the weary faem,
Frae far, outlandish pairts I came.
On ilka side o' me I fand
Fresh tokens o' my native land.

Wi' whatna joy I hailed them a'—
The hilltaps standin' raw by raw,
The public house, the Hielan' birks,
And a' the bonny U. P. kirks!
But maistly thee, the bluid o' Scots,
Frae Maidenkirk to John o' Grots,
The king o' drinks, as I conceive it,
Talisker, Isla, or Glenlivet!

For after years wi' a pockmantie
Frae Zanzibar to Alicante,
In mony a fash an' sair affliction
I gie't as my sincere conviction—
Of a' their foreign tricks an' pliskies,
I maist abominate their whiskies.
Nae doot, themsel's, they ken it weel,
An' wi' a hash o' leemon peel,
An' ice an' siccan filth, they ettle
The stawsome kind o' goo to settle;
Sic wersh apothecary's broos wi'
As Scotsmen scorn to fyle their moo's wi'.

An', man, I was a blithe hame-comer
Whan first I syndit out my rummer.
Ye should hae seen me then, wi' care
The less important pairts prepare;
Syne, weel contentit wi' it a',
Pour in the speerits wi' a jaw!

I didnae drink, I didnae speak—
I only snowkit up the reek.
I was sae pleased therein to paidle,
I sat an' plowtered wi' my ladle.

An' blithe was I, the morrow's morn,
To daunder through the stookit corn,
And after a' my strange mishanters,
Sit doun amang my ain dissenters.
An', man, it was a joy to me
The pu'pit an' the pews to see,
The pennies dirlin' in the plate,
The elders lookin' on in state;
An' 'mang the first, as it befell,
Wha should I see, sir, but yoursel'?

I was, and I will no deny it,
At the first gliff a hantle tryit
To see yoursel' in sic a station—
It seemed a doubtfü' dispensation.
The feeiin' was a mere digression;
For shüne I understood the session,
An' mindin Aiken an' M'Neil,
I wondered they had düne sae weel.
I saw I had mysel' to blame;
For had I but remained at hame,
Aiblins—though no ava' deservin' 't—
They micht hae named your humble servant.

The kirk was filled, the door was steeked;
Up to the pu'pit ance I keeked;
I was mair pleased than I can tell—
It was the minister himsel'!
Proud, proud was I to see his face,
After sae lang awa' frae grace.
Pleased as I was, I'm no denyin'
Some maitters were not edifyin';
For first I fand—an' here was news!—
Mere hymn-books cockin' in the pews—
A humanized abomination,
Unfit for ony congregation.
Syne, while I still was on the tenter,
I scunnered at the new prezentor;
I thocht him gesterin' an' cauld—
A sair declension frae the auld.
Syne, as though a' the faith was wreckit,
The prayer was not what I'd exspeckit.
Himsel', as it appeared to me,
Was no the man he üsed to be.
But just as I was growin' vext
He waled a maist judeecious text,
An' launchin' into his prelections,
Swoopt, wi' a skirl, on a' defections.

O what a gale was on my speerit
To hear the p'ints o' doctrine clearit,
And a' the horrors o' damnation
Set furth wi' faithfü' ministration!

Nae shauchlin' testimony here—
We were a' damned, an' that was clear.
I owned, wi' gratitude an' wonder,
He was a pleisure to sit under.

XIII

Late in the nicht in bed I lay,
The winds were at their weary play,
An' tirlin' wa's an' skirlin' wae
      Through heev'n they battered;—
On-ding o' hail, on-blaff o' spray,
      The tempest blattered.

The masoned house it dinled through;
It dung the ship, it cowped the coo';
The rankit aiks it overthrew,
      Had braved a' weathers;
The strang sea-gleds it took an' blew
      Awa' like feathers.

The thraes o' fear on a' were shed,
An' the hair rose, an' slumber fled,
An' lichts were lit an' prayers were said
      Through a' the kintry;
An' the cauld terror clum in bed
      Wi' a' an' sindry.

To hear in the pit-mirk on hie
The brangled collieshangie flie,
The warl' they thocht, wi' land an' sea,
  Itsel' wad cowpit;
An' for auld airn, the smashed debris
  By God be rowpit.

Meanwhile frae far Aldeboran,
To folks wi' talescopes in han',
O' ships that cowpit, winds that ran,
  Nae sign was seen,
But the wee warl' in sunshine span
  As bricht's a preen.

I, tae, by God's especial grace,
Dwall denty in a bieldy place,
Wi' hosened feet, wi' shaven face,
  Wi' dacent mainners:
A grand example to the race
  O' tautit sinners!

The wind may blaw, the heathen rage,
The deil may start on the rampage;—
The sick in bed, the thief in cage—
  What's a' to me?
Cosh in my house, a sober sage,
  I sit an' see.

An' whiles the bluid spangs to my bree,
To lie sae saft, to live sae free,

While better men maun do an' die
    In unco places.
"Whaur's God?" I cry, an' *" Whae is me*
    To hae sic graces?"

I mind the fecht the sailors keep,
But fire or can'le, rest or sleep,
In darkness an' the muckle deep;
    An' mind beside
The herd that on the hills o' sheep
    Has wandered wide.

I mind me on the hoastin' weans—
The penny joes on causey stanes—
The auld folk wi' the crazy banes,
    Baith auld an' puir,
That aye maun thole the winds an' rains
    An' labor sair.

An' whiles I'm kind o' pleased a blink,
An' kind o' fleyed forby, to think,
For a' my rowth o' meat an' drink
    An' waste o' crumb,
I'll mebbe have to thole wi' skink
    In Kingdom Come.

For God whan jowes the Judgment bell,
Wi' His ain Hand, His Leevin' Sel',

Sall ryve the guid (as Prophets **tell)**
    Frae them that had it;
And in the reamin' pat o' **hell,**
    The rich be scaddit.

O Lord, if this indeed be sae,
Let daw that sair an' happy day!
Again' the warl, grawn auld an' **gray,**
    Up wi' your aixe!
An' let the puir enjoy their play—
    I'll thole my paiks.

————

XIV

MY CONSCIENCE!

OF a' the ills that flesh can fear,
The loss o' frien's, the lack o' gear,
A yowlin' tyke, a glandered mear,
    A lassie's nonsense—
There's just ae thing I cannae bear,
    An' that's my conscience.

Whan day (an' a' excüse) has gane,
An' wark is düne, an' duty's plain,
An' to my chalmer a' my lane
    I creep apairt,
My conscience! hoo the yammerin' **pain**
    Stends to my heart!

A' day wi' various ends in view
The hairsts o' time I had to pu',
An' made a hash wad staw a soo,
    Let be a man!—
My conscience! whan my han's were fü',
    Whaur were ye than?

An' there were a' the lures o' life,
There pleesure skirlin' on the fife,
There anger, wi' the hotchin' knife
    Ground shairp in hell—
My conscience!—you that's like a wife!
    Whaur was yoursel'?

I ken it fine: just waitin' here,
To gar the evil waur appear,
To clart the guid, confüse the clear,
    Mis-ca' the great,
My conscience! an' to raise a steer
    Whan a's ower late.

Sic-like, some tyke grawn auld and blind,
Whan thieves brok' through the gear to
    p'ind,
Has lain his dozened length an' grinned
    At the disaster;
An' the morn's mornin', wud's the wind,
    Yokes on his master.

XV

TO DOCTOR JOHN BROWN

(Whan the dear doctor, dear to a',
Was still amang us here belaw,
I seb my pipes his praise to blaw
         Wi' a' my speerit;
But noo, Dear Doctor, he's awa',
         An' ne'er can hear it.)

By Lyne and Tyne, by Thames and Tees,
By a' the various river-Dee's,
In Mars and Manors 'yont the seas
         Or here at hame,
Whaure'er there's kindly folk to please,
         They ken your name.

They ken your name, they ken your tyke,
They ken the honey from your byke;
But mebbe after a' your fyke,
         (The trüth to tell)
It' just your honest Rab they like,
         An' no yoursel'.

As at the gowff, some canny play'r
Should tee a common ba' wi' care—
Should flourish and deleever fair
         His souple shintie—
An' the ba' rise into the air,
         A leevin' lintie:

Sae in the game we writers play,
There comes to some a bonny day,
When a dear ferlie shall repay
           Their years o' strife,
An' like your Rab, their things o' clay,
           Spreid wings o' life.

Ye scarce deserved it, I'm afraid—
You that had never learned the trade,
But just some idle mornin' strayed
           Into the schüle,
An' picked the fiddle up an' played
           Like Neil himsel'.

Your e'e was gleg, your fingers dink;
Ye didna fash yoursel' to think,
But wove, as fast as puss can link,
           Your denty wab;—
Ye stapped your pen into the ink,
           An' there was Rab!

Sinsyne, whaure'er your fortune lay
By dowie den, by canty brae,
Simmer an' winter, nicht an' day,
           Rab was aye wi' ye;
An' a' the folk on a' the way
           Were blithe to see ye.

O sir, the gods are kind indeed,
An' hauld ye for an honored heid,

That for a wee bit clarkit screed
      Sae weel reward ye,
An' lend—puir Rabbie bein' deid—
      His ghaist to guard ye.

For though, whaure'er yoursel' may be,
We've just to turn an' glisk a wee,
An' Rab at heel we're shüre to see
      Wi' gladsome caper:—
The bogle of a bogle, he—
      A ghaist o' paper!

And as the auld farrand hero sees
In hell a bogle Hercules,
Pit there the lesser deid to please,
      While he himsel'
Dwalls wi' the muckle gods at ease
      Far raised frae hell:

Sae the true Rabbie far has gane
On kindlier business o' his ain
Wi' aulder frien's; an' his breist-bane
      An' stumpie tailie,
He birstles at a new hearth stane
      By James and Ailie.

XVI

IT's an owercome sooth for age an' youth
  And it brooks wi' nae denial,
That the dearest friends are the auldest friends
  And the young are just on trial.

There's a rival bauld wi' young an' auld
  And it's him that has bereft me;
For the sürest friends are the auldest friends
  And the maist o' mine hae left me.

There are kind hearts still, for friends to fill
  And fools to take and break them;
But the nearest friends are the auldest friends
  And the grave's the place to seek them.

A CHILD'S GARDEN OF VERSES

TO ALISON CUNNINGHAM

(FROM HER BOY)

For the long nights you lay awake
And watched for my unworthy sake:
For your most comfortable hand
That led me through the uneven land:
For all the story-books you read:
For all the pains you comforted:
For all you pitied, all you bore,
In sad and happy days of yore:—
My second Mother, my first Wife,
The angel of my infant life—
From the sick child, now well and old
Take, nurse, the little book you hold!

And grant it, Heaven, that all who read
May find as dear a nurse at need,
And every child who lists my rhyme,
In the bright, fireside, nursery clime,
May hear it in as kind a voice
As made my childish days rejoice!

R. L. S.

I

BED IN SUMMER

In winter I get up at night
And dress by yellow candle-light.
In summer, quite the other way,
I have to go to bed by day

I have to go to bed and see
The birds still hopping on the tree,
Or hear the grown up people s feet
Still going past me in the street.

And does it not seem hard to you,
When all the sky is clear and blue,
And I should like so much to play,
To have to go to bed by day?

II

A THOUGHT

It is very nice to think
The world is full of meat and drink,
With little children saying grace
In every Christian kind of place.

III

AT THE SEASIDE

WHEN I was down beside the sea
A wooden spade they gave to me
   To dig the sandy shore.
My holes were empty like a cup,
In every hole the sea came up,
   Till it could come no more.

IV

YOUNG NIGHT THOUGHT

ALL night long and every night,
When my mamma puts out the light,
I see the people marching by,
As plain as day, before my eye.

Armies and emperors and kings,
All carrying different kinds of things,
And marching in so grand a way,
You never saw the like by day.

So fine a show was never seen,
At the great circus on the green;
For every kind of beast and man
Is marching in that caravan.

At first they move a little slow,
But still the faster on they go,
And still beside them close I keep
Until we reach the town of Sleep.

———

V

WHOLE DUTY OF CHILDREN

A CHILD should always say what's true
And speak when he is spoken to,
And behave mannerly at table:
At least as far as he is able.

———

VI

RAIN

THE rain is raining all around,
It falls on field and tree,
It rains on the umbrellas here,
And on the ships at sea.

VII

PIRATE STORY

THREE of us afloat in the meadow by the swing,
  Three of us aboard in the basket on the lea.
Winds are in the air, they are blowing in the
    spring,
  And waves are on the meadow like the waves
    there are at sea.

Where shall we adventure, to-day that we're afloat,
  Wary of the weather and steering by a star?
Shall it be to Africa, a-steering of the boat,
  To Providence, or Babylon, or off to Malabar?

Hi! but here's a squadron a-rowing on the sea—
  Cattle on the meadow a-charging with a roar!
Quick, and we'll escape them, they're as mad as
    they can be,
The wicket is the harbor and the garden is the
    shore.

VIII

FOREIGN LANDS

UP into the cherry tree
Who should climb but little me?
I held the trunk with both my hands
And looked abroad on foreign lands.

I saw the next door garden lie,
Adorned with flowers before my eye,
And many pleasant places more
That I had never seen before.

I saw the dimpling river pass
And be the sky's blue looking-glass;
The dusty roads go up and down
With people tramping into town.

If I could find a higher tree
Further and further I should see,
To where the grown up river slips
Into the sea among the ships,

To where the roads on either hand
Lead onward into fairy land,
Where all the children dine at five,
And all the playthings come alive.

IX

WINDY NIGHTS

WHENEVER the moon and stars are set,
  Whenever the wind is high,
All night long in the dark and wet,
  A man goes riding by.
Late in the night when the fires are
      out,
Why does he gallop and gallop about?

Whenever the trees are crying aloud,
  And ships are tossed at sea,
By, on the highway, low and loud,
  By at the gallop goes he.
By at the gallop he goes, and then
By he comes back at the gallop again.

———

X

TRAVEL

I SHOULD like to rise and go
Where the golden apples grow;—
Where below another sky
Parrot islands anchored lie,

And, watched by cockatoos and
    goats,
Lonely Crusoes building boats;—
Where in sunshine reaching out
Eastern cities, miles about,
Are with mosque and minaret
Among sandy gardens set,
And the rich goods from near
    and far
Hang for sale in the bazaar;—
Where the Great Wall round China
    goes,
And on one side the desert blows,
And with bell and voice and drum,
Cities on the other hum;—
Where are forests, hot as fire,
Wide as England, tall as a spire,
Full of apes and cocoa-nuts
And the negro hunters' huts;—
Where the knotty crocodile
Lies and blinks in the Nile,
And the red flamingo flies
Hunting fish before his eyes;—
Where in jungles, near and far,
Man devouring tigers are,
Lying close and giving ear
Lest the hunt be drawing near,
Or a comer-by be seen

Swinging in a palanquin;—
Where among the desert sands
Some deserted city stands,
All its children, sweep and prince
Grown to manhood ages since,
Not a foot in street or house,
Not a stir. of child or mouse,
And when kindly falls the night,
In all the town no spark of light.
There I'll come when I'm a man
With a camel caravan;
Light a fire in the gloom
Of some dusty dining-room;
See the pictures on the walls,
Heroes, fights and festivals;
And in a corner find the toys
Of the old Egyptian boys.

XI

SINGING

Of speckled eggs the birdie sings
 And nests among the trees;
The sailor sings of ropes and things
 In ships upon the seas.

The children sing in far Japan,
  The children sing in Spain;
The organ with the organ man
  Is singing in the rain.

———

XII

LOOKING FORWARD

WHEN I am grown to man's estate
I shall be very proud and great,
And tell the other girls and boys
Not to meddle with my toys.

———

XIII

A GOOD PLAY

WE built a ship upon the stairs
All made of the back-bedroom chairs,
And filled it full of sofa pillows
To go a-sailing on the billows.

We took a saw and several nails,
And water in the nursery pails;
And Tom said, "Let us also take
An apple and a slice of cake;"—

Which was enough for Tom and me
To go a-sailing on, till tea.

We sailed along for days and days
And had the very best of plays;
But Tom fell out and hurt his knee
So there was no one left but me.

———

XIV

WHERE GO THE BOATS?

DARK brown is the river,
  Golden is the sand.
It flows along forever,
  With trees on either hand.

Green leaves a-floating,
  Castles of the foam,
Boats of mine a-boating—
  Where will all come home?

On goes the river
  And out past the mill,
Away down the valley,
  Away down the hill.

Away down the river,
　A hundred miles or more,
Other little children
　Shall bring my boats ashore.

XV

AUNTIE'S SKIRTS

WHENEVER Auntie moves around,
Her dresses make a curious sound;
They trail behind her up the floor,
And trundle after through the door.

XVI

THE LAND OF COUNTERPANE

WHEN I was sick and lay a-bed,
I had two pillows at my head,
And all my toys beside me lay
To keep me happy all the day.

And sometimes for an hour or so
I watched my leaden soldiers go,
R—K & S—5

With different uniforms and drills,
Among the bed-clothes through the
    hills;

And sometimes sent my ships in fleets
All up and down among the sheets,
Or brought my trees and houses out,
And planted cities all about.

I was the giant great and still
That sits upon the pillow-hill,
And sees before him, dale and plain,
The pleasant land of counterpane.

XVII

THE LAND OF NOD

FROM breakfast on through all the
    day
At home among my friends I stay;
But every night I go abroad
Afar into the land of Nod.

All by myself I have to go,
With none to tell me what to do—
All alone beside the streams
And up the mountain-sides of dreams.

The strangest things are there for me,
Both things to eat and things to see
And many frightening sights abroad
Till morning in the land of Nod.

Try as I like to find the way,
I never can get back by day,
Nor can remember plain and clear
The curious music that I hear.

XVIII

MY SHADOW

I HAVE a little shadow that goes in and out with
    me,
And what can be the use of him is more than I
    can see.
He is very, very like me from the heels up to
    the head;
And I see him jump before me, when I jump
    into my bed.

The funniest thing about him is the way he likes
    to grow—
Not at all like proper children, which is always
    very slow;

For he sometimes shoots up taller like an india
  rubber ball

And he sometimes gets so little that there's none
  of him at all

He hasn t got a notion of how children ought to
  play

And can only make a fool of me in every sort
  of way

He stays so close beside me, he's a coward you
  can see

I'd think shame to stick to nursie as that shadow
  sticks to me.

One morning very early, before the sun was up,
I rose and found the shining dew on every
  buttercup

But my lazy little shadow, like an arrant sleepy-
  head,

Had stayed at home behind me and was fast
  asleep in bed.

XIX

SYSTEM

Every night my prayers I say,
And get my dinner every day:
And every day that I've been good,
I get an orange after food.

The child that is not clean and neat,
With lots of toys and things to eat,
He is a naughty child, I'm sure—
Or else his dear papa is poor.

XX

A GOOD BOY

I woke before the morning, I was happy all the
day,
I never said an ugly word, but smiled and stuck
to play.

And now at last the sun is going down behind
the wood,
And I am very happy, for I know that I've been
good.

My bed is waiting cool and fresh, with linen
smooth and fair,
And I must off to sleepsin-by, and not forget
my prayer.

I know that, till to-morrow I shall see the sun
arise,
No ugly dream shall fright my mind, no ugly
sight my eyes,

But slumber hold me tightly till I waken in the
    dawn,
And hear the thrushes singing in the lilacs
    round the lawn.

XXI

ESCAPE AT BEDTIME

THE lights from the parlor and kitchen shone out
    Through the blinds and the windows and bars,
And high overhead and all moving about,
    There were thousands of millions of stars.
There ne'er were such thousands of leaves on a
    tree,
    Nor of people in church or the Park,
As the crowds of the stars that looked down
    upon me,
    And that glittered and winked in the dark.

The Dog, and the Plow, and the Hunter, and all,
    And the star of the sailor, and Mars,
These shone in the sky, and the pail by the wall
    Would be half full of water and stars.
They saw me at last, and they chased me with
    cries,
    And they soon had me packed into bed.

But the glory kept shining and bright in my
   eyes,
And the stars going round in my head.

XXII

MARCHING SONG

BRING the comb and play upon it!
   Marching, here we come!
Willie cocks his highland bonnet,
   Johnnie beats the drum.

Mary Jane commands the party,
   Peter leads the rear;
Feet in time, alert and hearty,
   Each a Grenadier!

All in the most martial manner
   Marching double-quick;
While the napkin like a banner
   Waves upon the stick!

Here's enough of fame and pillage,
   Great commander Jane!
Now that we've been round the village,
   Let's go home again.

XXIII

THE COW

The friendly cow all red and white,
  I love with all my heart:
She gives me cream with all her might,
  To eat with apple-tart.

She wanders lowing here and there,
  And yet she cannot stray,
All in the pleasant open air,
  The pleasant light of day;

And blown by all the winds that pass
  And wet with all the showers,
She walks among the meadow grass
  And eats the meadow flowers.

XXIV

HAPPY THOUGHT

The world is so full of a number of things,
I'm sure we should all be as happy as kings.

XXV

THE WIND

I saw you toss the kites on high
And blow the birds about the sky;
And all around I heard you pass,
Like ladies' skirts across the grass—
    O wind, a-blowing all day long,
    O wind, that sings so loud a song!

I saw the different things you did,
But always you yourself you hid,
I felt you push, I heard you call,
I could not see yourself at all—
    O wind, a-blowing all day long,
    O wind, that sings so loud a song!

O you that are so strong and cold,
O blower, are you young or old?
Are you a beast of field and tree,
Or just a stronger child than me?
    O wind, a-blowing all day long,
    O wind, that sings so loud a song!

XXVI

KEEPSAKE MILL

Over the borders, a sin without pardon,
  Breaking the branches and crawling below,
Out through the breach in the wall of the
    garden,
  Down by the banks of the river, we go.

Here is the mill with the humming of thunder,
  Here is the weir with the wonder of foam,
Here is the sluice with the race running
    under—
  Marvelous places, though handy to home!

Sounds of the village grow stiller and stiller,
  Stiller the notes of the birds on the hill;
Dusty and dim are the eyes of the miller,
  Deaf are his ears with the moil of the mill.

Years may go by, and the wheel in the river
  Wheels as it wheels for us, children, to-day,
Wheel and keep roaring and foaming forever
  Long after all of the boys are away.

Home from the Indies and home from the ocean,
  Heroes and soldiers we all shall come home;
Still we shall find the old mill-wheel in motion,
  Turning and churning that river to foam.

You with the bean that I gave when we quar-
  reled,
I with your marble of Saturday last,
Honored and old and all gayly appareled,
  Here we shall meet and remember the past.

XXVII

GOOD AND BAD CHILDREN

CHILDREN, you are very little,
And your bones are very brittle;
If you would grow great and stately,
You must try to walk sedately.

You must still be bright and quiet,
And content with simple diet;
And remain through all bewild'ring,
Innocent and honest children.

Happy hearts and happy faces,
Happy play in grassy places—
That was how in ancient ages,
Children grew to kings and sages.

But the unkind and the unruly,
And the sort who eat unduly,
They must never hope for glory—
Theirs is quite a ifferent story!

Cruel children, crying babies,
All grow up as geese and gabies,
Hated, as their age increases,
By their nephews and their nieces.

XXVIII

FOREIGN CHILDREN

LITTLE Indian, Sioux or Crow,
Little frosty Eskimo,
Little Turk or Japanee,
O! don't you wish that you were
    me?

You have seen the scarlet trees
And the lions over seas;
You have eaten ostrich eggs,
And turned the turtles off their
    legs.

Such a life is very fine,
But it's not so nice as mine:
You must often, as you trod,
Have wearied *not* to be abroad.

You have curious things to eat,
I am fed on proper meat;

You must dwell beyond the foam,
But I am safe and live at home.

Little Indian, Sioux or Crow,
Little frosty Eskimo,
Little Turk or Japanee,
O! don't you wish that you were
      me?

———

XXIX

THE SUN'S TRAVELS

The sun is not a-bed, when I
At night upon my pillow lie;
Still round the earth his way he takes,
And morning after morning makes.

While here at home, in shining day,
We round the sunny garden play,
Each little Indian sleepy-head
Is being kissed and put to bed.

And when at eve I rise from tea,
Day dawns beyond the Atlantic Sea,
And all the children in the West
Are getting up and being dressed.

XXX

THE LAMPLIGHTER

My tea is nearly ready and the sun has left the
sky;
It's time to take the window to see Leerie going
by;
For every night at teatime and before you take
your seat,
With lantern and with ladder he comes posting
up the street.

Now Tom would be a driver and Maria go to
sea,
And my papa's a banker and as rich as he can
be;
But I, when I am stronger and can choose what
I'm to do,
O Leerie, I'll go round at night and light the
lamps with you.

For we are very lucky, with a lamp before the
door,
And Leerie stops to light it as he lights so many
more;
And O! before you hurry by with ladder and
with light,
O Leerie, see a little child and nod to him to-
night!

XXXI

MY BED IS A BOAT

My bed is like a little boat;
  Nurse helps me in when I em-
    bark;
She girds me in my sailor's coat
  And starts me in the dark.

At night I go on board and say
  Good-night to all my friends on
    shore;
I shut my eyes and sail away
  And see and hear no more.

And sometimes things to bed I take,
  As prudent sailors have to do:
Perhaps a slice of wedding-cake,
  Perhaps a toy or two.

All night across the dark we steer:
  But when the day returns at last,
Safe in my room beside the pier,
  I find my vessel fast.

XXXII

THE MOON

THE moon has a face like the clock in the
    hall;
She shines on thieves on the garden wall,
On streets and fields and harbor quays,
And birdies asleep in the forks of the trees.

The squalling cat and the squeaking mouse,
The howling dog by the door of the house,
The bat that lies in bed at noon,
All love to be out by the light of the moon.

But all of the things that belong to the day
Cuddle to sleep to be out of her way;
And flowers and children close their eyes
Till up in the morning the sun shall arise.

XXXIII

THE SWING

How do you like to go up in a
    swing,
    Up in the air so blue?
Oh, I do think it the pleasantest
    thing
    Ever a child can do!

Up in the air and over the wall,
  Till I can see so wide,
Rivers and trees and cattle and all
  Over the countryside—

Till I look down on the garden green,
    green,
  Down on the roof so brown—
Up in the air I go flying again,
  Up in the air and down!

XXXIV

TIME TO RISE

A BIRDIE with a yellow bill
Hopped upon the window-sill,
Cocked his shining eye and said:
"Ain't you 'shamed, you sleepy-head?"

XXXV

LOOKING-GLASS RIVER

SMOOTH it slides upon its travel,
  Here a wimple, there a gleam—
    O the clean gravel!
    O the smooth stream!

Sailing blossoms, silver fishes,
  Paven pools as clear as air—
    How a child wishes
    To live down there!

We can see our colored faces
  Floating on the shaken pool
    Down in cool places,
    Dim and very cool;

Till a wind or water wrinkle,
  Dipping martin, plumping trout,
    Spreads in a twinkle
    And blots all out.

See the rings pursue each other;
  All below grows black as night,
    Just as if mother
    Had blown out the light!

Patience, children, just a minute—
  See the spreading circles die;
    The stream and all in it
    Will clear by-and-by.

XXXVI

FAIRY BREAD

COME up here, O dusty feet!
Here is fairy bread to eat.
Here in my retiring room,
  Children, you may dine
On the golden smell of broom
  And the shade of pine;
And when you have eaten well,
Fairy stories hear and tell.

XXXVII

FROM A RAILWAY CARRIAGE

FASTER than fairies, faster than witches,
Bridges and houses, hedges and ditches;
And charging along like troops in a battle,
All through the meadows the horses and cattle:
All of the sights of the hill and the plain
Fly as thick as driving rain;
And ever again in the wink of an eye,
Painted stations whistle by.

Here is a child who clambers and scrambles,
All by himself and gathering brambles;
Here is a tramp who stands and gazes;
And there is the green for stringing the daisies!
Here is a cart run away in the road
Lumping along with man and load;
And here is a mill and there is a river:
Each a glimpse and gone forever!

XXXVIII

WINTER-TIME

LATE lies the wintry sun a-bed,
A frosty, fiery sleepy-head;
Blinks but an hour or two; and then.
A blood-red orange, sets again.

Before the stars have left the skies.
At morning in the dark I rise;
And shivering in my nakedness,
By the cold candle, bathe and dress.

Close by the jolly fire I sit
To warm my frozen bones a bit;
Or with a reindeer-sled explore
The colder countries round the door.

When to go out my nurse doth wrap
Me in my comforter and cap:
The cold wind burns my face, and blows
Its frosty pepper up my nose.

Black are my steps on silver sod;
Thick blows my frosty breath abroad;
And tree and house, and hill and lake,
Are frosted like a wedding-cake.

XXXIX

THE HAYLOFT

THROUGH all the pleasant meadow-side
  The grass grew shoulder-high,
Till the shining scythes went far and wide
  And cut it down to dry.

These green and sweetly-smelling crops
  They led in wagons home;
And they piled them here in mountain-tops
  For mountaineers to roam.

Here is Mount Clear, Mount Rusty Nail,
  Mount Eagle and Mount High;—
The mice that in these mountains dwell,
  No happier are than I!

O what a joy to clamber there,
  O what a place for play,
With the sweet, the dim, the dusty air,
  The happy hills of hay.

———

XL

FAREWELL TO THE FARM

THE coach is at the door at last;
The eager children mounting fast
And kissing hands, in chorus sing:
Good-by, good-by, to everything!

To house and garden, field and lawn,
The meadow-gates we swung upon,
To pump and stable, tree and swing,
Good-by, good-by, to everything!

And fare you well for evermore,
O ladder at the hayloft door,
O hayloft where the cobwebs cling,
Good-by, good-by, to everything!

Crack goes the whip, and off we go;
The trees and houses smaller grow;
Last, round the woody turn we swing:
Good-by, good-by, to everything!

XLI

NORTH-WEST PASSAGE

1. GOOD-NIGHT

WHEN the bright lamp is carried in,
The sunless hours again begin;
O'er all without, in field and lane,
The haunted night returns again.

Now we behold the embers flee
About the firelit hearth; and see
Our faces painted as we pass,
Like pictures, on the window-glass.

Must we to bed indeed? Well then,
Let us arise and go like men,
And face with an undaunted tread
The long black passage up to bed.

Farewell, O brother, sister, sire!
O pleasant party round the fire!
The songs you sing, the tales you tell,
Till far to-morrow, fare ye well!

2. SHADOW MARCH

All round the house is the jet-black night;
  It stares through the window-pane;
It crawls in the corners, hiding from the light,
  And it moves with the moving flame.

Now my little heart goes a-beating like a drum,
  With the breath of the Bogie in my hair;
And all round the candle the crooked shadows
    come
  And go marching along up the stair.

The shadow of the balusters, the shadow of
    the lamp,
  The shadow of the child that goes to bed—
All the wicked shadows coming, tramp, tramp,
    tramp,
  With the black night overhead.

3. IN PORT

Last, to the chamber where I lie
My fearful footsteps patter nigh,
And come from out the cold and gloom
Into my warm and cheerful room.

There, safe arrived, we turn about
To keep the coming shadows out,
And close the happy door at last
On all the perils that we past.

Then, when mamma goes by to bed,
She shall come in with tiptoe tread,
And see me lying warm and fast
And in the Land of Nod at last.

THE CHILD ALONE

———

I

THE UNSEEN PLAYMATE

WHEN children are playing alone on the green,
In comes the playmate that never was seen.
When children are happy and lonely and good,
The Friend of the Children comes out of the
    wood.

Nobody heard him and nobody saw,
His is a picture you never could draw,
But he's sure to be present, abroad or at home,
When children are happy and playing alone.

He lies in the laurels, he runs on the grass,
He sings when you tinkle the musical glass;
Whene'er you are happy and cannot tell why,
The Friend of the Children is sure to be by!

He loves to be little, he hates to be big,
'Tis he that inhabits the caves that you dig;
'Tis he when you play with your soldiers of tin
That sides with the Frenchmen and never can
    win.

'Tis he when at night you go off to your bed,
Bids you go to your sleep and not trouble your
    head;
For wherever they're lying, in cupboard or shelf,
'Tis he will take care of your playthings himself'

II

MY SHIP AND I

O it's I that am the captain of a tidy little ship,
    Of a ship that goes a-sailing on the pond;
And my ship it keeps a-turning all around and
    all about;
But when I'm a little older, I shall find the secret
    out
    How to send my vessel sailing on beyond.

For I mean to grow as little as the dolly at the
    helm,
    And the dolly I intend to come alive;
And with him beside to help me, it's a-sailing I
    shall go,
It's a sailing on the water, when the jolly breezes
    blow
    And the vessel goes a divie-divie-dive.

144 Works of Robert Louis Stevenson

O it's then you'll see me sailing through the
rushes and the reeds,
And you'll hear the water singing at the prow;
For beside the dolly sailor I'm to voyage and
explore,
To land upon the island where no dolly was be-
fore,
And to fire the penny cannon in the bow

———

III

MY KINGDOM

Down by a shining water well
I found a very little dell,
No higher than my head.
The heather and the gorse about
In summer bloom were coming out,
Some yellow and some red.

I called the little pool a sea;
The little hills were big to me;
For I am very small.
I made a boat, I made a town,
I searched the caverns up and down,
And named them one and all.

And all about was mine, I said,
The little sparrows overhead,
　　The little minnows too.
This was the world and I was king;
For me the bees came by to sing,
　　For me the swallows flew.

I played there were no deeper seas,
Nor any wider plains than these,
　　Nor other kings than me.
At last I heard my mother call
Out from the house at evenfall,
　　To call me home to tea.

And I must rise and leave my dell,
And leave my dimpled water well,
　　And leave my heather blooms.
Alas! and as my home I neared
How very big my nurse appeared,
　　How great and cool the rooms!

IV

PICTURE BOOKS IN WINTER

SUMMER fading, winter comes—
Frosty mornings, tingling thumbs,
Window robins, winter rooks,
And the picture story-books.

Water now is turned to stone
Nurse and I can walk upon;
Still we find the flowing brooks
In the picture story-books.

All the pretty things put by,
Wait upon the children's eye,
Sheep and shepherds, trees and crooks,
In the picture story-books.

We may see how all things are,
Seas and cities, near and far,
And the flying fairies' looks,
In the picture story-books.

How am I to sing your praise,
Happy chimney-corner days,
Sitting safe in nursery nooks,
Reading picture story-books?

V

MY TREASURES

THESE nuts that I keep in the back of the nest
Where all my lead soldiers are lying at rest,
Were gathered in autumn by nursie and me
In a wood with a well by the side of the sea.

This whistle we made (and how clearly it sounds!)
By the side of a field at the end of the grounds.
Of a branch of a plane, with a knife of my own,
It was nursie who made it, and nursie alone!

The stone, with the white and the yellow and
        gray,
We discovered I cannot tell *how* far away;
And I carried it back, although weary and cold,
For though father denies it, I'm sure it is gold.

But of all of my treasures the last is the king,
For there's very few children possess such a thing;
And that is a chisel, both handle and blade,
Which a man who was really a carpenter made.

VI

BLOCK CITY

WHAT are you able to build with your blocks?
Castles and palaces, temples and docks.
Rain may keep raining, and others go roam,
But I can be happy and building at home.

Let the sofa be mountains, the carpet be sea,
There I'll establish a city for me:
A kirk and a mill and a palace beside,
And a harbor as well where my vessels may
      ride.

Great is the palace with pillar and wall,
A sort of a tower on the top of it all,
And steps coming down in an orderly way
To where my toy vessels lie safe in the bay.

This one is sailing and that one is moored:
Hark to the song of the sailors on board!
And see on the steps of my palace the kings
Coming and going with presents and things!

Now I have done with it, down let it go!
All in a moment the town is laid low.
Block upon block lying scattered and free,
What is there left of my town by the sea?

Yet as I saw it, I see it again,
The kirk and the palace, the ships and the men,
And as long as I live and where'er I may be,
I'll always remember my town by the sea.

———

VII

THE LAND OF STORY-BOOKS

At evening when the lamp is lit,
Around the fire my parents sit;
They sit at home and talk and sing,
And do not play at anything.

Now, with my little gun, I crawl
All in the dark along the wall,
And follow round the forest track
Away behind the sofa back.

There, in the night, where none can
    spy,
All in my hunter's camp I lie,
And play at books that I have read
Till it is time to go to bed.

These are the hills, these are the
    woods,
These are my starry solitudes;

And there the river by whose brink
The roaring lions come to drink.

I see the others far away
As if in firelit camp they lay,
And I, like to an Indian scout,
Around their party prowled about.

So, when my nurse comes in for me,
Home I return across the sea,
And go to bed with backward looks
At my dear land of Story-books.

VIII

ARMIES IN THE FIRE

THE lamps now glitter down the street;
Faintly sound the falling feet;
And the blue even slowly falls
About the garden trees and walls.

Now in the falling of the gloom
The red fire paints the empty room:
And warmly on the roof it looks,
And flickers on the backs of books.

Armies march by tower and spire
Of cities blazing, in the fire;—
Till as I gaze with staring eyes,
The armies fade, the luster dies.

Then once again the glow returns;
Again the phantom city burns;
And down the red-hot valley, lo!
The phantom armies marching go!

Blinking embers, tell me true
Where are those armies marching to,
And what the burning city is
That crumbles in your furnaces!

IX

THE LITTLE LAND

WHEN at home alone I sit
And am very tired of it,
I have just to shut my eyes
To go sailing through the skies—
To go sailing far away
To the pleasant Land of Play;
To the fairy land afar
Where the Little People are;

Where the clover-tops are trees,
And the rain-pools are the seas,
And the leaves like little ships
Sail about on tiny trips;
And above the daisy tree
    Through the grasses,
High o'erhead the Bumble Bee
    Hums and passes.

In that forest to and fro
I can wander, I can go;
See the spider and the fly,
And the ants go marching by
Carrying parcels with their feet
Down the green and grassy street.
I can in the sorrel sit
Where the ladybird alit.
I can climb the jointed grass;
    And on high
See the greater swallows pass
    In the sky,
And the round sun rolling by
Heeding no such things as I.

Through that forest I can pass
Till, as in a looking-glass,
Humming fly and daisy tree
And my tiny self I see,

Painted very clear and neat
On the rain-pool at my feet.
Should a leaflet come to land
Drifting near to where I stand,
Straight I'll board that tiny boat
Round the rain-pool sea to float.

Little thoughtful creatures sit
On the grassy coasts of it;
Little things with lovely eyes
See me sailing with surprise.
Some are clad in armor green—
(These have sure to battle been!)—
Some are pied with ev'ry hue,
Black and crimson, gold and blue;
Some have wings and swift are
    gone;—
But they all look kindly on.

When my eyes I once again
Open, and see all things plain:
High bare walls, great bare floor;
Great big knobs on drawer and
    door;
Great big people perched on chairs,
Stitching tucks and mending tears,
Each a hill that I could climb,
And talking nonsense all the time—

O dear me,
That I could be
A sailor on the rain-pool sea,
A climber in the clover tree,
And just come back, a sleepy-head,
Late at night to go to bed.

GARDEN DAYS

———

I

NIGHT AND DAY

WHEN the golden day is done,
　Through the closing portal,
Child and garden, flower and sun,
　Vanish all things mortal.

As the blinding shadows fall,
　As the rays diminish,
Under evening's cloak, they all
　Roll away and vanish.

Garden darkened, daisy shut,
　Child in bed, they slumber—
Glow-worm in the highway rut,
　Mice among the lumber.

In the darkness houses shine,
　Parents move with candles;
Till on all the night divine
　Turns the bedroom handles.

Till at last the day begins
　In the east a-breaking,
In the hedges and the whins
　Sleeping birds a-waking.

In the darkness shapes of things,
　Houses, trees, and hedges,
Clearer grow; and sparrow's wings
　Beat on window ledges.

These shall wake the yawning maid;
　She the door shall open—
Finding dew on garden glade
　And the morning broken.

There my garden grows again
　Green and rosy painted,
As at eve behind the pane
　From my eyes it fainted.

Just as it was shut away,
　Toy-like in the even,
Here I see it glow with day
　Under glowing heaven.

Every path and every plot,
　Every bush of roses,
Every blue forget-me-not
　Where the dew reposes,

"Up!" they cry, "the day is come
On the smiling valleys:
We have beat the morning drum;
Playmate, join your allies!"

———

II

NEST EGGS

BIRDS all the sunny day
  Flutter and quarrel
Here in the arbor-like
  Tent of the laurel.

Here in the fork
  The brown nest is seated;
Four little blue eggs
  The mother keeps heated.

While we stand watching her,
  Staring like gabies,
Safe in each egg are the
  Bird's little babies.

Soon the frail eggs they shall
  Chip, and upspringing
Make all the April woods
  Merry with singing.

Younger than we are,
O children, and frailer,
Soon in blue air they'll be,
Singer and sailor.

We so much older,
Taller and stronger,
We shall look down on the
Birdies no longer.

They shall go flying
With musical speeches
High overhead in the
Tops of the beeches.

In spite of our wisdom
And sensible talking,
We on our feet must go
Plodding and walking.

III

THE FLOWERS

ALL the names I know from nurse:
Gardener's garters, Shepherd's purse,
Bachelor's buttons, Lady's smock,
And the Lady Hollyhock.

Fairy places, fairy things,
Fairy woods where the wild bee wings,
Tiny trees for tiny dames—
These must all be fairy names!

Tiny woods below whose boughs
Shady fairies weave a house;
Tiny tree-tops, rose or thyme,
Where the braver fairies climb!

Fair are grown-up people's trees,
But the fairest woods are these;
Where if I were not so tall,
I should live for good and all.

———

IV

SUMMER SUN

GREAT is the sun, and wide he goes
Through empty heaven without repose;
And in the blue and glowing days
More thick than rain he showers his rays.

Though closer still the blinds we pull
To keep the shady parlor cool,
Yet he will find a chink or two
To slip his golden fingers through.

The dusty attic, spider-clad,
He through the key-hole maketh glad;
And through the broken edge of tiles,
Into the laddered hayloft smiles.

Meantime his golden face around
He bares to all the garden ground,
And sheds a warm and glittering look
Among the ivy's inmost nook.

Above the hills, along the blue,
Round the bright air with footing true,
To please the child, to paint the rose,
The gardener of the World, he goes.

V

THE DUMB SOLDIER

WHEN the grass was closely mown,
Walking on the lawn alone,
In the turf a hole I found
And hid a soldier underground.

Spring and daisies came apace;
Grasses hide my hiding-place;
Grasses run like a green sea
O'er the lawn up to my knee.

Under grass alone he lies,
Looking up with leaden eyes,
Scarlet coat and pointed gun,
To the stars and to the sun.

When the grass is ripe like grain,
When the scythe is stoned again,
When the lawn is shaven clear,
Then my hole shall reappear.

I shall find him, never fear,
I shall find my grenadier;
But for all that's gone and come,
I shall find my soldier dumb.

He has lived, a little thing,
In the grassy woods of spring;
Done, if he could tell me true
Just as I should like to do.

He has seen the starry hours
And the springing of the flowers;
And the fairy things that pass
In the forests of the grass.

In the silence he has heard
Talking bee and ladybird,
And the butterfly has flown,
O'er him as he lay alone.

Not a word will he disclose,
Not a word of all he knows.
I must lay him on the shelf,
And make up the tale myself.

———

VI

AUTUMN FIRES

In the other gardens
  And all up the vale,
From the autumn bonfires
  See the smoke trail!

Pleasant summer over
  And all the summer flowers,
The red fire blazes,
  The gray smoke towers.

Sing a song of seasons!
  Something bright in all!
Flowers in the summer,
  Fires in the fall!

VII

THE GARDENER

THE gardener does not love to talk,
He makes me keep the gravel walk;
And when he puts his tools away,
He locks the door and takes the key.

Away behind the currant row
Where no one else but cook may go,
Far in the plots, I see him dig,
Old and serious, brown and big.

He digs the flowers, green, red, and
    blue,
Nor wishes to be spoken to.
He digs the flowers and cuts the hay,
And never seems to want to play.

Silly gardener! summer goes,
And winter comes with pinching toes,
When in the garden bare and brown
You must lay your barrow down.

Well now, and while the summer stays,
To profit by these garden days,
O how much wiser you would be
To play at Indian wars with me!

VIII

HISTORICAL ASSOCIATIONS

DEAR Uncle Jim, this garden ground
That now you smoke your pipe around,
Has seen immortal actions done
And valiant battles lost and won.

Here we had best on tip-toe tread,
While I for safety march ahead,
For this is that enchanted ground
Where all who loiter slumber sound.

Here is the sea, here is the sand,
Here is simple Shepherd's Land,
Here are the fairy hollyhocks,
And there are Ali Baba's rocks.

But yonder, see! apart and high,
Frozen Siberia lies; where I,
With Robert Bruce and William Tell,
Was bound by an enchanter's spell.

There, then, awhile in chains we lay,
In wintry dungeons, far from day;
But ris'n at length, with might and main,
Our iron fetters burst in twain.

Then all the horns were blown in town;
And to the ramparts clanging down,
All the giants leaped to horse
And charged behind us through the
    gorse.

On we rode, the others and I,
Over the mountains blue, and by
The Silver River, the sounding sea,
And the robber woods of Tartary.

A thousand miles we galloped fast,
And down the witches' lane we passed,
And rode amain, with brandished sword,
Up to the middle, through the ford.

Last we drew rein—a weary three—
Upon the lawn, in time for tea,
And from our steeds alighted down
Before the gates of Babylon.

ENVOYS

—

I

TO WILLIE AND HENRIETTA

Iғ two may read aright
These rhymes of old delight
And house and garden play,
You two, my cousins, and you only, may.

You in a garden green
With me were king and queen,
Were hunter, soldier, tar,
And all the thousand things that children are.

Now in the elders' seat
We rest with quiet feet,
And from the window-bay
We watch the children, our successors, play.

"Time was," the golden head
Irrevocably said;
But time which none can bind,
While flowing fast away, leaves love behind.

II

TO MY MOTHER

You too, my mother, read my rhymes
For love of unforgotten times,
And you may chance to hear once more
The little feet along the floor.

III

TO AUNTIE

Chief of our aunts—not only I,
But all your dozen of nurslings cry—
What did the other children do?
And what were childhood, wanting you?

IV

TO MINNIE

THE red room with the giant bed
Where none but elders laid their head;

The little room where you and I
Did for a while together lie
And, simple suitor, I your hand
In decent marriage did demand;
The great day nursery, best of all,
With pictures pasted on the wall
And leaves upon the blind—
A pleasant room wherein to wake
And hear the leafy garden shake
And rustle in the wind—
And pleasant there to lie in bed
And see the pictures overhead—
The wars about Sebastopol,
The grinning guns along the wall,
The daring escalade,
The plunging ships, the bleating sheep,
The happy children ankle-deep
And laughing as they wade:
All these are vanished clean away,
And the old manse is changed to-day;
It wears an altered face
And shields a stranger race.
The river, on from mill to mill,
Flows past our childhood's garden still;
But ah! we children nevermore
Shall watch it from the water-door!
Below the yew—it still is there—
Our phantom voices haunt the air

As we were still at play,
And I can hear them call and say:
"How far is it to Babylon?"

Ah, far enough, my dear,
Far, far enough from here—
Yet you have further gone!
"Can I get there by candle-light?"
So goes the old refrain.
I do not know—perchance you might—
But only, children, hear it right,
Ah, never to return again!
The eternal dawn, beyond a doubt,
Shall break on hill and plain,
And put all stars and candles out,
Ere we be young again.

To you in distant India, these
I send across the seas,
Nor count it far across.
For which of us forgets
The Indian cabinets,
The bones of antelope, the wings of albatross,
The pied and painted birds and beans,
The junks and bangles, beads and screens,
The gods and sacred bells,
And the loud-humming, twisted shells?
The level of the parlor floor
Was honest, homely, Scottish shore;

But when we climbed upon a chair,
Behold the gorgeous East was there!
Be this a fable; and behold
Me in the parlor as of old,
And Minnie just above me set
In the quaint Indian cabinet!
Smiling and kind, you grace a shelf
Too high for me to reach myself.
Reach down a hand, my dear, and take
These rhymes for old acquaintance' sake.

V

TO MY NAME-CHILD

1

SOME day soon this rhyming volume, if you learn
        with proper speed,
Little Louis Sanchez, will be given you to read.
Then shall you discover, that your name was
        printed down
By the English printers, long before, in London
        town.

In the great and busy city where the East and
	West are met,
All the little letters did the English printer set;
While you thought of nothing, and were still too
	young to play,
Foreign people thought of you in places far away.

Ay, and while you slept, a baby, over all the
	English lands
Other little children took the volume in their
	hands;
Other children questioned, in their homes across
	the seas:
Who was little Louis, won't you tell us, mother,
	please?

2

Now that you have spelt your lesson, lay it down
	and go and play,
Seeking shells and seaweed on the sands of
	Monterey,
Watching all the mighty whalebones, lying buried
	by the breeze,
Tiny sandy-pipers, and the huge Pacific seas.

And remember in your playing, as the sea-fog
	rolls to you,
Long ere you could read it, how I told you what
	to do;

And that while you thought of no one, nearly
    half the world away
Some one thought of Louis on the beach of
    Monterey!

———

VI

TO ANY READER

As from the house your mother sees
You playing round the garden trees,
So you may see, if you will look
Through the windows of this book,
Another child, far, far away,
And in another garden, play.
But do not think you can at all,
By knocking on the window, call
That child to hear you. He intent
Is all on his play-business bent.
He does not hear; he will not look,
Nor yet be lured out of this book.
For, long ago, the truth to say,
He has grown up and gone away,
And it is but a child of air
That lingers in the garden there.

www.ingramcontent.com/pod-product-compliance
Lightning Source LLC
Chambersburg PA
CBHW020923020726
47495CB00002B/324